To Vonda...

Cecelia

by

Patricia Strefling

Blessings

Patricia Strefling

Dedication

To each of us whose bad choices have taught us a measure of
wisdom and whose good ones a measure of grace.

Chapter 1

Dunnegin Castle – Edinburgh, Scotland

"Cecelia, you and Spencer have to go back to the States. There will be a wedding, but I have no notion of when or where or . . . ," Edwina said to her overbearing stepsister as they sipped tea in the formal dining room.

"Edwina, you know how you are. You'll wrap some oversized length of gauze around yourself and call it a wedding dress."

"So what if I do? If it makes me happy." Edwina knew her smile must look silly pasted on her face. Only days ago she had accepted Alex Dunnegin's proposal of marriage.

"There will be none of that talk." Cecelia's blue eyes were shining as her cup clattered into the saucer.

Edwina knew that was a bad sign.

"Look around you, Ed." Her sister swung her arms in wide arcs. "If you haven't noticed, you're living in a castle."

"We are not going to live here," Edwina said quietly and waited.

"Does he think you'll want to live in that farmhouse . . . cottage, or whatever you call that little ancient building, where all the dust and animals are?" she interrupted and turned to stare.

"It's only been three weeks since Paige's accident." A glance at Cecelia told Edwina she hadn't heard that last statement. Edwina sought to connect her sister's mind to other things and mused, "I think my wedding dress should . . ." She paused for effect.

"What? What are you thinking, Edwina Emily Blair? Because I can tell you right now Alex's family is going to expect a suitable affair."

Edwina knew "suitable" meant extravagant. Cecelia's prim English upbringing absolutely required her to make a good showing. Her sister was commandeering the wedding train, and it was flying down the track to Weddingville. Edwina knew there was no way to stop it. *There must be some way to convince her to go back home to Chicago.*

"Are you mumbling again?" Cecelia stood and picked at Edwina's hair. "Have you chosen a color for your bridesmaid's dresses? And I suppose if you insist on traipsing all over the Scottish hills in that gauzy dress idea of yours, we'll have to purchase special shoes."

Edwina planned on wearing simple white slippers on her wedding day, but that thought would never be spoken or she would have another battle on her hands. She preferred to be barefoot, if the truth were known.

"Oh, and Alex will want his family's traditions included too. His family crest and tartan must be considered." Cecelia's finger was tapping her chin. "Then the food. Heaven knows that will have to be Scottish and American cuisine. Spencer will help us with that. Did you know he has an aunt here in Edinburgh?"

"No, he didn't mention it." Edwina was glad for the diversion.

"She'll advise him on the preparation of the right Scottish dishes." Cecelia's pen scratched on the paper.

"Cece, please let Alex and I talk before you go any further." Edwina leaned in to catch her sister's eye. It was no use. Once she'd made up her mind, Cecelia—her beautiful, talented, entrepreneurial sister—would not be dissuaded. She hadn't heard a word.

"Cecelia Grace Giatano, are you interfering again?" Spencer Hallman walked into the dining room and snatched the paper out of Cecelia's hand.

"Stop it, Spencer." She turned angry blue eyes on him.

"What is this?" Spencer stepped away from the wild woman. "Can't you give them a chance to plan their own wedding?" he called out as he read the page and saw his aunt's name listed.

"My aunt is eighty-four years old." He laughed. "Past her prime in planning a wedding dinner, I would say."

"You have no idea what it takes to pull off a successful wedding." Cecelia snatched the paper back.

"Successful? Businesses are successful, Cecelia. Weddings are personal." He dropped his chin and widened his eyes as he peered over his trendy black glasses.

Spencer's blond hair stuck up everywhere, and the expression on his face nearly threw Edwina into fits, giddy as she was these days. She also knew Cecelia hated it when Spencer did that.

"Now listen you two, you have your bed-and-breakfast, Cece — Spencer, you have the new restaurant in Chicago to worry about. You don't need to plan anything. I am capable of handling our wedding," Edwina stated firmly and waited for the words to sink in.

"Now Ed, you know you don't have a single bit of sense when it comes to elegance, let alone planning a lavish affair." Cecelia smoothed her upswept blond hair.

"Aye, and I have nothing to say about me own wedding?" Alex Dunnegin stepped through the double doors as three pairs of eyes settled on him.

"What? Three voices hushed at my presence?" he teased. "Paige and I are aboot a ride. Anyone want to come along?"

"Sure, I'd love a ride." Cecelia started for the door. "Have you a convertible? It is such a beautiful day."

Edwina watched Alex's frown slowly turn into a smirk.

"Do you like the outdoors, Miss Giatano?" he said formally to the English-born lass.

"Of course I do." She lifted her chin.

"Then you will enjoy my offer. You will ride atop my best mare. She will guide you through the wooded paths more gently than a motor car."

"Horseback riding?" Cecelia's nose wrinkled. "Whatever gave you the idea I'd get upon a wild beast and let my hair fly about in such a fashion?"

Alex shrugged. "Suit yourself. Coming, Edwina?"

Edwina's heart pumped blood into her face again as she caught his handsome green eyes beckoning her. "Yes." Her voice escaped barely audible.

Someone had better pinch me. I am walking on some stage, the violins and flutes playing in the background, and my knight in shining armor has appeared and declared his love for me. Edwina chided herself for such silly thoughts.

Yet no one was more surprised that she had captured Alex Dunnegin's stubborn Scot heart. It had taken the last three days to convince herself, but she was beginning to believe he really meant all those things he'd said. For the life of her, she couldn't imagine that he was telling the truth until he kissed her in the field near his grandfather's cottage.

That kiss told her things she'd thought impossible.

Chapter 2

Edwina came to her senses and called over her shoulder. "Coming, Spencer?"

"Not a chance." He winked and turned to Cecelia.

Edwina noticed there was an indulgent smile on his face as he settled her sister's nerves with calm words. In that moment, as she followed her own beloved, she wondered if Cecelia had found her knight but did not yet see it.

Musing at the thought, she ran into Alex's back as a puff of air escaped her throat. He turned, and she saw a spark in his eyes. All thoughts of Cecelia's love life flew away like so many autumn leaves on a blustery day. Alex raised his hand and smoothed her hair.

"Is it standing out?" Her hands fluttered aimlessly at his touch.

"Aye."

Thankfully, five-year-old Paige, called from upstairs.

Alex grabbed her hand and took the stairs two at a time, heaving her along. As they strode into Paige's room, Alex sent her a backward glance and a wink.

"How's me bairn?" Alex's voice boomed.

"I'm ready, Da. I asked Mr. Gillespie to put Mama's saddle on my horse."

"Lass, ye are not riding alone. Ye have no sense in your cockle-burr brain. Ye'll ride with me, and that's the end of it."

At Paige's hopeful glance, Edwina forced her eyes to look away from the eager brown eyes. Accustomed to having Paige as her charge, she wanted to give in to her request. Surely the child could be placed upon her own horse, even with the casts on her legs. Edwina's heart still hurt over the fact that Paige had been injured under her watch. She'd been on the phone when Paige had ridden her bike into the path of a car.

This was not going to be easy. Now that her father was home and they were to be a family, she knew her place. She and Alex were going to have to talk later.

"Aye, look not at Miss Blair, lass. She and I will have a talk later, and I will inform her who will be making the decisions in this castle." He ruffled his daughter's hair.

Edwina smiled as the child acquiesced immediately, her mind reeling at the fact that Alex seemed always to repeat her very thoughts. He dropped her hand and swung Paige from the bed and up into his arms.

"I see your teacher has been feeding you extra dishes of ice cream."

"Aye. Do I look all right, Father?" The child peered into her father's eyes.

Edwina held her breath hoping Alex caught her meaning. *Am I beautiful to you?* Heaven knows the child had reason to wonder, with her father absent for the better part of the last year.

Alex whispered something in Paige's ear.

Edwina, satisfied with the child's smile, followed Alex down the hall and called out, "I'll get my boots." Sensing that Alex and Paige needed a few moments together, she headed for her room and slowly changed into jeans and a soft beige and orange cotton shirt. The warm midsummer weather was already upon them. Her thoughts turned to her wedding dress. *What would Alex want?*

It would take several weeks for family to arrive and notes to be sent out, especially now that they would be wed in Scotland. Her heart took a dive thinking about all the details. She wished for a small wedding, outdoors, the wind blowing on the Scottish moors. Who was she fooling? She didn't just want it for the character in her story—she wanted it for herself. *Am I acting selfish?* she wondered. Would Father and Victoria be able to travel across on such short notice?

Perhaps she and Cecelia should sit down and look at the family situation. All of a sudden Edwina, the normally detail-oriented sister, was at a loss as to how to plan her own wedding. But then, it was all new. This idea of her being married.

Edwina pushed the fearful thoughts aside and pulled on her boots. She was not going to run from this, no matter how unreal it seemed.

Chapter 3

"Spencer Hallman, stop talking down to me," Cecelia said grumpily.

Spencer leaned his backside against the kitchen counter, arms crossed over his chest, and smiled.

"Would you stop smiling like that? You look like the cat who ate the house."

"House? Wouldn't that be 'mouse,' Miss Giatano?" Spencer's eyes sharpened, aware that the woman was known to toss whatever she had in her hand at the moment when she was distressed.

"Oooh, you men have no idea how important a woman's wedding is to her." She tossed a pen his way. "Why don't you go riding about with the rest of them so I can be left alone long enough to plan a respectable wedding for my sister who seems to have no idea what an important affair this is, especially for a Scottish laird for goodness' sake." She threw her hands up and was off, her black heels clicking on the wood floor. "She has no idea of the European ways," she tossed over her shoulder.

Spencer smiled in spite of her ill temper. That woman was crazy, rich and spoiled, and beautiful and sassy all at the same time. He shrugged and pulled away from the counter. He had calls to make to his restaurant staff and escaped to the library.

An hour later he was packing. Cecelia appeared at the door of his room.

"Spencer, what are you doing? We can't leave now!" The woman had somehow gotten wind of his plans. "*I'm* leaving, Cecelia. The restaurant staff is short. Buffy the Bandit has stolen one of our employees!"

"Buffy the Bandit?"

Spencer could hardly contain himself at her confused look. Big blue eyes cast themselves on his face, and he knew he was in for a good one.

"Were you robbed?" She stalked up to him, hands at her slender waist, ready to fight for his rights.

"I was not robbed, at least not like you think."

She stomped her foot, causing a slight bit of harm, for she winced and cried out, then leaned down to massage her ankle.

"Now what have you done? You let your temper get the best of you. Ever heard of reaping and sowing?"

"Reaping and sewing? Spencer Hallman, what has sewing got to do with anything?" She straightened, still wincing.

He ignored her question. It would take too long to explain. Cecelia was forever misinterpreting clichés.

"Try walking." He leaned down to examine her slender ankle, but she pushed his hand away.

"Get up, I'm fine," she fumed.

"As you wish, milady." He bowed, his arm across his waist.

"You are avoiding my question. What has happened at *Winnie's*?"

Experience told him the woman would not stop yapping until she knew every detail. "Hattie has gone off and married Duncan."

"She's your cook. And isn't he your best server?"

"Yep."

"Oh, that is a bloody mess."

"You could say that. I need to go if you'll move out of the way, Cecelia." He stepped around her. "I have exactly two hours to make my flight."

"But . . ." Her hand reached out to stop him, and landed on his arm. "You can't go. Not now. You'll miss the wedding."

Spencer saw her confidence waver. "Cecelia, you will be fine. I trust you'll work it all out." He laid his hand over hers, and she snatched it away and gave him her back.

"Or you could come back with me and let Alex and Edwina plan their own wedding. . . ."

"Not a chance."

Spencer shrugged. "I have to go. Kitty is a good cook, but she can't work past three o'clock with four children to look after, which leaves her position open as well."

Cecelia turned to face him, and her countenance firmed right before his eyes. "Then go back. You have your restaurant to look after."

"It's not like I have a choice. It is my bread and butter." *Unlike you, Cecelia Grace, who is spoiled with too much money and too much power.*

He doubted the woman understood. Cecelia wanted what she wanted. Now. She was kind to a fault, but when you told her no, she always managed to find a way around it. This woman was his partner in business. Best to assuage her a bit.

"Will you be all right?"

"Of course I'll be all right. I've been all right all these years," she snapped.

Without you. He finished her sentence. "Right."

"Well then?" she hesitated.

Spencer knew she didn't know what to do. She'd brought down boardrooms full of business people with her savvy arguments, which were generally correct. But when it came to anything having to do with human nature or common sense, the bird flew right over her head with no place to land.

His conscience kicked in. It was her business sense that gave him the chance to start his own restaurant. If it wasn't for the arrangement she'd made for his restaurant and apartment on the entire second floor of her bed-and-breakfast building in downtown Chicago, he'd still be cleaning her apartment and working for peanuts. He had already paid off a sizeable chunk of his school loan.

"Stop stuffing your shirts in your suitcase like that," she sputtered, back to her old self, and refolded them neatly. He found himself standing to the side handing her his clothes.

She was onboard now. She charged back after a weak moment so quickly that he could hardly keep up with her. If nothing else, Cecelia Grace Giatano was a strong woman.

"And who is Buffy the Bandit?"

Chapter 4

"Spencer, where are you going?" Edwina arrived in time to see him heading for the car, Reardon waiting with open door.

"I'm glad you made it back. Listen, I have to go back to the States. A rumble at the restaurant."

"I'm so sorry. Anyone hurt?"

"No. Just me." Spencer smiled over his glasses when he saw Edwina begin to fret. "Not to worry, it's nothing like that. It seems that Hattie and Duncan have run off and gotten married while I was away, leaving the staff short of help."

"Oh no."

"I should have listened to Buffy the Bandit."

"Buffy the Bandit?

"That's what I call the employee gossip. I'd heard snippets here and there, but I didn't listen. And now you see . . . I am here in Scotland and *Winnie's* is falling apart in Chicago."

"Oh, Spencer, I'm so sorry."

"It seems we have a little bird that carries about such talk, but I was too busy to notice. From now on I'm going to pay attention to employee problems before Buffy the Bandit steals any more of my people. We were short-staffed to begin with. And I let Miss Cecilia persuade me to come. . . ." He shrugged.

Edwina smiled. "So she's got you in hand too?"

Spencer smiled that Brad Pitt smile of his and ducked into the waiting car. "Have a good wedding, Edwina, you and your knight in shining armor."

"Thank you. And I'll be praying that you arrive safely and everything works out."

Edwina waved as Reardon negotiated the circle drive and headed for the main road. There was a definite chill in the air. She stepped inside and heard nothing, which was strange. Where were Cecelia and Bertie? Her sister and Alex's housekeeper together were like gasoline and a lit match. Edwina picked up her pace and flew up the steps. She heard voices and walked quietly toward them.

They were in her bedroom. Edwina peeked between the small crack in the door and saw the contents of her closet splayed across the bed.

"Toss. Toss. Keep." Cecelia was ordering Bertie with each article of clothing the older woman held up.

"Hey you two, wait just a minute. That's my favorite skirt. And this shirt goes with my vest."

"You're back so soon?" Cecelia made it sound as though she was a pesky fly.

Edwina snatched her favorite skirt off the toss pile.

"How do you expect to be a laird's wife when you dress in such things?" Cecelia verbally pounced on her. "Ed, you have to keep up appearances. That's how I made it in business."

"Cece, marriage is not a business. It's . . . it's a family," Edwina tried to explain.

"Marriage *is* a business. Taxes have to be paid, papers signed, and meetings held to keep it going. Same thing." Cecelia tossed another skirt on the growing pile.

She sounded so smug that Edwina wanted to push her out of the room. "Look, could we do this another day? I need a bath. My backside hurts from all the bouncing around and . . .

Bertie and Cecelia looked up at the same time.

"Alex and I are going out to dinner this evening."

True to their nature, they both scattered. One to run the bath, the other to choose the right outfit from what was left of her closet contents.

Edwina smiled. It didn't seem to matter much these days what anyone thought about her. There was one person who thought her okay. Which, when she stopped to think about it, she really did want to please Alex.

"I have a white blouse. Basic, yet classy cut. You could wear it with this skirt if you put on pumps, Ed." Cecelia was holding up a black dress skirt.

"Pumps? You know I don't own any. We were thinking of a nice dinner, but not Hollywood style."

"Do you even know what Hollywood stars wear, Ed?"

Cecelia had her there. She hadn't been to a movie in almost a year.

"Something tells me you will need help with more than wardrobe," Cecelia tut-tutted enjoying her moment of glory.

"Come, Edwina, your bath is ready," Bertie called from the en suite bathroom.

"Are you on her side too?" she asked as she passed.

Bertie stuck her nose in the air. Oh boy, two of them. Would she ever have peace?

Sinking into the ancient claw-foot tub relinquished all duties at hand. Edwina eased herself into the warm, fragrant water for a good long soak. Half an hour later, she heard Bertie before she'd arrived.

"We have to dry your hair. The laird is aboot the place."

Edwina pulled herself up and let Bertie wrap her. "Now lass, your sister has laid out your evening wear."

"Oh boy, what has she chosen? You know if I don't like . . ."

Edwina's eyes widened as she came through the door. The skirt lay freshly ironed and a white blouse lay above it. "It's beautiful." She fingered the simple design. "I like it."

"Best that you do," Bertie grumped.

Edwina shot her a glance but said nothing. The towel came off, and she pulled on clean underclothes and stepped into the skirt while Bertie held up her hair.

"Sit, lass, I'll style your hair."

"Not too fancy, Bertie. We're just going out to dinner."

"Aye." She agreed too quickly, which meant she was up to something.

"I mean it, Bertie."

"Quiet yourself and let me work."

Cecelia was coming down the hall, her pumps clumping along the wood floors. "Done yet?" She stood in the doorway. "Blouse looks nice."

"Thank you, Cece, it really is nice. I like it. Where—" She stopped herself from asking where it came from. It may have cost several hundred dollars.

"Take good care of it. It's my favorite," Cecelia said.

"Oh no, you just blew my good intentions. I'll be worried the entire evening, Cece.

"Stop talking, Ed. Alex is waiting below stairs. We've been talking for thirty minutes, waiting for you to get ready."

A whiff of jealousy passed right by Edwina, and she felt its sting.

"I'm ready." She stood and bent her knees to catch her image in the mirror, then got on her hands and knees to look for her shoes under the bed.

"See? What did I tell you, Bertie?" Cecelia pointed at her sister.

Edwina got up in time to see Bertie's half smile. "She doesn't mind, do you?" Edwina sought Bertie's approval.

"Bertie wouldn't tell you if she did," Cecelia stated firmly. "The help knows their place."

Edwina's eyes opened wider. Had her sister really said that?

Bertie gave her a look—Edwina couldn't distinguish whether it was bad, good, or indifferent—and walked out.

"Bertie would tell me," she said smartly. "She has before."

"Well, it's not done in *well-run* English homes." Cecelia stuck her nose in the air.

Edwina was glad Bertie had gone. She only hoped she hadn't heard that last statement.

"Cece, we're not in England, and we're not highbrow people! Sometimes you should walk in someone else's shoes."

Chapter 5

Cecelia turned on her heel and started down the stairs. Edwina overheard her sister announce that she was ready, then ask, "What time are the reservations at the restaurant?"

"Reservations?" Edwina heard Alex exclaim. "One doesna usually need reservations for fish and chips, do they?"

"Fish and chips?" Cecelia whispered incredulously.

Edwina slipped off her shoes and flew to her room on tiptoes. Off came the skirt. She carefully hung Cecelia's white blouse on a hanger then changed into her best jeans and a short-waisted blue embroidered button-up jacket over a white shell, found her comfortable Birkenstocks buried in the closet, and put them on. That was one purchase Cecelia had been right about.

She dashed down the stairs and watched Bertie's and Cecelia's eyes widen at her appearance. "Ready?" She looked at Alex. "Where's Paige?"

"She's not coming," Alex stated firmly as his eyes settled on her.

"Oh." Edwina thought they would be together as a family, but her heart fluttered in excitement at his look and the idea that they would be alone.

"We're off." Alex grabbed her hand and made for the door. "Good night, ladies." He called back. "Don't wait up."

As soon as the door shut behind them, Edwina laughed out loud. "How did you do that?"

"What?" He laughed. "So you heard?"

"Yes. They had me dressed up like a stuffed turkey ready for the Thanksgiving meal."

"Ah, I know, my lass." His voice was deep.

Edwina shivered in the cool night.

"There's a shawl in the front seat. Bertie insisted," He opened the passenger door.

"Thank you. I didn't think about anything except getting changed." She laughed.

"How can ye think with those two afoot?" He settled into the driver's seat.

"So you see it too?"

"That's why I wanted to step out tonight. Get away from everyone so we can talk about Paige and where we will live . . . and the wedding." His voice had grown serious.

Edwina nodded and was quiet as she gazed out the window. This was still so new and fresh. She wondered if it were a dream that she would soon wake up from. But no, this was real, for the wind was blowing the tall grasses over like a concert. Back and forth they went, dancing to the slow beat of God's unheard music on these green, green hills.

Alex was quiet too as darkness began to settle over them. He was driving in new territory, and Edwina wondered where they were going, but had no desire to ask.

After a time he pulled into a parking lot, and lights were flashing. She ducked her head to read the sign above. *Fienie's Fish & Chips.* "It looks like an out-of-the-way place."

"I chose it so we could talk undisturbed."

Edwina gazed at him. His shoulders seemed tense. "We'll find a quiet corner."

"Aye," he agreed. They walked in, and the place was a veritable party. Teens had taken over the small shop, some tossing chips, others slurping their drinks, all shouting and boisterous. Chairs dragged across the black-and-white tiles, squealing as they went.

Edwina pulled on Alex's hand. "Come on, let's get out of here."

"Ye don't mind?"

"Of course not. We'll find another place," she assured him.

The door closed behind them and shut out all the noise. He drove several miles, and it seemed they would not find anything quiet, so he headed into Edinburgh to the *Pop & Top* where they'd eaten before. He pulled up, and they entered. The place was empty except for one couple. Alex headed for the table where he'd first proposed the idea of Edwina staying behind as Paige's teacher. It seemed an age ago.

He smiled as he pulled out the chair, and Edwina's heart did flip-flops. "Remember?"

She nodded, blushing.

Alex ordered at the counter, then returned with a number. While they waited, he pulled off his jacket and arranged it on the back of the chair. Same as before. Only this time it was not a suit jacket, it was worn brown leather. He was dressed in a casual shirt, open at the neck, and jeans.

He ran his fingers through his dark hair and mussed it. She wanted to reach over and fix it. She knew she could, but chose to see him like that. Not so perfect. When the number was called, he jumped up and came back with a loaded tray. "Thought you might enjoy a quiet night out."

"Oh goodness, yes. I am beginning to think the entire family is going to be upset with every decision we make. And I don't want that," she added softly.

"Lass, the wedding is ours, not theirs."

Edwina's heart skipped a beat as she watched his strong, and very tan hands, arrange the food containers and set the tray aside. "What I'm wanting is time to catch up. I've missed so much . . . especially with Paige." His voice dropped low.

"I know. It must have been difficult to leave so often and not know if you were going to lose her, . . ." Edwina couldn't utter another word.

"Ah, lass. It is past now. Elizabeth's father is in financial straits because of all the uncouth tricks he used. Others are now coming forward with their accusations and are not afraid to call him out. His lawyers will be busy."

"Too bad. For everyone." Edwina kept her hands in her lap. They had never prayed together before, so she shut her eyes for a moment and bowed her head.

Alex waited.

"Do ye believe God cares about little things?" He picked up his fork. Handsome green eyes searched hers.

"Oh yes. I do. Do you?"

He shrugged. "I used to. I guess losing Elizabeth and nearly losing Paige changed my outlook for a while. I was bitter."

"I can see why you were."

"Can you?" He looked up.

"Yes," she said softly, then pushed her jacket sleeves up and dug into her food, noting Alex's smile. "Bertie said you raise potatoes."

"At my instructions. We had to list employment on all my applications with the attorneys, so I listed meself as a potato farmer."

"So what *do* you do then?"

His face relaxed, then she saw a light come into his eyes. He was up to something.

"Nothing at the moment. My father left me with sufficient capital, but I've spent most of it on solicitors. I will have to find a vocation soon enough. My degree is in finance, but I'm thinkin' I may want to raise potatoes after all."

He paused for a bite.

"That is one of the reasons I wanted to get some time alone. I find myself wanting to live at the cottage after we are wed."

Edwina nodded and waited.

"Do ye disapprove?"

"No, it doesn't matter to me."

A smile of relief relaxed his features. "Ah, so Cecelia has not convinced her sister to desire the *good* things of life," he teased.

"The good things of life are not the same for Cecelia as for me."

"As I expected, lass." He was serious with both voice and eyes.

Edwina felt her face flush again. When would she stop turning ten shades of red around this man?

"What shall I do there at the cottage – besides raising potatoes?" he asked.

At first she thought him joking, but he was serious. She took another bite to gain some time, hating to answer something of such importance on the fly.

"Well, what do you want to do?"

She continued to eat and watch the emotions play over his face. He hesitated.

"What is it? You can be honest with me."

"Ye detect my ambivalence, lass."

Edwina laid her fork aside and folded her hands in her lap.

"I'd be hoping we would have sons, several of them." He added, "If you agree."

There she went again. Face red and splotchy, no doubt. She had not expected *that* "vocation."

"Ah, um, if you wish." She stared at her hands twisted in her lap.

"Look at me, lass." He reached across the table and lifted her chin, forcing eye contact. "Tell me what ye are thinking."

"I don't mind at all . . . having children . . . in fact, I never thought I'd marry, so I did not dare to . . . to . . .dream."

Alex noted her breathless, sweet apprehension. "Well lass I want to have them right away. Paige is five years of age, and if we are having several, it might be good to get started."

Edwina wanted to tell him to stop talking. She knew she was acting foolish, but did he know she had no experience whatsoever? He'd had a woman he adored, a loving marriage, and a child . . . all experiences she knew nothing about. Maybe she was a fool to think she could step into Elizabeth's shoes.

"Lass, your mind is working again."

"I'm . . . I'm not sure if I . . ." Alex dropped his hand, and immediately Edwina regretted her words.

"Lass, I am not here to be yer father. Ye may make decisions I'll not like. We'll fight it out in my Scottish way and make up later." He winked.

Edwina felt a new flush of color rushing to her face.

"Ye are a woman. And ye've made some decisions on your own. I have seen ye change. I am asking if ye want children soon after we're married and if ye'd like to raise them at the cottage."

"Yes . . . to both," she blurted out.

Chapter 6

W ithin minutes of her declaration, Edwina was having a case of
nerves.

"Lass, ye have left the planet." Alex's deep voice jerked her back
into reality.

Edwina garnered her thoughts. "I'm sorry. I. . ."

She noted his full-faced smile. Now that he was free of his burdens,
this Scot was going to be a handful. Her heart skittered in excitement as
the ring of his cell phone cut the conversation.

"Excuse me." He rose from his seat, walked several steps off, and
answered.

At his distance, she found herself pulling in deep breaths and letting
them out slowly. They'd rarely had time alone. Thoughts of running
home to Michigan zipped through her mind.

"Nothing to be concerned about," Alex said when he returned. "Are
ye finished?"

After her nod, he cleared the table. Edwina smiled as he worked.

"Ye smile lass." He pulled her up with his hand in hers. "Come, the
household awaits our return, I'm certain. Bertie will not sleep until you
are safely in your bed."

Edwina laughed. "I feel like they're watching us all the time. Cecelia
will do her best to pull off a highbrow wedding, you know."

The Scot smiled, a gleam in his eye.

She started for the passenger side and waited for Alex to open the
door when she found herself not inside, but with her back pressed against
the door, his arms on either side of her. "Lass, we have not had enough
of this."

He lowered his head and kissed her silly. Her thoughts scattered as he gently held her, his arms now wrapped around her middle. So this is what it would be like.

"Lass, we'd best set the wedding date soon. . . ."

* * *

"Edwina, is that you?" Cecelia called from her bedroom.

"Yes," she whispered. "Can I come in, Cece?"

"Of course. I've been waiting up for you and Alex to get back. I have a list. . . ."

"Oh, Cecelia. I—I can't believe it." She sighed, kicked off her shoes, and using the step, fell across the bed.

Cecelia smiled. "He's kissed you witless, hasn't he?"

Edwina stared. "How'd you know?"

"Well, believe it or not, I have had some pretty handsome men in my life too, you know!"

"I know. I just never thought it would be me, that's all." Edwina turned on her side and curved her body into a pillow.

"Why not you, Ed?" Her practical sister broke into her romantic bubble.

Edwina shrugged, unable to find the words to explain, so she changed the topic.

"You're used to having men about you all the time."

"Men use me."

"What do you mean?" Edwina sat straight up and stared at Cecelia.

"Not like that." She tapped Edwina's arm. "It's just that men see me as a means to their end. I've learned to put up walls."

"Walls?"

"Of course. You have no idea how many times I've wanted to engage in a simple conversation with a man when some woman, fiancée, or wife came up and gave me the evil eye."

Edwina relaxed, and her mind worked. "It's not easy being beautiful, rich and talented is it?" she said, amazed at her own words.

"Not exactly," Cecelia admitted. "But I'm used to it. I can hold my own. I saw the way my actress mother handled her admirers. Her stage persona was much different than the real person."

Edwina grabbed another pillow and found a comfortable position. "Tell me what it was like to grow up with your mother and father."

"Well, I grew up quickly, I do remember *that*. Beauty requires it, you know. I learned early on to keep men at bay, even as a young girl. My father was rarely around, and when he was, he was usually entertaining some young female behind my mother's back and I never had the fortitude to tell her."

Edwina felt her sister's pain.

"I learned to hide secrets and keep marching, no matter what happened. In the end, I guess it has served me well. Look at all that I have." Cecelia waved her arm in an arc.

Edwina felt the injustice. "You have done very well, Cece. I'm proud of you. I know it hasn't been easy, especially when your father died and left you no inheritance."

"He may have done me a courtesy. It made me realize I had to take care of myself and not depend on anyone. No man can guarantee a safe life. I have to do it my way."

Edwina nodded, thinking. "Do you want to marry, have children some day, Cece?"

Her sister shrugged. "Right now, no. I have too much to do. With the new building, I have to make a profit before I'll rest. Even then . . ." She fell silent.

"Spencer's restaurant is doing well, right? I mean, I know he has staff trouble right now, but do you think he'll make it?"

"Oh yes, Spencer has the gift."

"The gift?"

"Yes, you know—people skills. He knows how to handle difficult situations on the everyday, long-term level. Me, I can't stand slow-thinking, slow-moving people. I have to be in the middle of the fray to start some new enterprise, and once it's up and running, I'm on the road looking for a completely new adventure."

"Yes, that describes you well." Edwina laughed. "But, sis, do you want to be an entrepreneur all your life? I mean, would you like to settle down with someone or is that totally out of the picture?"

"Not totally," Cecelia admitted. "But there are some things I want to do."

"Like what?" Edwina noted the faraway look in her sister's soft blue eyes.

"Well, do you remember that huge Victorian at the corner of Washington and Squire? It's the one with the copper-roofed spire. I want that for a bed-and-breakfast. It's trashed at the moment, but I think I could bring it back to its original regal state. My English background helps." She smiled.

Edwina laughed aloud. "Goodness, you already have a plan, don't you? And I know nothing will stop you."

Cecelia's eyes gleamed at the prospect. "So, enough small talk. Tell me about your evening, Ed."

Edwina changed positions and murmured, "We ate at the *Pop & Top*. They serve the best fish and chips. We'd been there one other time, when Alex asked me to stay the first time."

Cecelia nodded, her fingers tapping her lips.

"He . . . I'm just so surprised. . . ." Edwina's voice faded away.

"What? That somebody loves you, Ed?"

"Well, in a way. I think I built a wall so if I didn't find anyone . . ."

"I know. Come, let's talk about the wedding. I have a lot to do tomorrow and with Spencer gone, I'll have to check into your food menu. And the photographer, if you can even find one at this late date."

Edwina paused, seeking words that would prepare Cecelia.

"Cece . . . I don't want a fancy wedding. Alex doesn't either."

"Edwina Emily Blair, this is your wedding day. Not some fly-by-day affair."

"It's fly-by-*night*, Cece."

"Whatever." Edwina saw her sister's hands flying. "You're marrying a laird, for goodness' sake. His people will expect it."

When Edwina thought she saw tears gathering in her sister's eyes, she acquiesced immediately.

"You're right. What are your thoughts?" Edwina watched her sister struggle to recover.

"Well, now that I have your attention, I'm thinking that you should find a huge, ancient church in Edinburgh, enough to seat Alex's family. You'll want a beautiful backdrop for your dress and your photos. And we'll need time to get Mother and Father here."

Edwina listened for ten minutes as her stomach churned.

"So what do you think?" Cece turned to her, excited.

"Do you really want to know?" Edwina's voice was low. "I mean really, Cece?" Edwina flipped onto her stomach and propped her chin up with both fists.

Cecelia shrugged. But Edwina could see disappointment displayed across her face.

"Alex wants to marry soon – without publicity, especially in light of the fact he's just gotten Paige safely through an ordeal the child knows nothing about."

Edwina knew Paige's grandfather had groomed his only daughter, Elizabeth from the beginning to take over his position in his billion-dollar tobacco business, effectively securing his own seat. But Elizabeth had wanted her own life. Her father's plan was to prepare Paige, his granddaughter, for the position Elizabeth had so foolishly tossed off by marrying Alex Dunnegin. And then Paige's mother had died. Alex had fought to keep Paige from being taken by her rich grandfather, but it had cost him a small fortune.

"Paige has rarely been out, and, well, we think it's best if we just have the wedding here. At the castle, perhaps, weather permitting, on the hills." She waited for Cecelia's look of despair.

"I see." Cecelia whispered.

"I don't want to hurt your feelings—really. It's just that . . ."

"Ed, you don't have to explain. I get it. If that's what you want, then do it."

Edwina jumped up to her knees and caught her eyes. "Do you mean that?"

"Of course I do. Once I make up my mind."

Edwina threw herself at her sister. "Thanks. I love you, Cece."

"You're mussing my hair. Now go to your own room. I have a new list to write out—especially if you two decide out of doors is going to be your *church*. If the weather is bad, you'll regret it. Most importantly"— Cecelia's mind was working again—"is what date have you chosen?"

"We don't have a date yet. He did say"—Edwina paused—"that he wanted it to be soon."

Cecelia laughed out loud. "Of course he does. Now scoot. Go on, get out of here. I'll work on some ideas."

Edwina slid off the bed, forgot all about her shoes, and tiptoed to her room to be alone with her thoughts.

Chapter 7

"What do you mean it's not for sale? It was when I left." Cecelia was on her cell talking in the hallway outside her door. Edwina peeped through one eye to check the clock. It was eight a.m.

"Tell them to put a bid on it. Today. Add twenty thousand to the top bid and get that house," Cecelia ordered.

Edwina heard Bertie's footsteps. For the life of her, she had fallen into the pattern and loved to see Bertie in the mornings. The noises about the castle today were loud. She heard Paige calling her father. Whenever he stayed over he slept below stairs next to his office.

Alex dashed up the stairs, two at a time. His little girl needed help getting out of bed, and her papa was the only one allowed to perform that task if he was in the castle.

Bertie found Edwina sitting up, the covers up to her chin, smiling.

"Lass, be aboot getting your feet on the floor. There's much to be done." Bertie stopped and stared at her. "What's that look on yer face, lass?" Her hands were on her hips.

"What look?" Edwina couldn't stop the smile. Bertie grabbed the cherry pink towel and shook it out, looking away. "Come lass, ye haven't got all the day. Laird Dunnegin has been waiting on ye."

"He has?" Edwina flew out of the bed.

"Aye. And patient 'e's been too." Bertie had the tub faucets running at full throttle.

"Do you like my hair?" Edwina asked as she swiped the steam off the mirror.

"Aye, well enough," she mumbled. "What will ye wear today, miss?"

"I'll dress myself, you can go to Paige." She waved her hand.

"And let you dawdle?" The woman's hands were on her hips again.

"Okay, my jeans, the washed-out ones. And that blue shirt you like so much. Nothing fancy. It's Saturday."

Bertie laid out her clothes and was off. Edwina was glad to soak in peace.

Some time later, noises in the hallway alerted her. That was the sound of Cecelia's luggage wheels rumbling over the ancient wood slats. What was that about?

Hurriedly, she dressed and ran a comb through her hair. It was easy enough. She'd had it layered, and it held its shape better.

Edwina leaned over the staircase, her hair dripping. "Cece, where are you going?" Dressed in a black skirt with a pristine white shell, black jacket over her arm, and her hair pulled up, her sister was on a mission. Especially with her three-inch black Dior heels. Reardon appeared at her service and stowed her luggage.

"Well, you're finally up. I've been making enough noise, hoping to see you before I left. I'm off to the States. The Victorian is suddenly taking bids, and I want that house. My agent tells me I'm in a bidding war against that old Mrs. King. Again," Cecelia called over her shoulder as she dug in her bag. "I've called for a standby seat, so I need to get to Edinburgh. Reardon will see me to the airport. Meantime, Ed, don't do anything. I'll be back in a few days."

Edwina ran down the stairs, still barefoot, and caught up with her. "Don't be gone long, okay? I want you here." Suddenly her eyes teared up.

"What? You think I'd miss your wedding, Ed?"

Edwina shook her head. "Of course not. Just be safe and call me when you get home, okay?"

"I will. Not to worry. Call Mother and Father, will you? I won't have time. Especially if your knight can't wait," she teased.

Edwina's face warmed. "It's not *that* . . ." Her voice faltered.

"Then what is it, Ed?" Cecelia slipped on her jacket and pulled her sister close.

Not a single word formed itself in Edwina's brain.

"That's what I thought." Cecelia winked and followed Reardon out the door.

"Good morning."

Alex Dunnegin's voice would forever cause her heart to beat too fast. Edwina dabbed her eyes and turned to the man she was going to marry.

"Cecelia is off to the States?"

"Business." Edwina shrugged, wondering if she looked all right.

"Jeans, 'ey? You up for a ride this morn? Paige is in the kitchen with her breakfast, but she's squirming to get outdoors. The sun is warm today." His six-foot frame stood inches above her five-foot-six one. "Y'er hair will dry in the wind." He fingered her wet hair.

"Sounds great." Her voice soft at his touch.

Paige called from the kitchen. Alex winked and headed there.

Even though her thighs were still screaming from the last ride, she had enjoyed the rocky pathways as they meandered through the green countryside. The stream near the cottage was her favorite place to stop and water the horses. Not to mention the fact that ingrained in her brain was the picture-perfect view as they gazed on the sun-sparkled waters gushing over the rocks, then slowly winding away through the low hills.

The idea of living in the cottage with the stream close enough to walk to brought more threats of tears. *What good thing in this world have I done to deserve this?* she wondered. *Lord, thank you for everything, for Paige, for Alex, for this land.*

"Lass?"

Edwina turned, her heart pounding at the way he called her *lass*.

"Paige is calling ye. I'll go out and saddle the horses while ye get ready."

Edwina hurried to the kitchen to find Paige seated on a chair with a stack of books beneath her.

"Are you all right?" Edwina worried about her legs still in casts.

"I'm fine. I don't like sitting on pillows. Are we riding today?"

"Yes." She smiled. "Are you up to it?"

"Aye, and I want to see Silsee too."

Edwina learned that five-year-old Paige was quite firm in her intentions and knew she would have to swerve around the little gal's determinations. "Does your father say it's all right?"

"Father has promised to take me down to the barn when we return."

It would be good for her to see her lamb. Edwina loved her happy voice. She thought perhaps they might lose the closeness they'd shared now that her father was home, and Edwina knew they would have to work on that. She'd find a good book about parenting and read up on it.

Chapter 8

Cecelia tapped her perfectly manicured fingernails on the airport counter. "I'm flying standby, but if you can get me into first-class I'd be willing to pay premium price," she said.

Cecelia turned slightly and noticed the man standing behind her. He was tall, dark, and wearing Armani. She'd know that label anywhere. Dark brown eyes in a tan face added to her view, and she looked away. When she glanced at him again, those dark chocolate eyes were gazing into hers.

"Business?" he asked.

"Yes, in Chicago. Rather a hurried situation, I'm afraid." She felt pulled into the man's presence as though they were the only two people in the airport.

"I see." He checked his watch and paused to reach for something in his jacket pocket.

Cecelia turned her chin upward a tiny bit and wondered if her hair looked halfway decent. Apparently it did, for the man, who seemed preoccupied a moment ago, now held out a boarding pass.

"What's this?"

"A seat in first-class. My business associate was to fly back with me but has been detained. I will inquire at the desk to see if you can have the seat."

She wanted to flutter about and make some sort of brilliant comment, but not a word came from her mouth except, "Thank you."

He motioned for the attendant's attention.

She listened as his deep voice stated that he had a first-class boarding pass and might the woman standing here have that seat. He spoke as one who was accustomed to being heard and deferred to. She knew that kind of man. Her heart did a silly flip-flop.

"I will check and call your name in a few minutes."

Cecelia turned to thank the man, but he was gone. She forced herself not to look around, but walked directly back to her seat and pulled out a magazine. It took every bit of professionalism she had learned *not* to seek the man out. Obviously he wished to stay incognito, which only warmed her blood more.

An agonizing twenty minutes later her name was called. She stepped up and found the man waiting. "It is taken care of. Seat 2B." He handed the adjusted boarding ticket to her. The woman behind the counter smiled at them.

"Thank you." She squared her shoulders, remembering her mother's words before walking onto the stage. *Wow them!* Cecelia felt she was on the stage and played the part exceedingly well. The man slipped his pass into his jacket pocket and with a slight smile, departed. Cecelia released her breath. How long had it been since Cecelia Grace Giatano had been breathless? She didn't have a clue.

She walked back to her seat and waited to board.

Suddenly she realized her thirtieth birthday was just a month away; it was time she made some sort of arrangement to start her life. Funny, but she hadn't desired anything like that until now. Why was that? She knew instantly. Watching Alex and Edwina interact, sharing secret looks, whispering, and trying to get time alone . . . that was it. And she hadn't been kissed silly in . . . sadly, she couldn't remember when.

Spencer had shot out of there too. She wondered if there was a real emergency at the restaurant or if he had scooted out so he wouldn't have to see Edwina in love. She may be busy, but she wasn't blind. She knew Edwina and Spencer had shared a kiss.

But there hadn't been time for Spencer to know Ed. Funny how events and circumstances shot people into your life like a cannonball and next thing you know they were shot back out again to some other part of the world.

She heard her name being called over the PA. "You're set for first-class boarding Miss Giatano, thanks to the gentleman."

She grabbed her carry-on and shook the cobwebs from her brain. She needed to focus. That Victorian would not stay on the market long, especially since Mrs. Quentin King had heard about it. That woman was a thorn in her skin. Anytime she heard that Cecelia was interested in a building, she was right there bidding against her.

Cecelia knew why. The woman thought her husband had a thing for her. Nothing could be further from the truth. Mr. King had a thing for every blonde that walked past him. Cecelia felt a stab of pity for Mrs. King, then remembered her purpose and walked faster.

She thanked the woman and hooked the handles of her carry-on over her shoulder. She was on a mission. Her Dior's clicked on the runway as she hustled to the plane.

After settling her bag in the overhead compartment, she took her seat, grateful to be on the flight. And first class was a bonus. She leaned her head back and closed her eyes, hoping that when she opened them she would see the handsome stranger.

When she did open her eyes, she checked her watch and gasped. Nearly an hour had passed.

"The princess must have slept on a mattress without a pea beneath it." He smiled at her.

"Evan Wyndham."

"Cecelia Giatano." She nodded.

She wanted to make some professional crack about fairy tales but nothing came to mind, so she reached for her purse at her feet where she'd stowed it before takeoff. She had never missed a takeoff in her life.

Sleeping. And with the handsome stranger next to her and no doubt watching. She hoped above all things that she hadn't let her mouth drop open—or worse.

"Did I snore?" She felt like a schoolgirl on a first date.

"No. But your head did fall on my shoulder."

Cecelia's eyes widened. He looked amused. Should she apologize or let it go?

She decided on the latter and took out her calendar and made a notation to keep her eyes averted until she could recover. What possessed her to ask him if she snored? That was the most humiliating comment she could have made.

By the time she had the courage to look his way, he was already interested in a magazine. She peeked. *Entrepreneur*. She wondered what business he worked in.

Half an hour later, he stood and reached above in the compartment and brought down a small notebook and made notations, then tucked it in his side pocket. As he did, he jostled her elbow and knocked the pen from her hand.

"I'll get it." He unbuckled and retrieved the pen.

Their hands touched, and Cecelia checked his left ring finger. Empty.

"So, what is your business?" She'd barely formed the words in her head before they'd popped out of her mouth.

"Publishing."

"I see." She nodded sagely, knowing that less was more, and waited for him to continue.

"And you?" he asked, turning toward her slightly.

"I buy buildings and turn them into B & B's or condominium units in downtown Chicago."

"Interesting."

He was a man of few words, she decided and thought it best to play along. She knew these types. They were self-made men who needed nothing from the rest of the world. They had it all. His quiet, reserved manner intrigued her.

"Yes it is." She reached for her bag and pulled out a magazine. *Business Week.* She would let him know that she too was savvy and his equal. She crossed her slender legs and modestly pushed her black skirt over her knees.

He did not speak for an hour. She read her magazine, which was three months old. Bored after she'd paged through it twice, she put it away and folded her hands in her lap. Should she offer her business card? Ask for his?

She loved his profile, having several opportunities to study his features when the flight attendant checked on them. Thick dark hair, dark eyes. She suspected Italian or perhaps Brazilian background. His well-manicured hands were tan like his face. That meant he'd probably been to the islands on a vacation recently.

Musing, she didn't hear him speak the first time and leaned closer. "I'm sorry?" she said and waited for him to repeat.

"May I order you a drink? It is *Miss* Giatano?"

"Yes, it is." Cecelia ordered a daiquiri.

Immediately she felt the doors open. Drinks in hand, they began to socialize the same way they would if at a business luncheon.

"So what is the name of your company, Mr. Wyndham?" Cecelia turned slightly.

"White Gate Publishing."

She nodded. "And yours?"

"Cecelia's Place."

"That would be on Michigan Street. The blue and gold awning."

"Why, yes. You know it then?"

"We've had several business luncheons at Winnie's."

Cecelia smiled. "And did you find the service acceptable?"

"Absolutely. In fact, the service is impeccable."

"An English background, if I guess correctly."

"Yes." She smiled.

"My father was from England. I recognize the slight variation in dialect." His voice was deep, sensual.

She watched his countenance change slightly. Women's intuition told her he was interested. She relaxed. Perhaps it was time she found a man too.

Edwina, her younger sister, would be married before her. Somehow she hadn't cared until this moment.

Chapter 9

"My card, should you need the services of a publisher." Their fingers touched slightly. "I'll get your things."

Cecelia took the card from his hand and stepped aside as he unsnapped the overhead compartment and handed down her bag. The plane had landed, the hours spent making her plan to claim that Victorian, and perhaps even Mr. Wyndham, as soon as her foot stepped in Chicago.

"Thank you for the seat." He accepted her handshake, and she shivered when he held her hand extra long. She bent to retrieve her purse from the seat to give him her business card, but he was already at the plane's exit door.

Heady, she fingered his card, still safely ensconced in the pocket of her jacket, and, smiling, hurried off. She had a job to do. Still, the hope of love kindled itself deep in her heart. Was she ready?

Her heels clip-clopped through O'Hare as she made her usual dash for a taxi once she'd retrieved her luggage. Heady stuff. Thinking about settling down.

Shaking her brain back into place, she took one last look around, hoping to get a glimpse of him, then slid into the taxi and called out her address to the driver.

* * *

"Spencer, have you got my keys?" She left her luggage at her door when she realized she'd forgotten her key. Edwina would not be around to keep track of her.

"You're back?" He appeared from the back of the restaurant office. "Are you okay?"

"Of course I'm okay. Just a business problem, that's all. I was hoping you had the extra key."

"No problem, Cecelia." Spencer retrieved the extra and dropped it into her hand. "So how are the wedding plans coming along?" He folded his arms across his chest.

She shrugged, her mind already working on whatever project brought her home. He wondered if she knew how beautiful she looked at the moment. Her hair was coming loose from its usual French twist and her eyes were tired, yet sparkling. The woman was a virtual robot. She needed someone to slow her down.

"What are you smiling at? Do you know something I don't? Has Edwina called?" She stared daggers at him just to let him know how serious she was.

"Nope. No calls, and I don't expect any. Alex Dunnegin is well able to handle his fiancée and his wedding." He knew that would start a fire.

"Since when does any man know how to plan a wedding?"

Spencer couldn't help the smile that crept across his face again. The woman had no clue. Not everyone wanted her to be their wedding planner.

"Spencer Hallman, you get on my nerves the way you look at me with that smirk on your face, never saying a word." She turned from him in a huff.

"Don't forget where you put that key, Cecelia. If you lose that one, I won't be there to rescue you and neither will Edwina."

Cecelia Grace Giatano was already halfway out of his office, the sound of her heels hitting the wood floors echoing in his brain. What would that woman do once her little sister was happily married off? Spencer only hoped he would be there to pick up the pieces.

* * *

The phone was ringing as Cecelia fussed with the door. She kicked off her heels and ran across the soft carpet. "Cecelia Giatano," she answered in her best formal English and hoped she'd hear Mr. Wyndham's deep voice. She'd already decided she would wear her newest Anne Klein designer suit on their first date.

Frustrated, because a tenant had lost their suite key and was down in the foyer unable to get into their room. Back to the second floor.

"Spencer, you still here?" She stuck her head into his office.

"He's lunching with a guest," Kitty called as she whirled past. "There." Kitty pointed with a nod of her head, hands and shoulder balancing the tray.

Cecelia eyed the throng of guests and found him. He was sitting with a beautiful woman. Blonde, slender, and sweet-faced. *Just his type.* So then why did she feel her heart pinch? *Well, if you aren't getting all soggy over something silly. . .* Cecelia scolded herself, then lassoed her thoughts and stomped over to the table.

"Key problems?" Spencer looked up.

"You might say that. Could I have a word with you?"

He excused himself from his guest and stepped behind a short wall.

"Cecelia, you can see I'm having lunch."

She noted his irritation. "I need the key to Suite 405.

Spencer gazed at the woman and without a word went to his office, retrieved the key, and handed it over.

"Thank you. I'll leave you to your guest," Cecelia said and walked away.

"I'm sorry, Deena, she's rather rude these days." He said to his sister.

Chapter 10

Chicago

Cecelia punched the elevator button, not waiting for James. She ignored him and thought about her next move. She realized she was clicking her pen when James looked rather annoyed. "Sorry," she said, but she wasn't. What was with her these days?

Three minutes later the guest had his key and she was on her way. The goal was to get her real estate agent, Rebecca Burke, on the phone, dress, and make her appearance. Mrs. Quentin King was not going to beat her this time, no matter how much she bid on that Victorian.

Within the hour, she was in her agent's office, sitting on the edge of her seat, tapping the table with her pen. Miss Burke had bid twenty thousand dollars over the asking price right up front. Her agent had warned her that was not the way to start the bid, but Cecelia didn't care. If Mrs. King wanted a bidding war, Cecelia would start it, not her.

Something burned in her heart. She felt anger, frustration, and unnamed feelings. She was angry, but at who? Not wishing to concede to those thoughts at the moment, she stood and paced.

Her agent appeared, and Cecelia knew it was not good news. "What?"

"She's upped the bid thirty thousand dollars over yours."

"Why, that—" Cecelia almost let unkind words slip out.

"It's not wise to keep going higher, Miss Giatano. I'm warning you, you'll pay triple what the house is worth if you continue."

"I want that house, Rebecca."

"I know you do. Believe me. But this isn't the way to get it. May I make a suggestion?"

Cecelia stopped fussing and turned. "What?" She waved her hand and paced.

"Stop the bid. Go home. Let Mrs. King think she's won."

"Are you kidding me? I'm not in the mood for silly advice," she spit out.

"You'll get the house, if you go home."

"Right, when chickens fly—or pigs or whatever it is. . . ."

"It's pigs." A gentle smile rested on Rebecca Burke's face.

Cecelia turned. "You're smiling, Miss Burke?"

"You know it says somewhere that a soft answer turns away wrath."

"Where does it say that?" Cecelia couldn't believe she was engaging in this conversation.

"The Bible."

"Oh, puff and fluff, that's all that is. I've tried that."

"You have?"

"Don't sound so shocked. I went to church with my sister several times. She's one of those too."

"Those?"

"You know, believers. At least, that's what she calls herself."

Miss Burke wisely decided to divert the subject back to the matter at hand. "Well, what do you say? Will you take my advice? You'll save yourself enough money to furnish an entire room quite handsomely if you do."

Cecelia turned, arms crossed over her chest. "I can't see how giving in gains anything."

"You'd be surprised." Rebecca Burke returned softly.

"What exactly do you want me to do?"

"Well, let's try this. I'll go in and kindly acquiesce and say we've decided not to bid on the house, that you have another one in mind . . . and you do. Remember the house on Third and Winston? That's a beautiful house, Miss Giatano, and you *did* want to see it."

"Call me Cecelia," she puffed out and narrowed her eyes.

"Okay . . . Cecelia. If you'll call me Rebecca."

Cecelia paced across the room several times, then waved her hand in the air. "If you think it's best, go ahead. I'm too tired to think straight."

Wisely Rebecca did not allow her emotions to surface. She hadn't thought Cecelia Giatano capable of backing down on anything she set her mind to. "I'll be right back."

Cecelia took a seat. What was it that Rebecca said? Something about a soft answer. Maybe she should read her Bible more. Edwina had given her one last year for her birthday, which was fast approaching. Thirty. Why in the world did turning thirty have her mind all tangled up? She had achieved a lot for her age. She straightened her shoulders. Not many single women owned two buildings in Chicago, half interest in a restaurant, and appeared on the *Oprah Winfrey* show. Plus she was about to sign the contract for a pilot for her own design show.

Not too shabby. Was that the right word? Her thoughts were interrupted.

"Well, it's done." Rebecca sat in the chair next to her. "Now for the wait."

"Wait. What do you mean, wait?" Cecelia noted her agent's slight nervous twitch.

"I'm thinking that since Mrs. King has no battle, she won't enjoy the war."

Cecelia just stared at her. What was it with these believers anyway? "Take me to see the other house." She needed to be busy.

"I'll get the keys." Rebecca stood and hustled away.

Cecelia tapped her nails on the chair's elegantly carved wooden arms.

"You've got jet lag, I'll drive, Cecelia. We'll leave your car in the lot."

An hour later, Cecelia was done in. "Thanks for showing me the house. I love the Victorian better, but this one has lots of possibilities if I get my own show?"

"Your own show?" Rebecca turned excited eyes toward her client.

"Yes. I've been working with the Home Channel for my own design show. We're in the process of contracting the pilot."

"What? Are you kidding me?" Rebecca knew she sounded like a child. "I've always wanted to use my creative—" She stopped suddenly.

"You were about to say?" Cecelia prodded.

"I guess I'm a frustrated designer."

"Why are you in real estate then?"

"Actually, I have no clue," Rebecca admitted. "Mostly because my mother is a Realtor and I grew up knowing the business. Maybe for the money since I did manage to get a great deal on your building." She laughed.

"Indeed you did. And I think you have great talent in matching people with locations. So don't jump too quickly. However . . . hmmm." Cecelia mused, following Rebecca to her car.

Rebecca drove in silence, knowing Cecelia was thinking outside the box. She loved that about her client, even if she was a bit heavy-handed at throwing thousands of dollars out the window just to assuage her insatiable need to win.

"If the Home Channel contract allows it, I could ask you to be my assistant."

"On a live or taped show? Oh, I don't do cameras. I freeze at the sight of them, not to mention a microphone put up to my face can send my thoughts flying and I'm left speechless. Entirely speechless." She finished.

"My thoughts were more along the line of buying an old Victorian, fixing it up for the show. I'll need someone to assist with paperwork, meetings, shopping, that sort of thing."

"Shopping? Now there's something I'm good at."

"Well, lets talk about your design ideas. It would only be part-time. Are you up for it?"

"I can work evenings and weekends. My dream has always been to be a designer."

"Well dreams do come true. My sister's certainly did."

Chapter 11

"Your sister. I don't remember your mentioning a sister." Rebecca turned her gaze to Cecelia.

"Recently moved to Scotland. She was from a small town in Michigan."

"Your family must be well-traveled."

Cecelia laughed. "If you knew her, you wouldn't have said that. The girl has hardly been out of her own town!"

"And now she's living in Scotland?"

"Funny, isn't it?" Cecelia paused. "My divorced mother married Edwina's widowed father and that's how we became family. She was just starting college, and I was just finishing."

"That sounds like a story I'd love to hear someday. Right now I have another client meeting." She checked the car clock.

"Right. Well, let me know about the Victorian, will you? I'm not sure I should have let you talk me out of making a bid." Cecelia was beginning to doubt her wisdom in stepping back. "Fact is, I need to go home and sleep. It's been a long day, and I've got a short fuse right now."

Rebecca nodded. "Sounds like a smart move. I'll call tomorrow."

"No. Call me as soon as you know anything. I can't wait to see what that woman does."

She smiled and parked the car. "I'll run in and get a copy from my file of this last house we looked at, just so you can think about it. It's really got good bones."

Cecelia grabbed her keys and unlocked her car door. The wind blew wayward strands of hair across her face. She breathed in deeply, but somehow the air wasn't as fresh as the winds on those green hills back in Scotland. She wondered what Edwina and Alex were doing.

* * *

The doorbell was ringing. Incessantly. "I'm coming!" she called out, straightening her hair.

"What?" She pulled the door open.

"Well, what have we here? A catnap in the middle of the afternoon?"

Spencer's wide smile irritated her immediately. "What do you want? And why did you keep ringing the bell? Aren't you supposed to be working?"

"Nope, got the rest of the day off. I was going to ask if you'd like to trot on over to *Chicago Firehouse* for dinner. I've got some things I'd like to talk to you about."

"What things, Spencer? And where is your key?"

Spencer leaned in the doorway and realized the woman was half crazy. "You picked it up earlier, remember? You were off to see the Victorian."

"Oh yes." She pushed strands of hair away from her face as she walked away.

He knew she was in no mood for teasing, so he followed her in and shut the door behind him. "I came for my bucket too."

"What bucket?" She looked over her shoulder.

"My cleaning bucket under your counter. Can't do without it. All my supplies are in it, and I have someone coming to clean my place—"

"What? Someone's coming to clean *your* place?" she interrupted. "Was it that woman you were having lunch with? Never mind, it couldn't be her. She was much too sophisticated to be cleaning houses."

Spencer gave her a look. "Oh, so you're still asking the questions and assuming the answers then?" He headed for the kitchen.

"Spencer, would you check to see if there's anything in the fridge? I'm starving," she called from the bathroom.

"Yep. Nope."

"Would you stop using that word? It's so not a word. Why you Americans talk like street people I'll never understand."

"Hey, whoa, street people? People are people, Cecelia, no matter where they're from or how they talk."

She shrugged. "Nothing, then?"

"Not a thing. Let me take you out. We'll eat and talk. I want to hear how Alex and Edwina are."

"They're fine."

"Last I remember you were planning their wedding. Did they send you packing?" He waited for the backlash. It came quick and like a flaming sword slicing into his midsection. She popped her head around the corner.

"I *will* be going back to plan that wedding."

Spencer knew when to hold 'em and when to fold 'em, and he was going to hold 'em. So he nodded, reached under the sink, and retrieved his cleaning container. He watched her jerk the cupboard doors open and then slam them shut. What he wanted to do was grab her and hold her. She needed someone to lean on and didn't know it.

"What happened to the woman I remember just a few months ago? The one who, when Alex made his feelings known about her sister, backed off and didn't think of herself?"

"That woman is me. And I'm still me, just tired of . . ."

She shot from the room. Could it be God was working in her? He'd never seen her cry. And didn't especially want to.

Giving her space is wise, he thought and went down to the restaurant, purposely leaving her door unlocked.

An hour later he knocked and heard nothing, so he tiptoed in and set up in the kitchen. He made familiar noises so she would know he was there.

"What are you doing here?" she croaked from the doorway.

"I went down to the restaurant and got some shrimp salad, made fresh this morning." He kept working, trying not to stare. She was without makeup. Her normally perfect hair was mussed. Also a first. Her baby blues were red and puffy, probably from crying. It was about time she learned to cry.

"Still hungry?"

She murmured something inaudible.

Pulling out plates and glasses, he set them up on the island as she pulled up a tall chair and sat. So she was going to stay.

Spencer set the plate in front of her. And poured a glass of iced tea, no sugar.

"You didn't have to add all these weeds," she complained. "I hate all that green stuff floating around your plate, and no one ever eats it anyway."

He shrugged, leaving that one alone.

Chapter 12

Early the next morning the phone jangled next to her elbow, causing Cecelia to drop her pencil. Without thinking she grabbed it and answered with a blend of professionalism and crankiness.

"Miss Giatano, Evan Wyndham here."

Cecelia sat up straighter and instantly changed her mood. "Good morning," she said brightly.

"Good morning. I have need of a favor. If you are free this evening, I need an escort for an event. It could be to your benefit, business-wise, if you'd be interested in accompanying me."

Pausing for effect, she said wisely, "I'll check my calendar and get back to you."

"Of course," he said and was gone.

Cecelia stared at the phone. "Well, he is rather rude. Calling at the last minute, expecting me to fill a need for him. And we just met!"

She paced, still in her blue silk pajamas, which was most unusual. Normally she was out the door at this hour. But today she was lonely. Edwina was gone. Her mother had her own life with Edwina's father. Spencer was busy with a beautiful blonde lunch companion.

Maybe what she needed was a love interest. *And Evan Roberto Wyndham*, she thought as she stared at his business card, *would suit me fine*. He was handsome enough. And she knew monied class when she saw it. She dropped the card on the glass coffee table and poured a cup of tea in the kitchen.

Cecelia spoke aloud as she paced. "But, can't be too quick, or he'll think I'm available. Should I refuse and hope he'll ask again? No, he's not a patient man. I'll wait a few hours."

There, that was settled. Depending on the event, she knew her electric blue dress with sequins or her basic black full-length dress with the faux fur stole would work for a ball or formal event, which no doubt this was. For official affairs, there was always her red suit. She picked up her cell.

"Rebecca, Cecelia. Any word on whether the good Mrs. King snapped up *my* house?"

"Actually, Cecelia, I'm waiting for a call from her agent. We should know in the next couple of hours."

"Perfect. I'll be waiting. Thanks."

With that, it was time to head down for a workout. Something sprung to life in her spirit again. Donning her bodysuit and shorts, she padded across the soft carpet, humming Celine Dion's *"The Power of Love."* A good workout would expend an hour, leaving plenty of time for a return call to Mr. Wyndham.

Spencer had suggested they convert several rooms on the lower level into a workout space, which she'd approved, and apparently he'd become a frequent visitor. She noticed he'd beefed up and looked quite good, actually.

"Miss Giatano." James bowed his head slightly.

"Good morning. To the workout room, please." She kept her shoulders straight and stiff.

One hour later, sweating and feeling more like herself, Cecelia rushed into her apartment. No calls on her cell. Hopefully her house phone had messages from Rebecca or Evan Wyndham.

She checked. No blinking lights. Sighing, she used the time to shower and sauntered into the living room wrapped in a huge white towel, her hair wet and spiky. The doorbell rang. "Darn." In one second she decided it was probably Rebecca here to tell her the Victorian was gone and she'd wanted to come in person to give her the sorry news. She swung the door open.

There stood Evan Roberto Wyndham in a black suit, pristine white shirt, silver blue tie.

"Oh! I thought . . ." Her face flushed.

"Obviously you expected someone else," he said calmly, raking his eyes over her slowly.

"Obviously." She was not happy that he'd come to her place without an invitation. "I'm sorry, but you'll have to call later." She started to shut the door.

"Miss Giatano, I believe you could give me the answer to my question now."

"Mr. Wyndham, you did not hear me. I'll call you later."

The man was the perfect specimen of male, standing right before her. But her temper and impatience got the better of her. What was she thinking turning him down? *Because he showed up and caught me like this!* She answered her own question, pushed the door closed, and shaking from frustration, locked it."How dare he come to my home unannounced," she spit out.

Cecelia made calls from her line phone. Rebecca Burke was a professional and would call immediately should there be news. Two hours later she was her old self. There were calls to be made concerning her television contract. She'd had no idea it would be so complicated a process, but if there was a goal, she would do whatever it took to close the deal.

Should she contact Mr. Wyndham and tell him she was not free this evening, or ignore his rude behavior and accept?

She decided on the former. Perhaps she was charmed by his looks and power and, no doubt, money but that didn't mean she had to lower herself to his obvious lack of propriety. She had a set of rules of her own, and it would do him well to see her working out her own objectives. For some odd reason, it gave her a sense of power. And she rather liked the feeling.

The phone jangled. "Cecelia, Good news. Mrs. King did not buy the Victorian."

Cecelia smiled, loving the excitement in her agent's voice. "How *did* you do that?"

"Do what?"

"Get her to the point that she didn't want that house?"

"Remember a soft answer turns away wrath?"

"Vaguely."

"Well, it worked. That and the fact that you did not bid against her," Rebecca said quietly.

"Well, then I've learned a new principle in my business." Cecelia was giddy. "Remove the competition from the competitor, and they fall like apples off a tree."

"So it seems." Rebecca kept her voice soft.

"Make an offer then. I want that house. My idea is to use it on the show as a redesign. All the while I'm filming and spending the money on it, I'll have free advertising and a newly refurbished house to rent or sell."

"Sounds like a win-win."

"Indeed." Cecelia was already mentally choosing paint colors.

"I suggest you bid at the house's value, without the twenty-thousand add-on,"

"Thank you. As you said, twenty thousand will be better utilized in renovation. You were right about that."

"So we have a price, then? Can you come and sign the papers now and I'll get on it? Or shall I come to you?"

"Do you have time for a late lunch? I want those papers in today." Cecelia ordered.

"I do, in fact."

"Good, you haven't seen my suite since I've redecorated. Twelfth floor."

"See you soon."

A quick change and Cecelia was ready for the day. The enticement of a new project fed her hunger for confidence. Thanks to her agent, she would soon be the owner of The Victorian. She needed a name for the place and set her mind to working while trying to do her own hair. There hadn't been time to make an appointment with her hairdresser.

The doorbell rang again. She pulled it open, wondering if she might see Mr. Wyndham standing there looking smug. He was not going to win her affections that way. After all, Edwina had been living her own life when her knight came along. Perhaps her little sister had a point.

"Rebecca, come in. Let's get these papers signed. You can fax them from my office so you can get the bid in quickly."

"Thanks, Cecelia, I will do that. Then I'll feel more at ease during lunch."

"That's right. Safe than sorrowful, that's what they say, right?"

"Well,"—Rebecca hesitated—"it's *better safe than sorry*, actually."

Cecelia repeated it as she took the seat on the sofa. Rebecca pulled out the papers. With a few flourishes of the pen, Cecelia was finished.

"If you'll show me to your office, I'll send this in," Rebecca said.

Cecelia took her agent down a short hall and stepped aside.

"Oh my goodness, it's so elegant," Rebecca exclaimed. "I love the color. It's such a cool gray, and the white beadboard touch is perfect. The crown molding makes the room."

"Thank you. We'll see the rest of the suite in a few moments."

"Right." Rebecca looked around. "Where's your fax?"

"Oh, stored right in here. I didn't want everything in view, you know." Cecelia opened a set of double doors revealing a desk, computer, and equipment in a large closet area.

"What a great idea. I thought a Murphy bed was hidden behind those doors."

"Good idea." Cecelia laughed. I rather like a clean atmosphere to work in."

"Perfect atmosphere is more like it. Which I also love." Rebecca fingered the pewter silk draperies and ran her hand along the smooth black granite desk surface.

"Looks like we have the same taste. Elegant, clean lines." Cecelia smiled.

"If the rest of your suite is anything like this, that's certain."

With a sigh of relief, Rebecca declared after sending the fax, "Well, that's that. We should know by the end of the day. Tomorrow morning at the latest."

"Great. I'm famished. Would you like to try lunch at *Winnie's* below stairs?"

"Below stairs? You have a restaurant in the building?"

"We haven't talked in a while have we, Rebecca?"

"Actually, we haven't. Over a year, I'd say, when you bought this building."

A lot has happened. We'll talk over lunch. I have a quick call to make, then I'll be back. Take a look around. The kitchen is to die for. Right this way." She walked Rebecca to the kitchen and left her to peruse.

She grabbed Mr. Wyndham's business card from the table and phoned her regrets to his answering service, then found Rebecca.

Cecelia noted her large brown eyes and medium brown hair with blonde highlights. "You ever thought of modeling?"

"Not a chance."

"Why?" Cecelia looked her over.

"My legs are too short, and my arms too long."

"Puff," she spit out. "You haven't the least desire?"

"I'd rather be thrown into Lake Michigan."

"Well, that settles it." Cecelia laughed.

Rebecca changed the topic. "Have you decided on the outside color of the Victorian, if the house is yours?"

"Oh yes, cream for the main part of the house with tan and pale green trim. The gingerbread border will be a strong peach."

"Sounds lovely."

"Here we are." Cecelia stepped off the elevator and walked through the restaurant's formal waiting area.

"It's so nice." Rebecca looked around. "I love the black accents against the blue-green walls."

"Cecelia." Spencer came flying through a side door. "Are you here for lunch?" He tucked her hand into his elbow.

"Yes, and I brought a friend."

"Oh, I'm sorry." Spencer turned.

"Spencer, this is my real estate agent, Miss Rebecca Burke."

"Miss Burke." Spencer offered his hand.

"Rebecca, this is Spencer, owner of *Winnie's*."

"Co-owner," he corrected Cecelia and smiled down at her. "Come this way, ladies."

As they walked through the maze of tables, Rebecca commented softly, "I like the atmosphere. The lighting is perfect."

"Right here." He pointed with a bow. "Your favorite table, Cecelia." He pulled out a chair. "Miss Burke." Then one for Cecelia. "Rico will be your server today." He handed each a menu and left them to their conversation.

"I like the deco. It's classy. Black barrel stuffed chairs, crème linens, blue and green accents. Beautiful and not too garish. Easy on the eyes. Love the simple art on the walls. Black frames are my favorite."

"Have you thought of becoming a designer, starting your own business perhaps?"

Rebecca turned to find Cecelia waiting for an answer.

"I can see from your look that you've never even entertained the idea." Cecelia smiled.

"Only in my dreams."

"Tell me about yourself." Cecelia placed her crème linen napkin across her lap.

"Well, there's not much to tell. My mother spent her career in real estate, so I heard about it growing up, took a few college courses in accounting because one of my career counselors thought I'd be good at it." She laughed.

Cecelia smiled. "You're not meant to be managing accounts and crunching numbers."

"Really? You think so?"

"Creative is what you are." She paused, her long fingernail tapping the tabletop. "Have you thought any more about the idea of assisting me with the Victorian? I'll need someone to run errands, choose accent pieces, draperies, rugs, frames; plus I'll need a good eye."

"You'd like me to help with the actual design of the Victorian?"

"Are you interested?"

"I would love to work with you." Rebecca hoped she didn't sound breathless.

"As soon as the papers are signed, we will begin then. You will need to keep your day job, and we can work in the evenings, if that suits you. You are single, correct?"

"Oh yes, that and more. I'm not even seeing anyone at the moment. I just broke off a two-year relationship."

"Oh, I'm sorry," Cecelia stated.

"It was going in the wrong direction. So I'm free. I'd love to learn all I can from you."

Chapter 13

Monday morning brought new excitements for Cecelia. The Victorian was officially hers, the contract with the Home Channel was waiting to be signed, and the producers loved her idea to purchase and redesign the Victorian. There would be an initial four-show pilot.

The doorbell buzzed into her thoughts. "Come in have a seat Rebecca."

"Thanks." She checked her watch then settled on the sofa."

"Rebecca, I owe you big time. Had it not been for your suggestion to hold back, I would be fighting the good Mrs. King. We are free to begin both projects. I sign the contract today. Would you like to come along?"

"Oh, could I? I'll have to check my calendar."

Cecelia saw the light in her eyes and waited while she paged through the day's appointments. "We have an agent meeting this afternoon." Her voice dropped with disappointment.

"Can't you miss it?"

"No, not really. I've never missed one."

"Call and explain you have a client meeting. With me."

"I could do that. I've just never missed a meeting—"

"Well, if you're going to grow, you have to step out." Cecelia looked her in the eye.

"That's true. And the meetings are usually—well, pretty useless."

"Then don't waste your time. You can represent your agency just by being at the signing of the contract. Couldn't hurt, your being there."

Rebecca nodded and called in her regrets.

"You didn't sound confident."

"I wasn't. My boss gave me grief over it. She was not happy with me."

"Rebecca, you can't be everywhere at once. Marketing is one of my best skills. And I'm telling you, your boss's business will be mentioned at this meeting. You're my agent, and I'll set it up. It's the least I can do to thank you for getting me the Victorian."

"Well, it works for me."

"There, that sounds better. Now go home and get dressed. The show's limo will pick you up in an hour. What's your address?"

Rebecca gave her the address and thanked her as she shoved out the door, her heart fluttering. Who knows what may come of it all? *Lord, help me to be wise.*

The steps up to her apartment were taken two at a time. She unlocked the door with trembling fingers and burst in.

"What's the matter?" Her mother turned large eyes on her.

"I have to change clothes. Is my black vest clean? I'm headed downtown with Cecelia Giatano to sign her first contract with the Home Channel."

"What? How—?"

"I'll explain later, mom. How're things going at the office?" Rebecca kept talking as she peeled her shirt over her head.

"Our boss is throwing fits again, and no one is in the mood for it. That's why I came home today...to get away from it all. She was not happy you're missing the meeting either."

"I know, but she'll be glad when she hears that Cecelia is going to mention the name of her Realtor today. Who knows what might become of *that*?" She talked around her toothbrush.

Rebecca was tossing skirts on the bed next to each other. The black vest was clean and hanging over a chair. The black-and-white geometric print pencil skirt paired with a clean, white blouse was perfect. She wore her best low-heeled black shoes and pulled her heavy hair into an upswing and hid the pins in the thickness.

"How do I look?" She dashed to the kitchen where her mother sat sipping tea.

"Great. Black and white suits you. Vest looks fine, actually."

"Good, I didn't want to wear a suit or anything that might overstate my purpose for being there, yet I need to represent our agency."

"I should say."

"Well, wish me luck, Mom. Miss Giatano's driver is here." We'll talk tonight.

Rebecca smoothed her skirt and hurried down the stairs, then slowed her step. She didn't want to appear too excited, but it was nearly impossible.

"Miss Burke," the man stated and opened the door for her.

"Yes. Thank you." She climbed into soft black leather seats and leaned back.

In less than ten minutes they were parked in front of Cecelia's building. The doorman signaled, and she came out wearing the most exquisite white blouse, silver gray skirt, matching short jacket and elegant gray pumps.

"You look fabulous," Rebecca said breathlessly.

"You sound the way I feel." Cecelia smoothed her skirt.

"You. Nervous? I can't imagine it."

"I just want to make sure everything goes right. This is my first attempt at doing a television show. My lawyer has already made concessions and changes to the contract, so it should be a schmooze and sign party today."

"You sound so sure of yourself."

In minutes the car pulled up and gained entrance to the production lot by special command.

Rebecca followed Cecelia without saying a word. They were shown to a large conference room. Cecelia's attorney arrived. "Thought it best to have representation in the event there are any moves to change anything." He spoke to Cecelia.

"Yes. Other than the items we talked about, is there anything I should be aware of?"

"I think we're in order. If anything questionable arises, let me answer," he suggested.

"Of course."

The large black marble conference table was encircled by four men and three women. Cecelia, her attorney, and Rebecca were invited to take seats.

Several comments were made by the producer. The attorneys talked to their clients, and it seemed all was agreeable.

When asked if she had any comments, Cecelia introduced Rebecca, and with a few well-chosen words hailed her agent's company as excellent and suggested anyone seeking real estate services to contact her.

Rebecca tried to keep her cheeks from turning a heated red and nodded quietly.

Then Cecelia shocked the entire group by asking if Rebecca Burke might be considered as her assistant on the show.

Her breath caught. She'd told Cecelia she didn't do cameras and microphones. What in the world was she thinking?

Rebecca started to protest until she caught Cecelia's look.

She was evidently schmoozing. Rebecca settled back in her seat.

"The producers choose from a pool of appropriate people. There is much criteria we have to consider."

Cecelia nodded in agreement. "As you wish."

Rebecca let out a long breath between her lips and hoped no one noticed.

"Well, then, Miss Giatano, welcome to *The English Victorian*."

"You've named the show then?" She stood to accept handshakes around the table.

"Yes, we liked the way you wrote your ideas about redoing the Victorian, and with your English accent and background plus the viewers' trend toward that era, we think your pilot will be a complete success."

Rebecca's heart beat like a thousand drums. Just like that, Cecelia's dream had come true. First the acquisition of the house, next the show. If only dreams were that easy to attain for everyone.

Thrilled at being present, she followed Cecelia and her attorney out into the hall. The building they were in was modern withTravertine floors, high ceilings, and walls of windows. She wouldn't mind working for one of the producers, which would require shopping for a new wardrobe. Surrounded by creative, talented designers and interacting with television crews sounded absolutely delightful. Behind the scenes, of course.

"Coming, Rebecca?"

"Oh yes." She felt like a kindergartner on her first day of school.

The attorney and Cecelia had a few words, a handshake, and then they parted.

"Did you notice he's got eyes for you?" Rebecca whispered.

"Who?" Cecelia turned to look at her agent.

"Your attorney. I didn't catch his name."

"Stuart Littleton. And he is handsome, but taken. I don't interfere with married men."

Rebecca smiled. Her regard for Cecelia lifted a notch.

"Let's celebrate. Dinner at *NoMI*. French cuisine and great views."

"Really! I've never been there. Do you think I'm dressed all right?"

"Of course. Let's go. I want to talk about ideas. *The English Victorian* is a perfect name for the show. We will turn it into a bed-and-breakfast for the world to salivate over. By the time we advertise on the show, we won't have a single vacancy for three years running."

Rebecca stepped up her pace. This was going to be one of the best days of her life.

Cecelia turned."Let's ask Spencer to join us. He's got really good ideas, and we could use a bit of male input."

"Sure."

Cecelia slid her phone open and dialed. "Spencer will meet us in an hour when *Winnie's* closes. We'll get a table and get some preliminary thoughts on paper, then run them by him."

Cecelia's driver dropped them at *NoMI*. Rebecca pulled in a breath, squared her shoulders, and prepared herself with a prayer. *Lord, please guide me to the right place.*

Once inside the restaurant, they were seated, at Cecelia's request, near a bank of windows overlooking Michigan Street from the seventh floor.

"Order anything you like." Cecelia's face shone with confidence.

"Cecelia, this place is stunning. So modern, and look at the views."

"French cuisine. It's one of my favorite places to take visitors."

"It's beautiful. The Chicago skyline from up here as the sun goes down is fabulous."

"It is." she stated. "I've seen it a dozen times." Cecelia smiled then changed the topic as she gazed at the menu. "Your hair looks good up like that."

"Do you know when you'll be starting?"

"Not until after my sister Edwina's wedding. I had that included in the contract. Plus it gives me time to prepare. I wasn't sure we would get a house this quickly. I expected it might take several tries before I'd secure one, so we have a few months. It appears we will tape our first show in early October. Of course, they will be filming all the *before* pictures in a few weeks.

Rebecca smiled, happy that she'd had a small part in Cecelia attaining the perfect house.

"Once I'm back from the wedding though, it will be push and pull to get the Victorian ready. Your evenings and weekends will be taken for months," she warned.

"Not to worry. I'm free and could use the extra cash. I want to get my own apartment."

Cecelia smiled. "You're twenty-five, right? It's time you were out on your own. Mother and I moved from one place to another and took whatever acting job she could get. I loved traveling, but I hated living in so many different homes."

"Maybe that's why you love B&B's so much."

Cecelia's gaze met Rebecca's. "I guess I never thought of it that way before."

Rebecca smiled. "I think I might feel that way, if I were you."

Cecelia put the menu aside and pulled out a notebook from her elegant black purse. "Let's talk paint colors. Are you familiar with the Victorian era colors?"

"Somewhat, but I can research all that on the Internet."

"Oh, would you mind doing some historical fact-checking? I absolutely abhor computers."

"I wouldn't mind at all. I rather like that part of things."

"Excellent. We'll make great partners."

The two discussed various facets of the design show. "Of course the producer will be directing us as to what they want to showcase, but we will have the opportunity for input," Cecelia reminded her.

"This is so exciting." Rebecca was bursting with joy.

"Ah, so the ladies have already begun their plans?"

Spencer joined them at the table. A waiter appeared instantly with a menu.

Rebecca noticed Spencer's black suit, white shirt minus the tie. His blond hair was spiked, and he looked like a model for a billboard. She wondered why Cecelia didn't notice the way he looked at her. Did the woman have every male acquaintance following in her wake and not notice? It was clear Spencer was more than her partner in the restaurant business.

Chapter 14

Edinburgh

Three weeks later, Cecelia and Spencer were on their way to Edinburgh. Alex and Edwina's wedding date had been set for July twenty-fifth.

The Scot said once he'd made up his mind they were to marry, it was pointless to wait. Paige was safely in his possession, and all was well at the castle.

Spencer lifted Cecelia's designer suitcases from the Edinburgh airport turnstile, then grabbed his case and muscled them toward the exit.

"Reardon is waiting." Cecelia's Christian Louboutin's clicked across the floor.

She saw Paige first then came Alex Dunnegin's booming voice from behind her. Cecelia turned and schooled her features. The man had charisma along with his good looks.

"Where's Edwina?"

"She is off to a fitting. We are to bring you to her." Alex laughed as he saw Spencer wrestling the luggage.

"Ah, the man needs assistance." He motioned to Reardon and took a large bag into his own hands.

"Thanks. The woman is impossible. It's Edwina's wedding, but you'd think *her* entire wedding trousseau is packed in these cases."

"The way of women," Alex stated. "Who can know it?"

Spencer smiled at the Scot's comment, and Cecelia noted his confidence. He had changed since he became co-owner of the restaurant. Where once he had been happy-go-lucky, he had settled down and taken up the partnership in the restaurant with boldness. The work suited him.

"Has she chosen a dress then?" Cecelia interrupted.

"Indeed she has," Alex Dunnegin pronounced.

"Well, take me to her. We've work to do. The wedding is merely six days off. I can't imagine Edwina's gotten everything together," she stated and picked up her pace.

"Father, does she know?" Paige whispered in her father's ear after tugging him down to her level.

"Nay, she does not. And we would be wise to let Edwina tell her, lass." He shifted the case to his other hand and caught his daughter's hand with his other.

Paige smiled up at her father, and Alex's heart lodged in his throat. He knew too well how close he came to losing his daughter and squeezed her hand more tightly.

"Shall we ride this evening, Da?"

"It seems best not to be underfoot with the ladies at the castle. We'll ride, but only if ye take care to wear yer breeches and boots and bring a coat along should the evening turn cool."

She nodded and picked up her pace.

"Slowly, lass. The bones in yer legs are still healing."

"Father, I have done well, haven't I? Since the accident, I mean?"

"Ye have done well, lass," he agreed, mussing her hair. "We are at the car. Reardon will drop off our guests. We'll change quickly and be gone before they pull us into the fray. Shall we ask Spencer to join us? I think he will be as lonely at the castle as we."

"Oh yes, Father. I like him. He's funny."

Alex Dunnegin smiled.

Chapter 15

"Edwina, where are you?" Cecelia called out as she dashed into Edwina's bedroom.

"Hello, Bertie. Is my sister decent?"

"Oh, you are here, Cecelia," came the response from a back room. Edwina put on a white terry robe and tied it at her waist, then ran out to meet her sister.

"I'm so glad you're here." She put her arms around Cecelia and hugged her. She leaned back, and the look on her sister's face nearly sent her into fits of laughter.

"I'm sorry. . . . I . . . didn't mean to . . ." Edwina had messed up Cecelia's hair in her rush.

"Not to worry. It's all water under the barn." Cecelia tried to repair the damage.

"*Bridge*," Edwina said softly.

"Well, whatever it is." She waved her hand in the air. "What dress have you chosen?"

Bertie disappeared into the dressing room.

Edwina saw those well-manicured fingers resting at the slender waist.

"I love your outfit, Cece."

"Puff. What does my outfit have to do with anything? Put on the dress." Cecelia would have none of it.

"Okay, if you promise not to try to change my mind, I'll show you the dress."

"Have you lost weight, Ed?" Cecelia was sizing her up.

"Oh, for goodness' sake, Cecelia. You always say that! I don't know, maybe. Wait here, I'll run up to the tower and put on my dress and come down."

Cecelia fingered the two veils that blew gently at the slightly open window. Should she be a bride, she would wear a tiara with miniature diamonds and a minimum twelve-foot veiled train. An off-the-shoulder, fitted, silk, full-length dress with diamonds, sequins, and pearls covering the bodice. That was her style. Elegant and classic, yet chic.

"Cece." Edwina walked into the room, her dress rustling.

Cecelia turned. Her hand flew to her mouth, and her blue eyes widened. "It's perfect Ed," she whispered, moving forward to touch the dress. "How . . . ?"

"Do you like it?"

"How did you decide on this dress? It fits you perfectly and, well, I love it. It's absolutely you."

"I'm so glad you like it," Edwina breathed out.

"And you chose it without me."

Edwina stepped forward as soon as she heard the words. "I had to, Cece. The wedding is coming up so quickly, and we've been so busy with the details and getting to know each other, that . . . well . . . we just decided this was the right dress."

"We? Who's we?" Cecelia demanded.

Oh no, I've done it now.

"It doesn't matter. The dress is perfect, isn't it? And you love it, which makes me very happy."

"Who helped you pick out the dress, Ed?"

Edwina wavered, turned her back, and called out as she hurried away before her sister made her tell. "I'll be back in a minute. Oh wait, I haven't chosen the veil. Would you do that for me, Cece? There are two hanging up at the windows."

"That ought to keep her busy," Edwina whispered to Bertie, who waited in the tower, as she toed off the white satin slippers, actually bedroom slippers, from her feet. It would not do to let her fussy sister see those. Bertie helped her out of the dress, and hung it gently. "Lass, this be yer very own wedding. No need to try to please anyone but Laird Dunnegin. And if me eyes tell me truth, the lad will be well-pleased." She winked and pushed Edwina out the door.

"Which veil do you think goes with the dress, Cece?" She made her appearance again.

"This one. It's the longest." Cecelia held it atop Edwina's head and studied her reflection in the mirror.

"I rather think I should choose the shorter one. The winds, you know."

"You are holding the ceremony out of doors, then?" Cecelia screeched. "I thought perhaps Alex may have tried to talk some sense into you."

Edwina felt her courage teeter.

"I suppose you've already decided that too. Ed, they have beautiful ancient churches in Scotland. You could have done so much better, especially for the pictures." Cecelia tut-tutted.

Edwina tried not to let her disappointment show.

"Don't be so reserved. The Scot has money, or haven't you thought of that?"

Edwina's heart dropped a notch into her stomach, but she said nothing.

Cecelia stopped fussing with the veil and caught the look in Edwina's eyes. "Oh, don't pay any attention to me, Ed. I just want what's best for you."

"You really do like my dress, Cece?"

"It is lovely. Really. But an outdoor wedding with all these wonderful churches around?"

"We want to be married on the hills." She kept her voice low.

Cecelia put the longer veil back on the wide hanger and brought down the shorter one. "If the wind is going to be blowing, this will be best." She set it atop Edwina's head and picked and pulled until it was just right. It pooled at Edwina's feet perfectly.

"Ed, you'll make a beautiful bride," she declared.

Edwina threw her arms around her sister. "I'm so glad you're here."

Chapter 16

"Spencer, where have you put my cosmetic case?" Cecelia was beside herself. "My face cream is in there." She leaned over the stairway.

Spencer heard his name, walked slowly to the large open foyer, and looked up. There she was, her hair wound up in a pink towel, her slender body wrapped in a huge, white bathrobe. He could see her bare toes sticking out between the spindles.

"I put everything in your room, Cece. Check again."

"Since when did I give him permission to call me Cece?" she muttered.

He smiled as she hurried off, mumbling and irritated. He waited for a few moments, arms crossed over his chest, until he heard, "I found it."

Alex chuckled as he walked by. "Game of chess in the library?"

A small table held the board and game pieces. Alex pulled up two chairs near the window. "Best to stay out of sight." He pulled the double pocket doors closed.

"Paige in bed, then?" Spencer asked.

"Yes, an hour ago. She still tires easily after she rides, thinking she's fully healed. The lass has some spit and fire."

Spencer smiled. "Like her father, I presume."

"Aye." Alex laughed and then cocked his ear. "Sounds like trouble is afoot."

The two studied the board and waited. Sure enough, there was a knock at the door.

Bertie appeared.

Alex's eyes questioned her. She hesitated. "I would have a word with ye." She stepped inside, looking behind her, and closed the doors. "Does Miss Cecelia know?"

"Not yet, but we will all know when she does." Alex made his move on the board.

"Aye, 'twill be a bit of noise when she does," Bertie agreed.

Spencer did not look up, but studied his play. "So what is the great secret, or dare I ask?"

"Man, you are a fool. If ye know, then ye'll be trapped too. Believe me, it is not that great a consequence, although your Miss Cecelia will no doubt have something ta say."

Spencer considered the man's words and said, "How's the weather tomorrow?"

"The winds have slowed a mite. If the good Lord continues this warm spell, it should be a grand day for the wedding."

Spencer envied and admired the man.

Bertie came with a tray of sandwiches and tea. "Thank you, Bertie. Now shouldn't ye be off to yer bed? There's much to do this week."

"Ach, as if I don't know it too." She busied herself with picking lint off the chair arms and made her way to the door, then turned. "Should ye need me, I will be abed," she said smartly and clicked the doors closed.

"We may want to make plans to steer out of 'ere tomorrow as well," Alex decided and picked up a sandwich. Spencer agreed.

* * *

Edwina woke to the dogs barking and Cecelia's frantic voice. She flew out of bed and grabbed her robe. The dogs had her sister cornered.

Down the stairs she raced, yelling, "Fife, Bailey, Duke! Come!" Instantly she heard the scratch of their claws on the wood floors. "Sit," she ordered. All three sat looking at her. "See, you've excited my guest. Naughty." But she couldn't help her smile. "Outside?" she asked.

The dogs flew to the door leading out to the gardens and waited. "Good boys." Edwina praised them and let them out, then ran back to find her sister.

"Cece, are you all right?"

"Barely," came the angry word. Edwina came round the corner, and there in the foyer stood her sister glued to the wall, afraid to move. "Are they gone?"

"Yes, I've put them outdoors. I am so sorry. The same thing happened to me the first time they came upon me . . . a new guest." She had to peel Cecelia away from the wall.

"I love cute little dogs, all we English do," she said, wiping the sweat from her hands, "but those are wild beasts, not dogs."

"Come, let's have tea. The house is quiet. We can talk."

"Good because I need to shop for a dress, and shoes, and what have you planned for Paige to wear? Or do I daresay, you've got nothing planned?"

Edwina saw those hands at her waist again and pulled in a breath. "Come, Cece, we're going to take a walk."

"Walk? This early in the morning? I only came down to get something for my headache and planned to go right back to bed."

"This may be the only time we have alone. I want to tell you all."

Cecelia's face portrayed a glimmer of interest, so Edwina went on. "We'll have some of Bertie's scones with cream and apricot jam and tea. It's so beautiful this time of morning here."

"I *am* famished. I don't remember if I ate yesterday," Cecelia mused.

"Probably the reason for your headache. Come to the kitchen."

"Now, like this?" Cecelia's voice was shrill. "No makeup, in a robe, for heaven's sake and no shoes." She picked up her foot and looked to see if it was dirty.

"Not to worry. No one will see us. It's 5:30 a.m., Cece."

Her sister hesitated a long moment and actually pulled her robe tighter around her and peered around. "Well, if you say so, I guess I could just this one time . . . but you know I hate to see anyone without my face on."

"I know. Really, it is hard to break your routine, isn't it?" Edwina's voice turned tender. Her sister ran by a certain set of rules, which gained her much success in her world, but Edwina wished Cecelia knew the simple joys of life.

"Come, I'll put the water on. I have some Earl Grey from Whittards."

"Oh, that does sound good. English tea *is* the best," she murmured and followed.

"So what about my dress and Paige's? Have you a color theme for the wedding? This affair is so out of control, Edwina. But then, I knew it would be if you were in charge."

Edwina knew her sister was not putting her down. She just wanted the best for her. She knew her wedding would be perfect—she just had to convince her sister.

"Sit," Edwina ordered.

"Here? Can't we at least eat out on the dining table? The atmosphere is so much—"

"What? More formal?"

"Well, yes. Why would you want to sit at this small . . . wooden . . . table?" Cecelia looked at it. "It's green, for heaven's sake. Parts of it anyway." She eyed the offensive object.

Edwina kept her lips in a straight line. "A table is a table. Not to mention that we don't want to draw attention to ourselves, now do we? I mean, in here the fire will keep us warm and cozy and we can talk. Plus no one will see us."

Cecelia reluctantly followed her sister's lead and pulled out a ladder-back chair. The paint was peeling off the green table and the mismatched chipped white chairs were ancient.

Edwina pulled down teacups and made sure to match the cups and saucers, set up napkins and flatware, then put out sugar cubes and cream. "Have you missed the English cream?"

"Oh, dearly. It's been months since I've had a good cup of English tea, not to mention a decent scone."

The teapot whistled. Edwina snatched it up and poured the steamy water into their cups. She watched her sister spoon leaves in the infuser and steep her tea. Edwina followed her sister's every move. "So this is the way the English drink their tea." Edwina caught Cecelia's eye.

"Indeed it is. Quite the proper way too." Cecelia was serious.

Edwina stirred in sugar and added cream for the first time. "The scones are warming in the oven and so is the jam."

"Excellent." Cecelia picked up her cup and sipped.

Edwina followed her sister's ladylike movements, but while the cup was coming to her mouth, her elbow hit something and splashed tea about.

Cecelia jumped up for a cloth and finding none, just sat back down. That's when it started.

Edwina could hold it in no longer. A giggle escaped from her lips, and at Cecelia's unawareness of what could be so funny in spilt tea, Edwina burst into a full-blown laugh. "I'm so sorry, Cece. It's just that I'm such a klutz. I will never be perfect like you." At first Edwina thought her sister might be hurt. And so she added, "I'm guessing you hope I never do, right? Then you wouldn't have anyone to scold."

Cecelia's eyes lit up. "That would be true. Who would I look after then?"

At that moment, Edwina saw her sister's eyes change again. Tears formed. And that last sentence came out in a whisper.

"Oh, now I've done it, haven't I? Acted silly and made you sad. You'll always take care of me, Cece."

"Not when you're here and I'm in America," she stuttered and set her cup down.

"I know. It will not be the same. But one day you'll get married too and have beautiful babies and . . ."

Her sister's eyes cooled, and she looked straight into Edwina's eyes. "Babies are not in my plan. A good, arranged marriage, but no babies. I cannot see myself changing nappies with, with . . . poo . . . in them. Not to mention, I do not intend to marry a man who wants such things. I have bigger plans."

Edwina, glad to get her sister back to safe subjects, nodded and agreed. "It's your choice, Cece...of course."

That settled, they set to drinking tea and talking about her father and Cecelia's mother. "They're scheduled to be here the day before the wedding. Father had planned a trip for this week, and your mother, well, she was not happy either. It seems she was about to start a new play. So you see, I have scrambled everyone's plans."

"Yes, that's true." Cecelia couldn't deny it. "You have to admit, it was quite sudden, Ed."

"I know it seems that way. But once a Scot makes up his mind, there is no stopping him,"

"Will you stop stirring your tea? The clinking is driving me crazy!" Cecelia's voice brought her out of her reverie.

Edwina put the spoon down. "Sorry."

Cecelia eyed her. "You are crossed in love, aren't you?"

"If that means crazy about the man I'm going to marry, then yes. I am crossed."

Cecelia shook her head. Edwina took that moment to look into her sister's beautiful blue eyes, without makeup, realizing for the very first time that she'd never seen her sister so free and unreserved.

Tears suddenly filled her own eyes.

"Now what's the matter?" Cecelia asked, putting her spoon down. "Have I said something?"

"Oh no, it's just that I'm so happy you are here. With me. Right now. Before I'm married. Just you and me."

Cecelia looked surprised. "It means that much to you, Ed?"

"It really, really does. Our parents are head over tails in love, and we can hardly get them to even notice us these days. And you with your business and Spencer . . . well, it seems we have to cling to each other. And now that we'll be in different countries . . . well . . . I just . . . want you to know that you mean very much to me."

Cecelia picked up her teacup. "Those scones ready? I'm starving."

Edwina lifted off her chair, knowing she'd put her proper sister in a mushy situation. "They're perfect." She set the scones on a pretty plate and burned her finger handling the hot jam.

"Oh, these are excellent." Cecelia buttered a scone and put on jam, then poured cream over the entire saucer.

Edwina's eyes nearly burst out of her head. "Not counting calories this morning, I see."

Cecelia waved her hand. "Not today. This is special. You and me before your wedding, sitting at this nasty table, at an ungodly hour. I deserve something for all this."

Her sister had effectively passed over the need-to-bleed moments, and Edwina was glad. The last thing she wanted was to get all mushy before the wedding . . . and make it more difficult for Cecelia to leave. She joined in and ate heartily.

Then gave her the news.

Chapter 17

"What do you mean, Bertilda *made* my dress? I know the best shops in Edinburgh, Edwina Emily Blair."

"Please, please just look at the dress, Cece. It's beautiful. Bertie designed it to look like mine. Just in a different color."

"What color is it?" she demanded. "And how long have you been planning this without telling me about it?" Cecelia's spoon was clinking loudly in her cup. Round and round it went.

"It's a soft champagne color. And Paige has one just like yours. They're beautiful."

"Beautiful? Are you out of your mind? Bertie is a maid. What does she know about style and sewing and design for goodness' sake?"

Cecelia was getting ugly now. "Look at the dress, Cece. Try it on. Please."

Her sister stopped stirring, placed her spoon rather heavily upon the saucer, and took a sip. Edwina gave her time to ease her temper. She waited without saying a word while her sister stared at the cupboards behind her.

"I'll look at the dress. But if I don't like it . . . I'll . . ."

Edwina finished her sentence. *I'll not wear it.* Cecelia was trying to push down her own desires, but Edwina knew it was nearly impossible for her to do it.

"Thank you, Cece. I know this is hard for you. You dress so beautifully all the time."

"And you could take a few lessons," she grumped.

"If only I had your looks and your shape, I might," Edwina spoke truthfully.

Cecelia suddenly stood up and proceeded to give her a piece of her mind. "Now there you go, Edwina. You could make yourself more beautiful if you'd try. Look at your hair. It's so plain. Get a designer cut. If you'd angle it just so,"—her sister demonstrated—"you'd look much more professional. Stand up."

Edwina stood and let her sister look her over.

"And you have lost weight. I've noticed, so don't deny it. You're thinner, and you look good. Your dress looked beautiful on you last night."

"You liked it then?"

"Of course, why wouldn't I? It's very classy. A bit simple for my taste. I'd add sequins and pearls and lengthen that train and add a diamond-studded tiara."

"So that means you liked what Bertie made?"

Cecelia shrugged as she paced, then turned. "Bertie *made* your dress, too?"

"Yes. And you love it, right?"

"I said I did, didn't I?" She said with a huff.

"Then come up and have a look at your dress. Bertie left the side seams open so we could fit it to you perfectly. I knew you would want that."

Cecelia stopped pacing and gazed at her sister, then shook her head. "You could get me to eat an entire pie at one sitting, I declare."

To Edwina that meant she would try the dress on. "Let's go, before anyone gets up. Just you and me. Tiptoe up the stairs because they creak loudly and Alex hears everything."

"Why are you whispering?" Cecelia fussed and followed her sister out of the kitchen, tiptoeing.

Edwina smiled. Her sister tiptoeing in bare feet.

Indeed the steps creaked several times, which nearly threw the two of them into laughing fits. Once at the top of the stairs, Edwina couldn't help herself. "Can you imagine two grown women sneaking about the castle as though we were doing something illegal?"

Cecelia actually giggled, and Edwina thought her heart would burst.

"In here." Edwina's heart beat faster.

They had crept up a third flight of narrow stairs, Cecelia complaining the entire way. "It's hot up here. Is this Bertie's work station? Honestly, Ed, you need a fan up here."

"There's one in the room. And Bertie has spent hours up here, first on my dress and then on yours and Paige's."

Edwina opened the door slowly. "Watch for pins. They are all over the place," she warned.

The small room was scattered about with sewing materials. White satin hung on a large hanger over a closet door. Two forms, one a woman's and one a child's, held the champagne material. Edwina watched as Cecelia made her way to the woman's form and inspected her dress. Her breath caught in her chest.

"It's beautiful."

"Yes, the very best. Alex insisted."

"Well, at least your knight has some taste," she murmured and walked around to view the back. "Hmmmm."

"Bertie thought it would look nice to add a wide chocolate brown silk band at the waist." Edwina tied the material into a bow for her sister to see.

Cecelia turned her head this way and that, fingering the material, and retied the bow. "There, that hangs better," she announced. "And Paige will have a matching bow?"

"Yes, we will have matching ties, except for the color. Mine is white like my dress."

"As it should be. You're the bride."

"Right," Edwina agreed.

"I'll wear the dress. But it will have to fit perfectly," Cecelia conceded.

"Oh, it will. Bertie will make sure of it."

Edwina took two steps and wrapped her arms around her sister.

"Ouch!"

"Oh, did I hurt you?" Edwina stepped back.

"No, one of those darn pins is stuck in my foot."

"Here, sit on this chair." Edwina dragged it across the floor. "Don't move."

Cecelia plopped into the chair, retrieved the pin stuck in her toe, and handed it to Edwina.

"Sorry. But I'm glad you like your dress."

"I didn't say I liked it, Ed. I said I'd wear it."

Edwina's face fell. "Oh. You don't like it then."

"Well, give me some time. Champagne is not my color but the shape is perfect for me. I'll give Bertie that."

"Good. It will be for only one day," she reminded her sister.

"Right. Now, have you retained a photographer?"

"Oh yes, Alex insisted we hire one. He has a good friend."

"Excellent. You don't want to have shoddy photos after Bertie went to all this work to make your dresses."

"Right." Edwina smiled.

Chapter 18

Deep in conversation, the two were interrupted when Paige burst into the room. "I heard you up here," she said, still in her nightgown.

"Paige, you're up early."

"I was thinking. . ."

"About what?" Edwina inquired softly, meeting the child's eyes.

"Well, if there's any silk left, can Bertie make me a ballerina skirt?" Paige twirled on her tiptoes.

"Of course." Edwina smiled. "And the leftover veiling can be added to the underskirt in layers, like real ballerinas. But don't speak to Bertie just yet. We mustn't make her work more difficult than it already is. The wedding is days away, and we have to fit our dresses."

"Okay, I'm going to see if papa is awake." She ran from the room.

"She speaks like an adult," Cecelia dragged a chair to the window.

"She was raised with mostly older people." Edwina joined her sister.

"Like me," Cecelia mused.

"Yes, like you. I try very hard to encourage her to engage her imagination, to be a child, read stories, think about her dreams, that sort of thing."

"I'm glad. Every child should be allowed a childhood. I had none. My father deserted us for another woman while mother and I moved from city to city. I played in dressing rooms, and my playtime was mostly in dress-up costumes. My dreams were to be on stage in front of people, making them happy."

"I didn't know that," Edwina said quietly.

"You wouldn't. I hardly allow myself to think about it, let alone speak of it."

"Maybe you should talk about it. Your childhood has so much to do with who you are today, Cece."

Cecelia shrugged. "No foolish talk now. It's time to get things done. Have you arranged a rehearsal dinner?"

Edwina noted the fact she'd changed the topic. "No. Alex doesn't want one. Our guests will be our small family and Alex's best friend Gavin MacDonald and his family. They are coming from Spain in a couple of days. He is a bullfighter."

"What?" Cecelia's face registered surprise.

"I haven't met him, but Alex said they were boyhood friends. Gavin is a Scot, married with two sons and a daughter. His wife is Verena. She's of Spanish descent."

"A Scottish bullfighter. I never heard of such a thing."

"I am so excited to meet their family."

"Are they all coming then? Children too?"

"Yes, it seems they are. So you see, it would be difficult to have a rehearsal since the wedding party is so small and it will be held outdoors. Gavin was able to get a few days away from work."

"Will there at least be a wedding dinner afterward?"

"Yes. Alex has planned it, and it will be a surprise to us all." Edwina felt the thrill of not knowing what Alex had arranged.

"You trust Alex to pull that off without a woman's hand in it?"

"Yes, I do."

"What about the minister or priest or whatever you call them?"

"Alex attended church with Elizabeth, and the pastor is a friend. He will perform the ceremony. I've met him twice at services."

"You and Alex go to church?"

"Yes, the last two Sundays. I've missed being at church, Cece."

"Whatever for, I can't imagine. God has enough to do. I can't believe He would want us wasting time in church every week, when there are plenty of things that can be done in the world." She ducked her head and peered out the small window. "The winds are blowing across the moors. I sure hope that doesn't mean rain is coming."

"Alex checked, and the weather should be perfect. Actually a bit warm this summer, he said." Edwina joined her sister at the window. "Beautiful isn't it?"

"That it is. I miss my English hills," Cecelia mused.

"Would you ever want to move back to England?" Edwina asked, her voice low.

"Someday maybe, but I'm bound in Chicago now." Then Cecelia turned to her sister. "Did I tell you I bought the Victorian?"

"No! Where is it located?"

"Washington and Squire. Perfect location. The area is slowly refurbishing the older homes, and property prices have shot through the attic."

Edwina smiled but did not correct her sister's use of "attic," which should have been *roof.* "Good for you. Please take pictures before you start and when you finish. I want to see what you've done." Edwina knew she would not be a part of her sister's life in that endeavor.

"Spencer will do that. He's the sentimental one."

"And what about your design show? Have you signed the contract?"

"Yes, just before I left. The pilot will film the redesign of the Victorian. The name of the show will be *The English Victorian.*"

"I love the name, and what a great idea, Cece—to buy the house you'll be decorating. I'm very proud of you, you know."

At this her sister stopped fidgeting with her nails and drew her gaze away from the view.

Edwina knew Cecelia didn't know what to say, so she artfully changed the topic. "We should go down and let Bertie know you can stand for a fitting—if that's okay with you."

"Well, I would rather have it done now as wait. Heaven knows there's going to be a rush. Best get Paige up here too so she can finish her dress. I can't believe you've waited so long, Ed."

"We were waiting to see if you'd like your dress," she said softly.

Cecelia jumped to her feet, anxious to be busy. This small talk was making her crazy. "I'll get my bath and be back in an hour. Have Bertie ready because I do have errands to take care of today."

"Okay, I'll let Bertie know. See you in an hour." Edwina watched her sister hurry away, then descended the stairs slowly, a smile settling easily on her lips.

Chapter 19

"Good morning, Bertie." Edwina burst into the kitchen. "Guess what? Cecelia likes the dress!"

"Hmm, aboot time the lass thinks of someone other than herself."

"Oh Bertie, that's not nice. Cecelia is used to ordering people around. She's accustomed to having things done for her."

Bertie grumped, but asked, "When can we finish?"

"She's having a bath and will join us in an hour. Will that give you time to get through breakfast?"

"It will lass. The men have pancakes and sausages in the warming oven. And there's fresh fruit. The least they can do is pour their own syrup."

"At the very least." Edwina agreed, knowing full well that underneath the tough façade, Bertie loved her charges.

"Paige should come up after yer sister. I'll be needin' to get those seams closed up and a last fittin' for the wee lass too."

"I'll do that. And Bertie . . . thanks for everything. I love the dresses."

"Ah, be away wit ya, lass. I've work ta do."

Edwina patted Bertie's shoulder and headed for her room, humming as she scurried barefoot up the protesting stairs. The house would soon be abuzz.

The water was running in the tub, and she knew Bertie would be upon her in moments once she heard that sound.

The older woman burst into the room. "Lass, call the florist. The woman has called twice this mornin', early enough to wake the dead."

"She did? Maybe I should do it now."

"In the water," Bertie ordered. "Freshen up. The woman is rude as a donkey. She can wait."

Edwina laughed as she sank low in the rose-scented water and groaned in delight. "This is heaven."

"Heaven it may be, but life awaits ye, lass. Be quick aboot yer bath. I've work ta do.'""

"Yes, Bertie." Edwina sighed.

After a short soak, Edwina grabbed the towel and wrapped it around her. Apparently Bertie was off on a mission. She walked into the bedroom and saw her clothes had been laid out. Her favorite jeans and two tops, her choice. She chose the white, soft T-shirt material and dressed. Black flats were on her feet, and she was clip-clopping down the stairs to see what duties she would be assigned today.

"Good morning." Spencer greeted her at the bottom. "You look fresh."

"Fresh?" Edwina laughed. "What, did I look sour yesterday?"

"No." He laughed and pulled her hand into his elbow. "How doth thy sister fare this lovely morn?" Spencer used his best old-English accent.

"She doth very well, indeed." Edwina played along.

"And doth she approve of all thy plans?"

"Sir, to my great delight, she approves of most of them."

"Ye, Miss Blair, are one lucky lady."

"Indeed I am."

They entered the kitchen, both looking for Bertie. Spencer for food, Edwina to remind her of the time.

She was nowhere to be found.

"I'll go upstairs to see if she and Cecelia are already doing the fitting."

"Fitting?" Spencer turned.

"Yes, Bertie made my dress and Cecelia's and Paige's." Edwina whispered and didn't know why.

"And she went for it?" Spencer crossed his arms over his chest and smiled.

"She did," Edwina said softly. "She actually did."

"Well, it must be the sister thing because I have it on good report, straight from her lips, that we were to go shopping for the dress in Edinburgh today."

"Really?" Edwina smiled. "Well, there's no need now, is there?"

Spencer couldn't seem to wipe the smile off his face. "The woman is just plain unpredictable, but I have always known that." He shrugged.

"Well, I'm off before she changes her mind. If those two are up there together, there's likely to be fire," she said and dashed off.

Spencer watched her go. The light in Edwina's eyes shone like a diamond. She was happy. He wished for Cecelia the same one day.

* * *

Alex came down the stairs blustering about his hunger, and Spencer joined him as they headed for the kitchen. "I've checked up there, but not a one of them can be found. Where's Bertie?" he called as he dove into the kitchen.

"She's upstairs fitting Cecelia's dress." Spencer waited for the words to sink in.

"Ah, then the lass knows? And has agreed?"

"It seems so." Spencer enjoyed watching Alex's face consider it all.

"Then there is to be peace aboot the castle today."

"Not for long, if I know Cecelia," he quipped.

Paige ran into the kitchen. "Papa!" She threw herself at her father as Spencer watched.

"Are you hungry like I am?" Her father growled in her ear.

Paige wriggled free and announced, "Bertie said we are to eat the pancakes and sausages from the oven and to pour our own syrup!"

Alex harrumphed. "Well, I guess it's better than porridge."

"Yuck." Paige made a face. "I'll get the plates." She pulled up a stool and stood atop the counter.

"Come down this minute, lass. You'll fall."

"I do it all the time, Papa. Bertie taught me so in case no one was about, I could get my own breakfast. While you were gone, she taught me lots of things. I can help baking the scones too."

"Ah, so the lass is becoming a woman." He smiled.

Spencer saw the softness in the man's green eyes. And the guilt. Alex grabbed the plates from his daughter as she handed them down, noting the fact that he held himself back from denying her the chance to be strong. *As it should be.*

Once the table was set for three, Paige made herself useful and poured juice into three small glasses. "Papa will get the hot plates out of the oven," she announced.

"What can I do?" Spencer asked.

"Get the syrup out of the refrigerator. We'll heat it up in the microwave. That's what Bertie does. Get the butter too. Please."

"Yes, ma'am." Spencer opened the refrigerator door and poked around. "There are two kinds of syrups."

"Bring them both, and we'll pour some from each into these bowls."

The men smiled at each other across the room. Soon the table was set to the lass's satisfaction, and all three sat to eat.

"I like this," Paige said excitedly, then dropped her fork. "We forgot to pray, Papa."

Spencer took his cue from Alex and set his fork down.

"We have indeed," he said. "Will ye, Paige?"

Paige bowed her brown head, her hair falling around her face, and with her little girl voice said, "Lord thank you for bringing my Papa back and Edwina back. And thank you that Aunt Cecelia likes her dress. And for the pancakes. Amen."

The three went back to their breakfast.

Chapter 20

"Let's walk, Papa." The men took Paige and quickly headed out the back door and into the morning sunshine.

They followed the worn path down the hill to the barn, and Alex showed Spencer his grandfather's old truck while he remembered the conversation with Edwina the day she finally understood he had chosen her, not Cecelia, to be his wife.

Paige ran off with Spencer in tow to show him her lamb. Alex could hear his child's voice calling, "Silsee. Silsee."

Musing, he shook his head, standing next to the truck. Edwina had been as stubborn as a Scot herself. Hadn't noticed the small signals he had given her. But then, they had been separated most of the time. And she had written that romance novel, clearly unaware that she had desired to be the heroine, but dared not dream it for even a moment, and had instead chosen Cecelia as the heroine.

His heart had warmed to the American lass the first time he walked into the library and found her atop the ladder, barefoot. He had frightened her with his voice, causing her to drop the book she was reaching for and, frustrated, she had spouted off a bit. With the sadness of losing Elizabeth and in the throes of losing Paige, he'd hardly had time to be decent. It was no wonder the lass didn't see she had stirred him heart and soul that day.

There had been something fresh about her approach to life. She had struggled with thinking beauty, success, and money were the appropriate paths to a beautiful relationship. He had been offered all those things from women, but not one had sassed him with a "whoop-de-do." He smiled, remembering.

Paige was running back to the house now. Mr. Gillespie was about the castle these days preparing the grounds for garden and flower planting. He had come at the bidding of the women to collect Paige.

"Where will the wedding be held?" Spencer met up with Alex. They stepped out of the barn, and Alex pointed. "Up there."

"Outdoors then?" He smiled.

"What?" Alex turned.

"Does Cecelia know about this?"

"I'm thinking she does by now," Alex murmured. "She would do well to go along. This was Edwina's one request. To be married on the hills, the wind blowing her veil." The view held the groom captive.

Spencer was quiet.

The moment broken, Alex asked Spencer if he'd like to walk along the stream. "Unless ye'd rather ride. It's about half a kilometer."

"Walk on." Spencer gestured, and the men set out.

* * *

When Paige walked into the third floor room, Cecelia was twirling in her dress for Bertie, her hair in a ponytail. The lass had gasped, "You look like a real princess. Right, Edwina?"

"Just like in the books, Paige." Edwina watched the little brown eyes dance dreamily. She was a little girl with visions of her own. Edwina wanted to cry and pressed her fingertips over her mouth. This little girl was hers.

"Unzip me?" Cecelia sat on a low stool so the child could reach.

Edwina thought it kind that her sister engaged Paige. Then it was Paige's turn to model her dress.

Edwina and Cecelia made lively talk about Paige's brown eyes matching the champagne color of the dress and how her dark hair would be put up for the wedding, Cecelia demonstrating the upsweep.

"Paige, turn 'round a bit more," Bertie said through the pins in her mouth. "There, we are done with ye, lass," Bertie announced. "Step out carefully so the pins don't move, mind ye."

Her part done, the child wriggled out of the dress and put on her riding clothes, announcing that Father had promised her a ride.

"Go on, but remember Mr. MacDonald and his family will be here. He was Papa's best friend when he was a boy."

"Papa had a best friend?" she inquired, her eyes large. "I didn't know."

"Perhaps you can talk with him during your ride. His friend's name is Gavin.

The set of the small mouth told Edwina there would be a long conversation during this morning's ride. "I'll come down and make you a sandwich. It's nearing lunchtime."

To her sister she said, "Cecelia, enjoy your day. Bertie will finish your dress."

"Do you have shoes for me too?" She straightened her slacks and gave her sister the evil eye.

"Did you bring any flats?" Edwina asked.

"No. Just my Birkenstocks and my black Louboutin's, neither of which will be suitable."

"Then wear something comfortable. No one will see, and the dress *is* long enough. It will be impossible to walk in heels."

"What're you wearing?" Blue eyes bore into hers.

"Slippers. White satin slippers." Strangely Cecelia didn't say a word. Edwina kept the fact that they were bedroom slippers to herself.

"Come on, Paige, let's find your father." Edwina sought to escape before her sister asked any more questions.

"I'm going into town," Cecelia called after her.

So she was going to Edinburgh to shop for shoes. Edwina was glad she didn't have to go.

"Want to go along? We could get you a traveling outfit for your honeymoon . . . which, by the way, where *are* you two going?"

Edwina hurried down the stairs, pulling Paige with her and pretending not to hear. Those were subjects she didn't want to talk about. Shopping and most especially not about the honeymoon.

Just as her foot hit the bottom step, Edwina heard the dogs coming in from the back patio. Paige let go of her hand and ran to her father.

Edwina stopped and watched the little girl throw herself into her father's arms. She smiled and stood behind a wall so she could watch. Spencer turned to let father and daughter talk and nearly ran into Edwina.

"What're you doing back here?" he whispered.

"Watching." She pointed.

"Yeah, I know what you mean. Cecelia around?"

"She's upstairs, and I'm thinking you're about to be wrestled into a trip to Edinburgh."

"Oh yeah?" He cocked his head. "I could do with some time away from the fort."

84

"Fort?"

"Fortress. Whatever you want to call this beast of a house. A person could get lost in here for years."

"The dogs would smell them out." Edwina laughed.

"I'll head upstairs. When Cecelia makes her way down from the loft up there, tell her I'm getting ready."

"What? You don't mind shopping?"

"Nah, it will be a barrel of laughs to watch her choose one pair of shoes now that she's been cheated out of searching for a dress. And who would carry the goods?"

"What's this?" The Scot's voice boomed from behind Edwina's head, and she turned.

The look in his face told her he was up to something. His eyes were narrowed, and she saw his hand twitch. "Don't you have to be somewhere, Spence?"

Edwina eyed him, waiting for . . . she didn't know what.

Spencer winked and shot up the stairs two at a time.

Alex grabbed her wrist and pulled her into his office, shutting the door. With his hands on her upper arms, he gently pushed her against the door. "I've been waiting all day to do this." His head came down slowly, his eyes never leaving her face. She wanted to bolt. She hadn't brushed her teeth after breakfast, and they were so busy. . . .

But he didn't seem to think about anything except kissing. "Relax." He lifted his head and whispered, "Where would you like to honeymoon?" His voice was low. "This weekend can't come soon enough." He leaned in for another kiss.

Edwina melted against the door. She had no feeling in her legs or arms. The man was cruel. Absolutely cruel to break into her day this way and expect her to have any brains left to finish what she had started. Which was . . . She couldn't string two thoughts together.

"Lass, is it in yer heart to travel someplace exotic for our honeymoon?" He now stood gazing down at her, his palms flat against the door on either side of her head.

She couldn't utter a single word and knew her face flushed red. Again. When would she stop turning all sorts of shades every time he kissed her?

"Unable to speak, are ye?" His intense gaze derailed any thoughts she might form.

"Hmm," she murmured.

"Now let's establish this before the wedding. Speak to me of yer thoughts. I can't read yer mind, lass, and I won't be having ye stuffing yer thoughts down into that head of yours. So speak up and tell me what ye're thinking. I might bluster if I've a different mind on the matter, but ye must speak up. Men are not good at reading minds. Especially women's minds."

"Well then, let me go so I can think."

"What, woman? I can barely hear yer voice."

"Move so I can think." She pushed at his chest gently.

He dropped his hands with a knowing smile on his handsome face. "Better?"

"Yes." Edwina crossed her arms at her waist, walked to the window on watery legs, and looked out at the grounds. "It's so beautiful today."

"Aye." He joined her at the window. She could feel his breath on the back of her neck.

For long minutes they said nothing, gazing across the hills. The stream sparkled in the noontime sun and sent glints of light shooting in myriad directions.

"What was your question?" she whispered.

"Where would you like to honeymoon? Have ye the wish to travel someplace far and away, lass?"

Edwina shook her head, tears starting to pool in her eyes. She couldn't believe she was having *this* conversation with *this* man. All thoughts of her former life were bits and threads of lonely times. She was almost afraid to let him love her. *What if . . . ? What about . . . ?*

"No honeymoon then?" He teased until he turned her around and saw her tears, then lifted her chin with gentle fingers. "What is it, lass?"

She couldn't speak, so he gathered her in his arms. She found her head in the cleft of his shoulder. He pulled her closer, and she felt his strength. His tallness. Safety in his embrace.

"Have ye dreamed as a little lass what yer weddin' would be like? I would have ye come as close to yer dreams as ye wish."

"Thank you," Edwina murmured against his chest. "I . . . this is larger than any dream I could ever create." Her voice wavered.

"Aye, it is then? Ye're not unhappy?"

She pulled back, her palms on his chest. "No, a thousand times no. I am too happy."

"Well then, where would ye like to honeymoon?"

"At the cottage," she whispered and allowed him full access to her gaze, returning look for look.

"Our guests will be at the cottage. Have ye forgotten?"

"Yes...yes, I think I did." Her mind was mush.

"Do ye trust me lass?"

"Of course I do." She heard the strength in her own voice.

"I've been working on a plan for a couple of weeks but I wanted to be sure...before..."

Edwina waited, breathless.

"To be sure ya didn't want to go someplace far and away."

She wanted to tell him she wanted only him when a thought hit her like an arrow in the heart. "Alex, did you have dreams of a special place you want to go? I'm so busy thinking about myself, that I didn't even consider you might have made plans already. I mean, I know you and Elizabeth must have traveled somewhere wonderful, and I wouldn't, and, well, I know you lived at the cottage and if that's not good...I mean...we don't have to live there...we could..."

Alex put his fingertips over her mouth. "Shush, lass, ye wear me out."

She nodded. Oh, that she could express herself in fewer words.

He released her reluctantly when they heard noises outside the office door. He was about to leave when she called him back.

"Alex, would you, would you . . ."

He knew what she wanted and kissed her, then abruptly let her go. "Woman, go aboot yer business," he said. And left her.

Edwina felt her breath come back slowly. Her hand rested over her heart. Had she ever known such sweetness? Such joy? She was grateful the wedding—and the honeymoon—was a few days away. Perhaps even more than Alex Dunnegin.

Chapter 21

"Do you want to drive the rental?" Cecelia asked Spencer. "It is my first time driving on the wrong side of the road, but I'll give it a shot. You can correct me if I make a mistake."

Cecelia climbed into the passenger seat, and Spencer, feeling strange, got in on the wrong side. "Weird." He laughed. "Reardon too busy to run us in then?"

"He's on holiday until tomorrow. That's why I rented the car," Cecelia said quietly.

"What, no excitement today?" Spencer drove slowly around the circle and down the long drive. He looked over at his passenger, dressed in black slacks and a soft lavender sweater with her Birkenstocks.

"Quite casual for the city girl today." It was not like Cecelia to be so docile.

"What?" She looked over at him, apparently lost in thought.

"What's on your mind today, Cecelia?" He softened his approach.

"Oh, nothing."

Nothing? Spence knew that was not true. The woman's brain was constantly cooking up something even when she was sitting still. Perhaps it was best to let her muse.

He drove along in silence, turning when she instructed him.

"Park there." She pointed.

He parked and ran around to let her out of the car. She always waited.

"Shoes today then?"

"Yes, Edwina already has my dress. But then I imagine you know that."

Spencer kept his mouth shut. This was a woman he didn't know.

He followed as she moseyed through one expensive store after another, picked up a shoe, and put it back down. For the next hour he did nothing but tag along and observe. He'd never seen her in indecision mode.

Finally he took her by the elbow, turned her to him and asked, "What are you looking for, Cecelia?"

"I don't know. I thought I knew."

Spencer's eyebrows shot up. The woman looked as though she was about to have a meltdown right here in the store. Also a first. What to do?

"Look, if you want, we can do something else and come back. How about lunch? Have you eaten today?"

She shook her head and fidgeted with her fingernails. Not a good sign.

He picked up her hand and pulled her along. "We're finding a restaurant. Where's the craziest restaurant in town? We'll get something to eat and check out the service and the food."

She seemed to rise out of her funk at that idea, and he took a deep breath. He had four sisters and knew a funk when he saw one. And this one was about to turn into a full-blown meltdown.

When she didn't protest, he knew for certain his hunch was right.

He followed her lead they exited the store and walked several blocks in downtown Edinburgh without a word.

"There." She pointed. "Larceny."

"Larceny? What? Do they embezzle your wallet at the door or something?"

"No. It's a hip place. The service is supposed to be exquisite, I've heard, but I haven't tried it."

"Excellent. Let's give it a go." Spencer slowed his pace, and they entered through double glass doors with *Larceny* sketched in white.

Tube lights of blue and white were everywhere. It was classy. Just blue and white. As his eyes adjusted, he noted the matching blue table covers and pristine white linen napkins. Blue-handled flatware sat crisscrossed on milk-white plates.

"Hey, this is nice. I like the lights and the simplicity."

Cecelia's gaze was taking in the scene too. "This shade of blue is heavenly." She smiled. "It's calming somehow."

The waiter, dressed in black pants and white shirt, a blue towel tucked over his arm, took them to a table in a bright corner. As they were seated, he touched a dimmer, and the lights dulled down. "I was wondering how I'd see you across the table." Spencer smiled as the waiter hurried away. Let's check out the menu. Maybe we can incorporate a new dish at *Winnie's* and name it the Edinburgh Special or something."

A soft, slow smile crept across Cecelia's face. Spencer enjoyed the view. So the woman was not all fur and diamonds after all. He handed her a menu.

Together they perused the choices. The names of the dishes were surprisingly funny: Burglary Burger, Absconding Albacore, Crime and Cream over Salmon, Looting Lobster, Pilfering Pork Chops, Purloining Sirloin, Petty Poultry with Orange Sauce.

Spencer made his choice and set the menu aside.

"Tell me about the dress." He hoped the topic was not upsetting to this woman who was not used to having her wardrobe chosen for her. *And handmade? Unheard of in Cecelia's world.*

"Mine or Edwina's?"

"Yours."

"It's a beautiful shade of champagne. Full-length and in the same design as Edwina's. She chose a wide chocolate brown sash that ties in the back. But hers will be white of course."

"Of course." He waited for her to go on. When she didn't and unhooked her gaze from his, he took a deep breath.

"Cece, tell me what's going on."

"What do you mean?" She lifted her chin.

"Look, I know you well enough that something's cooking in that lovely head of yours."

She looked away and for a moment he thought her reserve was going to break, which sent warnings to his brain. That was one thing about Cecelia he knew for sure. She would not cry in public. If it looked like she was going to, he would swoop her up, leave cash on the table, and get her out of there.

She looked back at him, and he waited, reading her features. He saw the stubborn resolve. She waved his comment away. "Weddings always do this to me." She smiled, at least with her mouth, but Spencer noticed not with her beautiful, sad, blue eyes.

"Well, let's eat first, and then we can mosey if you want."

"Mosey?" She smiled. "You'd mosey with me?"

"Right about that." He was glad for the turn of topic.

"Let's drink to that." She picked up her water glass, tapped his, and they sipped.

Spencer took in a big breath. The waiter came for their order and just in time.

She ordered the Crime and Cream over Salmon, he the Petty Poultry with Orange Sauce. When they said the words aloud, both smiled.

"A bit of humor is good, isn't it? Think we should rename some of our menu items and see how it works?" Spencer leaned across the table. "How about Theft of Turkey?"

"Stop, Spencer. We own an upscale restaurant," she mused. It would hardly be appropriate."

"Miss Proper." He smiled.

Her head tipped a bit, and he could tell he hurt her, even though she tried to cover it up with, "That's me, I guess."

"Hey now. Don't take me seriously. You are English and proper, but that's what I like about you." He gave her a wink to ward away the waver in her voice.

"Thanks."

"Why do you think I wanted to clean your apartment?" He turned serious.

Her eyes shot up. "What do you mean?"

"I thought you were the prettiest woman I'd ever seen."

"And you just out of college." She swiped at a crumb on the table.

"Six years of college, Cecelia," he shot back. "And that after two years of fooling around and messing up my life."

"That's right," she remembered. "Were you sowing your wild oats?"

"You might say that, but I'm not exactly proud of it, you know."

"Well, worse things have happened to good people."

Spencer's eyes lit up. "So you've known some hardships yourself?"

"Of course," she snapped. "Hasn't everyone?"

"Well, yes, but I thought your life was perfect."

"Well, it wasn't." In no uncertain terms.

"Would you like to talk about it, Cece?"

"Not really," she sputtered.

"Fine. But someday you're going to talk to me like a real person."

"What do you mean, a real person? Haven't I always treated you with respect?" She was leaning over the table now.

"Sometimes." He met her gaze head-on. Spencer decided it was time for some truth.

"What do you mean? I took you in as my partner. I don't do things like that lightly, Spencer Hallman."

"I know. You're right." He paused forming the words. "It's just that I think you don't see me—you just see someone who can be of assistance to you."

She leaned back and crossed her slender arms over her chest.

Had he blown it? Well what if he had? It was time she learned that using people to meet her ends was not really knowing them.

"I see," she snapped again.

"I'm not here to hurt you, Cecelia. It's just that you don't really know me, so don't act like you do, okay?" He lowered his voice and looked her in the eye.

"Okay," she acquiesced, and he knew it took a lot for her to do it.

"Hey. We are friends, right? Let's not ruin a good friendship." Spencer righted the matter quickly. "Maybe we can find some time back home to really get to know each other."

"Right."

Which Spencer interpreted as *not in this lifetime pal.*

The waiter came bringing their meals on glass-domed charger plates.

Spencer and Cecelia began their usual perusal of the presentation, the style of dishes, the placement of food and condiments accompanying the food.

"See, they don't throw on those ugly green plants for garnish. They drizzle sauces."

"As I see," Spencer agreed. "I do like the look of it better. And it adds an additional flavor. I need to sit down with Alonzo and hear some of his ideas."

"He attended Kendall College in Chicago, didn't he? He'll know the newest and latest trends." Cecelia's voice lifted.

"Right you are, Cece. Let's eat—I'm starved." Spencer watched as Cecelia picked up her fork and delicately cut her food, then laid the knife across the top of her plate. She was back.

Chapter 22

Two days before the wedding the castle was full of noise and activity. Gavin and Verena chose to stay at the farm while Edwina and Cecelia's parents were at the castle. Victoria Rose was in Edinburgh checking out the play houses to get the latest revues.

"It's Thursday already, Ed, and you haven't even told me where we will be standing for the wedding." Cecelia grabbed another scone. "I've missed these so much." She stuffed another bite into her mouth.

Edwina shook head in wonder. Her sister was more relaxed than she'd ever seen her. "I see that you do."

"What? Do I look awful? I can't afford to gain a single pound," she stated, then changed topics. "Which brings up another question. Who's doing our hair?"

Edwina's stomach always twisted up at Cecelia's questions. But today the world could collapse and she would still find something good about it. "Bertie's doing our hair—and dressing us."

She heard the scone drop to the plate. "You don't have hairdressers? Oh, Ed, my hair won't withstand the winds on those darn hills," she whined. "You know I need someone to . . . ."

Edwina waited, her eyes glued to Cecelia's.

"Okay. Okay. If that's what you want." Cecelia picked up her scone, took a bite then sipped her tea.

"Thank you, Cece. I know this is hard for you, but really, there will be just a few people there and no one will mind. Really. The wind will be blowing everyone's hair—if there are winds that day."

"Oh there will be winds." Cecelia grumped and scooted her chair back across the wooden floor as she went to the oven for another scone.

Edwina smiled. Her sister had become somewhat accustomed to eating in the small kitchen. Spencer appeared in the doorway. "You're up early," she said softly.

"Thanks to Paige." He leaned against the doorway arms crossed over his chest. "She wants to go riding, and she's very adept at talking me into it."

"She will do that. You have to be on guard at all times." Edwina stood and brought Spencer's plate to the table. "Eat hearty. You'll need it. The lass once on a horse will not dismount for hours."

"As I already know." He sat down easily. "Even my shins hurt."

"What you all see in riding a bunch of filthy, bug-infested beasts through the woods escapes me." Cecelia shook her head as she stood.

"Why don't you try it?"

"Me? Are you out of your mind, Spencer? I can't stand bugs, let alone imagine myself riding on the back of a mangy beast as being any sort of fun."

"Afraid Cecelia?" he tossed over his shoulder.

Edwina looked up and knew Spencer had done it now. Cecelia Grace Giatano would never admit she was afraid. She came marching back from the stove.

"Listen Cecelia,"—Edwina gave Spencer a look—"don't listen to him. He's just trying to bait you. It wouldn't be good for you to try something new just two days before the wedding. You could get hurt, and then where would we be?"

Edwina hoped Cecelia would listen to reason. There was no way Cecelia would ruin her wedding day, even if it meant admitting her fear.

Then just as if she hadn't heard a word, Cecelia said, "I will go riding with you, Spencer Hallman, just you see if I don't."

Spencer's smile was full-faced.

"Spencer, you are wicked." Edwina swatted at him.

With a shrug, he picked up his fork and ate like a man starved. Within ten minutes he was finished and stood. "See you down at the barn," he said to Cecelia and walked out.

"Ooooh, that, that—man," Cecelia sputtered. "He won't get away with this. I mean, how hard can it be to sit atop a horse. My backside isn't that wide. I should fit."

Edwina stood to clear the dishes. As soon as she turned, Bertie grabbed the saucers from her hands. "Lass, get to work on your errands. Ye have plenty to do. I'll clean the kitchen. Be off wit ye."

"Thanks, Bertie." Her thoughts were already elsewhere. What if something happened to Cecelia? She was an inexperienced rider. Maybe she should go along. Fairly new to the sport of horseback riding herself, Edwina might never have mounted a horse if it hadn't been for Alex's skills. Maybe she should go along.

"Ah, lass, don't you do it." Bertie looked up, her features certain. "Can't you see Spencer needs to be alone with 'er?"

Edwina turned her head and pressed her fingertips over her lips. "Oh my. I didn't think of that."

"'Ave ye no eyes in yer head, missy?"

"He is good for her. . . ."

"Ah, ye can't think two thoughts straight in a row, with ye being the bride," She said.

Edwina knew she was right. So much had changed she couldn't think. In two days she would be Alex Dunnegin's wife. Paige's mother. Pulling in a breath, she knew what she needed.

"Bertie, I'll be walking the hills."

"Ah, now there's a good place. Ye've got a lot o'thinkin' ta do, I'd be thinkin."

"Have you heard about the weather today?"

"Beautiful," Bertie said spritely. "A warm summer day, they say."

Up the stairs at a run, Edwina changed into old jeans and pulled on a T-shirt.

Alex was at the farm with his guests and had spent the night away. Cecelia would be with Spencer and Paige. Her parents were still abed, which left the perfect time to muse. She grabbed a yellow pad and sharpened a pencil.

The sky was blue as the ocean on a sunny day and the winds were easy, soft. Edwina pulled in a fresh breath, the smell of grasses and air awash with dew pervaded her senses. How good it was to be alive. To be loved. To belong to someone and yet be free.

She knew she wanted to be at the stream. To find a rock and sit while the noise of the water flowing over the rocks made music. In two days her life would change completely. It was thrilling and frightening all at the same time. Excitement pulsed through her veins.

Birds flew overhead calling to each other. The sun was just coming up past the stand of trees behind the castle. She found her favorite rock and leaned on the crooked branch that hung out over the water. The pad and pencil lay together nearby.

Her life had become like one of the many romance novels she'd read—almost too good to be true. She held out her left hand. It was bare. They had stopped at Alex's jeweler and returned a ring. He told her he had bought it for Ilana and glad he was to be rid of it. Together they chose simple gold wedding bands.

Edwina had not wanted diamonds. The circle of gold was more than enough to remind her she would be Alex's wife. Paige had already asked if she might call her mother. The child had never known Elizabeth, her beautiful mother who loved to dance. How large a set of shoes they would be to fill.

She scolded herself aloud. "Stop thinking you can fill anyone's shoes, Edwina Emily Blair," she whispered.

Grabbing the pad and unhooking the pencil from the top edge, she wrote down her fears. Fears that she wouldn't be enough. How could anyone be enough for Alex and Paige? Her heart teetered on the edge of hope and what-ifs.

She wrote until her pencil was dull, then tucked it back into the top edge and laid it aside, satisfied that she'd unloaded her worries onto paper. Somehow that was the one way she could move forward.

That settled, she leaned onto the branch and gazed out to the hills. They would stand up there on the greens and blues of the summer grasses and wed.

The sounds of hooves drew her eyes downward. Dust arose from the path coming out of the stand of trees behind her. Lifting her hands against the sun, she waited. Spencer appeared. Where was Cecelia? She jumped up. Then she saw another puff of dust a good distance off. Cecelia was coming out of the woods as her horse clip-clopped slowly along. She'd gotten Slowpoke Patty, the oldest mare in the barn.

A giggle escaped her throat. Sure enough, a full minute later her sister rode into full sunlight. Cecelia's beautiful blonde hair was flying about her face, the ponytail she had earlier all but gone. She was hanging on for dear life.

"Oh Cecelia, how you must hate me."

The familiar look of a new rider, bouncing on the horse instead of riding with it, nearly sent her into fits.

Her sister would never forgive her for this one.

Voices riding on the winds alerted her. Someone else was coming. She looked up the pathway. Alex led his horse ahead of a line. First a man, followed by two boys and a girl. Hand over her eyes, she squinted against the sun. Gavin and his children, then Paige. At age five the lass already knew how to handle her horse. Edwina smiled, and her heart turned stone-still as she gazed upon them. She sat down on the rock again, hoping to stay out of view. She wanted to be alone, and they needed their time together.

Turning her back to the riders, she picked up her pad and began writing her heart's thoughts until she heard a horse approaching. Alex was riding toward her. Alone.

She stuffed the pad under the rock, turned her back to the stream, and waited for him.

"Ah, lass, it is here ye have found yer solace?"

He dismounted and walked toward her. Her eyes could not fathom why such a man would love her, but it was too late now. She had fallen hopelessly in love with him. She kept her seat on the rock and let him come to her.

"How did you know I was here?" She smiled up at him.

"Ah, lass, this is yer favorite place. I know it." He sat beside her.

Quick and sure was love. Deadly in its target of the heart. She thought that could be a song. When had she become so melancholy?

"Are ye all right?"

"Yes."

"No wedding jitters then?"

"I didn't say that." She felt her face warm.

"Second thoughts?" She saw his eyes darken.

"Absolutely not—at least, not on my end." She laughed lightly.

"Lass, am I going to have to kiss you every time we see each other to remind you how much I love ye?"

Edwina picked up a rock and looked it over. Did the man have to see everything in her face? Suddenly she sensed his own fear at not knowing if she loved him. Had she said it enough? Had she really let *him* know? Especially since she'd been so daft at his attempt to propose.

She patted the rock and scooted over a mite. Reigns in hand, he pulled his horse and sat, gazing out at the view. Long moments passed.

"Do you love the view?" she whispered.

"Aye."

"Well, I love you like that," she said, voice wavering.

He never moved. Just sat staring.

"I know it, lass."

"Do you, Alex?"

"I do." His green eyes locked with hers.

Chapter 23

The wedding day arrived. Edwina was soaking in a tub of lavender water. Bertie was busy managing Cecelia and Paige while she mused. For some reason, unknown even to herself, Edwina was not nervous. The sound of a CD playing the bagpipes with flutes pressed her into the realization: this is where she would make her new life. In Scotland.

They'd all breakfasted together at the castle, the MacDonald clan included. The huge formal dining room had been an eruption of noise and busyness and talking. She and Alex sat back and watched it all play out as though they were the guests.

He had caught her in the garden and said a few words, then let her go with a promise to see her on the hills in a few hours.

Cecelia moved with a great deal of care. Edwina noticed and smiled. Spencer had been busy meeting her sister's every need. Mostly because Cecelia told him he owed her. Big time. Paige had a new friend in Gavin and Verena's daughter, Anabel, who also loved to dance the ballet. Her own father had found himself enjoying his new role as Paige's grandfather. And Victoria spent hours teaching the girls exciting new dance steps.

The day was perfect. The blue skies with white puffy clouds added to the intense ideal of the perfect wedding on a perfect day with the perfect man.

That thought barely finished, she heard her name. Well, at least Bertie's name for her. "Lass, up and out. We have to dry yer hair. And it soaked from yer bath."

Edwina smiled and wondered if her sister's hair had turned out all right. The plan was to dress and do makeup and hair for Cecelia and Paige, then come for the bride last. The dream was over, and reality was upon her. She lifted herself out of the tub and into the cherry pink towel.

"Lass, move yer feet. Everyone is waiting below stairs. Have ye no senses?"

Edwina's eyebrows lifted, and she felt a smile curl her lips.

"Come. Sit.. I'll plug in the dryer. Let me press the water out o' yer hair with a towel."

Obeying her, she found the seat and let Bertie perform her ministrations. "Oh, that feels so nice when you do that," Edwina purred as Bertie finished drying her hair.

"Well then I'll stop it because ye'll be here all day letting folks stand around, and here ye are the bride," she huffed.

"Not to worry, Bertie. Everything will be all right. As long as we are married, everything else will work out."

"Ah, the queen of romantic foolishness. A Jane Austen fan, no doubt."

Edwina snickered.

Bertie tapped her head with the comb and turned her back, and Edwina tried to control her emotions. She couldn't help it. She leaned over, slapping her hand over her mouth.

"Lass, stop. This is not . . ."

For a full minute, both were out of control. "Remember when I slid off the bed?" She cracked up again. "That silk nightgown?"

Bertie was waving the comb in the air, trying to gather strength enough to speak.

"Child, ye are going to be me undoing!" She screeched.

"You screeched!" Edwina yelled and gasped for air.

The loud knock at the door stopped the giggling, and Bertie and Edwina stared at each other. It was Alex. They knew that knock.

The door creaked open a bit. "Are ye aboot ready?"

Edwina jumped up and hid behind the bedpost, or at least tried to, while Bertie fished in the closet.

"We'll be down in a few minutes," Edwina said, holding her towel tight around her, glad he hadn't stepped in.

"Well make it quick, lass. Yer groom awaits ye."

"Come, Bertie, we'd best get things going, or we're both going to be in trouble." Edwina tried her best to wipe the silliness from her face.

"Lass, sit down and do as yer bid," she scolded.

Edwina felt the comb tearing through her hair. "Ouch."

Bertie did not stop until she was dressed, the wedding gown pooling at her feet. "I'll swing your hair up and hope we can get this veil tucked in wi'out any trouble."

When all was finished, Edwina stood and turned. "Do I look all right?"

Bertie's eyes filled with tears, and she pressed her fingers over her lips. "Aye, ye are beautiful, lass. And don't forget yer slippers."

Edwina grabbed the bed post and stuck a foot out for Bertie, then the other.

"Now go on down and meet yer man," she ordered and pushed her out the door.

"Get your dress on, Bertie. I'll see you downstairs."

"Aye. Ye took so long, look at me hair all astray."

"Astray?" Edwina teased and shut the door before both of them starting crying.

Edwina stood at the top of the stairs and looked at everyone below talking quietly in the foyer. Cecelia was beautiful, her silky blond hair swept up in a French twist. But...she was walking slowly. Thankfully her sister had given up on the idea of wearing heels and had actually decided on wearing a pair of satin slippers that Bertie had quickly dyed with tea leaves to match her champagne-colored dress. Spencer was doting on Cecelia. He looked drop-dead handsome in a black tux with his spiked blond hair. They made the perfect couple.

The MacDonald family was dressed in their finery, and her Father wore a suit, Victoria a beautiful, flowing soft blue dress. She must remind Victoria to hold onto that full skirt or the Scottish winds would be showing her underthings. They looked so happy.

Mr. and Mrs. Gillespie stood to the side, smiling. And Paige stood alongside Anabel twirling in her new dress, the two of them trying new dance steps.

Edwina wanted to cry. Every person who meant anything to her was there.

When the front door opened, she saw Alex come in. She hadn't known what he would wear, but there he was in full Scottish dress, his family's plaid and crest for all to see. She pressed her fingers over her lips and prayed. Her heart leapt with joy. She was marrying this wonderful, handsome man. *Lord, help me be a good wife to him.*

Alex came directly to the stairs and looked up. She gazed down and held his eyes, not caring a whit if he saw her before the wedding.

He moved to the bottom of the stairs and raised his hand, beckoning her to come to him. Slowly she moved to the top stair, lifted her dress, and made her way down.

When she reached the bottom step, he took her hand and whispered, "Lass, ye are beautiful."

Her face warmed.

"Where's Reardon?" Edwina suddenly realized he was missing.

"He is waiting outdoors to lead us," Alex said and tucked her hand into his elbow.

Cecelia caught her eye, and Edwina nearly lost her resolve. Her sister knew her duty. "Don't forget your bouquet." She handed it to the bride.

"Thank you. Cece, you look beautiful."

"Thank you. Ed, let's go. I can't believe you let Alex see you before the wedding." She pushed her sister forward. "Fashionably late is one thing. Extremely late is an entirely different matter altogether."

Edwina tried lifting her dress while managing the bouquet.

"Here, let me have your bouquet," Cecelia ordered. "Lift your dress—you can't have it stained with grass before you even arrive," she scolded, then mumbled, "Imagine walking down the *aisle* on grassy hills."

"Imagine indeed," Alex said and headed for the door leaving his bride to the care of her maid of honor. "I'll see ya at the top o' the hill." He winked and was gone.

The men walked briskly ahead of the women and took their places at the top of the hill.

Reardon led the ladies across the expansive meadow of yellow and lavender flowers. The pastor was already there, and they had only to get to him. Gazing as they went, Edwina noted every flower, every nuance as they climbed upward. The crowd stopped to gather their breath and continued. Once there, the pastor turned his back to the stream and said, "The view down the hill is yours to enjoy as you say your vows."

She accepted her father's whispered words of blessings and allowed herself to be escorted to Alex's side. Edwina stood next to Alex and pulled in a long breath to steady her sudden case of nerves. She felt as though she were dreaming—nothing seemed real all of a sudden. She remembered the moment she'd fainted dead away and found herself on his arm at the airport. Hopefully her legs would not wither and fail her now.

"Okay?" Alex looked down at her.

"Yes."

He patted her hand, the one that he held so tightly in his elbow, and winked.

Together they looked up at the pastor, the stream sparkling below and the wind blowing across the hills. Her veil, so light and airy, was whipping in one direction. She didn't even try to manage it. It was exactly the way she wanted it to be.

Vows were spoken, and the moment came when the pastor announced they were husband and wife. Alex turned to her, his green eyes seeking hers. He leaned her back over his arm and placed a chaste kiss on her lips. She saw the promises to come in his eyes.

Chapter 24

The photographer, Ethan Chance, followed the wedding party at a discreet distance and snapped pictures. Once the group pictures were finished, Reardon, per Alex's orders, quietly informed the wedding party they were to go back to the castle, change into casual clothes, and bring along a jacket or sweater. They had one hour to prepare since the bride and groom would be busy with photos. Ethan posed and reposed them, and Edwina loved his ideas. She longed to see the picture of her veil blowing parallel to the ground, wrapping both her and Alex in its folds. Ethan had caught the significance of the powerful veil of wind entwining the two as one.

Alex sent Ethan down to the see if the wedding party was ready, and he took advantage of the moment to say a few words to his bride as they stood under a white birch tree. Ethan turned and snapped the picture.

After a soft, slow kiss Alex stood straight and peered down into his bride's dark blue eyes. Pinned against the tree Edwina felt trapped in his love. She gazed into his green eyes, this handsome man standing with her who moments before had promised to be hers for a lifetime.

Edwina told him with her eyes just how much she loved him Tears formed as she realized she had written her dream story, but in the end it was God who'd made it come true.

Alex grabbed her hand, and they walked down their wedding hill together, stopping to look back every now and again. "I hope we remember this moment forever, Alex. When things get difficult."

"We will lass. We will."

Her veil whipped in the Scottish winds, just like she'd dreamed.

* * *

Once back to the castle, there was chaos. Everyone was dressed in casual attire. Edwina looked to Alex. "Go up. Bertie awaits ye. Follow her instructions. We're off for the wedding dinner."

Edwina lifted her bridal dress and slowly climbed the steps, each one a reminder that she was now Alex's wife. She had only to gaze at her left hand to set her heart racing again.

Bertie waited for her, already changed herself. "Are you coming with us?" Edwina burst out excitedly.

"Aye. The laird insists. I don't know what has gotten into the lad's mind." She waved her hand. "That is what ye are to wear. He insists upon that too," she grumped.

Edwina's eyes followed Bertie's hand. "My old pink shirt? My old jeans? And my flats?

Alex chose these things?" Her heart did another flip-flop.

"Aye." Bertie cocked her head. "As I said, the lad has gone daft."

Edwina smiled. "Works for me," she said and turned her back.

"All this work and for an hour or two." She unzipped Edwina's dress and pulled it down. "Step out now and mind ye don't get it dirty."

"What? You think I'll wear it again?" Edwina laughed.

Bertie looked hurt.

"Oh dear, I'm sorry. That was so unkind. You put a lot of work into this dress." She was truly contrite. "I'm so full of myself today—I wasn't even thinking." She placed her hands on Bertie's shoulders and dipped her head to catch her eyes.

"Seein' as it could be Paige's dress someday . . . I was just thinking . . ."

"Of course." Edwina saw her meaning. "I'm so daft." She winked. "What will ye do with the two of us, Bertie?"

"Oh, be off wit ya, child," Bertie snapped. "They are waiting below stairs for the bride. Again." she announced, hands at her hips.

"Not to worry. I'm ready. That was quick, and I'm so comfortable. Thank you for washing everything up. You even ironed my jeans and T-shirt, didn't you?"

"Aye, it seems these are to be your wedding dinner clothes." She shrugged. "How could one *not* iron them?"

Edwina sensed they were about to enter dangerous territory. But perhaps she should go ahead. "Bertie, I love you like a grandmother—which is really what you are to me. . . ." She couldn't finish.

"Oh, now there ye go gettin' sappy." Bertie pulled a lace handkerchief out of her pocket. "A lass young and silly as ye needs someone to look after 'er. Since her own ma is gone," she added.

"Had it not been for you, Bertie, I don't know where I'd be. I was so determined to live my life the way I thought it was set up to be. You made me laugh. And you laughed with me."

"Oh, be on your way, lass. I have a mess ta clean up, and yer making yer new husband wait."

"Right." Edwina's hands fluttered at her waist. She reached out and pulled Bertie into her arms, and they clung to each other for a long minute.

Once released, Bertie picked up the damp towel from her morning bath and swatted her backside.

Edwina laughed and scurried out the door. "Hurry, Bertie!"

She ran down the stairs to chaos. There were noises out front of the castle. Where was everybody? She opened the door and stepped out. Four black cars sat in a line.

"Ah, the bride has come down," Alex's voice boomed. "Everyone into the cars."

Edwina laughed out loud, excited to the tips of her toes. "Where are we going?" she asked her new husband.

"Well, it wouldna be a surprise if I told ye, lass."

"Right."

Alex pulled her to the front car, and they got into the back seat. Alone. Paige had insisted she wanted to ride with Anabel. Alex let her.

"Reardon drive on," he ordered.

The trip lasted a full half hour, which was just perfect because Alex and Edwina could be alone and enjoy their first moments together.

"You hired all these cars and drivers?" Edwina twisted in her seat to see the entourage.

"Reardon's brother Claude came down from Glasgow to join us. He is a driver, same as 'is brother."

"Really? I had no idea Reardon had any family."

"Just Claude. Claude's wife passed two years ago, and he's thinking of coming to Edinburgh to seek a position here."

"Oh really? Maybe we could help. Do you know someone who might need a driver?"

Alex laughed.

"What?"

"Just that ye think of everyone but yerself."

She leaned her head on Alex's shoulder and closed her eyes.

When the cars stopped, they were at a dock of some sort. Edwina dipped her head. "Clock's Dock. What a funny name."

"Jeremiah Clock was me mother's eldest brother. Died young out at sea."

"I'm sorry."

"The man has been gone thirty years. His son, my cousin Seamus Clock, is proprietor."

The car came to a stop. "I have so much to learn about your family, Alex."

"Aye." They'll be plenty of time for that. He extended his hand and pulled her up.

Alex instructed Reardon. The entourage was to return at half past midnight.

Edwina watched their group form a line. Even Cecelia had on jeans. Who in the world had gotten her to go that route? She never, ever wore jeans in public—had, in fact, declared she never would. Spencer's jeans were thin and worn. He had on a white T-shirt with a brown corduroy jacket, handsome as always. Cecelia was even letting him hold her hand.

Paige and Anabel were inseparable now. As were Gavin and Verena. Then she saw the strangest thing. An older man sidled up next to Bertie and spoke to her. Bertie stepped sideways to give herself more space. She looked affronted at first, then surprised, then shocked. What had the man said to her? Edwina found herself ready to go to her aid. No way was someone going to hurt Bertie. Then she smiled. Bertilda could take of herself. Soon she could see there was a mutual conversation between them, so she relaxed. They boarded the yacht, she and Alex last.

"A dinner cruise," he said in her ear. "Not a formal one," he added.

"I love it."

"Knew you would." He gave instructions to the captain, and the small yacht pulled out of port. "Come on, we're going forward." They stood together as the ship moved.

Edwina looked out over the waters. She had been on a yacht only once. In Italy at her father's wedding. Suddenly she saw the escutcheon. It read simply *The Edwina*. Her brain did a double take, and she turned to Alex.

"Your wedding gift. I plan to spend a lot of hours out on the water together, you, me, and Paige."

"You own this?" she stuttered, pulling windblown strands of hair from across her face.

"We own this. Seamus and I work together."

Edwina needed time to think, so she said nothing, just stared out over the North Sea as they set out.

Alex tucked her into his side as the ship entered rougher waters.

Should she die this instant, she had been blessed beyond anything she could have imagined.

Chapter 25

It seemed there was an unspoken rule about the ship, for the two of them were undisturbed, except an occasional visit from the steward who kept them well served with drinks and snacks.

She could hear the voices of the others laughing, talking, and children running.

"Dinner is served," the steward announced some time later.

Alex caught her hand and guided her below. There in the middle of the large space was an oval glass table, the chair backs covered in champagne satin with matching chocolate-colored bows. Milk-white roses and carnations sat in clear vases everywhere. The fragrance of yeasty bread and browned meat drew them toward the table.

"How did you . . . ?"

"With a great deal of help," Alex admitted.

"When did you even have time?" She felt guilty because she had done nothing for him.

"Yer mind is working, lass. Come, let's eat. I'm starved."

Edwina smiled. The man was always starving.

Music was playing from unknown sources, all of it Scottish. She loved the powerful sensations that rained over her. Alex was proud of his heritage, as all Scots were. She would have to learn more about his family's history so she could teach Paige.

Something grew strong and powerful within her.

She took her seat next to Alex and closed her eyes for a silent prayer. Then she heard Alex, now standing, preparing to make a toast with their water glasses.

"To my bride. Her family and mine joined forever."

Glasses clinked and well wishes were spoken aloud. Edwina couldn't help but state one of her own. "To the joy of knowing love still exists," she said and blushed.

"Aye." Alex winked at the group and sent them all to tittering.

Edwina's face burned.

The servers came and began setting dishes in the middle of the table and stashing others on a sideboard. Chicken and fish and steak and mashed potatoes came out. Green beans with almonds, brown breads, and sweet breads covered the table. Salads and side dishes galore, Scottish and American cuisine.

Everyone ate heartily as Alex suggested they do.Edwina watched the faces around the table. The pairs. Even Bertie seemed to blush now and again as the man she now knew as Claude, Reardon's brother, spoke to her. Cecelia and Spencer were lost in conversation. Her Father and Victoria were smiling, heads leaning together in some secret remembrance of their own wedding day, perhaps. Gavin and Verena sat together with Anabel and Paige to their left and the two boys to their right. The Gillespies were at the opposite end, and she leaned forward to see how they fared. They spoke quietly as was their usual manner. Edwina sighed. Her world was complete.

"Happy?" Alex leaned down to whisper in her ear.

"Aye."

Gavin and Verena had eyes only for each other until one of the boys dropped his fork and upon retrieving it from under the table upset his water glass, spraying his youngest brother in the face. The boys tried not to laugh. Unsuccessful, they hit at each other while their sister rolled her eyes, far above them in station, if not in age. Paige had taken it all in as she sat next to Anabel. Edwina's heart squeezed as she watched Paige laughing.

When dinner was finished, Alex invited everyone up to the top deck to view the sunset. The sun's slow descent toward the horizon had all eyes watching as it appeared to slip into the water. The reflection of the orange and lavender hues soon softened. The evening quickly turned cooler after the brightness gave way to dusk. Even Gavin and Verena's handsome dark-eyed sons had settled down. The water could be heard lapping the side, and waves were gently rising and falling now.

By midnight the group had tired from the long day. The yacht was guided into position by the handlers pulling in the thick ropes securing her to the dock. As they walked down the gangplank, Paige's hand in her father's, the sound of water lapping in the background was the last reminder of Edwina's wedding day.

The cars sat ready to escort them to the castle. "It was so beautiful, Alex."

He opened the door for her.

Chapter 26

Once back at the castle, Alex carried Paige to her in bed, instructing Reardon to take the Gillespies and the MacDonalds back to the farm.

Everyone, tired from the long day, had gone to their rooms. Spencer and Cecelia were the last ones in. Alex came down and stood beside his bride. While Spencer and Cecelia were putting up their wrappings, he pulled Edwina into his office. With that look in his eye, he backed her up against the door and kissed her. He hadn't even bothered to turn on the light.

"I'll be back for ya Mrs. Dunnegin." He opened the door and stalked out of the room.

Breathless, she gained her senses and came around to find Cecelia and Spencer in near the same circumstance. Quickly, she stepped back inside the dark office and slipped off her shoes, opened the door slowly and tiptoed toward the stairs, and tried her foot. Two steps later the wood creaked loudly in the quiet house.

"Edwina, is that you?" Cecelia sounded breathless.

"Yes," she answered quietly. "Just going up."

"What do you mean going up?" Cecelia was at the bottom of the stairs, one hand on her hip the other on the newel post.

"I'm going up." Edwina thought her sister must have caught a draft.

"By yourself?"

Oh, so that was it. "Yes, I'm going up. Are you coming?"

"Don't change the subject, Ed. Where's Alex?" Cecelia demanded from below.

"He'll be back in a little bit." She whispered.

"What?" Where is he? You two should be headed for your honeymoon, wherever in the world *that* is . . ." she paused, hands fluttering.

Edwina noted the softness of her sister's features and the high color still on her cheeks.

"What is going on? You're standing there smiling when by all rights and means you should be with Alex. It's after midnight Ed, for heaven's sake. Where is he?"

Edwina shot a grateful glance at Spencer, who was walking up behind Cecelia, his blond hair awry, white tux shirt open at the top, tie and cumberbund dangling from his back pants pocket.

"Time to go up, Cecelia." Spencer whispered something in her ear, took hold of her elbow and steered her directly up the stairs, past Edwina and off to her room.

Edwina gave Spencer a grateful look as he passed. She heard them whispering and smiled. Perhaps her sister was beginning to realize what real love looked like.

Chapter 27

She'd left Spencer and Cecelia talking in the dimly lit hallway and made her way down to the foyer. Standing there alone, she heard the front door open and waited, hands clasped tightly behind her back, heart beating against her ribs, knowing it was Alex. When he came into view, she had the strangest urge to run and throw herself into his arms. Instead, she watched as he came toward her.

"Ready." He handed her the small bag Bertie had packed, at his instruction.

"I'm ready." She whispered knowing full well she didn't have a clue what he had planned for their first night together. Then her practical senses became alarmed, "Do I need to bring some different clothes... food...a bag...some...

"Alex caught her hands in his and interrupted. "Trust me lass."

Edwina slowed her thoughts and focused on his eyes as he stood looking down at her. "Aye." She whispered. He was forever asking her to trust him. It was time she did.

Alex let go of her hands and she felt his strong hand at her waist as he pulled her close. He whooshed them out the door to his car.

"It's too dark to walk..." he hinted and put her in the passenger seat. Alex slid in behind the wheel and looked at her. First he leaned over and gave her a chaste kiss then began to drive down an unfamiliar bumpy road that became so narrow he had to stop.

"We'll walk from here."

He grabbed a flashlight from the rear seat and lit the way. It was a slow climb; uphill along a well-worn path. A few minutes later he stopped and turned his head.

Edwina followed his gaze as the flashlight revealed a miniature rock house with a thatched roof. A soft yellow light danced in a tiny yellowed window.

"My grandparent's first home." His voice deep, Alex turned to her. "Built with their own hands."

Edwina couldn't see his face in the dark, but she read in his tone that this was a sacred place.

"This is where we will spend our first married night together. Same as they did."

Her heart began to pump double time. Hot tears formed and fell. Questions surfaced but she forced herself not to ask them. She let him show her the way.

"Watch your step. I put flat rocks down in front of the door, but they're not settled yet." Alex reached in front of her and pushed the door open.

Before she could utter another word, she gasped as she was swept up and carried over the threshold.

"God bless us and this home." Alex declared as he ducked under the short doorway and brought her into the cozy one-room cottage.

Instead of setting her down, he turned full circle slowly. In one corner stood a rough-hewn table and two well-cut tree stumps for chairs, a miniature fireplace, lit with logs burning and popping, and a bedstead made with ropes.

Field flowers sat in an old tin cup on the wooden table. Edwina's eyes went to the bed, which was made up with soft looking pillows and blankets. Alex had done all of this?

"What say ye lass?" Tis me grandfather's house I've been working on so we could come here alone."

"Alex, I . . . I . . ." Edwina's eyes filled with tears.

"Ah lass," he let her legs loose and her feet slid down to the wood floor. "Tis not a time to cry, but a time to love."

She felt his arms go around her waist and he pulled her to him. Freely, she kissed her husband. She knew they were no longer two, but one. Suddenly he stepped away, leaving her bereft. He carried the flickering candle from the fireplace mantel to the miniature twig table next to the bed, put another log on the fire and drew her back into his arms.

Edwina felt his heart beating furiously against hers.

Chapter 28

"What do you mean, you're leaving?" Spencer said to Cecelia at dawn two days later. She was dressed and already gulping down a cup of tea. "At this hour?"

"Reardon's coming. I've arranged for an early flight home."

"I thought we were going back together." He ran his fingers through his hair and pushed his hands into the back pockets of his jeans.

"I have a new house to look after, and besides that the show needs me to tape opening scenes. There's so much to do. Rebecca called this morning. I may as well get ahead while I can." She whipped her head around. "Everything all right at the restaurant?"

Which means she doesn't want to talk about why she is fleeing. He already knew. He had gotten too close and she was jealous of Edwina. It was so clear, and she didn't even know it. Spencer stepped back and put his hands up, giving her space. "Everything's fine, Cecelia."

Paige rounded the corner in her nightclothes, her hair sticking out around her small face. "What have we here? A sleepyhead?" Spencer squatted in front of her.

"Could you hold me?" she said sleepily. "Until I wake up?"

Spencer lifted her up where she could lay her head on his shoulder, and she closed her eyes. "Have a bad dream?"

The little brown head nodded against his cheek. "Want to tell me about it?" He walked slowly to the library.

Cecelia watched, eyes wide, then suddenly snapped her cup down on the glass table in the foyer and walked out the door.

Edwina saw everything from the top of the stairs where she had been sitting. Cecelia was upset and dashing off again. Her sister flew out of the nest each time anyone was about to get too close for comfort. Afraid of commitment.

At dawn that morning she and Alex had come home quietly and found Cecelia in the kitchen. She tried to talk Cecelia out of leaving, but once her beautiful, entrepreneurial sister made up her mind, it was like trying to empty Lake Michigan with a coffee cup.

They had already said their good-byes. Edwina had gazed into Cecelia's blue eyes, hoping to see the same girl the night they lay laughing at themselves like children at a slumber party. Instead her eyes had turned icy blue and determined.

* * *

Thirty minutes later the front door slammed again. "Where's me wife?"

Edwina could not keep the smile from her face, nor the burst of joy that erupted from her heart. She wanted to run to him and throw herself in his arms while he twirled her round and round until she was dizzy. Her knight.

She tiptoed to the top of the stairs and peeked down. He wasn't there, and she saw movement in the library. He, Spencer and Paige were talking. Rather seriously, it seemed.

Turning on her bare heel, Edwina walked quickly back to her old room and went to the window. Pulling back the heavy plaid drapery, she noticed the sunlight filtering through the thick-glassed panes, the iron crisscross pattern repeated on the wooden floor. Below Mr. Gillespie was walking about with a wheelbarrow pulling weeds and gathering sticks.

Edwina wondered where Bertie could be. She checked her watch. Perhaps in all the chaos she had forgotten her duty. Shrugging, she pulled her hair up into a short ponytail, knowing full well Bertie would frown at her with those dark eyes of hers.

Slowly and quietly descending the stairs, she gazed about. The threesome was still in the library, their voices low. She stepped into the kitchen calling quietly, "Bertie, you in here?"

Silence.

What could be the matter? She checked her watch again and then the one over the stove. At this precise hour every morning, Bertie was stirring oatmeal or flipping pancakes. But no smells emanated from the kitchen.

Suddenly the back door burst open and in rushed Bertie. She pressed her hat to the nail and grabbed her apron, tying it as she scurried about and babbled aloud like the brook outdoors. Pots and pans were flying off the pot rack and hurriedly set on the stove.

"Bertie, did you wake late?" Edwina spoke loud enough to get her attention.

The woman's arms flew upward; the pot she was holding went soaring into the air and landed on the kitchen floor with a crash. "Lass, what ye be aboot at this hour and shoutin' fer?"

"I'm sorry. I thought you saw me standing here."

"Ach, I wouldna dropped this 'ere pan if I did, now would I?" she grumped.

"Need any help?" The woman actually looked like a reptile ready to strike.

"I'll 'ave ye know, ye and Laird Dunnegin were naught but bairns when I was in charge of this castle. Be aboot your affairs and leave me to mine." She waved a wooden spoon. "If for once in me life I didna hear the clock . . ."

Edwina obeyed instantly, but not before she saw the trouble. Bertie hadn't heard her alarm. She must have been out late with Claude, Reardon's handsome brother, or her name wasn't Edwina Emily Blair . . . Dunnegin.

Chapter 29

Edwina left Bertie to her duties and wandered out into the gardens in the early morning sun. Her heart beat faster as she remembered Alex's call for her earlier. He would know where to find her.

After a walk through sun-dappled gardens, she moseyed back inside and peeked through the swinging door. The kitchen was empty again, yet the need of food grabbed at her stomach. She slipped in and brought down a teacup and saucer and was waiting for the teapot to whistle on the stove when she heard low voices somewhere in the vicinity of the broom closet. It was large enough that several people could stand in it. She put her fingers over her mouth and couldn't help but draw closer.

When the knob on the door turned, she hurried back to the stove and turned her back, her hearing sharp as a steak knife. Someone was having a tête-à-tête in there, but who?

One second later her question was answered. Out popped Bertie, pressing her hands to her cheeks. Claude followed behind, a huge smile on his face. "There ye go, lass. A kiss for the day," he said sprightly and exited through the back door.

Edwina felt a smile creep to her lips. She straightened her back and did not move.

When Bertie turned to find her standing there, her mouth flew open but not a single word came out. And her face was suspiciously red. The woman started stirring the oatmeal and fanning her face with a small paper bag, ignoring her.

"Just came in for some tea," Edwina said, knowing her voice was loaded with juicy sarcasm. She stepped out the back door with her teacup and left Bertie to her duties.

* * *

"Winnie?" Spencer called from the back door. "Good, I'm glad I found you. Paige is sick."

Edwina jumped to her feet. "Does she have a fever?"

"I don't know. She just started throwing up. Alex was here. We talked for quite a while in the library, then he got a call from Gavin. Seems one of the sheep has a problem, so he rushed off to see what that was about. He wanted me to let you know. Right after he left, Paige asked me to carry her to her room and that's when she got sick."

"Does Bertie know?" she said over her shoulder.

"No, I came straight for you."

Together they hurried up the stairs, and Edwina found Paige lying across her bed.

"Paige, Spencer said you were sick. Did you throw up?" She sat on the edge of the bed, reaching to touch her forehead. "You seem a bit warm," she murmured.

"Spencer, would you mind getting a wet cloth from the bathroom?" After Spencer left, she peered at Paige. "What seems to be the problem?" her voice gentle. She leaned down and saw Paige's tearstained face, her dark hair wrapped in wet strands around her face. Gently she pulled the wayward strands away and realized this was a woman thing. "Spencer, thank you for the cloth. I think we can take it from here."

Edwina saw Spencer's look of understanding, and he nodded slightly and left.

"Sweetheart, did someone or something hurt you?"

The little girl's face screwed up, and she burst out, "Miss Edwina, do you think Mummy is mad or crying up in heaven because, because . . ."

"Because you have another mommy?" she finished for her.

"Mm-hm." She hiccupped.

Edwina remembered when her father married Victoria, and even though she was an adult, she still wondered if her mother would be angry at her father for having another woman. She contemplated before answering.

"I don't think so. Mommy's in heaven, and she sees things differently than we do.

I think . . . I really think she's very happy, actually."

"You do?" Paige sat up straighter.

"Aye, I do."

"Why?"

"Well, because if I were your mommy first and I had to go to heaven, I'd want someone to come and make my little girl happy. Wouldn't you?"

"Aye."

"Well then. There you have it." She smiled down at the little body curled up in her lap.

"You mean like if I died and Silsee was here, you'd be her mummy for me?"

"Exactly." Edwina smiled. "Exactly."

The matter settled, she held Paige until she fell asleep, carefully laid her on the bed, covered her and tiptoed out.

Hopefully Miss Bertie was well over the embarrassment of her romantic liaison with Mr. Claude in the pantry. Edwina was hungry.

"Well, it looks like you'll have to join me for a late breakfast, Winnie." Spencer laughed. "Bertie must be off running bath water somewhere, Alex is playing doctor to a sheep, and Cecelia has run off to Chicago, whereupon I plan on using every minute I have left to enjoy someone else's cooking . . . and serving."

She pulled out a chair, noting Spencer preferred eating in the kitchen as opposed to the huge formal dining table.

"Is Paige all right?"

"Yes, I think it was all the activity. And . . . she was worried her mother might be sad or angry because she had a new mother."

"Hey, no tears." Spencer smiled. "She will soon be used to you and no doubt all those brothers her father is planning on siring."

Edwina's mouth opened, then snapped shut as her face burned. "Alex told you that?"

"Alex is happy, Winnie." Spencer shrugged and noted her far-off gaze. Her smile was that of a woman loved.

Spencer carried two plates to the oven and piled on blueberry pancakes and sausages. Edwina poured tea and they ate.

"How is Cecelia doing? I know she is having a hard time with all of this." Edwina chose a more suitable topic.

"You have no idea, Winnie. She changes moods like she does her shoes—three or four times a day. If she doesn't have some driving force behind her, she's lost."

Edwina leaned forward. "I know. I worry about her, Spencer."

"As I do. But I'm powerless to do anything. She sees me as a nice guy with no class."

Edwina put her teacup down a bit carelessly. "Don't say that."

"Well, it's true. You know it, and I know it."

She couldn't disagree. Cecelia had eluded that to her as well.

"It's all right. I've always figured God had a plan of some sort in Cecelia and I meeting in the first place. The rest, well, we'll see what happens from here." He shrugged.

"I admire you, Spencer. You're cool when things get crazy in her life, and I know you bring her peace, even though she doesn't recognize it."

"What else can I do? I just pray that one day she sees how much I care about her."

The moment was interrupted when Alex appeared in the kitchen. "Ah, so there's me beautiful wife." He strode over and planted a kiss on top of her head.

Spencer stood and stretched. "Tell Bertie those pancakes were great. Think I'll head out for a walk before the rains come. It's looking rather hazy to the north."

"Aye. The clouds are gathering." Alex reported.

"How's the sheep situation?" Spencer asked as he stood.

"All's well."

"Good, then I'll be on my way." He saluted and left.

"Where's Paige? And for that matter, Bertie?" Alex looked around as he pulled out a chair and sat.

"Paige is upstairs in bed. She was sick earlier, throwing up."

Alex started to rise, and she caught his arm with her fingertips. "She's all right. I think it was a case of overstimulation with everyone about and the fact that she thought her mother might be sad or angry because she has a new mother."

"Ah." He paused. "And how is it with ye, lass?"

"We talked it over, and I think she understands that her mother is happy for her."

Edwina saw the now familiar look come across his face and felt her heart swell.

Some time passed in silence and Edwina, usually nervous at moments of quietness, found herself satisfied. Soon her parents would be coming down for breakfast, then off to the airport for their afternoon flight.

"Gavin and Verena are leaving this evening." He winked.

Edwina held his gaze.

"Business calls him back. And Verena has announced she is pregnant and wants to be at home."

"Oh!" Edwina was happy. Both sets of eyes turned at the sound of a small voice.

"Hey, lass. Are ye feeling better?" Alex strode to the doorway and carefully lifted Paige up in his arms. "Are ye hungry like ye're father?"

She nodded sleepily. "Aye."

Edwina stood and felt her forehead. "Have I got a fever Miss Edwina?" She had a worried look on her face.

"No. It's gone. You look much better too."

"Lass, would ye like to call Edwina, mother?"

Edwina almost gasped. It was too soon . . . only the day after. She started to speak when she saw a smile creep to Alex's face. He motioned with his head, and she followed his lead. Paige was nodding.

"Do ye think yer mother Elizabeth is okay with it?" he asked her.

Edwina looked at Alex and then back at Paige. "Aye, I do," she said, and Edwina knew the child-woman had already decided. She just needed someone to tell her it was okay.

Edwina felt tears burn her eyes, and she gazed into Paige's brown ones and felt sincerely sad for Elizabeth. But her arms went out just in time to catch Paige. She held her tight, rocking back and forth. God was in his heaven, and Edwina's world was perfect.

Chapter 30

Chicago

"What did you say happened?" Cecelia raised her voice. "I'll call Stuart and get him on it."

Rebecca Burke agreed. "Mrs. King has retracted her statement and is now saying she *did* make a bid on the Victorian."

"The papers have been signed. What does she think she can do now?" Cecelia tapped her fingernails on the counter. "So much for soft answers...or whatever that saying was."

"She can't do anything. Except stall your purchase. Which is exactly her motive at this point." Rebecca sighed. "There are plenty of other houses she could choose from. There's no way she will get this house, unless you renege."

"Which I will never do!"

Cecelia reacted the way Rebecca thought she would. Mrs. King was attracted to making certain she was seen by Chicago's society as one who was not easily crossed.

"Prepare to spend money, Cecelia. I'll get the paperwork together. You can't afford to have a holdup, especially with the new show." Rebecca knew her client would not sit still on this one.

"I'll call Stuart now."

Ten minutes later she had an appointment, and by late afternoon Stuart Littleton had already made his first inquiry and informed Cecelia she had nothing to worry about. But it may take a little time to work out.

"We don't have time, Stuart. Filming starts in two months, and I need to get into the house to prepare. Get on this right away. Rebecca's faxed you the paperwork, correct?"

"Yes. And signatures and dates are legal. The problem is that as long as there are any legal matters pending, Miss Burke will not be able to turn the keys over to you."

"Are you joking?" Cecelia's voice teetered on the edge.

"Unfortunately, that is the problem we have right now."

"I own a home I cannot get into?"

"I'll file the proper papers. Mrs. King has paperwork that may have been backdated at her attorney's suggestion."

"That's illegal!"

"Yes, it is. But we have the burden of proof."

"While you are taking care of this, I'm going to get that key."

"I wouldn't advise that, Cecelia," Stuart suggested strongly. "You'll only set yourself up to look bad. Remember, Mrs. King is in the wrong. Don't join her."

"You're right." Cecelia grudgingly admitted.

"We've been through the house, and I have a good memory. I'll spend my time shopping for the linens and draperies."

"Good idea. I'll be in touch." Stuart ended the call.

Cecelia pushed the button on her phone and mumbled, "That woman." Then called Rebecca and made plans to meet her after work.

It was her first day back, and truthfully, she was glad to have something to do. Her normally practical mind had been all mushy with Edwina's wedding, and Spencer's kindness had confused her. They had shared a sweet kiss downstairs in the castle. She shook off the memory.

The phone rang as she was walking out the door, interrupting her angry thoughts that Mrs. Quentin King could upset her life so much. And heaven knows the woman's husband had little constraint over his wife to do anything about it.

Cecelia decided she would never put herself in that position again.

"Hello?" She was hoping to hear news from Stuart or Rebecca.

"Miss Giatano."

"Mr. Wyndham." She kept her voice formal. His past behavior showing up at her door unannounced went down as a point against him.

"I am sincerely contrite for my actions the other day. Will you forgive me?"

Unprepared for that comment, she stuttered, "Of course."

"It was ungentlemanly of me to expect you to fulfill my schedule needs."

"Yes, it was." Cecelia softened at his apology.

"May I take you out to dinner then? I would like for us to make a fresh start."

"That's fair," Cecelia responded, her anger assuaged.

"When would you be available?"

"I am busy today, but the next two evenings are free."

"Would Friday evening be suitable? Perhaps dinner then a play?"

"Sounds fabulous."

"Great. You choose the play, and I'll choose the restaurant."

"*A Woman Scorned* sounds like a good one right now." Cecelia laughed lightly, she heard him chuckle.

"I've just returned from my sister's wedding in Scotland and home to a legal problem."

"Sorry to hear that.I'll arrange for the tickets. Pick you up at six? Play starts at 9 p.m."

"I'll see you then." She pressed the button on her phone, her heart lighter. The man had a bit of character after all, not to mention he was handsome and probably very rich. Maybe there was a God…the timing was perfect. She needed a diversion right now.

* * *

"Spencer, you're home," she answered her cell. "Rebecca and I just came in from a 2-day shopping spree. We're purchasing accessories for the Victorian. I didn't know you were back," Cecelia said breathlessly.

"Do you have dinner plans? I'd like to see you."

"Sorry, I'm not available tonight. I have a date. Everything all right with Edwina?"

"Everything's fine, Cece. I'll catch you later."

Cecelia pressed the button, annoyed at his curt hang up.

She tossed her phone on the sofa, and deposited the purchases on her bed. She and Rebecca shopped for designer fabric and accessories at several downtown boutiques. Cecelia learned her friend was an excellent seamstress, and offered to sew the draperies for a fee.

"I'm so excited about the paint colors you've chosen," Rebecca gushed as she hurried out of the bathroom.

"You have good taste. And you sew!" Cecelia smiled. "I'm thrilled that we can work together. You have no idea."

"Not a problem. I'm just excited to be a part of this whole project. My designer juices are flowing—which reminds me, what are your plans for the foyer? The chandelier is too small for the space. It needs to be replaced with something in the correct time period and much classier."

"Agreed. Any ideas?"

"There is an older house in the same neighborhood that is in disre- pair. I might be able to contact the owner and ask for a tour. The house sported a huge chandelier that could work."

"Really. Get on that today if you wouldn't mind."

"Can do. In fact, I need to get back to work, but I can make some phone calls. Will you be free this evening if I can reach the owner?"

"No. I have a date."

"Oooh, you didn't mention that!" Rebecca teased. "Spencer?"

"Spencer and I are business partners. That's all," she said smartly.

"Ah, got that." Rebecca saluted.

"Besides, if I remember right, I've seen you with Spencer a time or two."

"Oh, now don't go reading into that. We're just friends," Rebecca shot back. "I know two of his sisters."

"Sure." Cecelia twisted her head and caught Rebecca's eyes.

"Honest. I think Spencer is the cutest guy, but I know he has no more thoughts of romance with me than he does one of his sisters." She tossed her long hair over her shoulders.

"You never know," Cecelia teased back.

"True enough. Listen, I need to make some calls before the end of the day. See you tomorrow then?"

Cecelia sent off her new protégé, grateful for an assistant. After a quick time check, she hurried to set out her clothes and shower. She had to look good. This man was a bit of a mystery, difficult one day, a perfect gentleman the next—which she rather liked.

Wrapped in a towel, she stepped into the huge walk-in closet and filed through the choices. A black skirt with points that flowed when she walked, a cream-colored knit top with three-quarter sleeves and elegant gold and bronze sequins. She decided on basic black heels.

That done, she bent over and combed out her hair, remembering how Edwina had brushed hers out one evening. Smiling, she tossed her hair back and sprayed and scrunched it. It would have to do. No time to put it up formally. Simple black earrings with dangles and a matching bracelet completed her outfit. She turned at the mirror, pleased, sprayed her favorite scent, Celine Dion's *Belong*, into the air and stepped into it.

The doorbell reverberated throughout the tall ceilings, and her heart quickened in anticipation. She needed something exciting in her life right at the moment.

Chapter 31

"Well, Miss Giatano, have I accounted for my previous bad behavior?" Evan stood outside her door at the end of the perfect evening, his handsome dark eyes boring into hers.

She noticed he didn't push to invite himself in. In fact, he had been most accommodating all evening. Something stirred inside her. Perhaps it was that knight-in-shining-armor thing. Whatever it was, she needed someone in her life. Now.

"Of course." She found herself taken in with his good looks, his bearing and manner of dress, impeccable. Things she loved in a man.

"Then I will bid you good evening." He turned to leave, stopped and turned back. "May I call again Miss Giatano?"

Cecelia fished through her purse, hoping he'd ask to come in. Best to play along. "If you wish." She put on her best smile, turned her back, and keyed the door. He had complimented her several times during the evening and spoken entirely about what was going on in her life. She turned slightly, a confident smile on her face. "Next time we'll talk about you." Then she slipped in the door without a backward glance. Cecelia shivered. Those eyes had been focused on her the entire evening, and she knew when a man appreciated her. And Evan did.

Tossing her black pearled-and-sequined purse on the sofa, she kicked off her shoes and hummed as she went to undress. The evening had been a complete success. She was back.

Confidence filled her thoughts. Unable to sleep, she put on her turquoise silk pajamas and rifled through the purchases she and Rebecca had made earlier in the day. Satisfied that the color scheme was decided, she grabbed a pencil and pad and sketched window designs and furniture placement for the foyer, living room, and library. Several times she stopped drawing and, with the pencil between her teeth, wondered where

Evan Wyndham lived. The man was so handsome and self-assured, she wondered jealously how many women must be after him. He would definitely be a catch. Was she up to the challenge? Cecelia Grace Giatano knew she was.

What she needed was some new clothes, a fresh new hairstyle. She picked up her cell and left her hairdresser a voice mail.

* * *

"A man's stomach is not always the way to his heart," Cecelia teased Rebecca the next day while they shopped. "The right dress does wonders." She laughed, passing several mannequins and stopping to view each outfit. "Now *this* is an evening dress. I love the narrow form-fitting style. Black is so classic. Let's go inside."

"It does look good," Rebecca agreed and followed.

"Rebecca, do you enjoy style?" She turned her head.

"Call me Becca, okay? I can't stand being called Rebecca unless I'm at work."

"Sure. No problem. You like this?" Cecelia held up a full-length red wraparound dress.

"For me? Are you kidding? I'd never make it to the car without tripping on it. I'm such a klutz when it comes to stuff wrapped around my ankles. I have an aversion to long dresses."

"Really?" Cecelia wondered if Becca was joking.

"Hate formal dress." Becca grabbed a shorter version of the dress and said, "This is more my style. But only if I have to."

"You sound just like Edwina. I bet you don't own a single pair of Birkenstocks, do you?"

"Not a single pair."

"Well, we'll see about that when I'm done with you. When's your birthday?"

"Why?" Becca put the dress back on the rack.

"Because I'm buying you Birkenstocks for your birthday. Today."

"My birthday isn't until September, and besides, you don't have to buy me anything. I'm loving all this, remember?"

"Pooh. You'll never regret wearing Birkenstocks, I guarantee it."

"Well then, I'm on board, if you say so. Take me there." Becca pointed. "I'll sew something at no charge for you."

"Don't worry about it. I'm glad for the company, not to mention someone I can talk to that won't tell me about the latest *Wall Street Journal* business prediction."

"Not to worry. I'm unaware of anything except my own simple life," Rebecca joked. "Besides, I'm here to learn, so teach me all you know."

Cecelia felt her joy return. She liked the idea of sharing her skills with someone who really wanted to learn.

"So, we've been out for two hours now, and you haven't mentioned a thing about your date last night," Becca baited her. "Big secret?"

"No. No secret," she murmured.

"Oh my gosh, Cecelia, it's that bad, isn't it? Tell me," she gushed.

"Well, he is handsome. And a perfect gentleman."

"Okay . . . that will do for starters. What's he do?"

"He's a publisher. But he didn't talk about himself last night."

"It was all about you then? Jeesh, where did you *find* this man?"

"That's what I'm saying."

"When do I get to meet him? Of course, he asked you out again? Of course he did. Look, you're blushing!"

"Me, blushing? I don't think so. Am I?" Cecelia put the dress back on the rack and turned, looking for something in Rebecca's . . . Becca's eyes.

"Well, let's just say it's pretty apparent he liked you."

"I think he does. We did start off on a bad shoe."

"That's *bad foot*," Rebecca corrected.

"Whatever." Cecelia grumped. She was just like Edwina. We're here. "Now sit down and try these three styles on for size."

Becca walked out, at Cecelia's insistence, wearing her new Birkenstocks and exclaimed, "You are so right about these shoes. I'll be spoiled for life."

"Good . . . you're going to need those shoes, dahling. Because you're going to be my major shopper. You'll be doing the running."

"Oh, like I would hate that?"

"Just want you to know. There was a method to my gladness."

"*Madness*. But it doesn't matter."

Cecelia huffed. "You should pull your hair up. It would look rather elegant with your heart-shaped face."

After a moment, "So, do you think I need a makeover since I'll be working with you? I realize I'll be representing you, and heaven knows, once your show is public . . ."

"Smart woman." Cecelia gave her shoulder a tap. "Design isn't just for rooms and landscapes, my dear." Cecelia hailed a taxi.

Becca caught her lip between her teeth. It wouldn't hurt to prop up her image a bit. Arriving at the same small office every day working with the same no-fun people had become a bore. She entertained thoughts of meeting someone new. Her mother had reminded her only that morning that she needed to go out more since her recent two-year relationship that was going nowhere finally died. This job would certainly throw her into the path of new people.

"Well, the packages are safely in your condo. My arms have had a great workout these past few days! I'm off. I'll take the fabric for the swag with me. Maybe I should wait while you check your fax. Wasn't your attorney supposed to get back with you?"

"He said he would. But it's Saturday, and he's likely schmoozing with his golf buddies." Cecelia headed for her office anyway. "I'll check while you're here."

"Good because once I sit down at the sewing machine, I'll be there all evening!"

Cecelia laughed, and it felt good. She had someone to talk to since Edwina would not be back anytime soon. Especially if she had all those sons the Scot was talking about.

"Hey, there is something." Cecelia scanned the paperwork. "Nothing much. I just have to sign something and send it back."

"Oh well, trouble will come soon enough. No sense borrowing it early."

Cecelia looked at her. "Becca, you need to get out more."

"Right," she agreed. "I'll be in touch. Have a good weekend."

Chapter 32

Sunday morning Spencer was knocking at Cecelia's door. "Good. I wanted to talk to you. How is everything with Alex and Ed?"

Spencer cocked his head. "Do you know that Edwina hates it when you call her Ed?"

"She never told me."

"Maybe you never gave her the chance," Spencer shot back.

"What? You have jet lag or something?" Cecelia walked to the sofa and sat with a gesture inviting him to do the same. "We need to talk Spencer."

Spencer chose to sit across from her. "What's on your mind?" He propped his feet on the coffee table, which, he noted, irritated her.

"Well, I'm going to be very busy with the show. I won't be around much."

"And?"

"Well, we're partners in the restaurant. I just thought you might want to know."

"Know what? I've been running the place for eight months, and if I remember correctly, you've eaten there, but I've never asked you for anything, have I?"

The woman got up, miffed, and stalked to the kitchen.

He was not going to be one of her thrown-off suitors. "Got anything to eat up here?" Spencer followed her.

"I haven't even thought about food today."

"What? You on a diet again?"

"I'm not on a diet, Spencer. What is your problem anyway?"

"Nothing." He held up both hands. "Peace, okay?"

"Okay, but get to the point. Why did you come up here?"

"Just to let you know I was back, that's all." He turned a quick corner in the conversation. "I talked to Alonzo, my new chef. He's good, really good. I took your advice and sat down with him yesterday. We have some new menu items. I think the clients will appreciate the changes."

"Good."

"Good food with excellent service is what we need, Cece. I've hired two more waitresses to accommodate the new chef. He's quick to prepare a plate, so we are seating more clients per day, which is good for all of us."

"Great."

Her one-word sentences were beginning to annoy him. "I decided to sell Winnie's." he baited her.

"Really?" she said absently.

"Cecelia, you are not listening."

"You're right. I'm not. Sorry, Spencer. I have a lot on my mind."

"I'll leave you to your work then. We'll talk later."

* * *

Cecelia heard the door shut. Why was she so spacey today? She knew. Her cell had not rung.

Thoughts began to creep into her mind. Maybe Evan Wyndham wasn't going to call her again. Why did it matter so much? She had plenty of opportunities with men of the same caliber, maybe not as handsome, but just as wealthy and at the same pinnacle of success.

Determined, she got up and thought about calling a girlfriend and heading out to the clubs this evening. But that didn't suit her mood. Most of her female associates were married. And she felt uncomfortable when they went along partying as though they were single.

She thought about the kiss she and Spencer shared the night of the wedding. Her face warmed at the thought. He had been so gentle and so sweet. Why did he irritate her so?

It was not kind to compare him to Evan, but she couldn't help it. Spencer was so together, so regular, so everyday. She wanted excitement in a man. The thrill of the catch consumed her. Spencer was always there. And she knew he would come closer if she opened the door. She wanted to travel, meet new people, start new businesses. If she knew anything about herself, she knew she would never be able to settle down to Spencer's kind of lifestyle.

She needed more. She wanted white roses. Diamonds. New sleek cars. A townhouse in New York. A beach house in the Bahamas. Beautiful surroundings. And she would have that and more. Especially once the show exposed her to the world. Perhaps she would be offered talk-show appearances. She might be asked to write a design book. Or travel to other locations to design homes. The world was hers, and she didn't want to block any opportunities.

Cecelia knew she would not call Evan Roberto Wyndham, no matter how much she wanted to. But when a week passed and still no call, she'd picked up her cell three times in the last hour to make a call.

The problem with Mrs. King had worked itself out quick enough when Cecelia picked up the phone and suggested they meet. She gave her an ultimatum: Stay out of her business or hear one more story of her husband's infidelities. There were plenty of those floating around in the moneyed circles. Cecelia knew her claws were out, but the woman would cause her to waste too much money; money she would need for the Victorian.

Becca had tried to talk her out of it, but to no avail this time. Cecelia felt a certain hardness creep over her. Evan hadn't called, and Edwina, too busy with her own family now, had not called either. Cecelia was one woman that should the rest fall away, she would stand.

At least that's what she told herself.

Chapter 33

"Spencer, I need someone to clean my place. Have you got time?" Cecelia asked from her cell.

"I could make time, Cece. When do you need it done?" *And this after you told her you wouldn't have time to clean for her*, Spencer scolded himself.

"Tomorrow afternoon. I'm arranging a showing. There are three possible tenants, and I want to make sure everything is perfect."

"Tomorrow? That doesn't give me much headway."

"I know. I just found out. And since the Victorian is mine free and clear, Becca and I have been over there every evening. There are three levels, so it's taking time. We have to get the tulips planted this fall, not to mention the brickwork design needs to be done before we can even plant them. And the English garden has to be prepared before the snow flies."

"Not to worry. I'll get over there tomorrow early. Your place hardly gets dirty anyway."

"You're a peach, Spencer. Thanks."

"Right."

"I do appreciate you."

She sounded tired. "I know. Leave your key under the mat. I'll let myself in about seven in the morning, unless you have other plans."

"No, that's perfect. I'll be gone by six a.m."

"Got it." Spencer paused. "You okay?"

"I'm fine. Just a little overworked."

"Make time for yourself, Cece."

"I will."

Spencer shut his phone. *Something's on that woman's mind.* But he was not privy to it. She acted like they'd never gone to Scotland, let alone shared a long, sweet kiss. She had warmed and relaxed in his arms. He'd felt it. What had happened?

Clueless, he called Deena and invited her to lunch.

* * *

"Becca, did you have time to order the area rug?"

"It won't be here for another week, Cecelia. Something about a backup at the factory."

"Figures."

"Hey, that handsome guy, what's his name—Evan something. Has he called?"

"No, he hasn't, and it's been nearly two weeks."

"I'm sorry." Becca regretted her off-the-wall question.

Cecelia shrugged. "I'm busy anyway."

"I do have some good news though. Remember the house I told you about that was trashed? It's three streets over from here. I have the key. The owner said we could make an offer on anything in the house. He said the mansion belonged to his great grandfather and he has no use for it. He lives in Wisconsin."

"Want to run over now?" Cecelia's voice excited at the prospect of finding a treasure.

"Let's go." Rebecca pulled out her keys. "Let me drive. I know where to park."

Within minutes, the two were foraging through the dusty house. The black-and-white marble tiles positioned diagonally on the foyer floor needed a good cleaning, but were still in mint condition. At the same moment, both looked up and gasped. The French-style crystal chandelier looked as though it belonged in a cathedral.

"Do you think it will it fit the Victorian?"

Rebecca's sensible question prompted Cecelia to whisper. "Yes, I believe it will."

"That's a keeper then. Let's see the rest of the house."

Reluctantly, Cecelia pulled her eyes away from the beautiful creation, and they began a slow walk-through. "There isn't much furniture. The bones of the house are good though," Cecelia murmured. "Is the house available?"

"The owner doesn't care what they do with it. He's got a large family, and he is well set. Enough to ignore the historical value of this house," Rebecca grumped.

"I'm stalled now. I'm involved in the Victorian. However, if the show goes well, I *could* pull enough equity out of the restaurant and the downtown place to finance it."

"Oh, Cecelia, that could put you over the top. Unless this guy will give it to you."

"Give it to me?" Cecelia turned.

"Well, sometimes owners will sell for a dollar to someone who will bring back and maintain the historical integrity of the house."

"Check on that, would you? Oh, look at this settee. It's the perfect size for the foyer. We'll take that too. The fabric is coarse, but it's original. We can have it recovered in period fabric and the wood oiled. Becca, you've found a treasure."

"I had no idea it was this beautiful inside. The way the owner talked, I thought it was trashed. Let's check out the other two levels."

"Well, if this is trashed, I'll take it off his hands for a dollar and bring it back to life."

"Let me check into it first, Cecelia. You don't want to get in over your head."

"Miss Practical." She smiled. "We're going to need to hire one of the contractors to come and get this chandelier and remove it piece by precious piece."

"Right. It will be an excellent showpiece."

"That's settled. Let's go. I'm starving. How about *Winnie's*? We can tell Spencer about our finds." Cecelia checked her watch. "It's just about time for him to close—if we hurry, we won't have to change and we can eat whatever's left in the kitchen."

Rebecca took one look around and shook her head. Maybe she hadn't been smart in bringing Cecelia here. The woman had no boundaries. Thirty minutes later, the two were talking at the same time as they walked into the restaurant. The staff had just turned off the open sign and were about to lock the entry.

"Hold on." Cecelia called from the elevator. "Is Spencer in?"

"He's here. I'll get him." The girl dashed away.

"She must be new. I haven't seen her before. Spencer said he had two new employees."

"Good. He needs more staff. Spencer is handling the clients too often," Becca piped up.

"Really. He didn't mention that to me. He said everything was fine."

Becca gazed at Cecelia. "He didn't want to bother you," she said nonchalantly.

"Why?"

"You've been busy, remember? Spencer handles any problems that arise."

Cecelia started to ask Becca how she knew so much about Spencer, but stopped. She shrugged, all of that forgotten when Spencer appeared. "We're starved."

Becca noticed Spencer's blond hair sticking up all around his head. "Stick your finger in a light socket?" she teased.

"That bad, huh?"

"Worse. But hey who cares, we came as we were, a bit dusty, I'm afraid."

"Sit down, ladies." He pulled out two chairs. "I'll get water."

He was back in a moment and called, "I'll see what's left. Alonzo wants to get out of here. Long day."

"I'm so excited. My mind is racing, trying to think of a way to finance that other house. It's calling me."

"Maybe so, Cecelia, but count your costs first. You can't afford to lose anything, especially now that you're committed to the design show."

"I know, I know."

"Besides the money, when will you ever find time to spend hours on the set and come home to another huge project? You'll end up a spinster because you have no social life."

Cecelia actually laughed. "Well, at least I'll be a busy one."

Rebecca smiled and took a sip of water. The woman would not be dissuaded.

Spencer served them. "Oh, vegetable soup and fresh French bread and warm butter. It doesn't get any better than this." Becca waved the steam toward her nose.

"Haven't you anything a bit lighter?" Cecelia eyed Becca's plate.

Becca's eyes widened. The man was serving food from his kitchen after-hours. What did she expect?

"It's this or nothing," Spencer said with a firmness Becca hadn't noticed before. The man was a saint, and Cecelia didn't even see it.

"Well, a small bowl, maybe. But no butter."

"Right." Spencer headed back to the kitchen and brought Cecelia another plate.

Becca nearly burst out with a reprimand to Cecelia. To keep from spouting out loud, she slurped a spoon of hot soup into her mouth, then reached for her water glass to slow the burn.

Spencer, with nary a facial feature out of place returned, sat a tiny butter bowl of soup on a large plate with a slice, a very thin slice, of bread. No butter.

Cecelia snapped a look at him, ready for a fight, but Spencer would have none of it. He walked away.

"He expects me to fill up on this?" She picked up her spoon.

"That's what you asked for." Becca dug in, ignoring her friend. "I'm starved, and this is good." She reached for the butter.

Some time passed, and Becca noticed Spencer did not come back. She didn't blame him. Getting hotter by the minute, Cecelia jumped up from her chair and headed for the kitchen.

"You going to eat your bread?" Rebecca called out.

"No. If you're that hungry, take it," Cecelia grumped over her shoulder.

She did, slathering butter on it and finishing her soup.

It wasn't long before Cecelia came back, her lips pressed together. "Spencer left."

"Oh." Becca stood up and started to clear the table. "I'll just take these back."

"That's their job," Cecelia sputtered, snatching her purse from the table. "Let them clear the table. People know their place."

Becca stopped halfway and turned, stunned that Cecelia could actually say those words. She thought she knew her better. Shrugging, she continued to the kitchen with dishes in hand.

"Thank you guys, this was great. Who made the soup? Loved the broth."

One of the younger guys looked up from his work at the sink and raised his hand.

"I'm having this when I come back. Is it served daily?"

"Yes," he said and smiled, wiping sweat from his forehead.

"See you all later. Thanks for staying open for us." She waved and went back through the restaurant, tossing a generous tip on the table.

Cecelia was pacing back and forth in front of the elevator. "Come on. I'm tired, and there's more work to be done tomorrow."

"Actually, Cecelia, I don't work on Sundays."

"What do you mean?" Her hands were on her hips.

"I don't work on Sundays," Becca repeated.

"Well, how do you expect to be my assistant?"

"Design and furniture stores usually close early on Sundays. Besides, you have to take a rest sometime or you'll keel over."

"Keel over?"

"Yes, you know, drop dead."

"As in gorgeous?"

"Not exactly." Becca rolled her eyes. "We are too tired. We'd better get some sleep. My car's downstairs, so I'll be on my way. Call me Sunday night if you want to talk about the schedule this week."

Cecelia nodded and waved as she stepped onto the elevator.

Jeesh, the woman is not only a powerhouse, but she's power hungry. She knew now she'd have to set some boundaries or Cecelia would run her over like she was roadkill. But she remembered they were both tired from the long day and overrun with too many projects and short deadlines. Anyone would be a bit touchy.

Becca climbed in her car, glad to be alone for the first time today. *A good night's sleep is what we need.* She yawned and the night lights elongated in her vision. She popped out her cell and called her mother to tell her she was on the way.

Chapter 34

Sunday morning Cecelia was up and dressed early. Spencer would be here in an hour.

Now that she had a project, she was happier, more motivated. The fact that Evan Wyndham hadn't called somehow seemed less important. Until the phone rang and she ran for it, tripping over her shoes.

"Cecelia speaking," she answered with her most professional voice, just in case.

"Evan here," he stated.

She pressed her fingers over her lips to keep from blurting out something stupid.

"Can we talk?"

"Yes."

"I have been in Italy."

"Really?" Cecelia could play this one-word game.

"Family problems."

"I see."

"This is short notice, but I wondered if you might have time to meet for a late lunch."

Cecelia's heart accelerated from ten miles per hour to forty in less than five seconds. She forced herself to pause. "Let me see. I have several papers I must finish today, but I could free myself say, three o'clock?"

"Yes. Do you have a favorite restaurant? Besides your own, of course." His mood seemed to lighten.

"*Blacktop* is one of my personal favorites, if you want to do casual."

"That sounds good. Jeans then?"

"Jeans." She tried not to sound too excited.

"That's out on Lake Shore Drive, right on the lake."

"Yes, it is." She was genuinely surprised he knew about the place. "I'll meet you there at three thirty, Cecelia."

He was gone before she could react at the tender way he said her name. It was obvious something was wrong. He had been too quiet, not in charge like usual. She was intrigued.

She dressed in her grey sweats and planned on going down to exercise while Spencer was cleaning. The invitation sparked her energy level, as had the fact that she now had a mission. Several of them. One, to have the best design show on television. Two, to get that second house. And finally, to make Evan Roberto Wyndham fall in love with her. And maybe it was time to have someone who cared about her the way Alex Dunnegin cared about Edwina.

She was instantly furious with herself. Why should she be jealous of Edwina? Indeed, Cecelia had the things in life she wanted. She was well-known in Chicago society—if not at the top echelon—close enough. She'd worked hard for that position.

She knew Spencer's knock and sprinted to the door. "Come in. You're early." She smiled. "I'm going down to exercise while you work. About an hour?"

Spencer, still half asleep, grunted in agreement as she flew past him. He got to work and within the hour had the kitchen and bathrooms spick-and-span. They required little cleaning since they were hardly ever used. He vacuumed, put the cleaning supplies underneath the sink and shot out of there. He wasn't in the mood to talk to Miss Giatano this morning.

Cecelia returned, her home smelling of roses and French vanilla. She headed for the bathroom and turned on the shower, letting the warm water run over her. She decided she might just soak in a tub full of scented bubbles one of these nights. *Just like Edwina.*

Renewed, she stepped out of the huge glass-encased shower, grabbed her white robe, and went to her closet to search out an appropriate outfit for the occasion. Passing over the sequins, she finally realized she had very little in the way of casual tops. Designer jeans she owned. Cotton tops, she didn't. She settled for the baby blue button-down blouse with jeans and playfully pulled her hair back into a ponytail. It reminded her of the time she had fallen in love. Micah, an older boy, was playing the part of Archie in one of her mother's plays, and she'd been smitten with the way he carried himself, the way he knew his lines, and the way he looked at her. Like she was special.

Victoria was always so busy, she hardly seemed like a mother. She was either dressing or practicing her lines somewhere on or near the stage, usually with a man half her age. Her mother still possessed a girlish figure and beautiful eyes and could dress up and carry herself like the Queen of England should she desire.

Thing is, as a child Cecelia never knew what was truth and what was fiction. They lived in a dream world. Go out, perform in full regalia, bow, and come back to your dressing room and become . . . whom?

The next few hours were spent in busywork in the office for half the time, the other half musing. Shaking her head, she wondered what in the world had prompted her to go back to those days. Then she realized. The ponytail. Scooping her hair up, she anchored a rubber band tightly around her pony tail and tied a blue ribbon around the band. She wasn't going to let a little thing like her undressed hair detract from the fact Evan had called her.

Smelling of rose-scented soap, she decided against squirting on her one-hundred-dollar-an-ounce perfume in favor of going as is. She sensed this meeting could possibly be a turning point in her life if she played her cards right. Caught up in the easy Sunday reverie, she decided to leave early. Traffic would be light, so she called down to the garage and had her black Cadillac brought to the entrance.

Snatching her beaded and sequined purse, she dumped out the contents on the coffee table, and fished in her closet for the exact right one. After some time she decided that a small handheld number would do. Satisfied, she punched the button on the elevator and waited.

Stepping out into daylight, she noted the dark clouds covering the sky. Looked like a rain shower was headed their way—at least from the view straight up. She slipped into the black leather seat, lowered her window, and pulled in a deep breath of fresh air, pushing it out through her lips. The darkened windows protected her perfect skin from the sun's rays. She'd worked at that too—and had been told many times what creamy smooth skin she had been blessed with. She pulled down the visor mirror and peeked. Indeed she was clear-skinned and pink-cheeked.

The drive would take about twenty minutes, but today she felt there was no need to hurry. She tapped the wheel with her newly manicured fingernails, choosing a lighter nail color this time instead of the garish red she and most of her friends wore when they were out on the town. Should she be fashionably late? Or on time? She chose the latter, her intuition telling her the man wanted to talk. She planned what she would say, how she would gaze into his black-brown eyes and he into her blue ones. And how they might connect.

Taxi horns honking reverberated from somewhere outside her hearing, for she was dreaming, hoping that this would be nothing less than a Jane Austen *Pride and Prejudice* ending.

"How silly!" she said aloud, her voice echoing in the car. "You know better than to trust a man or give your heart away too soon." She repeated her mother's words. Yet her mother had married Edwina's father within months after meeting him. He had supported her acting, and whenever he could, joined her wherever she was playing. They were head over tail in love.

Dark thoughts began to invade her mind. She doubted Edwina's father knew her mother went from one man to another during her entire childhood. That she lived with men, but married only one of them—her father. And that had been disastrous. Shaking the thoughts from her head, she forced them out of her mind with a pound of her fist on the steering wheel.

She would be different than her mother. She had determined that early on. When some of those men gave her the eye, her mother had protected her. And for that, she owed her. What possessed her to be reliving her childhood, she had no idea.

Suddenly, the name *Blacktop* caught her eye, and she slammed on the brakes, nearly missing the drive. The building was small and nondescript, but you could get the best breakfast in town. Bar none. And hamburgers were juicy and huge. She was early, so she parked under a small tree for shade, lay her head back, and listened to a new CD. The performers from Scotland called *Classie Lassies* consisted of fifteen- to seventeen-year-olds who played violins and cello and harp with a skill unmatched by any troupe she'd seen. The Scottish dances and costumes had been outstanding at the live show. The music was uplifting and deeply moving all at once.

Lost in the sound track, she realized several minutes had passed. She opened her eyes and gazed around the lot. It was still a little early. The lot was full of mostly trucks and older model cars, so when a sleek, black car drove past, she knew it was Evan.She kept her gaze slightly averted, then saw him from the corner of her eye. He was wearing a black shirt tucked into a pair of faded blue jeans. He could have walked straight off a commercial shoot. His hair was jet black and blowing, adding to his good looks. She wished she'd have chosen the sequined top after all.

"Too late now," she murmured and opened the door and stepped out as graciously as she could manage. At least she wasn't overdressed, which to her was as inappropriate as being underdressed. Her Birkenstocks were comfortable; she felt at ease for the first time in days.

"Hello," he greeted her solemnly. "It's good to see you."

"Thank you," she said brightly, noting his melancholy voice.

"So this is your favorite place?" A slight smile slipped across his face.

"It is when I'm not schmoozing." She thought that sounded pretty humble.

"Schmoozing is, unfortunately, a part of the job."

"Yes, it is. That's how the game is played in business and politics." *And*, she almost added, *in marriage*.

Without a word he took her elbow and led her to the front entrance when they easily could have entered through the small screened back door.

"You've been here before?" she questioned as they stepped into the small space.

"Yes. They happen to serve the best breakfast, although I won't allow myself more than one visit a month."

They waited to be seated and slid into the well-worn burgundy leather booth seats. The waitress already had a coffeepot in her hand ready to pour.

"Hot tea," Cecelia said quickly.

"Coffee for me."

She poured, and Cecelia noticed the woman giving Evan the once-over. Who wouldn't? She sat up straighter and enjoyed the fact that she was with him.

"So what brings us here today?" she asked to break the ice.

He reached for his spoon, added two teaspoons of sugar, and stirred.

"It seems I have inherited a villa in Italy."

"What? That doesn't sound so bad."

"If you could see the condition it's in, you'd think differently. I don't have the time to hire contractors nor do I wish to."

"Sell it."

"I would do that except my aunt's papers require that I keep it in the family."

"Oh, that is a problem, if you really don't want it. Could you fix it up and rent it out?"

"I hadn't thought of that." He looked hopeful. "I was all set to move my business and live there while the repairs were being made. They'll take two years, minimum. There's a wine press and acres of grapes to be harvested. The crew is there now and has been working for my aunt for years. She set aside money to pay them for their services. I would have to manage the estate."

"Hmmm . . . and with your business here in Chicago, that does present a problem. Do you have anyone here in the States who could cover for two years while you work in Italy?"

"No. My grandfather and father worked in the business, and it must be held by a family member."

Cecelia nodded, noting his flare of temper. When the waitress appeared, he waited for her to order and then ordered himself. She rested her right index finger at her jaw and let her mind visualize an Italian villa, which she herself should have inherited from her father.

"Are you familiar with the city of Perugia?" His eyes softened.

"Actually, I haven't been there. My father lived in Salerno."

"Ah, beautiful country."

"Your family dates back from Italy then," Cecelia inquired.

"Yes. My mother was full-blooded Italian. My father was English."

"The reason for your dark eyes," she blurted out before thinking.

He returned her gaze.

"Do you have to return soon?"

"Next week."

"Next week?" she repeated. "It's that serious then?"

"Yes. I have been here a few days, and already everything is in chaos. My employees have no idea how to run the company without me. I can't leave them. But I can't stay."

Cecelia understood his dilemma. He was not the type of man to admit a weakness, let alone talk about it. She guessed this was something new to him. "Well, let's eat," she said when the plates were set in front of them. "Get some sustenance and talk."

"Good idea." He picked up his fork and ate heartily.

Cecelia sensed this man needed her, and she knew for certain she needed him.

"So, tell me what's going on in your life. Since I don't know you very well and have taken all this time telling you my woes, why don't you enlighten me?" He sat back and crossed his arms, in a completely relaxed stance.

Cecelia, sensing his mood change, told him about her newly acquired Victorian, about the design show and how she herself had been busy trying to pull all the pieces together.

"Ah, two alike."

"It seems so." She sipped her tea, a serene calm settling over her.

He listened without a word while she talked about her business plans, then set his elbows on the table and gazed at her. "I'm really grateful that you had time to meet with me today."

Cecelia dabbed her mouth with the paper napkin and smiled.

Chapter 35

During the next three days Evan called Cecelia half a dozen times. She began carrying her cell in a pocket for such occasions, causing a great stir with Rebecca. "Gosh, woman, does he need you *that* much?"

Cecelia smiled and shrugged. "He's going through a tough time. And we both know business. It works."

"I guess it does. I'll be glad when he gets himself over to Italy, and then maybe we can get something done here."

Cecelia would not allow herself to think about him leaving. The last three evenings, they'd had dinner together at small cafés where they could sit in a quiet corner and talk about the day's events. She'd become accustomed to letting him lead. Something she rarely let a man do.

"Why don't we work on hanging the drapes? I don't relish ironing them again." Rebecca looked up from the makeshift plywood table where she sat at the sewing machine

"I have lunch plans," Cecelia called from the corner.

"Lunch plans again? I've used three days of vacation thus far, and we haven't had one full workday, Cecelia."

"Okay, okay, you're right." Cecelia noted Becca's crisp voice." We're so close. I'll call Evan and cancel lunch."

"Great. All we need is a couple of hours, and we will have these drapes up."

"I'll get the ladder." Cecelia borrowed a landscape worker who carried in an eight-foot ladder and set it up.

"I'll get up here because I know how I made them to hang." Rebecca slung the heavy material over her forearm and started up the ladder with one hand.

"Take your time," Cecelia ordered. "I can't afford to—"

"What are you doing?" Spencer's voice echoed from the tall ceilings. "Come down. You can't hold onto the ladder and hang those at the same time. You'll break your neck."

Cecelia's long-fingered hands landed at her hips. "What're you doing here?"

Spencer gave her a look and walked past. "Looks like I came just in time."

Rebecca's toes sought the next rung as she backed down several steps. "I was a bit worried how I was going to get the rings over the bar."

"Have you got another ladder?"

Cecelia stalked away and brought the worker back with another eight-footer.

"That'll work. Cece, why don't you get on the other end and balance the bar while I sling the rings on?" Spencer ordered. "Can you handle that?" He remembered she hated heights.

"I can do it Spencer." She grumped.

"Rebecca, you can stand at the bottom and see if the hem lands where you want it to. It looks like we have several length choices up here," he said as he reached the top.

"Yes, we had them install two levels since there'll be a matching cornice to cover the draperies at the top. They have to hang at floor level to look right," Becca explained.

"Got it." Spencer carried up one set, slung the rings over the correct level bar while Cecelia balanced the other end.

"Hey, how did you know where to find us?" Cecelia turned to him as she descended ever so slowly.

"Rebecca and I had lunch a couple of times. She fills me in."

Cecelia's brain worked. "I see. Well, what do you think?"

"I didn't see the place before you started, but the landscaping out front looks really good, especially the blue stone pavers curving up to the front door."

"We're trying to keep it authentic."

"And as always, your taste is impeccable."

Cecelia turned her head and gained his gaze. Was he being facetious?

Satisfied that he meant it, she answered a call from a contractor to verify that the faucets were correct so the driver could be on his way. She was glad to get away from Spencer. Guilt tried to weasel in, but she pushed it away. She and Evan were more suited—by far.

"The arc of that leaded window is beautiful there above the plate-glass view." Rebecca pointed upward. "It was totally covered by a piece of plasterboard. No one knew it was there until this afternoon. It will let in morning sun and shine on the wood floors. Isn't it grand?" She hurried to show Spencer around since Miss Cecelia was such a snob today. She had not offered Spencer a thank-you. The woman was daft.

"Have time for lunch today?" he asked Rebecca.

"Sorry, I can't. Cecelia's staying in, and we're going to work through the lunch hour for once. We have to scrape paint off the trim around the windows today.

"Want some help?"

"Sure, if you have time."

"I had a huge breakfast this morning, so I can stay a few hours and then back to the restaurant."

"Oh, we need you! Come on. I'll show you where the supplies are."

Twenty minutes later they were hacking at layers of paint.

"This is the worst job," Rebecca complained. "My arms are already sore from sewing and lifting my arms above my head too many times these last few days."

Spencer laughed heartily. "That really hurts, doesn't it?"

"Deena introduced me to your other sister."

"Which one? I have four."

"Symond. A very unusual name."

"Yeah, she gets that all the time. My parents were not exactly into popular names."

"She looks so much like you. She could be your twin."

"She is my twin."

"What? I didn't know you had a twin."

He shrugged. "No need to announce it unless it comes up I guess."

"You sure are laid-back." Rebecca laughed. "Nothing seems to motivate you to scream or get angry or upset."

"Oh, it's definitely in there. I just don't show it as often as I used to."

Rebecca turned her head to read his eyes, but he hadn't looked up, just kept working. "By the way, if we're going to work together, call me Becca. I only use my given name for business."

"Okay, Becca it is then. So do you have brothers and sisters?"

"Not a one. Spoiled rotten by my mother. My father died a couple years ago. . . . But that was years after he left me and mom."

Spencer made eye contact, nodded, and kept working. After a time, he asked, "Where did you get your highlights done?"

"What?" Becca couldn't believe her ears.

"I have four sisters. Symond wanted me to ask you. She liked the reddish golds with your dark brown hair."

"At *Elle's*."

"I know exactly where that's at." He smiled.

"And how do you know that?" Becca was laughing.

"Cecelia says it's the best place in town."

"It is, really."

"Well, glad to know it. I'll tell Sy tonight."

Becca's heart started to whisper sweet things. This guy was a keeper. Quiet. Hard-working. Brad-Pitt cute and that spiked blond hair. She could just see his towhead kids. And with four sisters, he obviously knew what women were about.

One thought stunted her hopes. Spencer cared for Cecelia, and from the looks of it would be willing to wait for her. He also knew about Evan but had never said as much.

"Hey where is Cecelia anyway? She was supposed to help with the windows."

"I saw her out instructing the landscape crew awhile ago." Spencer kept on working.

"This is the perfect day for it, so best get that done." Becca said, noting the workers scurrying around as Cecelia pointed. After a time Spencer yelled from across the huge empty room.

"Well that's four finished and two more to go. These old houses are amazingly built."

"And tall! Twelve-foot walls at least. I should know. I sewed the drapes for these long but very beautiful windows!"

Spencer laughed easily. "I don't know about you, but pizza is sounding really good right about now." There's a pizza joint right around the corner. Want to head over there?"

"Sounds good, but look at me. Paint chips in my hair…and my jeans look like painter pants," she laughed. "Actually they are."

Spencer's face lit up with a smile. "Charge a new pair to Cecelia." He joked "We're business partners. I"ll see it gets done."

"Of course." But she knew it was way more than that, at least on Spencer's part.

"Come on, let's get out of here. The landscape crew left an hour ago, and Cecelia doesn't know when to stop. Besides, she'll probably be out with her new boyfriend tonight."

"Probably." Becca agreed. "I'll let her know we're leaving."

Spencer put his tool belt away. Hands on jeaned hips, he looked around. "Made good headway on those windows today…"

"We did." She agreed, as hands on hips, she assessed their progress.

"I'm going to wash up."

"I guess Cecelia took off." Rebecca felt a sting of guilt knowing Cecelia had a date with Evan. "Well, you look better," she teased.

"Better than what?" The laugh lines around his blue eyes crinkled.

She ignored that comment with a smile and followed Spencer out to the small parking lot in back. "We can walk if you'd like. It's only five blocks, and fairly warm tonight."

"I'm just glad for a breeze. I'm not sure they'll want us in their restaurant after we've been sweating all day."

"Ya think?" He laughed and took her elbow.

Chapter 36

"This is good pizza." Rebecca pushed another bite into her mouth.

"Well, I can see that," Spencer quipped over the sound of Rod Stewart's *I'll Stand by You* playing in the background.

"Oh, I love this song," Rebecca mused as she leaned back into her chair and closed her eyes. "I'm so full."

"You should be. You ate half a large pizza."

"Really? I did?" She sat up straight.

Spencer's huge smile warned her that he'd been fibbing again.

"What? Do you lie all the time or just some of the time?"

He shrugged. "Only when necessary. Hey, do you need to rest, or do you want to walk?"

"Oh, let's walk. I know I didn't eat half that huge pizza, but it feels like it." She moaned and pressed a hand to her middle.

Spencer motioned for the bill and pulled out his wallet.

"I'll get us next time," she offered.

"Not when you're with me."

Rebecca looked at him. He wasn't angry, just firm. She let that go.

He took her elbow, and they walked out into the late afternoon leaving the loud music behind.

"I have to check in at the office. Do you mind?"

"I'll wait over here."

Spencer walked a few paces ahead, hands resting easily in his back pockets, looking up at the sky. A couple of young girls stopped to ask directions, it appeared, for he was pointing up the street. Rebecca smiled. He had no idea the girls were flirting with him. He had already given directions and stopped talking, and the girls were making small talk, from the way it looked. She knew what young girls did to catch guys.

The man was clueless.
And she liked that about him.

Chapter 37

"Evan, I can't make it for dinner tonight. Something's come up. I have an important meeting."

"I'm leaving in two days, Cecelia."

His soft voice and announcement stunned her. "Two days? I thought you had at least another week."

"Something's come up."

His simple statement echoing her own words set off a signal. Cecelia didn't know what, but something was wrong.

"What came up, Evan?"

"The crew has finished their work schedule on the villa. I have to go and meet with the architects to plan the next phase of the project."

"Can't you manage the work online?"

"Not on this one. It's too big, and if I make an error, it'll cost more than if I travel to Italy."

"What about White Gate Publishing?"

"Right now my associate, Aiden McClure who has been with me for several years, will take over. I have no other choice."

Cecelia's mind began working. She had totally forgotten a very important meeting. If she asked Becca to make some design decisions, she could possibly get away for dinner tonight.

"Let me make a call. I'll get back with you." She hung up and dialed Becca.

"Listen, I need a favor. A big one. I need you to meet with the fabric team this evening. They're the best in Chicago. Do you think you could choose the fabrics for the library, sitting room, and great room? Ms. Gervase is aware of my color scheme and my likes and dislikes."

"Whoa—are you sure you want to miss that meeting, Cecelia? I mean, this is a big one."

"I know. You're free then?"

Becca heard her fingernails tapping the phone. "If you're sure." She felt her stomach twirl. "What's so important anyway?"

Cecelia felt her hackles rise. "I have another engagement."

"All right. But you realize I've never done this before. I was hoping to learn from you tonight, not the other way around."

"I wouldn't ask if I could be there myself," Cecelia answered in clipped tones. "The meeting starts at seven p.m. Don't be late."

"I'll do my best, Cecelia. I'll run home and change into my best suit. I just hope I can represent your tastes. It makes me really nervous that you won't be there."

"Not to worry. You and I have been discussing color schemes and designs for two weeks. I'm looking for the icy cool blues to match the curtains you made. I don't like monotone, as you know, but a bit of soft greens and browns will suffice for background in the carpets. She knows that I want toile in blue and black."

"Okay, toile in blue and black," Becca repeated, making notes.

"Good. Giovanna's office is at 110 Philadelphia Court. That's down by the courthouse— fifth floor. I'll call and tell her you'll be representing me. She will be a bit huffy at first, but she loves her work. She'll settle down."

"Will she be showing me materials for the other pieces in the room? On the settee, you wanted a silver-blue period fabric, right?"

"Right. She'll show you some silks from India and Persian carpet samples. As I said, we've met once, and she knows my style and taste."

"Got it." Writing verbatim to remind Cecelia later, should she change her mind. Rebecca felt a headache coming on.

"Thanks. I'll call you as soon as I get in tonight," Cecelia stated firmly and clicked off before the very shrewd Becca could make her tell her where she was going.

The woman could spot a smidgen of ambivalence a mile away. This was one area of her life that belonged to her and Evan alone.

* * *

Cecelia called Giovanna Gervase and listened quietly while she ranted and complained that she would not be responsible if the fabrics were not to Cecelia's liking.

"Giovanna, Rebecca Burke has been working closely with me and knows my taste and style. As you do." She let that sink in. "Unfortunately I cannot be there tonight. I've been called away on important business."

She knew that was the truth, but a stretch nonetheless. Edwina would have given her the eye at that last statement. To assuage the woman, she added, "It's just one meeting. The fabrics will be chosen, and I will stop by early next week to look them over. Should there be any problems, we can correct them at that time."

"It is your choice," came the snipped words.

"You are right. I will be in touch, Giovanna."

* * *

Evan Wyndham was on her mind now. They had spent many evenings together these last weeks. The summer flowers in Illinois were in full bloom, and Cecelia felt the sun invade her windows and her heart as she drove home. She knew Evan trusted her, and she liked the feeling. But he was leaving and had no idea when he would be back.

She would like to make the most of tonight, and wandered into her walk-in closet when she arrived home, looking for something feminine and special. She planned to treat Evan to dinner at a nice restaurant. A quiet place where they could talk.

Winnie's would have been her first choice, but Spencer would be eyeing them all evening. Something about that made her sad. They had shared a sweet kiss, but that's all it would be because Evan had found a place in her heart. And he needed her. Spencer didn't. Not to mention the fact that Spencer and Becca had been spending a lot of time together lately.

That alone prompted her to point her heart toward Evan. They had become close during the last several dates. He had dropped his guise, and she knew it couldn't have been easy for him. She was already planning to travel to Italy for the upcoming holidays.

He had no clue as to her true feelings, however, because she had not dropped her guard completely. She had let it down in increments, making sure she knew the man before she allowed him any inroads into her heart. Cecelia knew enough about life to know when men wanted her money and not her. She'd watched her mother skim across her world breaking men's hearts, never committing to any of them for any longer than she needed them.

She refused to live like that. In fact, she had thought about remaining a woman free of marital commitments, except she would *not* leave a trail of wounded men to do it. Her life had been deliberately planned. Business first, friendships next, and family third.

Until Edwina's wedding, she had been happy with her life.

Chapter 38

Her cell jangled as "Beethoven's Fifth" rang off the high ceilings. It tripped her heart into overdrive. She picked up the phone and sighed when she saw Evan's name.

"Were you able to work something out?"

A smile crept across her lips. "Yes."

"Excellent."

She noticed his voice sounded more positive. "Did you have any plans?"

"I didn't want to do anything until I heard from you." He spoke softly.

"I've freed myself from the evening's obligations," she said cheerfully.

"What would you like to do?"

She loved his low voice and the tenderness she heard in it. "Well, if you wouldn't mind, I'd like to take you to a new restaurant where we could sit and talk. I want to hear about your plans, what you're going to do. Perhaps we could do some design brainstorming for your villa."

"Thanks, Cecelia, it's exactly what I need tonight. I'm overwhelmed."

She knew instinctively that was an understatement and one he would not normally make. No business entrepreneur would ever let people know they weren't prepared to handle whatever came up. It was in their nature to figure something out. Even if they didn't know what to do, they'd think of a way.

Excited, she bubbled over. "I'll pick you up. What time will you be ready?"

"It's four o'clock now. Let's get an early start. I'd like to go out for drinks beforehand. How about six?"

"Sounds like a plan. I'll be there." Cecelia closed her phone and tossed it toward her purse on the sofa, then trotted to her bedroom. She was falling in love.

The plan was to wear something nice but simple. She didn't want to wow him, she wanted to woo him. And that required soft and pastel. She chose a warm white blouse with no sequins. Not too flashy. A dark chocolate brown straight-line skirt. Low brown heels. "Just right," she whispered, tipping her head and viewing the outfit laid out on the bed. She headed for the tub. This time she would soak in soft fragrant bubbles and think about what a life with Evan Wyndham would be like. What they could do together. Where they might live. The places they would travel.

He had a house in Italy, most likely a fine villa with plenty of land. She forgot how many acres he mentioned. They could live in Chicago since they both owned businesses and travel to Italy for summers and holidays. By that time Evan could have someone trained to run his office effectively while he still remained the owner. Cecelia shivered deliciously at the thought of how easy it would all be.

And with a man as handsome as Evan, she could actually picture herself married to him.

Perhaps she had found her knight in shining armor too.

The tub was filling with water, and already the rose scent she squirted in was filling the bathroom. She ran for her cell in the event Evan called, placed it nearby, tossed off her clothes, and sank into the tub. She laid her head back on a rolled towel and wondered what Edwina and Alex were doing.

If things worked out, she might be having a wedding of her own. Thoughts of a designer gown, complete with veil, sequins, pearls, and an exotic honeymoon, traipsed through her mind.

Chapter 39

Forty minutes later, Cecelia pulled herself out of the tub, humming. She blow-dried her hair and decided tonight was the night to use a couple of sparkly combs to pull her hair back from her face. She wanted Evan to notice her beautiful skin and turned her face this way and that in the mirror. Her cheeks, pink from the hot water, were perfect. She smelled divine.

Walking over to her makeup mirror, she sat at the marble-topped counter and applied a softer version of her regular routine. If all went as she hoped it would, she would be wearing a rock the size of Texas on her left finger to let every man she met know she was taken. The thought thrilled her. She pressed down nagging thoughts—like they'd only known each other a few weeks, she didn't really know his background, and she hadn't even asked if he had been married, perhaps even fathered children. But each time a negative thought pricked her conscience, she came up with a viable reason why she should not worry about it.

Cecelia dressed carefully and after a viewing at the mirror was satisfied. She checked her watch and dashed around the living room, punching the pillows and rearranging the flower vases in the event Evan wanted to come back here tonight. Just as her hand pressed the button for the elevator, her cell rang. She answered immediately. "I'm on my way."

"Cece?" Spencer said.

She was stunned into silence for a moment. "I'm on my way out." Why was it Spencer always seemed to call at the most inconvenient times?

"So I hear." He laughed. "Working on the Victorian today?"

"No." She knew her one-syllable answer was not exactly kind.

"I'll be quick then. I was calling to see if you'd be available day after tomorrow for lunch at the restaurant. I have a few ideas I'd like to discuss with you."

"Not this weekend, Spencer. I'll be busy. Sorry. Listen, I have to run."

"Okay. I'll wait until you're free." He forced his voice to stay at the same decibel. "Cece, be careful, okay?"

Cecelia heard something in his tone, but she ignored it. Spencer was a friend. Just a friend. She nearly flipped her phone shut, but he was still there. "I will."

"If you ever need to talk, I'm here."

"Thanks, Spencer. I've got to go."

* * *

"Bloody traffic. Fridays are like holidays," she mumbled, slamming on her brakes for a bicyclist that darted in and out between vehicles. A light rain began to pelt her windshield. She reached for the wiper mechanism, and the blades squealed across the glass as though in pain.

It was already late August and the fall season would be upon them soon, which meant she would be alone. Unless—she stopped at the red light—there would be a chance to visit him in Italy. But the Victorian. She had to make sure it was ready for the show. For the first time in her life, she felt pressed to perform and had no desire to do so.

Pressing her foot to the accelerator, she checked in the mirror. She looked fine. Pushing her thoughts deeper down, she hurried on. Evan was waiting.

Chapter 40

Cecelia leaned down to check the street names through the rain-covered windshield. She knew this area of town. Definitely exclusive. Her heart thrilled at the idea of seeing Evan's place for the first time. She pulled up to the valet and gave the young man her name.

"Mr. Wyndham is expecting you," he said courteously. "I'll park for you."

Cecelia reached for her purse and stepped out of the car.

The doorman appeared from beneath the gold and green awning with an umbrella and escorted her to the door. "Whom do you wish to see, madam?"

"Mr. Evan Wyndham." She looked him in the eye in her usual manner.

"I'll ring."

He disappeared into a miniature office and returned with a smile. "Mr. Wyndham is in the lounge, Miss Giatano. Right this way." He stood beside the entry and let her pass.

"Thank you." Cecelia was duly impressed. Evan must have given him her name, which meant he intended for the doorman to become accustomed to her visits.

Her heart performed a slight flip-flop all on its own. It settled again, burrowing in at her next thought that Evan Wyndham was leaving for Italy in two days and she didn't know when she'd see him again.

She suppressed negative thoughts and walked in the direction of the lounge. A small purple neon sign pointed the way. She entered the darkened area, Frank Sinatra singing *My Way* in the background, patrons gathered around small tables talking.

"Ah, the princess arrives." Evan rose from his seat, placed her hand in his elbow, and sought her eyes.

Cecelia noted the sadness in them and instantly decided she would be a good listener this evening. "It's raining tonight."

"Like my heart," he whispered and drew her toward a corner table away from other patrons. "We'll have a drink and be on our way."

She acquiesced and allowed him to take her hand.

"You look beautiful. Different somehow." He spoke over her shoulder, his low voice next to her ear. He paused a moment, then pulled out her chair.

"Thank you." She gave him a smile, placed her small purse on the table, and leaned into her seat comfortably. "Nice atmosphere."

"The best."

Without warning Cecelia's brain flashed back to *Larceny's* in Edinburgh—the blue tube lights turned down low and Spencer talking over the table, his blue eyes looking into hers. She refocused her eyes and looked directly into the handsome brown eyes of the man sitting across from her.

"I'm going to miss you," he said, gazing directly into her eyes.

"And I you." She smiled and picked up her water glass and sipped. She pressed her lips together, forcing herself to stay quiet. When he didn't speak, she said softly, "Tell me about your plans."

"I leave Sunday on the overnight flight. Aiden is handling *White Gate* until I return."

"When will that be?"

"I'm not sure, Cecelia."

"Hmm." She watched him comb his fingers through his thick hair.

The waiter came and Evan ordered her favorite drink and one for himself. "You're quiet tonight," he stated.

"I'm waiting for you to tell me what's going on, Evan."

He stared at her for a moment. She knew instinctively he was measuring his words.

"I'm falling in love with you."

Cecelia nearly let her guard down, but wisely kept her face from showing her feelings. "I see," she said softly.

"Is that all you've got to say?" He leaned closer.

The waiter reappeared with the tray, Evan clearly disturbed at the interruption. When they were alone, he picked up his glass and drank, his eyes never leaving her face.

She picked up hers and sipped, giving her time to school her emotions.

"I feel the same way."

His glass came down hard, sloshing liquid over the side. "Why didn't you say so?"

"I just did." She stayed cool.

"Come on. I'm starving." He finished his drink and came for her.

"You choose the restaurant." Her heart sped up. She sipped quickly, picked up her purse, and stood.

Evan slipped his hand around her waist and drew her close.

If she could have, she would have sighed aloud.

Chapter 41

Within minutes Evan had called for his car. They were slowly pulling away from the curb, the rain-slicked lights of the evening reflecting on every surface. The night was unusually warm. Cracking the window, Cecelia laid her head back on the soft leather seats. Thoughts of Evan's leaving curtained around her heart. In days past, she had rarely allowed anyone entrance to her inner heart. Why this man? Why now?

"Penny for your thoughts." The low, deep voice interrupted her reverie.

She turned to face him and smiled.

"Ah, no repartee from the female? Unusual."

Cecelia merely closed her eyes and let the world go by.

Evan drove through the night, and Cecelia felt as though she'd been swept away and out into the ocean on a sailboat, just the two of them. For a few hours they would be free from phone calls, business decisions, meetings, even the weight of living every day without someone who cared for you. *It doesn't matter what you own*, she mused, *as long as you own it with someone.*

Even her mother had found someone.

When the car stopped, she raised her head and opened her eyes. They were back at Evan's place. "Do you mind?" he asked gently. "I don't feel much like going out."

She shook her head slowly and waited while he handed the keys to the valet. Evan came around and opened the door for her. So this is what it was like. To love someone. Her mind warned her they had only been together for a short time. But the look in his eyes washed away any wariness she may have been feeling.

Within minutes he had ushered her through the elegant lobby and into the elevator.

"The penthouse," he instructed the elevator attendant.

Cecelia forbade her face to register surprise. Suddenly she felt as though she were in a vacuum, swept up in the moment, as if in a dream.

The doorman pressed the button, and Evan slipped him a bill, took her hand, and invited her in when they arrived at his suite. She stepped into overstated elegance. Soft tan walls with cream trim provided a subtle background. Floor to ceiling windows overlooking the Chicago skyline and Lake Michigan filled her eyes. In all her dealings with Chicago's elite, she had never seen this particular view.

"Properly impressed?" He smiled and tossed his keys on a glass table.

Cecelia disengaged her hand from his and walked to the windows, gasping as she noticed the carpet seemed to signify the edge where the room stopped and only the clear glass prevented them from walking off the end into oblivion.

"Afraid of heights?"

"A little." She shivered at his whisper in her ear.

"Don't be afraid. I've got you." His hands rested on her shoulders.

Cecelia kept her eyes glued to the lights that reflected over the rain-washed city. "This is beautiful."

"The best."

He had moved to stand beside her. She felt a chill.

"I'll start a fire."

Cecelia finally turned from the wall of windows and the scene before her eyes to see him push a remote button and the fire leap up in the grate. Then he pushed another button, and the tan wall of drapes slowly began to close.

Her heart beat faster, and she knew.

Chapter 42

Sunday afternoon Cecelia left Evan Wyndham's apartment for the short drive home. She took one look behind her and shut the door to the penthouse. Somehow the click sounded so final that she felt tears burn her eyes.

He had already gone that morning to finish up details at work and have a final meeting with Aiden. She'd left Evan a note, stating her love for him. They had already said their good-byes.

The elevator opened, and she looked down at her shoes. The doorman averted his eyes and pushed the ground-floor button.

She stepped off, glad to be alone, and walked to her car. Evan had called her driver and had her car brought around at the precise hour. The familiar smell of her car and the little pillow Edwina had sewn lying on the front seat comforted her somehow. She drove away slowly.

Tears fell freely once she was alone. She remembered her and her mother, driving away from yet another town, another stage, another play. The loneliness was still there. She felt like the little girl who had no daddy and no home. Hot, burning tears fell as she pulled into her space. She wiped her eyes and gave the valet her keys.

"Welcome back, Miss Giatano," he called out happily. "Nice weather we're having."

She smiled lightly, pretending everything was all right.

When it would never be again.

She keyed her door and was met with the smell of bleach. Spencer.

She had no desire to see him, or anyone else for that matter. Cecelia shut herself up in her bedroom and locked the door. She would pretend to be asleep, knowing Spencer would not wake her. She showered, changed into her blue silk pajamas, climbed in between her sheets just like when she was little, and hugged the pillow. The other side of the bed was empty and so was her heart. She sobbed into the pillows until there were no more tears, then finally fell asleep.

* * *

Spencer walked through and saw her shoes at the door. He called her name quietly before he saw her bedroom door was closed. He raised his hand to knock and make a joke, but he heard her sobbing. What he wanted to do was break in there and find out what was hurting her, but he held his own desire in check. The pastor had said just that morning at church that our job was to let the Lord do his work. Spencer's hands dropped to his side. After a quick prayer for her he finished up, leaving the vacuuming for another day. At least she'd have a pot of soup ready when she woke. He left a note that Edwina had called on the countertop so she would see it when she reached for her coffee cup, then smoothed the tablecloth and made his way to the door, letting himself out.

* * *

Hours passed and Cecelia slept. She turned and opened her eyes, stretched, and remembered the last few hours. Her eyes burned from crying, and she wanted nothing more than to go back to sleep and forget her troubles. Evan was leaving. She squinted at the blue numbers on the digital clock, and it was the exact moment his plane was taking off. She pulled the covers over her head and let the tears burn her eyes again.

Why was it so hard? She'd only known Evan a few weeks and already she was confused. Why didn't God love her like he loved Edwina? And worse, would she turn out like her mother?

Her life had been sideswiped when she met Evan, and she had not liked his ways, then over time he had persuaded her he cared for her. And she had always worn her armor so tightly. Now he was leaving.

She argued with herself, knowing she had the perfect life. Well-liked, honest in her business dealings, and heaven knows she was about to have her own design show. What was her problem anyway?

There'd been many times when she was growing up that they packed up and left. She should be totally used to this. Then why did it seem like Evan had abandoned her? Sleep came but in troubled spurts.

Monday morning Cecelia threw the covers off and did the only thing she knew to do: Get to work. She turned on the radio and showered.

Today was a new day, and she had to get going. Becca had already stood in for her Friday evening. She knew her duty. And she would do it.

She chose her favorite comfortable pantsuit—the nut brown with embroidery—and called her hairdresser for a quick appointment. Leaning closer to the mirror, she looked into her own eyes and saw the sadness there. She wiped her face with a cloth and headed out the door. She would have her makeup done today too. Her cell rang, and she nearly tripped running to get it out of her purse. It was Spencer. Not Evan. Her resolve nearly crumbled. She ignored the call. Nothing was going to stop her from being who she was. Not even Evan Roberto Wyndham, who was by now,she assumed, in Italy. He hadn't even bothered to call to let her know he'd arrived.

Chapter 43

The doorman greeted her quietly, and she smiled at him just like every other day.

"Your car is waiting," he informed.

"Thank you, James."

He ushered her out on the first floor with a slight bow. "Have a good day, Miss Giatano."

She waved and was on her way. Back to her life, just as it should be. Two hours later she was coiffed and safely behind her makeup.

"Becca, Cecelia here. How did the meeting go Friday?"

"Cecelia, I'm so glad it's you. I tried calling twice. Can we meet for lunch? I've got several issues you'll want to know about."

Cecelia's heart nearly plummeted. At any other time, she would be glad to get her teeth into a problem. Today she felt like turning her back on anything that would interrupt her sadness and regret.

"Of course." She felt her voice wobble.

"Are you okay?" Becca asked softly.

"I'm fine."

"I'll meet you at *Winnie's* then, around noon?"

"Not there. How about the *Moonstruck Chocolate Café* down by my hairdresser on Michigan Street?"

"Okay." Becca knew she sounded surprised and tried to recover. "Noon, it is. I like trying new places."

"Good." Cecelia snapped her phone shut. *I have got to get myself together.*

* * *

Cecelia drove around the block several times and finally squeezed her car into a tight parking space that had just opened up. She was glad for the extra long walk, which gave her time to refresh her thoughts and drag her wayward anxieties back into the business of choosing fabrics for the Victorian. Plus, time was counting down until the production company would be requiring her presence for prepping and taping. She *had* to get that Victorian ready.

The Windy City wrecked her new do, which set her nerves on edge. She stopped at Starbucks, grabbed her favorite brew, and sipped it, burning the roof of her mouth. The door snapped shut behind her when she left as the wind whooshed its powerful force against her back. Lifting her hand to straighten her mussed hair, she grumped, "All this for what?"

When her neck scarf whipped free and flew into a man's face, she wanted to swear. He swatted at it. It caught on his hand and went flying upward and away like a balloon.

"Well if that doesn't take the pie," she muttered and hurried toward Moonstruck's to meet Becca. "What else could go wrong today?"

Becca was already seated and stood to wave.

Cecelia sat down hard on the chair and exhaled sharply. "I've just had the worst morning," she sputtered.

Becca, cool as a cucumber, sat there smiling.

"What?" Cecelia gave her the eye.

"It's just that your hair is sticking up. Almost like Spencer's."

"Where?" She smoothed it as best she could. "I must look a fright. And I have a horrible headache."

"Well, I have some good news. I found the perfect carpet, thanks to Spencer's sister."

Why was it everywhere she went Spencer's name kept coming up? She averted her eyes and watched a young family at a nearby table— anything to keep her mouth from saying what she was thinking.

"It's perfect for the library."

"Great. I'll stop by the Victorian and have a look."

Becca sat back and crossed her arms over her chest. "You look different, Cecelia."

"How?" She avoided Becca's eyes and cast about in her bag trying to find a pen.

"Oh I don't know. Just different."

"Okay, let's get started. How did the meeting with Giovanna go?"

"Not good at first. She was annoyed that you weren't there, but I was able to get her to settle down and finally convinced her that both of us were familiar with your tastes and knew what you were looking for. Cecelia, I have to tell you, we chose the softest color palette and it's perfect. The fabric for the love seat is a light ice-blue sateen. It will look gorgeous with the antique white finished wood. And for the walls, Ms. Gervase suggested we use matching material on that short wall behind the chair, which will be covered in the same fabric as the settee with the addition of gossamer silver gray streaks. The curtains we already have were a perfect match when we held the material up."

"Giovanna came to the Victorian?" Cecelia's eyes grew large. "She has totally refused to travel anywhere unless she absolutely has to. All this time she required me to take pictures and then was miffed if she had to look at them."

Becca shrugged. "She didn't seem to mind when I suggested she use her excellent taste and eye to see for herself." Then she winked.

"You persuaded her with flattery."

"If you say so."

Cecelia laughed out loud.

"I like your laugh. You should do that more often," Becca said smoothly.

"Weasel."

"Jaybird."

The two bent toward each other over the table, putting their hands over their mouth to stop the flow of giggles.

"I . . . I haven't laughed this much since . . . I can't even remember when!" Cecelia sputtered, feeling totally out of control.

"Stop. Stop. I have to go back to work, and my mascara is running down my face," Becca nearly shouted as she dabbed her eyes with a napkin.

When patrons began to smile and whisper, Cecelia pulled herself together and tapped her pen on the table, trying to bring some order.

"Stop that," Becca giggled again. "You look like Judge Judy." And they were off again.

"Okay. Okay." Cecelia took a deep breath. "Now I know you have some bad news, but since the wind blew my newly coiffed hair out of style, I burned the roof of my mouth with hot coffee, and then my favorite designer scarf flew away like a balloon, it's been one bad day up until now."

"Your scarf flew away?" Becca tried not to laugh. She could only guess at how much money Cecelia had spent on that scarf.

"My headache is slowing up though," she realized.

"That's because you're laughing, Cecelia!"

Suddenly Cecelia felt herself crossing from laughter to tears. She grabbed a napkin off the table and dabbed at her eyes, forcing her mouth to smile.

Becca saw the problem and changed the topic. "Listen, I've got to run. Do you have time to catch up later?" She looked at her watch, grabbing her bag at the same time.

"Yes," Cecelia blurted. "Good idea." She kept her eyes averted.

"Okay, then, I'm on my way. Call when you have a few moments."

Chapter 44

Cecelia pulled in a deep breath, stuffed her notes into her bag, and shot out the door. Her phone jingled. Glad for an aversion, she answered.

"Hey, I've been trying to get ahold of you." Spencer's voice floated into her ear.

She rolled her eyes. "Not now, Spencer," she said quietly.

"Where are you?"

"What does it matter?"

A few seconds of silence. "Is everything all right?" He forced himself to be patient.

"Yes."

"Look, Cecelia. I know you're running from something. Why don't you let me help?"

The gentleness in his voice undid Cecelia. She wanted to sob. On his shoulder. She knew he could help, but something inside her wouldn't let him. "Thanks, Spencer. But not this time."

"Okay. I understand you need your space. But if you need anything, call okay?"

She answered in the affirmative and hung up before she was sobbing in the streets then tossed her phone deep in her bag, and stepped up her pace, the wind blowing her hair backward.

Unable to sit through even a short meeting with Becca, she mentally gave herself a good, stiff lecture, the same way she did when she was a child and her mother told her they were moving again. *What does it matter if we move? New people, new places. That's good, right?* But in the end, it always felt like running away.

By the time she was at the door of her condo, she had succeeded in burying her deepest needs and instead threw her anxiety into another round of planning. At the end of the evening, she had sketched the three rooms of the Victorian with the colors and design aspects that the show would require. Satisfied, she set the drawings aside and made a cup of tea.

Tomorrow she would force herself to face Spencer. To show him she was fine.

* * *

She rang up Spencer. "I'm meeting Becca for lunch today. Can you save us a table?" It was early in the morning, and she'd showered and dressed for the day.

"Of course."

"About one o'clock then?"

With that settled she set out her fabric samples. Throwing herself back into work was the only comfort she knew. Still, like the smell of bad garbage in a clean house, the thought lingered that Evan had not called.

The rain pelted her twelfth-story windows. She hadn't seen the Victorian for several days and needed to drive over and check out the landscaping. It was supposed to be finished by now. With these things in mind, she slowly began to recall her original plans before Evan Roberto Wyndham had showed up in her life. Which was to make a name for herself. If he didn't call by the end of the week, she was going to call him. Firm resolve created a sense of strength in her. She had made it this far by herself. And she would make it the rest of the way whether Evan called or not. For some strange reason, she withheld her heart and her phone call. Today would be the beginning of her new life.

By noon she'd spoken to Giovanna, met with two prospective tenants, both promising, and had to rush down to Winnie's to meet Becca. She felt her old self begin to return.

"Sorry I'm late." She dashed in and tossed her fabric samples on a chair. "Two meetings with possible tenants."

"Great." Becca smiled, glad to see Cecelia back. "That'll be good for the bottom line. You're going to need a manager pretty soon. You'll have your hands full with the new show. Speaking of which . . . ," she hinted.

"What?" Cecelia's eyes lit up, glad to be about business again.

"Well . . . it seems that *Better Homes and Gardens* magazine wants to do an interview."

"Really?"

"Yes. While you were gone this weekend, this really strange-looking guy came into the Victorian while we were working and asked us a few questions, then left."

Cecelia's eyes widened. "Well, what did he say?"

"Oh, the normal stuff. Spencer talked to him for more than thirty minutes, walking him around, discussing the changes, your new show."

"Spencer? What was he doing there? And on the weekend?"

Becca shrugged. "He knew I had my hands full, so he offered to stop in and help. His new staff is working so well, he feels free enough to step out on weekends. Cool, huh?"

Cecelia pressed the matter of Spencer's help into a mental file and continued. "So this guy got in contact with you?"

"Yes! That was part of my good news." Becca knew she was overly excited. "And—get this—he wants to do a series of shots as we move through the process of designing the house. So that means he'll do an update in each issue until we finish!"

"What? Unheard of." Cecelia *knew* she was back. "An entire series, until we finish?"

"Exactly. Okay, here's more news. He'll be contacting you. He tried this weekend, but didn't get through. No problem though. He seemed so laid-back I wondered if he was who he said he was. But Spencer gave the man his cell number to be sure you didn't miss the opp."

"So that's what Spencer wanted to talk to me about?"

"Yep, that was it. I just couldn't keep my mouth shut. And Spencer said I could tell you today at lunch."

"I see." Cecelia bit her bottom lip.

"Look, we don't have time to sit around here. Talk to me about the colors. I've seen the swatches. Have you talked to Ms. Gervase yet?"

"Yes, this morning. We're meeting at the Vic this afternoon to verify choices so she can place her orders. I trust your choices, Becca, yours and Giovanna's, so we're going to decide on the other two rooms today and get those fabrics ordered."

"Good. Because, girl, we are in this thing lock, stock, and barrel." Becca didn't care who heard her.

Cecelia stared at her for a moment. "You know, I never did understand that saying. What does it mean?"

"Oh, sort of like hook, line, and sinker. You either fish or get out of the boat."

"Okay." Cecelia tried to make heads and tails of that.

"Your proper English upbringing is getting in the way," Becca teased, then said seriously, "Cecelia, do you know what you've got here? The chance of a lifetime to make it big. If that is your goal in life, honey it is sitting in your lap."

"What do you mean, if it's my goal in life?"

"Well, isn't this what you've been dreaming of for like, forever?"

"Yes." Cecelia thought about it for a moment. It *was* what she wanted in life, right? To be successful—self-sufficient. To be on top. At this moment, there was nothing else. "Yes, it is!" she said quickly. And the die was cast.

For the next hour, Rebecca and Cecelia tossed ideas at each other quicker than a pitcher throws strikes to the last batter before the win. Cecelia loved the interaction and forgot all about her troubles until Spencer walked in, hair askew.

"Where have you been?" Rebecca laughed.

Cecelia turned and found his blue eyes looking deep into hers, as though he was trying to read her. The resolve in her melted for a nano-second, then she recovered, smiling at him. "I hear you've talked to the man from *Better Homes and Gardens* magazine."

Cecelia watched as he ran his fingers through his blond hair, which didn't do much to tame it, and pulled out a chair next to her. Rebecca had a silly smile pasted on her face, which was catching.

In the space of the next half hour, the three were talking at once, then listening as the thrill of success pushed them. This was a chance of a lifetime, all agreed. And Cecelia was right in the middle of it all. She smiled, sat back and listened as Spencer and Becca threw one idea at her, then another until her head swam with the joy of it all.

Cecelia Grace Giatano was back.

Chapter 45

Rebecca's phone tones jangled into their conversation. She grabbed it and snapped it open, still talking, then gasped. "I blew a meeting with a client," she sputtered, stuffing items into her purse. "I have to run. My boss is livid," she said as she hurried away. "I'll catch up with you tonight, Spencer."

"Right. Seven, as usual." He waved her off with a smile and turned it to Cecelia.

"What?" She laughed lightly, tapping her fingers on the table.

"You nervous?" he teased.

"No. Are you?"

"Not a bit. What will be, will be. And it sounds like you've got it going bigtime, Cece."

She thought about that for a minute. "Well, if you say so."

"What? You aren't the least bit happy about all this?" He waved his arm in a circular motion. "Co-owner of Winnie's, two buildings nearly filled with tenants and a new show, now a regular spread in *Better Homes and Gardens*. What more could a girl ask for?"

"Meaning what?" She turned serious.

"Isn't this what you've been wanting?" He crossed his arms over his chest and sat back.

She wanted to cuff him. What did he mean? That she was supposed to be guilty of something, when she'd earned every success she had?

"You're not talking," he teased again. "Does that mean you're actually speechless?"

"Maybe I am," she clipped back. "It seems you're full of questions today. Maybe you should be answering them for me, since you seem to know me so well."

"Whew—I touched a nerve." He smiled and leaned his elbows on the table, closing the space between them, then whispered, "You've got it all, Cece. Does it make you happy?"

"Of course it does," she shot back. "And why shouldn't it? I've made it this far on my own. Why shouldn't I be proud of my work?"

"You're right. You have made it this far. And believe me, you've done a lot. But you didn't do it alone. We never do. You've got the best friends and associates. Becca really stood in for you this weekend."

"Now you're meddling in my life, Spencer."

"Absolutely right." He changed the topic. "So, I'm free as a bird today. It's nearly four o'clock, want to run over to the Victorian and look around? We've got a surprise for you."

"Another surprise?" Her brown eyebrows raised as her blue eyes widened.

"Come on, let's go. I'll go change out of this suit. I'm driving, so meet me downstairs in the lobby." He stood and was gone before she could tell him she'd go on her own.

She shrugged a shoulder, remembering her mother hated that, and smiled. Even after living in America for nearly eight years, she still remembered her English upbringing. And she rather liked the fact that Spencer had told her what to do.

With a quick trip upstairs, she stepped out of her business outfit and into a pair of designer jeans and chose a simple white shirt. Then she did the strangest thing. Knowing full well the man from *Better Homes and Gardens* just might show up, she put her hair in a ponytail.

She didn't even look in the mirror, just dashed for the door and greeted James with a full smile and rode the elevator, her heart beating like a teenager at her first high school dance.

Too late, she realized that should she be stopped by a tenant, she would have to apologize for her lack of professional appearance. The thought became a reality in the very next moment when she turned and found one of the prospective tenants walking up to her.

"Miss Giatano. My wife and I have decided. We love it here. The views. The restaurant on the second floor, everything. We'd like to arrange a meeting. We were about to call you when my wife spotted you."

Cecelia smiled and looked up. Spencer was standing a ways off, arms across his chest, smiling like a schoolboy. She turned her back and stuttered as she began to talk. "I'm so pleased. Would you be available tomorrow? I have commitments the rest of the afternoon, but I would be most happy to accommodate you, say, around noon? We could meet at *Winnie's* or you can come to the conference room."

"Let's meet at the restaurant. We've already had the pleasure of dining there, and the service is excellent. We love Chicago and want to get to know people here since we'll be coming over six months out of the year."

"Wonderful." Cecelia shook the man's offered hand, then the wife's. They were from Ipswich, England, and looking for a condo to rent. Two of their four children lived in the States, and they wanted to be nearby.

"Tomorrow then at *Winnie's*. Noon. I'll bring the contract. My attorney will be present for any questions you may have." Cecelia made a mental note to call Stuart the moment she could, hoping he would be available on such short notice.

Spencer walked up after they left. "Looks like you've got some happy people."

"A contract." She smiled, pulling out her phone. "I need to call Stuart right away." She stepped away and put a hand over one ear. A moment later, she went back to Spencer.

"Done deal?" he asked.

"Yes, and by a New York minute. He is about to leave the country on holiday."

"Great news. Come on, let's get going before anything else interrupts."

She followed his quick step, feeling euphoric. The day was bright and warmer than earlier in the week with the cold rain. They didn't speak, just enjoyed the streets full of people.

Spencer asked her to wait and he would pull around. He sprinted to his car, drove under the awning, parked, and got out to open her door.

"Really, you don't have to be so chivalrous."

He shrugged. "You're a woman, and I'm a man.

"Now tell me about this surprise." She watched him pull out into the noisy traffic and noted he wore jeans with holes in the knees, a worn black T-shirt, and brown work boots.

"I hope you don't intend to put me at the top of a ladder today." She laughed lightly.

"Nope. I'll do the laddering stuff. I know you hate heights."

She settled into her seat, remembering Evan's floor to ceiling windows and her fear of looking down. She would not let Evan interrupt her joy today.

Ten minutes later, Spencer was talking and pointing out the wind-shield. "Lean forward. Look at the pavers curving to the front door."

She gasped. "They're beautiful."

"Wait until you see the rest." He parked and came around for her, pulling her out with his hand in hers. Spencer let go of her, then with his hands on her shoulders placed her directly in front of the house. "Do you like it?"

"The wall. They built a curved wall. I didn't—"

"Right. We know you didn't order this, but Becca and I talked to the landscaper and he said it would enhance the front and make it stand out from the other homes in the neighborhood. It's not too high, just subtle enough to make a statement."

"You're right. I love it." She ran her hands along the light gray wall. "And the red geraniums hanging on the porch set it off perfectly."

"Great, you like it then? We were not sure about going ahead without you here, but we had to let the landscaper know so he could get the stones delivered. Both of us tried to reach you, but we knew you wanted to be left alone."

Cecelia turned at that statement to read Spencer's eyes. Did he know she was with Evan?

Chapter 46

"Come inside. There's more." He grabbed her hand.

"I forgot my key," she moaned.

"Not to worry. Becca had one made for me. Hope you don't mind." She didn't have time to answer.

"Let me go first. I want you to see something else." Spencer stepped inside and pulled her to a stop. "Look up Cecelia."

The French crystal lamp hung like a jewel in the foyer.

"Oh Spencer, it's beautiful. And sparkling clean. How did you . . ." Spencer noted the joy in her blue eyes as she turned to him.

"Well, it wasn't easy. We had a small crew over here to clean each and every one of those crystals. There were nearly three hundred of them. Symond and a couple of her friends agreed to come and help. It took the better part of a day. And when the construction guys came, we weaseled all four of them into hanging it for us. It cost me five large pizzas!"

Cecelia turned and threw herself into Spencer's arms. "Thank you. It was so good of all of you. And I was so . . . unavailable." She felt guilt crawl into her thoughts.

"Don't worry. We wanted to help." He hugged her close, then released her quick before he ruined everything and kissed her. "One more thing, and then we'd better get to work. Becca will be here after her appointment, if she still has a job," he joked. "She's been on her boss's bad side since she started working for you. She's trying to please both you and her. And I don't think it's working."

Cecelia stepped back and said, "You don't think she could lose her job, do you? I mean, this is all she's known for her entire life. What if she—"

"I wouldn't worry, Cece. If she does lose her job, she would be happy."

"What? I thought it meant everything to her."

"Well, it did before all this came along. She really likes working with you, and the more I get to know her the more I see she is cut out for design, not for real estate. She's happier."

Cecelia discerned that Spencer and Becca knew each other better than she realized. Another guard went up around her heart. They might be an item by now.

"I'm glad. We'd better get going."

"Right you are. Okay, Miss Giatano, step this way." He took her elbow.

"Now close your eyes and don't peek. I'll direct you."

"This is so silly, Spencer. Why don't you just show me?"

"Because this is much more fun," he teased and pressed her hand into his elbow.

She felt his strength as he pulled her close and directed her steps.

"Okay, we're in the doorway. Remember, there's a slight incline here. Stay put while I turn on the lights."

He came back, and she held on tighter, feeling ridiculous. She felt his hands on her shoulders. "Okay open."

She did, and immediately her hand flew to her mouth as she tried to take it all in. The entire room was finished, right down to the carpet.

"Now, we know that you wanted this room to be part of the show, but while speaking with Ms. Gervase—she was here, you know—she mentioned that the kitchen would be a much more interesting show than the library. So we finished this room. Becca talked with the production crew to make sure it would be all right. And they agreed. What do you think?"

"You did all this in one weekend?"

"Remember the curtains were already hung, and we still have to recover the love seat and hang the matching fabric on the one wall, but it is a good start. We draped it so you could at least get an eye for how it would look. "It was Becca's idea to do this for you. She knew your original plans and carried them out."

She walked away from Spencer, feeling he was too close in proximity to her body and her heart. Tears popped out as she ran her hands over the fireplace with a new marble mantle and then the silver blue fabric. "It's perfect. The blue paint reflects in the lighting fixtures."

Spencer stayed where he was and watched her reaction. He doubted anyone had ever given the self-made Cecelia a surprise. She was always the one in charge. He smiled thinking how good it was for her to *receive* a gift. He watched as she bent down to run her hand over the plush carpet.

"We know you would have chosen a larger carpet piece, but Becca thought it would be nice to have the wood floors showing around the edges."

"I really don't know what to say." She turned.

"What's there to say? We wanted to do something for you. The good Ms. Gervase was able to bring an entire bolt of fabric over that you had chosen. She and her crew even stayed and helped us paint the walls."

"What? Are you kidding me? She was painting? That woman refused to lower herself to come to a location, preferring we bring pictures to her office. I can't imagine her picking up a paint roller."

Spencer shrugged. "What can I say?"

"You are persuasive," she concluded aloud, but knew it was his kindness that drew people.

"Okay, I am totally and completely indebted to you all." She bowed at the waist.

He smiled. Those words told him what he needed to know.

"What's the project for today?" she asked.

"We're tearing out the kitchen tiles—if you agree, that is. We wanted to be sure it's what you wanted before we start. They're in really bad shape, and I pulled one up. No wood floors underneath. So I'm thinking we need to start with new underlayment."

They walked to the kitchen. "It's so small—kitchens of that period were, you know." She was talking to herself. "And we have the butler's pantry to think about, whether we want to incorporate that into the kitchen area or leave it as a separate space." She gazed at the floor space. "Since we'll be doing the kitchen in the show—and I do think it's a good idea—I think we'd better wait. Tearing up the original floor should be part of the filming."

"You're right, Cece. We were so excited to get things moving that we didn't even think that far ahead."

"Is there anything else we could work on today?" She was excited to be doing something.

"We could sweep. The contractors left a mess. There's sawdust, marble dust, and all kinds of nails and shavings on the floors. When the camera crew comes in, it'll need to be clean anyway."

"Okay," Cecelia agreed. "So where are the brooms?"

"Back room behind the kitchen. That porch was added sometime in the late 1800s, one of the contractors said."

"Really? That's news to me."

"Yep, he looked at the foundation. There's a small closet out there that was used for cleaning materials. Want to take a look?"

Cecelia followed and took the large broom he offered. "We can start at the front and work our way back."

"Right." They chose the foyer and began raising the dust.

"Hey, we need masks or we won't last long. This place has spider-webs from the 1800s," he quipped and came back with two white masks.

He stood in front of her, pulled out the band, put it over her head, and adjusted it to fit. "I like your hair in a ponytail."

"Thank you," she mumbled. His closeness unnerved her. She backed away and began sweeping furiously.

He adjusted his mask and went to the other side of the room.

The woman was making him crazy.

Chapter 47

Spencer removed his mask and coughed up dust from his throat. "Almost finished here," he called to Cecelia, who turned and put her hand behind her ear. He set his broom against the wall and walked closer.

"Finished?" he asked

"Yes, just about. Would you mind moving that picture? It's heavier than it looks." Cecelia pointed, pulling her mask off for a moment.

Spencer hefted the heavy framed oil painting and set it against another wall.

The sound of voices broke into the quiet house. "Hey Spence, we're here. We saw your car out there."

Becca and two gals came around the corner laughing and talking. Cecelia met the first gal, dressed in jeans and T-shirt, her bright red hair pulled back from her face with a large black band. No makeup. The other girl was blonde and very pretty, and she too had no makeup and was dressed to work.

"Hey, Cecelia! We didn't know you were here." Becca came dashing up. "What did you think of the chandelier? And the library?" She talked excitedly.

The two other girls went straight to Spencer for instructions.

Rebecca and Cecelia went to the library and stood in the doorway.

"Don't you just love this room?"

"I do. It's perfect, Becca. You really did a good job."

"Well thanks, but it was more than just me. Did you know Ms. Gervase stayed and painted?"

"I heard. Spencer said she was rolling the walls. I could hardly believe it."

"What did you think of the carpet?" She looked for Cecelia's response. "I hoped you didn't mind we went ahead and made the purchase."

"Not at all."

"Ms. Gervase helped us get twenty percent off the original price, saving a whopping three hundred dollars right off the top."

"Really?" Cecelia countered, wondering how she would pay them all back for their kindnesses to her. And after all the guilt she felt inside, their kindness seemed almost painful.

"I'll introduce you to the girls." They headed back to the gathering, and Becca quickly began the introductions. "This is Symond, Spencer's sister—twin sister. And her friend Edris."

Cecelia took her offered hand. "Edris, so nice to meet you. I didn't know Spencer had a twin."

"Yep, that would be me. He was born first, so that makes me the youngest."

"Well, better to be young than smart," Spencer joked.

Symond cuffed him on the shoulder. "Always comparing yourself." She teased.

"Okay, so what are we doing tonight?" Becca stopped the fussing. "It's already late, so we'd better get started."

"We're sweeping the place. It's dusty from all the workers in here." Cecelia grabbed her broom. "How about pulling some of that nasty wallpaper off the foyer walls? Just at eye level and below. No ladders," she ordered.

"Okay, with five of us we should be able to get at least some of it off." Becca turned.

"Spray the walls with warm water and clothes softener in a spray bottle and let it set," Spencer suggested. "I heard that on the design show the other day."

"Right. I'd forgotten that was a good trick. There's probably three or four layers underneath so we may be here awhile," Symond added.

"I'll get the spray bottles. If you want to come with me, I'll show you where all the cleaning supplies are kept." Spencer led the way.

Spencer and Cecelia finished cleaning up while the girls worked on the wallpaper.

Two hours passed so quickly that Cecelia barely realized the time. She found her purse and checked for calls. Two from the contractor, two others—unimportant, but no call from Evan. She dashed back to work.

"Cece, Spencer, Edris and I are out of here. We made good headway. I sprayed the walls heavily with the solution. We may be able to come back tomorrow evening. We all have tight schedules," Symond said.

"Thank you for coming, girls." Cecelia came to see their work. "You've done a really good job. I can pay you Friday."

"We didn't come for pay," Symond spoke up. "We just came to help."

"But I thought you needed some extra cash."

"Oh, we do, but not this time," she said firmly and looked to her brother.

Spencer shrugged, a wicked look on his face.

Cecelia could tell he was waiting to see if she would accept their offer.

"Thank you so much," Cecelia said. "I'll remember this." She felt her voice waver.

"We're outta here." Symond saluted and Edris laughed as they left calling over their shoulder, "We'll come and finish the job as soon as we can." And they were gone.

Cecelia put her cloth down. They had raised so much dust sweeping that she had gone along the flat surfaces with a damp cloth and dusted. She found Becca in the small room still working.

"Becca, you'd better get home for some sleep. Spencer says your employer isn't too happy with you. I don't want you to jeopardize your job."

"I'm not too worried. I love this work so much. It's my mother who's going to have a fit. She trained me and expects me to walk in her shoes."

"And now?" Cecelia asked.

"Well, now I know I'm not cut out for sales. Selling real estate was a job. I never really had the opportunity to try something else. This design and decorating thing is for me."

"You're sure? I mean, you don't want to step away from something sure. We're just starting out here."

"Not to worry." Becca waved off her comment. "No matter what it takes, I'm in."

"You know what you want!" Cecelia laughed.

"Yes, I do. Always have. The only difference is now I have the confidence to go after it."

Spencer joined them, pulling his mask off.

"Well ladies, it's time to go. We've done enough for tonight."

"Right you are. I'm heading out." Becca kicked the wallpaper scraps into a corner, waved, and slammed the door behind her.

Cecelia just stood there. She was tired. A good tired.

"I'll get the lights and lock up." Spencer started for the back of the house.

With the dust rag in hand, she finished the last fireplace mantle. It had been a good day.

Spencer came from the back. "Ready?"

"Yes." She couldn't help looking into his eyes. Would he be disappointed in her? For some reason it seemed to matter.

Cecelia's heart beat faster. She saw the look in his eyes. He wanted to kiss her.

She set her lips together and moved out of his presence. "I'll get my purse."

Spencer stuffed his hands in his back pockets and looked away.

Chapter 48

The ride home was silent. The evening lights of Chicago stung her eyes. From the dust no doubt.

"You shouldn't rub your eyes like that. It'll make it worse." Spencer's voice was gentle.

Cecelia wondered why he didn't drop her off in front then park his car. Instead they pulled into his space, and he came around for her.

They walked through the parking garage and headed for the elevator. "I'll see you up."

"That's all right. You're tired. Spencer. Thanks for helping."

"Not a problem." He punched the button to call the elevator and walked away.

Cecelia watched him go. He ran his fingers through his hair—one of his quirks. She smiled and felt sad.

Her phone rang before the elevator door opened. It was Evan.

For a moment, she thought not to answer. Instead she snapped it open and answered breathlessly. "Cecelia here."

"Cecelia. I just wanted to let you know I made it across. How are you doing?"

"I'm fine. And you?" She hated that they were talking like this.

"Busy. Listen, I probably won't be in touch for a while. Too much going on here."

Her heart plummeted. *Too busy?* She forced herself to think a moment before responding.

"I see."

"I'm sorry. Really. It's just that—"

"Don't worry," she interrupted. "I don't expect anything."

"Thanks."

She snapped the phone shut and tears fell down her dusty cheeks.

* * *

For the next three days, Cecelia managed to fill her calendar with meetings. She avoided Spencer and did not visit the Victorian, making enough appointments to keep her busy for a month.

It was the only way to keep Evan's deadpan voice from entering her thoughts over and over. She had been such a fool.

The new tenant's contract was signed, and they were heading back to England to bring a few favorite furniture items back. The couple had contracted Spencer to paint the entire space a soft creamy pale vanilla. She knew from Becca that she and her friends had gone to help him. The new tenants would be back in two weeks.

Somehow she had managed to stay out of that situation. She was in the car on her way to another appointment with her attorney. Television shows were not easy contracts to negotiate.

Her phone rang. Mrs. King? What in the world could that woman want? She wanted to let it go, but couldn't. She'd love nothing more than to give her a piece of her mind.

"Cecelia here," she answered, ready to fight.

"Miss Giatano, this is Mrs. Quentin King."

"Yes."

"I wanted to thank you for your recent purchase."

Oh she wanted to scream. So she knew about the rug. Unknown to Cecelia, Edris worked at Mrs. Quentin's designer carpet store. Becca and Edris had worked out the deal without telling her who owned the store.

At least *she* hadn't made the purchase. "My associate made the purchase," she said stiffly.

"I see. Edris is my great niece. She has told me all about your Victorian and the new show."

Cecelia wanted to snub her with a few unkind words, but nothing came except Becca's words, something about soft answers. She couldn't remember, so she said nothing.

"Well, I would like to come and see your house, if you wouldn't mind."

The woman actually sounded timid. Timid?

"Well, I'm quite busy at the moment. Would you mind calling again? I am not at my calendar and have meetings this entire week."

"Of course," Mrs. King said.

"Thank you." Cecelia thought she sounded kind enough and snapped her phone shut.

"I can't believe that woman is calling me. She probably wants to see what I'm doing so she can start her own show. Or better yet, buy something right next door and do it better. What nerve!" Cecelia talked out loud, nearly running a red light. "What next?"

Her phone rang again, and she tried to ignore it. She looked, expecting Mrs. King again. It was not a number she recognized. Something told her to answer it.

"Cecelia here," she said.

"Cecelia?" Edwina asked.

"Ed. I'm so glad to hear your voice."

"You'll never believe this, Cece, but I'm at your place."

"What? Here in the States?"

"Yes. Alex had to come to sign final papers with his lawyer. Paige and I came along."

"I wish you would have called."

"I know. It was so quick—we barely had time to arrange for a flight for the three of us."

"I'm sorry, Ed. I have to do this next meeting with my attorney, but I'll cancel everything else for the next couple of days. You do have two or three days, right?"

"Yes, three to be exact. Alex has to get back. We want to stay longer, but couldn't manage it."

"Great. You say you're at my place?"

"Yes. Spencer let us in. I hope you don't mind."

"Of course not, silly. I'll be there in a couple of hours. And . . . Ed, I'm glad you're here."

"Me too, Cece. Drive careful, okay? I can hear you're in the car."

"Okay. Help yourself to the fridge if there's anything in there. Otherwise you can order pizza and put it on my tab. See you soon."

Cecelia was thrilled, yet reticent. Everything had changed so much these last couple of months that she hardly knew what to think. Edwina was here. She hurried to park and intended to tell Stuart Littleton he had best hurry.

Less than two hours later, she was on her way home. Excited, she pulled into her marked space and rushed up. The door was unlocked. She stepped in and smelled food cooking.

Slipping off her heels, she tiptoed over the carpet and appeared in the kitchen doorway. "Cece, you're home!" Edwina ran and threw her arms around her.

For the first time she and Edwina had actually fully embraced. She hugged her sister, feeling the pinch of tears at her eyes, then pulled away. "You look so good."

"Thank you." Edwina couldn't help but grin. "You look different somehow." She gazed into her sister's eyes.

Cecelia looked away quickly and changed the topic. "Where is Paige?"

"She's napping. Spencer promised to take her down to the restaurant later tonight."

"I see. I'm going to change clothes. What have you got planned for tonight?"

"I just cooked supper for us. I asked Spencer to come. I hope that was all right."

"Smells delightful. Be right back."

Why does everyone think they have to invite Spencer? Cecelia grumped as she changed into tan slacks and a black long-sleeved sweater, then went back to the kitchen. "What are you making?" She lifted the lid on the pot.

"I cooked a roast with carrots and potatoes. Spencer said he'd bring a pie from the restaurant."

"Great. Should we set the table?"

"It might be another hour, maybe a bit longer before Alex is free. He's going to call. Could we just sit and talk?"

"Sure. It'll probably be the only time we have to catch up." Cecelia talked with an upbeat voice. "You should wear blue more often, Ed. It suits you."

"Oh really?" Edwina looked down at her blue sweater over black capris. "Thank you."

"So how is married life?"

Edwina sat down on the sofa, her sister at the other end, and looked at her hands. "I'm very happy, Cece. More than I ever thought to be."

"I'm happy for you, Ed. Do your dad and my mom know you're here?"

"Yes. Dad's in the middle of school, and your mom is in Los Angeles."

"She is? I didn't even know. We don't keep in touch like we used to. But then we're both so busy."

"I know. So tell me, how is the television program going? I'm so excited to see you on the show. You'll have tapes so we can watch every episode, right?"

"Of course. That's the easy part. Things are slow. There was a slight delay in the contract negotiations. Our attorneys are working on that now. But I was able to acquire the Victorian, and we've been preparing it for the show."

"How exciting, Cece. Spencer said the restaurant is doing well and that you have new tenants coming in, that both buildings are nearly full."

"Yes, all's well here." She tapped her fingers on the table.

Chapter 49

"What's this I hear that you've got a boyfriend?" Edwina scooted closer to her sister.

"How did you know about that?" Cecelia spoke before she meant to.

"Well, Spencer said Becca told him you were seeing someone."

"I was. Am. Oh, I don't know, Ed. It's such a mess."

"Hey, hold on. Are you falling for someone?" Edwina gentled her voice and waited.

"Not exactly. Already fell." She felt tears coming.

"Did he hurt you?" Edwina knew she sounded defensive.

"No, not like that. It's just that, well, I really care for him a lot, but I'm beginning to think he doesn't feel the same way."

"Maybe you haven't given it enough time," Edwina offered.

"He's in Italy. And he's not coming back anytime soon."

"Italy? Where did you meet him?"

"On my way home from Edinburgh. We met at the airport. He managed to get me a seat in first class after his associate cancelled."

"I see." Edwina wanted to ask more questions. Instead she let Cecelia talk.

"He's so handsome, Ed. At first I didn't like him at all. But then we spent quite a bit of time together, and I really thought he needed me."

Edwina nodded. Her sister wanted someone to need her. She could certainly understand why. Her father left when she was a little girl, and her mother was a beautiful and famous stage actress. Where did that leave her? She suddenly realized in a deeper sense why Cecelia had to be successful and in charge of her life.

And why she wanted the best for her younger sister. "Cecelia, is there any chance at all you'll see him again?"

"He called about a week after he left and said he wouldn't be available much. That was just a few days ago. I've been trying to keep busy and not think about it."

"Did Spencer meet him?"

"No. Why would he?"

Cecelia seemed surprised at her question. "Spencer cares about you, Cece. I guess you haven't noticed since you met this guy. What is his name?"

"Evan Wyndham. He owns White Gate Publishing here in Chicago. Ed, Spencer and I are friends. Nothing more."

Edwina nodded. "So tell me what happened when he left."

"It was so strange, really. We got really close at the last minute, and then he announced he had to leave. Just like that."

"Hmm." Edwina's phone rang, interrupting her. "Hold onto your thought, Cece. It's Alex." She flipped open her phone. "Hi, Alex. Yes, I'm talking to Cecelia. Paige is napping so she can go down to the restaurant with Spencer. He promised her she could cook something. Is everything going as planned? Good. Well, dinner is on, and we'll wait for you then. Love you too. Bye."

Cecelia felt like an intruder. The way those two talked to each other made her happy for them, but reminded her she was missing something. What was it? She stood up. "I'm going to shower."

Edwina noted the abrupt end of the conversation.

"Okay. I think I'll go wake Paige. She won't want to miss anything. Spencer is coming up in half an hour. We can eat and shoo those two downstairs, and while Alex is making his phone calls, we can go for a walk, if you're up to it."

"Sounds good. I need to get out of here and quit thinking so much."

"Good. We'll head out as soon as we get those guys out of here. Just you and me."

One thing she learned about her sister; when their conversations swerved anywhere near her emotions, she skedaddled.

Chapter 50

Cecelia showered and wondered how Spencer knew she was seeing someone. She hadn't mentioned it to him. *Of course, Becca and Spencer are close, silly.* Becca would have thought nothing of it.

She heard Spencer's voice out in the living room. His laughter rang out, and then she heard Paige running. Something flipped in her stomach. She dreaded dinner this evening—pretending she was fine when she wasn't. She pulled in a breath and let it out while selecting a pair of worn jeans and an orange and brown sweater. It was going to be chilly later. Her wet hair was blow-dried and put in a ponytail. She thought about Spencer's compliment and took it back down and rearranged it around her ears.

Becca called while she was dressing to talk about the good news. "I'm so glad your sister is here, Cecelia. Would you like me to run over to the Victorian and finish that wallpaper? Edris and Symond said they'd come along. They're bored stiff."

"Really?" Cecelia laughed lightly. "Sure, if you feel like it. Just record your hours."

"All right, if you insist," Becca teased.

"Ed and I are going out after dinner for a walk. Perhaps we'll show up."

"Great! Love to meet your sister and her husband, especially since he's a Scottish laird."

Cecelia felt a tinge of jealousy slip through the cracks of her soul. "Yes, he's a nice guy."

"Great. See you later then." Becca was gone.

A knock at her door brought Paige's hearty request that she come for dinner. "I'm coming," Cecelia called back and made her way to the kitchen.

Spencer was leaning against the counter, still in his suit. Edwina was dishing up food. Alex walked in, rubbing his hands together. "Smells great." His stride took him straight to Edwina. He wrapped his arms around her waist from behind and kissed the top of her head.

Cecelia smiled wanly then looked away. Straight into Spencer's eyes.

"You are my Aunt Cecelia now, aren't you?" Paige asked her.

"Yes, I am. Let me see my new niece." Cecelia played along, glad for the interruption. "Dinner's ready," Edwina announced.

There was a dignified scramble for chairs. Spencer tossed his suit jacket off and then his tie. Alex, always the gentleman, made sure everyone was seated before he sat.

Cecelia swept away her negative thoughts. It was so rare to have company at her own formal dining table that her heart warmed. Caught up in the moment, she suddenly realized everyone seemed to be waiting for something.

"Are we going to pray?" Paige asked.

"Of course. Anyone?" Cecelia felt the color rise in her face.

"Alex, would you mind?" Spencer asked.

"Of course not." He prayed a short prayer and looked up with a smile. "Aye, blessed food is good food." He laughed out loud.

Edwina's look of love flowed from her face. Cecelia didn't remember Alex being a religious man. Shrugging, she took the offered dishes and filled her plate.

"Did you bring a pie from below stairs?" Paige asked.

"You mean from the basement?" Spencer asked straight-faced.

"Is that where your restaurant is? In the basement?" She made a face.

"Well, not exactly. We're on the second floor."

"But did you bring the pie?" Paige's fork was waving around.

"Yep. Sure did. Two of them. They're in the oven."

"I didn't see you do that." Paige stared at Spencer.

"Well, I'm quick." Spencer laughed. "Now eat."

Cecelia thought Spencer would make the best father. And it was evident from Edwina's face that she was happy. And so was Alex. For the first time in her life an old memory of her and her mother eating alone skittered through her mind. They had both cried. She for her father. Her mother for her husband. It was their first meal alone, without daddy. Why in the world she thought of that, she didn't know. Determined to push away such thoughts, she ate heartily.

The meal finished, Alex and Spencer shooed the girls out, all except Paige who was not leaving her daddy, and cleaned the kitchen.

Later Spencer wandered in the living room to retrieve his jacket and tie. "Thanks for having us." He winked at Cecelia.

"It was fun. I'm glad they're here. I've missed my sister."

"Yeah, it's great they're here. I'm headed down to the restaurant with Paige. Later..."

The man walked out with his coat over one arm, his other hand holding a little girl's. She noticed Paige led the way, even though she didn't know where they were going. Cecelia felt the same way. Edwina came from the bedroom at that moment and kissed her husband good-bye. Retrieving their jackets, Edwina and Cecelia headed for the elevator and found that the weather was mild. "Which way, Cece?"

"Let's head for the Victorian. Becca is there with her friends. I told her we'd try to make it over. It's only a few blocks from here."

"Great I'd love to see the Victorian and meet your friends."

Cecelia pulled a fresh breath of air into her lungs and exhaled. "The landscaping is finished—just in time. The rest of the show can be shot inside, so no problem. And did I tell you *Better Homes and Gardens* is doing a spread on the house once a month until we're done?"

"No. Really?" Edwina was excited. "You've done well, Cece. I'm shocked at how you can pull this big stuff off. I'd be going crazy. My mind is compartmentalized. Needs structure and simplicity. It's amazing to me that you can keep all the balls in the air at once."

Cecelia wanted to tell her sister just how many times she'd dropped the ball lately, but didn't. Pride kept her from exposing her weaknesses. She knew it was a trust issue. But she wasn't quite sure how to handle this part of her life. She'd been able to square off with business owners, the elite, even the pompous Mrs. King, but knowing what to do with trust issues . . . she didn't have a clue.

"Well, it isn't easy sometimes. But I do it because it's what I love."

"I'm glad for you. But I wish Evan would call. You say he owns a publishing company? That's pretty cool. What does he like to do for fun?"

"Actually, I don't know. We mostly met for dinner and talked. We went to a few social affairs, but we both preferred quiet evenings after running businesses all day long."

"I can understand that. Do his parents live here?"

Cecelia didn't know and changed the topic. "I've never met his parents. Speaking of parents maybe we should call them.

"Yes, let's do. Dad said your mother was extremely happy with her part. I think it has something to do with a bag lady."

"Bag lady?" Cecelia laughed. "Can you just see my proper British mum playing that part?"

"She's an actor." Edwina laughed at herself. "I'm sure she'll do it up right."

"Oh that she will. She's nothing if not a perfectionist." Cecelia knew her voice was accusing.

"Don't we all have that somewhere deep inside us, Cece? We want things to be perfect. Either in ourselves or someone else."

"Or both!" Cecelia quipped. "I'm surprised we can find anyone who is willing to put up with our idiosyncrasies for a long-term period—like marriage."

"I know. If God didn't plan this entire thing called marriage, I think we would all be in trouble."

"What do you mean God planned it?" Cecelia wanted to know.

Edwina thought for a moment, then answered, "You know we didn't think up this idea of marriage ourselves. God wanted us to be with someone who loved us and could balance us and help us be all that we can be."

"Whew . . . that's a big order."

"It is. That's why we need so much help."

"You mean like therapy and counseling?"

"Well, that's helpful. But we can pray to God and ask for things you know."

"I know that," Cecelia stated firmly but realized she didn't know how to do it. *Isn't God too busy for things like our small and silly requests for love?*

Edwina decided to let her sister muse and after a couple minutes asked, "Since your buildings are almost full, the restaurant is doing well, and no doubt you'll pull off your seasonal show and the Victorian is done, what then?"

Cecelia dashed a sideways glance at Edwina, who was looking ahead in thought. "I have no idea." She paused. "Right now I'm just happy to know the show is coming up."

Edwina thought her last comment did not have the joy she was used to hearing in her sister's voice. She began to think things had changed for Cecelia since she'd left. She just couldn't put her finger on what it was that was different. Maybe lack of confidence in herself.

They walked on in silence.

"Here we are." Cecelia pointed to the house as they walked up. "Isn't the color beautiful? It really stands out in the neighborhood, which was what we wanted."

"Oh, Cece, I love the soft cream color, the tan and green trim." As they walked closer, she said, "Oh the dark peach is a good contrast. Period colors, right?"

"Absolutely," Cecelia said proudly. "Doing our best to bring it back to its original state."

Dusk was beginning to fall over the house. Lights sparkled from every window of the huge house, lighting up the wraparound porch.

"It's so warm and welcoming. I could see you living here when you settle down, Cece!" Edwina stepped up onto the porch and gasped. "It's perfect. I love the curved walkway. The curved arches and the curved posts. So inviting." She ran her hand along the railing.

Cecelia smiled. This was her life. To redeem buildings and make them livable for people who wanted to be surrounded by beautiful things. She only wished she could redeem herself. She forced herself to push the negative thoughts away and enjoyed her sister's open appreciation of what she had accomplished.

Edwina turned back excitedly. "Do you plan on living here when it's finished, Cece?"

"No, not really. I like my modern place. I love seeing Lake Michigan in the mornings.

"That's true," Edwina agreed. "You can sell it to someone who will appreciate it."

"I plan on turning it into a B&B and since it will be viewed by millions on the show I don't think there will be a problem getting clients."

"Oh that is perfect," Edwina agreed.

"Come in. Take note of the French crystal chandelier in the foyer. Spencer had it cleaned and hung while I was gone."

"You mean as a surprise?"

"Yes," Cecelia said softly.

"It's lovely, Cece. Each crystal reflects off the walls. It's magical," Edwina whispered.

"It's one of my favorite pieces."

As they walked through each room, Cecelia felt her joy return. Edwina loved everything, just like she did. "What color for the sitting room?" Edwina turned in a complete circle, her eyes skimming the decorative ceilings, and arced windows.

"Becca and I chose softer colors since the ladies were the ones who used this room the most. The rest of the house is in disorder. But I'm glad you're seeing it in the early stages so you can see it when it's done." Cecelia's hands were on her hips.

Edwina saw her sister coming back.

"Well, I can't wait to see it finished. That's for sure." Her voice grew soft.

Chapter 51

"Hey, you made it!" Becca came bouncing out from a back room, her hair pushed away from her face and wallpaper scraps hanging from her jeans.

"Becca, this is my sister, Edwina. Edwina, this is my partner, Becca."

"You two are going to turn Chicago upside down!" Edwina smiled.

"We plan on doing exactly that," Becca stated. "Want to see what we're doing?" She waved her hand for them to follow.

"You girls have almost got the wallpaper layers down to the original base." Cecelia smoothed her hand over the walls and smiled.

"This is Symond, Spencer's sister, and Edris her friend." Cecelia introduced the other girls. "My sister, Edwina."

"Shall we sweep this up while you're finishing?" Edwina asked.

"Sure. The brooms are around here someplace." Cecelia went searching.

"I love what you girls have done *and* for helping my sister," Edwina complimented them.

"Thanks. We love working here. No one's here to boss us around, and we get to deconstruct things. That's what's fun!" Becca laughed. "Besides, we get caught up on all the stuff going on in our lives when we're together."

Edwina smiled.

Cecelia brought two brooms, and they began the difficult work of sweeping wet, sticky wallpaper into a pile. They worked for an hour and together finished the room. The wallpaper was off and the droppings out in the trash.

"The floors actually look pretty good. I think we'll just have to get them refinished," Cecelia said happily. "Have you girls eaten?"

"Nope. We're starved," they said at once.

"I'll call for a huge pizza." Cecelia laughed. "Can't have my girls starving." She popped her cell phone open and walked off.

"So, we hear you married a Scottish laird." Becca sidled up next to Edwina.

Edwina felt her face warm. "Yes."

"What's he like?" Edris took two steps closer so she could hear Edwina's soft voice.

"Well, he is a good man."

"How did you meet him?" From Symond.

"I ended up taking a trip to Scotland alone that Cecelia planned. Her father passed, and she was called away last minute, just as we were about to board the plane. I was there alone, and I'd never been to Scotland." Edwina heard them gasp. "And . . . well . . . Alex rescued me, sort of." She shrugged.

"Rescued you? How?" Becca wanted to know.

"Something went wrong with my hotel reservations, which left me with no place to stay. Alex was standing behind me, waiting to secure a room."

"In his own town?" Becca questioned.

"Yes, he was, well, getting married and was there to obtain the bridal suite, and I was holding him up."

All three girls' eyes widened.

"What happened?" Becca again.

"He brought me to his castle, and—"

"Castle?" the girls whooped out.

"Yes. I didn't know anyone in Scotland, and since he was in a bit of a hurry to be rid of me, he brought me to his home. I was already scheduled to leave Monday on a Scottish bus tour, so I only needed a place for a couple of days."

"So in one weekend you stole his heart?"

"Oh no. Nothing like that. I was rather a problem, it seemed to me. But he was kind."

"I guess!" Edris exclaimed. "So how did you guys end up married?"

"I took the tour, and when I returned he asked if I might work for him and I declined."

"You *declined*? Why would you do that?" Becca threw her hands up.

"I wasn't sure about myself, and I knew nothing about Scotland. My home was in Michigan."

"*So?*" Becca interrupted.

"I wasn't very open to new things. I came home, and something inside me said I should not have said no."

"Duh!" All three said at once.

Edwina smiled at the attentive girls.

"Anyway, I ended up going back, and the rest is history."

"It's the history part I want to hear about," Becca said. "What happened to his fiancée?"

"She wasn't the woman Alex had hoped she was. And I just happened to be there at the right time." She shrugged.

"Yeah right. If only!" Becca nearly shouted.

"So now you live in a castle, right?" Symond's soft voice interrupted.

"No, we live in a little farmhouse called Beaufort Manor."

"Farmhouse? Why in the world would you do that?" Becca asked.

"Calm down, Becca," Symond laughed. "It could happen to us too, you know!"

"Right. Yeah, like the Mississippi River will change its course next week?"

"What's all the shouting about?" Cecelia returned. "Pizza's on the way."

"Edwina was telling us about her knight."

Cecelia saw her sister's discomfort at being the center of attention. "See, dreams do come true, gals," she said lightly.

"Hey, I hear Spencer's voice," Symond said, walking toward the front of the house.

The group followed. "We brought you gals some chocolate chip cookies straight from the oven." He set a large pan on the table. "Paige made them. Still warm."

Paige ran to stand next to Edwina.

"Still warm?" Edwina winked at Paige as she nodded.

"Well, I'm all for dessert *before* pizza," Becca spoke up, and the three girls helped themselves. "Whoa, these are huge. Just the way I like 'em."

Cecelia declined. Spencer stood aside and enjoyed the view, Edwina noted, and twice looked at Cecelia with concern before her sister fled the room.

"Spence, come look at the room we just finished." Becca caught his hand and hauled him off. "All the wallpaper is off, and Cecelia and Edwina helped us clean up the floor or else we might have been here most of the night." She laughed. "Wallpaper scraps were stuck to the floors."

"Looks great." He ran his hand over the walls. "Smooth too. Won't be too difficult to repaper. Is that what Cecelia's planning?" He turned to Becca.

"Yes, I think so. We haven't talked about that yet. But Ms. Gervase had a great idea to cover some of the smaller walls with fabric. Unique application, but I like the idea."

"Hmm, not sure about that. I'll leave that one up to you designers." He laughed.

Cecelia popped into the room. "Where's the broom? There's a mess in the foyer to clean up." She dashed out, noting Spencer and Becca's easy way they talked. So they *were* an item?

She wondered why in the world she'd care about that. Maybe it seemed as though everyone had someone—but her. *Stop feeling sorry for yourself, Cecelia Grace Giatano. You have someone. He's just acting like a jerk right now. He'll be calling any day.*

Spotting the broom—it was right where she had left it—she grabbed it and hurried to the foyer. It was almost nine o'clock. Alex would be waiting for Edwina.

Her cell had not rung once.

She shook her head and scattered her thoughts. *What I need right now is to stay busy.* She swept furiously. The front door opened sending her small pile of trash flying across the floor.

"Oh, sorry," Spencer said as Becca followed him in. "We went out back to check the landscaping behind the house. Nice job."

"Thanks." Cecelia gathered up the stuff on the floor.

"I'll get the dustpan." Spencer picked up his pace.

Cecelia leaned on the broom and waited. Becca dashed inside to talk to the other girls.

"Here." Spencer bent down and waited for her. "I'll take it out to the dumpster. Too much dust to leave it inside." He headed out.

Cecelia tossed the broom in a side room and huffed about for a moment. What she wanted was to fly to Italy and force Evan Roberto Wyndham to look her in the face. At least she could read what was written there.

Chapter 52

Cecelia crossed her arms over her chest as she walked about gazing into each room. Right now her creative juices were all but nil. Maybe she should just fly over and surprise Evan. Perhaps he was overrun with business. That was something she understood. She scolded herself for reading into things. What had gotten into her these days?

The high-pitched ring of her cell made her nerves tingle. Her mother.

"Mom, how're you doing?" She found an empty room at the back in the butler's pantry and closed the door to the noise. "Did the play go well?"

"Wow, that's nice, really nice, Mum." Cecelia listened for several minutes while her mother expounded on the success of the play. "Mother, would you have time to stop here on your way home?"

"Right. Maybe next time then." She paused. "Did you know Edwina and Alex are here?"

"You knew? Oh . . ."

"Okay, glad it went well for you, Mum." Cecelia heard the ruckus in the background. "Yes, congratulations." She raised her voice.

Her mum had already hung up. She snapped the phone shut while little-girl feelings swept over her from the past. Never enough time to talk. There were a constant stream of well-wishers and important visitors. It was no wonder she *had* to excel in something other than her mother's chosen vocation. And she had. *Let bygones be bygones*. She admonished herself and stuffed the memories into a secret place, checking her watch as she stepped through the door and straight into the arms of Spencer Hallman.

"Whoa." He did not remove his hands from her upper arms where he had stopped them from crashing into each other. Instead he relished the unplanned moment and sought her eyes.

Cecelia wiggled out of his embrace, but he stood square in the doorway and she couldn't get around him so she stepped back.

Spencer placed his empty hands in the doorway, one on either side. "You've been awfully busy since we returned from Edwina's wedding." He knew enough not to try to engage her in any personal talk.

"Yes, I have been." She crossed her arms over her chest and took another step backward.

"Whoa, body language says, 'Do not disturb.'" He smiled down at the slender woman.

"Why do you say things like that?" she grumped. "You know I have a lot on my mind."

"I do know. I hear your boyfriend went back to Italy."

Cecelia turned her face away for a moment, but knew her frustration was showing. "What does that have to do with you?" She eyed him.

"Not a thing. Not a thing. Just making conversation. Is that what's bothering you, Cecelia?"

"Spencer, I don't really want to talk right now."

"Okay. Not a problem." He dropped his arms and stepped aside. "But if you need to talk, remember I'm not the enemy, I'm your friend."

"Right," she spouted, not sure why she was angry and stalked off, glad to hear the doorbell ring. "Pizza's here," she announced.

The crowd gathered around and ate. She didn't see Spencer anywhere. After some time, someone noticed he was missing.

Edwina spoke up. "He left. Said he had cleanup tonight at the restaurant," she explained.

"Ed, I'm tired. Let's head out if you're finished."

"Good idea Cece. Alex is probably missing his daughter." She glanced at Paige who was beginning to show signs of jet lag.

Cecelia suddenly remembered they had walked, and it was dark now—and no doubt colder. She expressed her thoughts aloud.

Becca reached for her phone. "I'll call Spencer. He won't mind coming back. I've got my car, but it'll be full with the three of us."

Before Cecelia could intervene, her cell phone rang. It was Evan. Her heart beat double time. She pulled in a deep breath, hurrying away from the girls, and let it ring twice more. "Cecelia here." She hoped her voice was confident.

"Cecelia, Evan Wyndham."

His voice, dull and flat, indicated this would not be a loving reunion call. Not to mention he used his last name as though he were on a business call.

"Yes." She thought her anger at him had thinned, but her own voice told her it hadn't.

"It seems I will be forced to fly home in two weeks."

"Forced?"

"There's a problem at White Gate."

"You sound disappointed."

"The timing is imperfect."

"A lot of things are imperfect, Evan."

"Have you made your contract with the show?"

Cecelia noted the lift in his voice and wondered, for the first time, why she even thought he cared about her. "Just about." She didn't owe him anything.

"I see. Would you like me to be present for your first taping—if I can manage it."

"No need, Evan."

Silence. "Listen I have to go. I'll call you when I get in."

Cecelia heard the call end and nearly tossed her phone across the room. "He has no intention of calling," she blurted out, careful to keep her voice low. *Why didn't he just say so?*

Tears popped into her eyes, and she swatted them away like pesky flies. She stalked across the room several times. Finally she pulled herself together, and, as always, presented a good face to the crowd.

"What's the plan?" She inserted herself in the middle of the chaos.

"Spencer's coming for you guys," Becca stated. "And I'll take the girls back with me."

Cecelia pressed her lips together, then smiled. "Would you mind terribly if I went back with you? It's a bit closer, and I have some business that must be attended to this evening."

"We're not going straight home." Becca asserted herself, knowing Cecelia didn't want to ride with Spencer. "Spencer will get you gals home quicker than I can. We have to make a stopover at Symond's for a tool she left at home." Becca gave Symond the eye.

"Sorry," Symond apologized.

"Okay, girls, we'd better get going. It's late, and we have plenty to do tomorrow." Becca corralled the girls and slammed the door.

"What was that all about?" Symond looked at her friend when they were out of earshot.

"I'm playing Robin Hood. Only it's not stealing from the rich to pay the poor," Becca answered. "It's way more than that." She huffed.

Edris just shook her head. "You are always up to something, Bec."

Becca just smiled. "Well, someone's got to do it."

Chapter 53

"Everyone ready?" Spencer called out the minute he opened the door. Paige ran to him and took his hand. "Well, there's one gal who's ready."

"I've got to check the back door." Cecelia turned.

"Let me take care of it. You ladies get in the car. I'll make sure everything is secure."

Cecelia knew not to argue with him. He was the protector and would take no guff, not even from her, so she followed Edwina out and found herself sitting in the front with Spencer. She almost rolled her eyes. Why did it bother her so much?

"We're going straight to bed, Cece, if you don't mind. Alex and Paige can visit a little bit, and then we can talk tomorrow when we're all rested."

"Sounds like a good idea, Ed. I have several tasks to finish in my office."

Spencer jumped in the car. He pulled up beneath the awning and opened the doors for the girls. "Out with you and to bed." He patted Paige's head and was completely surprised when she threw her arms around his legs.

Cecelia watched out of the corner of her eye as Spencer leaned down and picked up the little girl and held her close, his muscular arms around the tiny body. Something in her broke. She stalked inside and into the elevator without a word to James.

Edwina and Spencer shared a look. "She's different, Spencer. I'm not sure how, but she seems more vulnerable."

Spencer didn't say a word, but agreed with a nod. "Up to bed with you girls," he whispered to Paige. "See you tomorrow."

* * *

Spencer washed pots and pans at the restaurant with a vengeance. Didn't the woman see anything? Didn't she see she was heading down a dead-end road with this guy? He hadn't even met him, but knew from Becca that he had all the makings of a man who used women. Good looks, big money, no heart.

"And she sure doesn't want anything to do with me," he said to himself. She had made that clear. He cleaned the entire kitchen until it was spick-and-span and went down to the lower level to work off his frustration in the weight room. While he pulled the handles until his muscles were screaming, he realized he was in deeper than he wanted to be. Living so close to her, he knew too much. And right now there was no way out. They owned the restaurant together. And he lived in the same building. The second and twelfth floor were *not* far enough apart. He set the machine levels higher and tried to work it out of his system.

Superman he was not. As much as he wanted to be, he knew there was only one way to handle this, and that was to wait and pray. He'd run ahead before and made a mess of everything. He promised himself he would never walk that way again.

* * *

Cecelia dashed into her office, clicked her door closed, and looked around. Papers sat ready for signatures. A stack of checks waited for Spencer's employees—their employees. Spencer had already been up here and taken care of everything. Tears burned her eyes. Why was she so resentful of him? All he'd ever tried to do was help. She pushed her fears and emotions down to a safe place, shut off her office light, and went to the kitchen. Spick-and-span in there too. He had cleaned up even the dessert dishes. Everywhere she went Spencer seemed to be standing there looking at her. The way his blues eyes stared into hers when they ran into each other in the doorway did things to her she didn't want to admit. And that spiky blond hair of his. She'd wanted to smooth it back into place more times than she cared to think about right now. She dashed such foolishness from her mind, remembering how he was always there in her face, acting like he knew everything about her. Cecelia felt instant fear. *What if he knew? Could he know somehow? Was that why he was looking at her the way he did?* Cecelia answered her own questions. *No one needs to tell me how to run my life. I am a grown woman, capable of taking care of myself.* Then another unwilling thought popped into her head. *Then why am I so miserable?*

Shaking her head, she stirred sugar into a cup of hot tea and carried it to her room. After a quick change into her favorite blue silk pajamas, she grabbed a book from the shelf and climbed into bed. The warmth of the cup in her hands set her imagination on fire. She knew one thing. She was a woman who needed some romance in her life. She cracked open a book that promised a happy ending and began to read.

Two hours later, eyes burning, she snapped the book shut and pressed the dimmer button, lowering the lights. Curled up with her pillow, hot tears began slipping down her cheeks. The story may have well been written about her. The character had everything. Except love. She stared out the window feeling alone. She squeezed the water from her eyes and squinted, wondering if she were seeing things that weren't there. Just like in her life. Evan Wyndham hadn't been worthy of her love. But it was too late and too dreadful to think it may be true.

The book lay on the table, the corner of the page turned down where she'd stopped reading. Mostly because it was going someplace she knew she would not be going. The reserve she'd established as a young woman had kept her safe from the wiles of men who were rich and handsome and didn't care a whit about the women they dated. She'd seen enough of it in her life to know how they operated. The hard-and-fast reserve built itself up in her mind again, except this time the dam burst as tears burned down her cheeks. She had been a fool. And reading a sappy romance had only shown her the truth.

Cecelia felt her heart harden. It was safer than being swept away by foolish dreams. Maybe Alex and Edwina had something special, but it was not for her. She was a savvy woman whose success in this world would be found in business not in a romance novel. She was at her best in front of a conference room full of colleagues, making plans and decisions that mattered. Her design skills and ability to perform, and look good in front of a camera, *were* her talents. The mastery of her professional dreams was what made her heart beat fast. Slowly, methodically, she redefined her goals. Look good, sound good, put on a tough exterior, and by all means, make money. This was her destination. And she would do it by herself. She didn't need Evan Wyndham *or* Spencer Hallman, for that matter.

Throwing back the covers, she grabbed a tissue, wiped away the silly tears, tossed the book in the trash, and grabbed her empty teacup. The stomp to the kitchen and the loud twang as she set the cup in the sink fired her resolve. She was born to this kind of life. Time to act like it. Hours later she shut her office door and exhausted, crawled back into bed.

Chapter 54

"Aunt Cece, can I come in?"

Cecelia groaned, turned in her bed, and sat up. Where was she? The voice came again. She managed a groggy response. "Yes."

The door opened slowly. "I just wanted to see you." The little girl, still in her pink ballerina-print pajamas, all but ran and tossed herself on the bed.

Cecelia grabbed her head.

"Did I hurt you?" Paige, now on her knees, was in her face with a truly repentant look in her huge brown eyes.

"No, I just went to bed very late last night," she murmured.

"Oh." Paige gently crawled over to the extra pillow and lay down.

"What are you doing up so early?" Cecelia checked the blue digits with squinted eyes. "It's only six o'clock. I've had exactly two hours of sleep," she murmured.

"Do you like it here?" The child's chin was suddenly resting in her palms as she turned and landed on her elbows.

"Yes, I like I here." Cecelia winced.

"Have you got a headache?" Paige wanted to know.

"Yes, as a matter of fact I do," Cecelia grumped.

"Bertie always had headaches too."

Cecelia kept silent. She sensed more was coming.

"But she doesn't anymore. Not after she got a boyfriend."

Cecelia's face turned to gaze in those eyes. What was she getting at?

"Claude is her boyfriend. That's Reardon's brother."

"I see." Cecelia couldn't help but smile at the child's unaffected statement.

"Bertie doesn't have headaches anymore. She said that."

"She did now, did she?"

"Yes. Maybe you could get a boyfriend."

"Since I have a headache?"

"Yes." Paige turned to lie on her back and noticed the sun as it came in through the window. "Look at the rays on the floor." She leaned over the side of the bed.

Cecelia sincerely wished Paige would quit moving.

"Can you see them?"

"Not right now. I'm not feeling too well." Cecelia thought she might be coming down with something. She scolded herself, it was the late-night dance with her emotions last evening.

"Okay, I'll go away. Father says we should let people rest when they're sick."

Paige flipped herself off the bed, sending Cecelia's hand to her head to calm the motion.

"Breakfast is almost ready."Paige whispered and tried to tiptoe quietly over the carpet.

Cecelia jumped as the door slammed shut, then groaned and turned back into her pillow. So much for her plans today.

* * *

Two weeks passed quickly and Cecelia found herself face to face with Evan Wyndham as she walked into the foyer of her building one evening after working on the Victorian.

"Cecelia?" She heard her name, schooled her face and turned, hoping he would get a good look at her when she was at her worst.

"I wasn't sure it was you." He stared at her rather rudely, then looked around.

"Afraid someone might see us?" She lifted her chin and looked him squarely in the eye.

"No."

"Really?" she pressed him as his eyes checked left and then right.

"I was just coming by to let you know I'll be in town for four more days. I thought you might want to go out for dinner."

"Well, you know, it is a little late. If I would have known yesterday or even earlier this morning . . ." She let him surmise her meaning.

"I didn't have time. Problems as soon as I walked off the plane. That *is* why I'm here."

"That's terribly unfortunate, but as you see, I'm not really up to an evening out, Evan." She noticed he took a step back. Did she look that awful?

"As you wish." He turned and walked away, his shiny black shoes clicking as he went.

Cecelia took a deep breath and turned. Her eyes met Spencer's immediately. He obviously had stepped off the elevator and had seen the entire ugly scene.

"Your Mr. Wyndham?" He unbuttoned his suit jacket and loosened his tie.

"He's not *my* Mr. Wyndham, Spencer."

"Mind if I ride up with you?"

"No," she said with a curtness she didn't really mean.

"I haven't talked to you since Alex and Edwina left. Didn't want to disturb you."

"Thanks. It has been rather busy. Getting closer to our goal."

"Great. You gals have worked hard."

"Yes, we have. I've learned a lot. It's been enlightening to see how wallboard actually goes up." Cecelia smiled slightly.

"You hung wallboard?"

"Not exactly. I said I saw it go up. It's so messy that I'm drenched in white dust."

"I can see that." Spencer leaned his shoulder against the wall and crossed his arms.

She hit him back verbally. "You look pretty snobbish."

"Does it show?" He played along. "You're usually the one in the designer suit."

"And I can't wait to get back into my designer suits."

"I rather like you a bit mussed up."

"What?" She gave him the sly eye."

"Just telling the truth." He smiled at her, glad to see her in her not-so-perfect realm.

"Spencer, you need to grow up." She swatted him.

Chapter 55

Spencer drew back at her comment as he followed her in. *Why does she have to bring that up? Like I'm some kid out of high school. Does she see me as beneath her?* He was going to set that straight first chance he had.

"I'll shower quickly. I can't even think with all this dust in my hair," she called as she hurried away.

Spencer slipped off his jacket, folded it neatly, and laid it across her sofa, then tossed his tie, rolled up his white shirtsleeves, and dug into the dishes sitting in the sink. He was standing with the refrigerator door open perusing when he heard her voice, soft and low.

"Don't you ever get tired of cooking and cleaning up?"

"No. It's my work," he shot back. "Why?"

"Just wondering. I am starving. Anything in there? I haven't been shopping in ages."

"What, you're not going out with your boyfriend tonight?" Spencer knew he sounded grumpy. But he was tired of playing games with this woman. On one minute, off the next. He intended to get to the bottom of things, boyfriend or no.

"No. And it's none of your business." She gave him her back as she rummaged through the cupboards. "There isn't even bread in the house."

"I have an idea." He turned to her. "Let's go down and eat in the restaurant. We have two new dishes you haven't tried yet."

"What are they?" She combed her fingers through her damp hair.

"One dish is Italian angel hair with chicken and spinach and a creamy Parmesan white sauce, the other is a new sandwich. Roasted turkey slices with sage dressing and a pineapple slice on marbled rye served with a spinach salad."

"Oh, the Italian sounds wonderful. Isn't turkey rather old-fashioned to serve to upscale clients."

"We're trying out the new turkey recipe in time for Thanksgiving," he explained. "Besides, when is it old-fashioned to serve good down-home cooking to anyone?"

"Down-home cooking? That sounds rather low class."

"Good food, cooked well and served well, is never low class, Cecelia."

"Well, you're the manager." She straightened her button-up white shirt.

"Touché."

"I don't feel like dressing up tonight though."

"That's okay. We'll eat in the back. I've got a small table set up in the kitchen. It's warm and aromatic."

"Aromatic?" She turned smiling.

"Yes, you know, smells good in there."

"I know what you meant, Spencer. Give me a bit of credit will you?"

Spencer sensed the conversation was going south. "Right, lass," he quipped.

She stared daggers into him, then squared her shoulders and brushed her pants with her hand. "As long as we aren't schmoozing, I guess it won't matter how I'm dressed. Just make sure we're not seen."

"Got it. Let's go." He grabbed her hand and then suddenly found she'd slipped it out.

"I'll get my shoes."

Spencer looked down and saw those small bare feet and guffawed.

"What?" She followed his eyes.

"Just like Edwina. Caught with your shoes off." He smiled. "Go get your shoes, Miss Giatano. We've got some business to discuss."

She felt her face flush and rushed off to her room. What was it about Spencer that he kept getting on her last nerve? She retrieved a pair of tennis shoes from the back of her closet. She wanted nothing more than to be comfortable.

"What, no Birkenstocks?" Spencer gasped.

"No. You said we'd be eating in the kitchen. You're sure, right?" She stopped and stared.

"Of course." He winked. "Would I lead you down the wrong path?"

Cecelia looked a moment longer into his eyes and realized something. Spencer Hallman would not lead her down the wrong path. She leaned down and tied her shoes.

"So, are you free all evening?" He punched the elevator button.

"All evening."

Spencer knew a foxy smile rested on his face. He couldn't help it. "We're eating at the restaurant." He informed James, who smiled ever so slightly and nodded.

Spencer whistled, which probably set Cecelia's nerves on edge these days. "Business has been up these last few weeks. Due, I think, in part to our sponsoring the local clubs."

"Which ones?" she demanded. "You didn't tell me about that."

"You haven't been around," he stated simply.

"We'll use the servant's door, won't we? Really, Spencer, I don't want to be seen."

"Not to worry, little lady. Your English manners will not be compromised. Follow me."

They slipped through a tiny door, and she found herself in the kitchen.

"Right over here." He pulled out a chair in a far corner, away from the action.

"It's perfect." She looked around. "Very French." Small table covered with a long white cloth. Miniature vase of flowers in the center. Black wrought iron chairs. "Did you design this?"

"On my honor, no. One of the gals set up the table. I just implemented the idea of inviting people to the back to eat in peace—away from the politics of professionalism and posh people."

Cecelia gave him a hard look.

"Coffee is in the carafe. Sugar's over there." He pointed. "I'll go and change."

She helped herself to coffee and two sugar blocks, wondering what Evan was doing. Strangely, she had no desire to call him. Yet something hurt inside at the knowledge he expected her to be instantly available. Just like the first time. Perhaps if she'd have seen it then . . .

Several minutes passed, and her stomach reminded her it was time to eat. She stood and looked around for anything she could snack on when Spencer walked in.

"Need something?" His black glasses rested low on his nose. An ancient white T-shirt stretched over his wide shoulders and narrowed at his jeaned hips.

"Yes," she answered properly. "I was looking for a bite of something."

"Sit. Our dishes are in the oven."

"It smells delicious." She heard the swinging door squeak on its hinges.

"Miss Giatano." Chef Alonzo wiped his hands on the towel at his waist and bowed.

Immediately she felt a kinship. He had the darkest eyes and the easy manner of the Europeans. "It is good to see you again." He spoke with an accent.

"Oui," she answered. Then she asked him in French whether he liked his job.

"Oui, but I must go. It is busy this evening. We will talk again." He flew away.

"Coming up." Spencer opened the oven and pulled out two plates covered with silver domes. "Alonzo saved these for us. The dish has been a hit thus far, but it's only been on the menu this week. We wanted your English tongue to taste it and tell us if you like what we've created."

"So you knew I'd come?"

"I could only hope." He winked and set the plates just so and turned hers slightly. "I'll bring water." He didn't need to ask. Cecelia, always health conscious, drank water.

"It looks good." She eyed the plated food. "Lots of color and smells divine."

"The spices are Alonzo's mix. He learned French and Italian cuisine from his French grandmother who was married to an Italian chef."

Cecelia picked up her fork. It stopped in midair at Spencer's last comment.

She never knew a grandmother. Would she ever be someone's grandmother?

Spencer watched the light in her eyes harden. She put her fork down and slowly placed her linen napkin across her lap, and with a sadness he hadn't seen before, Cecelia lifted her fork to her mouth and ate.

He forced himself to eat without talking.

After a few moments passed, she spoke. "Spencer, this is good, really good."

"You think so? It's light enough that if we cut the portion in half we can serve it for lunch as well with a salad, maybe a dish of green beans with sesame seeds on the side. What do you think?"

"That's really your department, Spencer. I trust your judgment."

"With food." He waited for a verbal comeback, but none came.

"What?" She tapped her napkin at the corners of her mouth and glared at him. "You know it isn't easy for me trust people."

Spencer nodded, waiting for her to go on. He knew she had a definite issue with trust. He felt sucker punched each time she inadvertently reminded him. Didn't she know he understood that about her?

Chapter 56

How much more proof did the woman need? He had worked the restaurant and cleaned her condo, helped without asking for pay on her Victorian, and was available anytime she needed him. Time to turn the subject elsewhere.

"So does your Mr. Wyndham have plans for you tomorrow evening?"

Cecelia's eyes shot up and she glared at him. "What does it matter to you?"

The woman was dense. For as much skill as she had as an entrepreneur, she lacked equally in knowing anything about relationships, especially those that required trust. Spencer found himself smiling.

"What now?" She put her fork down and glared some more.

"Don't ruin a perfectly good meal with your trust issues." He dug into the food. "Relax. No one's going to sweep you off your feet without your approval."

"Oooh, you just . . . just . . ."

Spencer shrugged, took another bite, and then let her have it. "What? I couldn't possibly understand?"

"You bloody well know that I'm not good at that sort of thing."

"Indeed I do," he agreed.

She noted his crooked smile and wished she had not been brought up so properly. She would have tossed a forkful of mashed potatoes at his smug face. Instead she straightened her shoulders and decided to play the game by turning the tables on him.

"So, what is this I hear about you and Becca?" She felt a certain sense of power as she watched his smiling eyes turn serious.

"What did you hear?"

His coolness goaded her further. "Why don't you tell me?"

"What, that we're friends? Go to the same church? That she and Symond are friends? That about does it."

"What? You don't want to discuss *your* romantic life?" *Punch line delivered.*

"You want to discuss *my* romantic life?" He tripped her up this time.

"Sure, why not? It seems you're all interested in mine."

"Well, all right. Why don't we head over to my place, and I'll tell you all about it." That ought to set her running.

Cecelia heard the challenge in his voice. She wasn't afraid of Spencer Hallman.

"I'm free this evening." She laid her fork down and gave him a look.

"Good. Dessert?"

"None, thank you. I'm full." She dabbed her mouth and set her napkin across her plate.

"Ever the lady." He did the same and went to pull her chair out.

"Oh, for heaven's sake, Spencer, we're in the kitchen. No one's looking."

"I don't do it for those who are looking. I was brought up to respect women."

His low voice and smug smile seemed to mock her. "Whatever." She felt the light touch of his fingers at the small of her back.

Spencer wisely chose not to engage in any more talk. The woman was likely to change her mind before they got to his apartment.

The strained silence had his thoughts bouncing around. How much should he tell her about his life? Would she understand, or would he push her away? Suddenly it seemed very important. *Lord, lead me in my speech.*

He reached in his pocket and unlocked the door. "You've never been to my place."

"No. There was no need. Your space is your space."

Spencer stood by and let her go ahead of him. He'd left lamps lit, and it looked cozy.

"Smells like pumpkin pie in here."

"My sisters burn candles whenever they're here."

She ran her hands along his brown leather sofa. "Did you decorate or your sisters?"

She had turned to him, he knew, to check his eyes for the truth. "I decorated, but the girls added the candles and the afghans. They crochet and knit you know."

"No, I didn't." She picked up a dark-colored blanket and looked closely. "I've always wanted to knit or sew or something like that."

"Really?" He tried not to register his surprise. "It's easy from what I hear. When they come, they usually bring their stuff and work on it while we watch a movie."

"Do they come often?" Cecelia tried to be nonchalant.

"Mom and Dad are busy with their retired lives, so we meet here, usually on weekends. The girls bring their guys if they're dating, and we hang out."

"Becca too?" She hated herself for asking.

"Yep. So, what's your next step at the Victorian?" He switched to her interests.

She shrugged, running her hand along the back of the sofa. "I've lost touch with the calendar. The Victorian needs to be ready next month. They want to start filming."

"Great timing."

"Yes, I thought so."

"And then with the show premiering in the spring, people will be looking to buy old houses and fix them up to look like yours." He eyed her. She was way too passive.

"That's the plan." She fingered the leaves of a plant.

"Also from a sister." He gestured with a nod. "I'm not good with plants. Usually forget to water them."

"Me too." She sighed.

"Here, sit. You probably need to get off your feet for a while. Once your show starts, you won't have a minute's rest."

"You're right. I know how much work it will be, but it will give me the exposure I'm wanting. It'll be enough to set me apart, especially if they offer a long-term contract. Not to mention television and radio interviews will increase."

"Yep, you've got the world by the tail."

"What in the world does that mean?" Cecelia stared at him as she sat down on the sofa.

"Means you'll have it all." Spencer chose a side chair near the fireplace rather than sitting next to her on his sofa. "Everything you've always wanted, Cecelia."

"Hmm." Her mind was already working. "It's chilly in here."

226

"I'll start the fire." He jumped up and flipped a switch. The fireplace lit up, then he pulled the afghan off the back of his chair and laid it across her knees. Her feet were curled underneath her. "Better?"

"Much," she murmured. "So we came up here to talk about you." She was glad Spencer didn't traipse her through his entire apartment. She didn't want to get too close to him.

"Well, what do you want to know?" He leaned forward, elbows on his knees, and looked at her.

"I don't know. You tell me."

"You'd never make a good interviewer."

"I never said I would," she shot back.

"True," he agreed. "Where did we leave off? Something about my romantic life?"

"Yes, since you were nosing into mine, I thought to nose into yours."

"Good enough. I'll start at the beginning. I have four sisters. Two married, two single. One nephew, one niece. My folks were born and raised here in Chicago. My mother owned a hair salon, my father worked as an engineer for the city. Both are retired, travel a lot, work with our church and with Habit for Humanity."

"You went to church all your life?"

"Yep, born and raised in church. Took a sabbatical for a couple of years and learned enough of the world to bring me running back."

"Hmm." She had no idea what that meant and wasn't about to ask.

"Your parents take you to church?" he asked.

"Only to confess their sins and go out and live any which way they wanted."

Spencer listened and nodded as she nipped at her fingernails, then tucked her hands beneath her.

"Mother was too busy with her work and father seeing to his newest conquest. Sometimes it was a business, sometimes a woman."

"I see. Your trust issues came out of that?"

"As you can see." She grabbed a magazine off a side table and leafed through it like a wild March wind.

"Where did you grow up?" Spencer asked.

Cecelia sighed, uncomfortable with the subject, but unable to get up. "All over the place. I was born in England. My parents met in London. Then my mother and I came here, first to New York, Los Angeles, and finally Chicago. I spent my college years here."

"Ah, were you a cute little cheerleader?"

She glared at him. "I was a cheerleader, yes. Does that mean something?"

"Just trying to get to know you." He wiped the smile from his face and held his hands up in surrender. The woman was testy.

"So, did you play football?" She turned the tables.

"Some. Wasn't very good at it, but did fairly well at baseball. Did you do sports?"

"Oh heavens, no. Mother would never allow that. Very unladylike."

"Would you have *liked* to play sports?" Spencer wanted to know about her desires.

"Well, I love baseball. I'm a Cubs fan, you know. At least I used to be." Her voice fell away."

"I had no idea." Spencer pulled his chair closer.

"I dated one of the players a long time ago." She tossed the magazine aside.

"Who?" he asked before thinking.

"Does it matter? He . . . well . . . he . . ."

Spencer saw her lips press together. Trouble was afoot.

"Do you want to talk about it?" He lowered his voice. "It's okay if you don't."

Cecelia lifted her eyes and gazed at him for a long time.

Spencer forced himself to relax and listen. He saw her eyes go soft.

"It doesn't matter who he was. The thing is . . . he was married. I met him through some friends, and they told me he was divorced. I learned later that he wasn't."

Spencer nodded and let the silence float between them.

After a time she spoke. "I really cared for him. When I learned that he was married, I ran off to my father in Italy."

"Was he there for you?" Spencer asked quietly.

"Not really. He had another woman living with him. She did not like me interrupting their lives. I stayed for a while. It gave me time to think. To unwrap my heart strings, which were tied up in knots." She managed a smile. "It was my first broken heart."

"First? You probably left a trail of broken hearts from elementary upward," he teased. And noticed her dull smile.

"Thanks for trying, Spencer."

"I'm not trying for anything, Cecelia. I'm telling you what I think."

She laid her head back, and Spencer knew tears were going to follow. They did.

"I can't believe I was so stupid to believe everything his buddies said," she murmured. "By the time I got back home, he'd filed for divorce from his wife and had another girlfriend. Younger than me."

"Men do stupid things."

"You can say that again. But so do women. We fall for the first guy who gives us a scrap and then find out we're not as special as we thought."

"Not to every guy."

"No. I managed to find something more exciting."

"Work," he answered for her.

"Yes. Work. It gives me what I need. Accolades, a job well done, all of that. And I do well at it."

Spencer nodded in agreement. "That you do."

Silence.

"Is it enough, Cecelia?"

"What?" Her head jerked up.

"Work? Success? Money?"

"It is for me." She stiffened. "You know, I think it's time I got back to work."

"Whoa." He held up his hands. "Stay put. I have something to show you."

Chapter 57

Cecelia could hear him rummaging through stuff in the other room before he came back with a picture frame. Without a word, he handed it to her.

"You played? For the Cubs?"

"Well, let's just say I was on the team for a short time."

"You never told me." She gazed at him, eyes clear.

"Wasn't exactly the best time of my life."

"What do you mean? Do you know how many guys want to play for the Chicago Cubs?"

"Of course I do. I got drafted in my senior year of college."

"What happened?"

"You really want to hear the whole sordid tale?"

"Of course. I wouldn't ask if I didn't," she puffed.

"Okay, here give me that." He took the picture from her hand and laid it face down on the side table. "There isn't much to tell really. I got drafted. I hung out. Made some huge mistakes and left. Simple."

"You're not telling me the whole story are you?"

"Does it really matter?" Spencer dug his heels in.

"Well. It's your story, isn't it?"

He shrugged. "That's true. It's just that I don't especially like talking about my past."

"We all have one, Spencer." She gave him a look.

"I guess." Spencer said a silent prayer and began. "Somehow I got lucky and was at the right place at the right time. At least that's what I thought."

Cecelia tucked her hands between her knees and settled deeper into the sofa. She was in.

Spencer leaned forward, elbows on his knees again, hands clamped together. It was his turn to trust someone, and it wasn't as easy now that it was him doing the trusting.

"Hard to trust, isn't it?" She smiled.

"Yep." Silence. "I met this girl my senior year of college. She was head cheer, smart, beautiful, and well, her father had money and he threw it around freely. When we hooked up, her father said he saw promise in me and pretty much opened the doors. I should have known it was too easy. Within a month I was signed up. Dead last, but nevertheless on the team. My parents were really proud of me, even though I had hardly talked to them the last two years of college."

"Why not?" Cecelia's soft voice came from his right.

"I was walking my own way. Everything I'd learned from my parents I dumped for a new way of thinking. There's an extreme amount of power, money, wine, and women in the sports arena. And I wanted a piece of it. So I went along with pretty much everything."

"And . . . ?"

"That's about it," Spencer said and silently asked God to forgive him. He wasn't ready to tell Cecelia the rest.

"So why did you leave?"

"I knew it would break me. You want anything to drink?" He was up on his feet, hands in back pockets, uncomfortable enough to wish he'd never asked her to open up.

"Do you have any popcorn?"

"Popcorn?" He stared at her. "Never seen you eat the stuff."

"I don't know—it just sounds good. Do you have any good movies we could watch?"

Had the woman grown donkey ears? He found himself staring.

"Sure. Lots of them. I'm outnumbered by the female gender, remember? *Twenty-Seven Dresses*, *The Bachelor*, *Ever After*, *Pride and Prejudice*?"

"How about the first one. Isn't that where some woman is a brides-maid twenty-seven times or something?"

"Yep, that's the one. Katherine Heigl and James Marsden. One hour fifty-one minutes. Seen it four times."

Spencer watched as a genuine smile slowly lit her face. "Microwave popcorn okay? The gals won't let me use my peanut oil for the good stuff, afraid of the calories they'll consume."

"I hate microwave popcorn. How about we go all out and make it from scratch. I'll work it off tomorrow."

"You kidding?" Spencer, glad for the interruption, almost danced to the kitchen before she changed her mind. "Come on, I'll show you how to make real popcorn."

Cecelia unwound herself from the sofa, and, having tossed off her shoes earlier, padded in socked feet behind Spencer. "Nice. I like the dark cherry cupboards. Stainless appliances. Black granite countertops." She rubbed her hand along the smooth surface. "Love the backsplash tiles too. Taupe with black accents. Simple. Classic."

"Yep, that's me. At least that's what the girls tell me. I like a well-thought-out kitchen plan, since it's where I do most of my work."

"Why did you want to be a chef when you could have chosen baseball, with the Cubs?" Cecelia, one hand resting on her narrow hip and the other leaning against his countertop, waited for him to answer.

"I don't know. I just loved food. My mom was the worst cook, and the girls followed in her footsteps. The only way Dad and I got anything decent to eat was if I watched Rachel Ray after school and whipped up whatever she was having. I was good enough at it that I became resident grocery shopper and cook. Everybody loved me." He shrugged. "Besides, a chef makes good money, and anytime you get paid well for something you love to do . . ."

"Exactly."

"Would you mind grabbing that large bowl from that cupboard?" He pointed. "You're in my way." Spencer placed his hands on her upper arms and moved her to his left.

"Sure." She felt her face flame like a schoolgirl's. Spencer's kitchen wasn't *that* large.

"Good, hand me that pan there before you go." He pointed and stepped aside. "It gets pretty messy. You have to let plenty of air escape so the kernels will pop big and crunchy."

"Another occupational secret?"

"Common sense, mostly." He concentrated on getting the right amount of oil and popcorn mix and waited. "When's the last time you watched a good movie?"

Cecelia shrugged. "If you'd asked me that about a play, I could give you dates and times. But a movie?" She lifted her eyes upward in thought. "Very long time."

"That's what I thought." He shook the pan as the room filled with noise.

"That smells divine." She took a long sniff. "Do you have butter?"

232

"Butter? Whoa girl, you really are going all out. You want butter, we'll get butter. Reach in the fridge. It's in the door."

She poked around and came out with a stick. "Hmmm, real butter. Want it in the pan?"

"Nope." He pulled out a thick glass measuring cup. "Put 'er in here, and we'll microwave the moisture out."

"Really? Microwave, huh? I'm learning a lot here." She felt giddy. "The whole thing?"

"Whatever you want." Spencer laughed and poured fresh-popped corn into a huge bowl. "We share around here."

"Fine with me." She shot her hand out and grabbed a fistful before he tipped the saltshaker. "This is wonderful," she purred and reached again.

Spencer, happy that they had finally shared some common ground—popcorn, of all things—slapped her hand away. "You'll be full before we get the butter on."

"Not likely. For some reason, even after our great dinner, I'm still hungry."

"Good. Now do you think you can stay awake for the movie?"

"I don't fall asleep at movies. Of course, I haven't been to one for a while . . ."

Spencer smiled down at her, careful not to push things too quickly. He liked what was happening so far. "What to drink? Water?"

"Got anything else?"

"I have a small refrigerator in my room, if you want to check the juice and pop supply."

"You have another fridge?"

"College days. Reach in from the bed and get whatever you want when you want."

"Which way?"

Spencer pointed. "Don't look at my mess in there. I hate a perfectly made bed."

"Well, finally you have a fault." She laughed.

"Oh, there's plenty more," he called to her back.

Cecelia went toward the appointed room and felt on the wall for a switch. Lights on, she noticed the huge bedroom. Posters hung in frames on one wall. Sports. Mostly football. One had something on it about Jesus, but she ignored that one. He had good taste. The walls were a light gray, and his furnishings were black. Accents were blue and green. His black and gray comforter looked thick and was hanging off the bed.

She noticed a huge black velvet upholstered headboard. A built-in book-case, floor to ceiling, also black, surrounded the headboard. She stepped forward and checked the titles. Stacks of cookbooks, zillions of restau-rant magazines, and then a small group of books on one entire shelf. Religious stuff.

She wondered who Spencer Hallman really was. She'd found out more about him tonight than any other time. Quickly, she tucked her thoughts away. She stepped to the miniature black fridge and chose a drink, then called out, "What do you want?" He named Cherry Coke, and she found one easily.

"About time you came back. The butter is done, and the movie is in. Come on." He pulled her arm, grabbing two napkins off the table as he went. "To wipe up the grease."

She gave him a side-glance. "That bad?"

"Yep. Trust me, you'll need it, especially if you add all that butter."

She eyed the butter all melted, picked up the glass cup, poured most of it into the bowl.

"Going all out I see."

"Might as well. It smells so good. And it's been an age since I've had real popcorn."

"Good. Eat up, girl."

Their eyes met, and Cecelia's need to control almost bid her to put a wall between them. Instead she took her place on the brown leather sofa and watched while he set up the movie.

Spencer scooted his chair closer to the sofa so he could eat out of the bowl and view the television without craning his neck. Still, he had to reach across the table to get popcorn.

"This is ridiculous," he muttered as he grabbed his pop, sat on the opposite end of the sofa, and plopped the can down on the end table to his right.

Cecelia didn't even try to scoot away.

Chapter 58

Two hours passed quickly. Spencer noted that Cecelia had barely uttered a word throughout the entire movie, which was very strange to him. Anytime he watched with his sisters, they didn't stop talking about who was doing what and why.

Together they had devoured the entire bowl of popcorn. Instead of speaking, Spencer glanced sideways. She was staring at the screen as the final song played and the credits rolled. Mesmerized, it seemed. Did she love the movie? Hate it?

"Did you like it?" He kept his voice low, watched her carefully. She nodded, her fists moving to rest under her chin. She looked so vulnerable. He wanted to comfort her, if that's what she needed, but she didn't give him any clue. So he waited.

"How many times have you seen this?" she mumbled through her knuckles.

"This makes the fifth time," he admitted.

"You watch movies like this with Becca and your sisters?"

"Yeah." His voice raised in question. "Does that surprise you?"

She shrugged. "I don't know. I guess I really don't know you very well, do I?"

"Well, not personally. We've done business together. Traveled to your sister's wedding."

Again she nodded. "I've never even been to your place. And you've been here, what? Almost a year?"

"Yeah. So? You've been busy, Cecelia. I didn't expect you to come calling on me. I have my life, you have yours. Nothing wrong with that. Is there?"

She didn't answer.

Spencer kept his seat and let her muse. He wasn't going to upset the apple cart now that they'd come this far.

"I guess I'd better be going." She tossed off the afghan.

"Hot date tomorrow? That guy is heading back to Italy any day now, isn't he?" Spencer knew he stepped on icy pavement.

"How did you know?"

"Girls talk." He shrugged. "Especially about good-looking, rich men."

Cecelia shook her head. "It's—we're not . . . I don't know." She let the words fall away.

Spencer slowly lifted himself off the sofa and picked up the bowl from her lap. He had nearly gone too far. He could see he was stepping into her territory and ragged at himself for bringing up the subject. He'd probably ruined a perfectly good start with his impatience.

"Bathroom?" she asked.

He pointed, first door on your right. "Just clap when you walk in."

"Why?" She stopped midway off the sofa. "You have something creepy in there or something? Turtles in the tub?"

"What? Turtles in the tub?" Now he laughed out loud.

"I used to have turtles in the tub. That was the only animal my mother would let me have. No fish. They always died."

Spencer snapped his mouth shut. "You had fish?"

"Yes we did. Didn't you?"

"No, but we had cats, which by the way I'm allergic to."

"Hmm. We had a cat once when we lived in Italy. My father adored them."

"What was your turtle's name? Or was there more than one?"

"I had four. Paul, John, George, and Ringo."

"That makes sense, you being from London."

"We had to leave them when we moved."

"In the tub?"

Cecelia felt her eyes burn. She turned from Spencer and headed for the bathroom. He heard her stumble.

"Clap!" he called out. He heard a soft clap and then the door shut.

Spencer cleaned up the living room, rinsed the dishes out, and still no Cecelia. Finally he knocked. "You okay in there?"

"Just a minute." Her voice was low.

The door opened and out came another woman. "I hurled."

"You threw up?" He was astonished. She looked fine when she went in.

"Yes. Sorry. I found a cloth and wet it. I was dizzy too. Guess I ate too much butter." She groaned.

"Here, lay down. I'll get you some ice chips."

He brought a pillow and then the ice chips. "Lay your head back. Try not to close your eyes if you're feeling dizzy. It'll make it worse."

"Okay," she croaked. "Have you got a wastebasket? Just in case," she whispered.

"Yeah, here." He put one next to her then lifted the afghan from the back of the sofa and laid it lightly over her slender body. "You've been working too hard. Better let me handle some of your concerns at the Victorian this week. I can free some time from the restaurant."

She didn't answer. He looked closer. She was asleep, her face pale. He checked her forehead for fever.

Chapter 59

"Feeling better?" Spencer eyed Cecelia when she came down to the restaurant the next morning.

"Yes. Thank you for letting me sleep in at your place. I don't think I could have moved from that sofa last night."

"No problem. Busy day?" He held her gaze, noting her colorless cheeks.

"Yes." She looked away, feeling slightly guilty. She had a date with Evan this evening. He'd called earlier with an apology for his previous behavior and that he wanted to see her before he left. She'd caved.

Spencer did not ask any more questions.

"Well, thank you. I have to get going, but wanted to stop down before I left."

A large group of clients stepped off the elevator. Spencer looked, and she was punching the button. Her upswept hair and professional suit told him everything he needed to know. It was pretty obvious Evan Wyndham was snooping around again.

He plastered on a smile and greeted his guests. "Ladies."

* * *

"In two weeks they start filming, girls." Spencer removed his face mask.

Becca, Edris, and Symond all stopped working.

"Take a break. We need to let the dust settle."

The three girls found five-gallon buckets to sit on or scrambled to the floor. "This place still looks like a wreck." Edris sighed. "And after all the work we've done."

"It's supposed to look like this. How else will Cecelia look good on the makeover show if it isn't downright ugly at the beginning?" Becca laughed.

"You're right about that." Symond sighed. "The entire place is covered in dust from the wallboard install. And look at the beautiful French chandelier. Each crystal is going to have to be washed and polished all over again!"

"It was not very smart to clean it up so early in the game, was it?" Spencer said.

"Not really." Becca snapped her fingers. "We'd better keep going. It's getting late." She lifted herself off the floor slowly. "At least the walls will be smoothed over," she assured herself and the others.

"Right again." Spence laughed as he slapped his hands against his jeans, which sent a cloud of white powder into the air. "When this project is done and the chandelier cleaned, we're pretty much finished."

"Someone's here. I heard the front door open," Edris ran.

Cecelia and Evan walked in, Edris trailing behind.

Becca and Symond shot a glance at Spencer.

"Hello, everyone. I just wanted to stop by and introduce Evan to the people who have been helping." Cecelia's voice echoed in the empty room.

Spencer noticed she looked much better than she had earlier that morning. He also noticed the scowl on Evan Wyndham's face as Spencer walked over to shake his hand.

"Evan, this is Spencer Hallman, my associate."

Spencer offered his hand and read the man's dark eyes rather than the false smile that was pasted on his face. He was a ladies' man to be sure. All the qualities were there—at least the outward ones. He looked a bit like Cary Grant, except a little chunkier.

Two minutes later, the two left. Spencer noted the man dusting off his coat sleeves as he hurried out the door.

The room was quiet. Spencer went back to scraping the walls with a vengeance. He had better get used to the idea that Cecelia would never see him as anything other than a big brother. Someone turned on a radio, and Spencer was glad. He didn't want to talk.

The girls were silent at his back. First time he could remember.

Chapter 60

Two weeks flew by at *Winnie's*. Two of Alonzo's new dishes seemed to go over well because their customer base had increased nearly nine percent, which gave the servers more tips. Chef Alonzo's name was being whispered around Chicago's other venues.

"Hey Spencer, it's me your sister. Remember me?" Symond walked into *Winnie's* early Monday morning for breakfast. "We haven't seen you around." She hugged her brother. "Table for two. Becca's meeting me." She followed him to a two-seat table in a quiet corner. "Thanks. Just what we need. We're making plans for the last-minute color choices for the accessories. The film crew is coming at the end of the week after another delay."

Spencer smiled openly.

"I've heard through the grapevine—mostly mother—that things are going well here."

"Customer count is up. By Thanksgiving we'll have two more new dishes to introduce, and we should be climbing upward of a twelve percent increase by the end of the year." He looked up and saw Rico motioning, so Spencer excused himself and hurried away.

"Becca, over here." Symond waved.

Becca came dashing up. "I've got the best idea for popping some color into those rooms, Sy." She put down her large bag and took a seat. "I've been awake half the night staring at color wheels and checking out Web sites for authenticity." She pulled out a designer magazine. "Check this out." Becca whirled the book around, her brown eyes large. "Do you think it's too much?"

"Black for accent? Isn't that a more modern look?"

"Yes and no. It is a modern look, but check out these pictures from other houses. It's there, just not so prominent as we display today. I think black lamp shades and an occasional really dark table against the silver-blue walls will look great. See, right here." Becca pointed to a magazine article touting the idea. "There was so much gold in the prominent houses of that day that it becomes too much. I think if we tone it down, it'll appear more sophisticated with black accents and not so gaudy. And still fit into the Victorian era."

"I see. Hmm . . . what does Cecelia think?"

"She has been hard to get ahold of lately, so I haven't asked her. Every time I call she seems preoccupied. But"—she shrugged—"it's okay because everything else is done except for our concept idea, and we'll have to run those past the television station's producer."

"True. Hey, we all need a break from that place."

"Can you believe we actually get to be part of this Sy?" Becca was shrieking quietly.

"I know. It is exciting."

"Cecelia knows how to put on a production, let me tell you. I've already learned so much from her. And to think I was going to stay in real estate the rest of my very boring life."

Spencer carried water glasses and greeted the girls. "Good morning, ladies. What will you have today?"

"You're waiting on us?" Becca laughed. "Since when do you have time?"

"Since I own the place and make sure each one of my special customers is well-served." He bowed at the waist.

"My, aren't we formal today?" Symond teased, glad to see her brother happy. She'd known meeting Evan Wyndham had not been easy.

Spencer waited and took their order, memorizing it without a pad.

"You remembered I love tea," Becca laughed as Spencer set down two tea bags.

"It's my job to remember."

"Well, I'm glad it's you and not me. I can't remember what I had for lunch yesterday, let alone every customer's preferred drink."

"See, the Lord has a place for each of us according to our gifts." He winked.

"Whew, you remembered what the pastor said at church yesterday. I barely heard with all the noise in my head about this color-matching stuff."

"But you did remember once I quoted it, right?"

Becca stared. "Are you able to find the good in everything?" She shook her head. "Gosh, Spencer, I give you that."

Spencer shrugged his shoulders an easy smile on his lips as he hurried away.

"Sy, could you tell me again why Cecelia doesn't go after that man?"

Laughing, Symond said, "One day when the time is right, maybe it'll become apparent to her. Cecelia isn't ready yet. She has too much on her plate right now, and that plate is gold!"

"True," Becca agreed stirring her tea. "I'm just glad you and Spencer invited me back to church. I was so angry with my father for leaving us. I couldn't understand why God could see that and not *do* something, you know?"

"I know. It's hard to understand things of this world. It's a pretty mean place sometimes."

"True enough. But as I listen to the pastor, I see more and more good in the world, Sy."

Symond smiled.

"Here he comes. I'm starved." Becca moved her teacup aside.

"You're always starved." Symond laughed again. "That's because you never sit still. You're constantly on the move, using every one of those calories you scarf down."

"Right you are." Becca quieted as she forked her eggs. "Mmm, they make my eggs just right every time."

Spencer was schmoozing with some new clients, then made his way to the table while Becca was in the ladies' room. "Have you seen Cecelia, sis?" He took Becca's seat.

"No. In fact, I was wondering if you'd run into her. She hasn't been in touch with anyone that I know of. Do you think you should check in on her Spencer?"

"I'll do it today. Mr. Wyndham went back to Italy more than a week ago, I heard."

"Well, you know more than I do. Since we finished our projects at the Victorian, I thought I'd hear from her. Even Becca has had little contact. She takes care of the paperwork for Cecelia at her place and hasn't seen her either."

"Maybe she took a vacation," Spencer mused.

"Not to Italy. Is that what you're thinking?" Symond's eyes grew large.

"Maybe she did," Spencer agreed. "Maybe she did."

"Look, I can see that you care for her. She doesn't care about the same things you do, Spencer. Please promise me you'll be careful with your heart, okay?"

Spencer looked across the table at his very wise sister and said, "You're right. I get too involved and I need to remember to let the Lord lead."

"Your heart is right. It just needs time. Let God do the work, Spencer, not you."

"Absolutely right. Thanks for the reminder. Here comes Becca. You two have a good day." Spencer patted his sister's shoulder as he hurried to greet new customers.

Chapter 61

Spencer headed to the twelfth floor and rang Cecelia's bell Saturday just before noon.

He was walking away and pressed the elevator button when he heard the door open. "What do you want?" Cecelia peeped through the crack.

"Are you sick?" he asked softly.

"Yeah, I have what's going around. You'd better not come in."

Spencer paused, then pushed the door slightly. He wasn't going to be deterred this time.

"You shouldn't be here. It's really bad, this stuff." She coughed into a tissue.

"Things could be worse," he stated. "Do you have any chicken soup?"

"No, I don't feel like eating anything. Besides, I'm flushed with fever and have no energy at all. I have to rest. We're filming on Monday."

"Step aside woman," he ordered. She did. "Chicken soup works. I'll make some, if you have anything in this kitchen," he grumbled.

Cecelia headed for her room, leaving him to the kitchen. An hour later, he barely heard her screech. "Spencer, can you come?"

He stepped into the bedroom doorway. "What do you need?"

"It really smells good. I'm surprised I can smell anything."

"I'll get you a small bowl."

He returned with a miniature bowl of hot soup on a plate. She sat upright and with the plate on her lap sipped the broth.

Spencer took a side chair. "So where have you been?"

Cecelia gazed at him through pale blue eyes.

"You've really got it bad."

"Do you think?" she mumbled and sipped another spoonful.

"You didn't answer my question, Cecelia."

"I don't have to report to you, Spencer."

"Yes you do. Real friends do that."

She cast him a side-glance. He waited.

"I've been busy with the television producer."

"Suit yourself." He stood and took her empty bowl, stalked back to the kitchen, cleaned it up, and made some hot tea with sugar and lemon.

"Drink this. I'll see you another day."

She stared at his back. She tried to speak, but nothing came from her throat.

* * *

"Spencer, Cecelia's here to see you."

It was already Wednesday, and business was booming. He set aside his jacket and went to her with white shirt untucked and loosened tie.

"Finished for the day?" she asked quietly.

"Yep. Just now, in fact. What's up, Cecelia?"

"I wanted to thank you for coming up the other day and putting up with me."

"No problem. Friends do that, remember?"

"You're grumpy today. Do you have time for a movie this evening or no?"

"You mean at my place? Or out?" he asked.

"Your place."

"Sure. Want me to make dinner—something easy on the stomach?"

"No popcorn," She almost gagged at the thought.

"No popcorn. Chicken salad sandwiches on croissants?"

"Sounds good. What time?"

Spencer checked his watch, mostly so he wouldn't show his surprise. "How about seven."

"Works for me. I'll see you at seven."

She trotted away. And Spencer's blood pressure slowed. What had gotten into her? He was ready for battle, and *she* had dissuaded *him*.

Chapter 62

Spencer checked his watch again. It was half past one and he was free the rest of the day. He changed into work jeans and an old sweat-shirt, then took off to the market for vegetables and cheeses. A stop at the bakery gave him some fresh croissants.

Humming, he carried his packages home and started chopping celery and peeling sweet onions, making enough to send some home with Cecelia. Fifties music played from his CD. His heart was happy, but tentative. He had to let Cecelia make up her own mind. It wasn't his job to change her. He set a guard on his heart, along with a prayer for strength.

Time for cookies. Her favorite were chocolate chip with pecans and oatmeal. He whipped up a batch and spent the next hour baking and taste testing. Now for a nap. Spencer found a pillow, collapsed on the sofa, and slept. Thankfully, the phone never rang. He sat up, ran his fingers through his unruly hair, and checked the clock. It was still early. He found a puzzle he had from last Christmas, set it up on a card table nearby, and picked out the edges.

Then it was time to meet Rico in the weight room. After an hour workout, Spencer came up and showered, inviting Rico to join them later. He wondered why he'd done that, when all this time he'd been waiting to be alone with Cecelia long enough to really talk to her. After a moment he realized what it was. He was not exactly excited to know if Evan Wyndham had stolen Cecelia's heart. Maybe that's why she wanted to talk to him. To tell him her *good* news.

Frustrated at his own negative thoughts, he pulled out another CD. It was David Gray's *Life in Slow Motion*. It more closely matched his current mood.

Even though Rico declined the offer, he almost wished he would have accepted. It seemed Rico had his own set of problems.

Spencer realized he and Rico's lives were very much alike. They both wanted something they couldn't have. He shared his failures with Rico, who understood completely. It was the first time Spencer had opened up completely about his past.

It was six o'clock. He paced the rooms, praying God would imbue his spirit with truth, then pulled out the vacuum and freshened the carpet. The doorbell rang just as he was fitting the machine back into the closet. It rang again before he could get there. *Impatient woman.*

"What, is there a time clock to punch?" He opened the door with those words.

"Nope, just that my hands are freezing. Do you have that fireplace on?" Cecelia shivered.

"Come in. Give me your coat. Hit the sofa—it's closest to the heat."

Five minutes later she was already cozy in the corner with the afghan.

"Smells divine in here. I'm starving."

"What have you been up to today?" he inquired and sat on the chair.

"Good news. They are giving us another week before we start the difficult scenes."

"And you're happy about that?"

"Yes. I've been under the weather lately, and I need the extra time. You haven't seen the Victorian recently, have you? They did the preliminary filming already. And we've worked with the producers to give it a fresh image. It looks really good."

"No. Lots going on at the restaurant."

"That's good," she murmured. "So what movie did you choose?"

"Thought I'd let you do that." He hopped up and grabbed several from the cabinet and handed them to her. "I'll get dinner."

"Great." Cecelia chose *Pride and Prejudice*, the most recent version with Matthew MacFayden and Kiera Knightly.

Spencer called from the kitchen. "Dinner's ready."

Cecelia eyed the table. Perfect setting as usual, right down to the butter yellow placemats and matching napkins sitting atop the navy blue table cloth. Not too formal, but classy.

"Have a seat," he gestured.

Spencer set a glass of ice water next to her plate. He always remembered. Part of his duty, she guessed. A flame danced in the orange candle in the center of the table. The pumpkin scent filled her senses. He sat two plates out and cut the bread. "There's plenty of chicken salad. Butter for your bread, if you want it. I'll pray, and we can eat."

Cecelia set down her spoon and waited.

Spencer's short prayer fell between their awkwardness and hunger. "Eat up. You need to put some of that weight back on."

"You noticed." She made a thick sandwich and ate heartily.

"Yep." Spencer buttered his bread lightly.

"So you're happy at the restaurant?" She looked across the short space into his eyes.

Spencer nodded. "Of course. Why do you ask?"

"Look, I'm here tonight to try and be friends. You were right about us being friends."

He noted her quick speech. She must have practiced the words because he knew she was not comfortable talking about feelings. "To friends then?" He lifted his glass to her.

They clinked in the quiet room. Spencer jumped up and changed the CD to a livelier one.

"Want to dance?"

"Not in the middle of dinner," She frowned.

"Miss Scrooge."

For all the fun he meant that to be, he saw the hurt look on her face. "Cece, look, I'm uncomfortable here. Can I be truthful with you?"

"Of course." She lifted her chin.

"Why did you come here tonight?" He said the words gently.

Silence. Then tears formed in her eyes. "I don't know."

Chapter 63

After the awkward meal, Cecelia had watched the movie in complete silence. *Pride and Prejudice* was a love story of two unlikely characters finding love. As the credits rolled, she picked up her coat, slipped on her shoes, and walked out the door. He didn't even try to stop her. Spencer picked up their glasses off the coffee table and wanted to crash them into the wall at full speed. What had gone wrong? He knew enough about the woman to know something was dreadfully wrong, but he could not read Cecelia, no matter what tact he tried.

* * *

The week had been especially long and difficult. Rico and his girl were getting married and moving into their new apartment all in the same weekend. Spencer had run down to the courthouse and stood up for them, then hurried back to the restaurant. Rico had become his best waiter, and Spencer had a difficult time keeping up without him. Rico was going to get a raise when he got back from his honeymoon, Spencer decided.

Hard knocking woke him from a deep sleep, and he stumbled to the door in his bathrobe.

"You still in bed on Christmas Eve? Must have been some party you had last night." Becca teased.

"No party. Just business." His voice croaked.

"Well, in that case, I'm sorry to wake you. Say, I don't want to sound paranoid or anything, but I haven't seen Cecelia for four days. She told me she was going to sign the checks, but they're still sitting on her desk. Have you seen her?"

"Not for over a week, I think. *Winnie's* has been crazy with Christmas parties."

"She left me a note, saying she'd be out and that she wanted you to clean her place while she was gone. But she didn't say where she was going. If you haven't noticed, she's been acting strange lately. Something's eating her Spencer, but I can't figure out what it is."

"Yeah, I've noticed too. Think it's that Wyndham guy?" His voice lowered to a growl.

"I don't know. She hasn't talked about him for a while. But then you know Cecelia, she keeps most things to herself unless it has to do with business."

"Yeah, I know. You say she wanted me to clean her place? Probably having his family over for the holidays."

"She mentioned it in a note...about the cleaning. Something about not wanting to worry about anything when she got home."

"Okay. I'll head over tomorrow." Spencer shoved his hands through his hair. "She's probably off with Wyndham."

"She might be, but the whole situation is pretty strange. Well, I have to get going. Mother and I are going out to a swanky place for dinner tonight."

"Uh, Did you forget *Winnie's* is closed for Christmas Eve so employees can spend time with their families."

"I said . . . someplace *swanky!*"

"Ouch!" Spencer found himself smiling.

"Then we're heading off for the Christmas play at church tonight. You coming?"

"I hope so. My family will be there."

"I'll look for you." Becca laughed and was gone.

Spencer, glad for the wake-up call, hurried to the shower. Besides the fact that he'd missed his family's annual get-together last evening, he was starving.

He came out wet and refreshed. Running his fingers through his blond hair, he stood in front of the mirror and gave up trying to manage it. He headed for the fridge. Eggs and toast. That was going to be about it for now. He hadn't shopped for days. Hoping his family had some leftovers, he called and made arrangements to come for dinner and afterward they'd head to the church.

His father had made a beef roast, real mashed potatoes, and gravy for their gathering the night before. His mother made her favorite dish—green bean casserole. That was about the only thing she could put together without ruining it. He microwaved a plate of leftovers.

Laughing, the family piled into two vehicles and drove to the church. Inside candles burned from every corner. There were whisperings, sounds of violins tuning, and children running in period clothing. One little girl, a ruffian angel from the looks of her, dragged a blanket behind her as she sucked her thumb looking for her mother.

Laughing, Spencer loved the noise and activity. He wondered how in the world he could ever think he could be with Cecelia. Although his heart hurt, he pushed down the thoughts that she was made of different stuff and their backgrounds couldn't possibly merge into a marriage.

The thought wounded his heart.

Chapter 64

Friday morning, the day after Christmas Spencer was up early, showered, and ready to clean Cecelia's place. The restaurant staff had shooed him out for the day, thinking they would likely have light business.

Whistling, he unlocked her door and called as he entered. The place was a dump. What had gone on here? Dishes with dried food sat on the coffee table. He knew Cecelia would never allow that. Two guest bedrooms were in shambles. Hurrying to the kitchen, he checked and, sure enough, bottles and cans sat on the granite countertops with full ashtrays scattered about. He frowned, tried to make sense of it all, and figured she probably had some party for her business friends she had to schmooze with. Maybe the show's producers. Maybe Wyndham's friends. At that thought, he grabbed a large garbage bag and began cleaning up trash first. He lit several candles to cover the smell of cigarette smoke. Two hours later, he was just finishing up. The place was spick-and-span. He sprayed some fragrance into the air.

Cecelia hated cigarette smoke. He wondered at the change in her. Maybe she was in some sort of situation. Trying not to borrow trouble, he stepped into her room and looked around. Her bedcover was lying helter-skelter over the bed. The lamp had been moved to the dresser, and several pillows were strewn on the floor. Maybe she'd had kids in here. They were known for messes like this. He ripped off the sheets and replaced them with clean ones. Her scent was on the pillows. The washer and dryer were already going, so he tossed the dirty laundry into the small room. Everything was in order after a good vacuum. He just had to clean her en suite bathroom. Whistling, he tossed the trash into the big bag and noticed three strips. All with a pink plus. He eyed them and knew exactly what they were. Pregnancy tests. Probably her guests. The way the room looked, he knew Cecelia hadn't slept here. Yet her scent was on the pillows.

Something in his mind clicked. He started thinking about Cecelia's behavior these last few weeks. If he knew anything, he knew women acted strangely when they were pregnant. Maybe that was it. A sense of urgency began to pound in his head. He had to talk to her. Now.

He grabbed her bedside phone and dialed Becca. "When did you say she left?"

"I haven't talked to her in four days. Count the last two days, and it's been six days."

"Any idea where she could be?"

"No. Why? You're scaring me, Spencer."

"Did she say anything about a party at her house?"

"You know, she did . . . something about Evan's friends. I think."

Spencer's heart sank. Cecelia was in trouble.

"I'm calling her sister," he said and hung up.

Fishing for Cecelia's address book—he'd seen it a dozen times on her bedside table—he poked the buttons for Edwina and stared through the long windows at the snow covered streets and the barely visible Chicago skyline.

He didn't even think about the time difference and heard Edwina's sleepy voice. "Winnie, I'm so sorry to wake you up. Have you talked to Cecelia?"

"Not for a few days. I tried to call her a couple of days ago and again yesterday. Is something wrong, Spencer?"

"I'm not sure. Did she mention anything about a trip?"

"She did say something about coming over to Italy. But I never heard for sure. She was supposed to visit us if she made it over, but she never called."

"Okay, I'm calling Wyndham."

"Spencer, what are you thinking?"

"I'm not sure. Let me try to reach him, and then I'll get back to you, okay? Sorry to wake you. I'll catch up with her, not to worry."

He paged through and found Wyndham's phone number easily. Cecelia was nothing if not organized. He dialed, heart beating fiercely. If that guy . . .

A man answered.

"Wyndham?"

"Yes," he answered gruffly.

"Spencer Hallman here. Is Cecelia there?"

"She just left."

"What do you mean she just left? It's the middle of the night over there.

"I know what time it is Mr. Hallman."

"Where is she headed?" Spencer's ire was at level ten. He forced his voice to stay calm.

"To her sister's, I think."

"You think?"

When there was no response Spencer spit out, "Thanks," and pressed the end button, then grumbled, "For nothing."

He dialed Edwina and told her it sounded like Cecelia was heading her way. "Call me the second you hear from her." Spencer slowly snapped his cell shut and began praying and pacing. Something was definitely wrong.

Chapter 65

Lord, take care of her, Spencer prayed as he knelt at her soft white sofa.

He snatched his cell and placed it in his back jeans pocket. With one last look at her clean apartment, he exited and locked the door. Things would be different from now on.

He rode the elevator down to his place, grabbed the key to the Victorian, and set out walking. Head down against the Chicago's blustering wind, he stuffed his hands in his pockets and pulled the black-and-white beanie lower over his ears. The world passed by—people laughing, taxi horns honking, red lights flashing, shoppers' arms heavy with bags. He found himself standing in front of the Victorian, blinking against the sun that was just coming from behind a cloud and wishing he was in Scotland. He unlocked the door and stepped inside.

Dodging the lighting equipment, he snapped on the light switch and looked up at the chandelier. That was one thing they'd overlooked. He went to the back porch, grabbed a ladder, and set it up. Tossing off his coat, he found a stash of cleaning rags, filled a bucket with cleaning solution, and climbed up. He couldn't bring the elements down without help, so he cleaned each crystal meticulously, constantly pressing his back pocket to make sure his cell was there.

Two hours and twenty minutes later, he stepped down, rubbed his stiff neck, clicked on the switch, and looked up. It sparkled like the noonday sun. Satisfied, he put the ladder back and placed the rags in the laundry area, then walked every room thinking about life. And material things. He wanted Cecelia to have her dream, but at what cost? Everything seemed too fixed and too set in stone. There was no room in her life for anything but her need to succeed.

Cecelia was pregnant. He knew it and blamed himself for not knowing. All the signs had been there. Her moods, the fact that she threw up that night at his place and had been sick off and on for weeks. He knew the symptoms. His sisters talked about these things all the time. He wanted to punch his fist through one of those perfect walls. The whole scenario was too familiar.

His stomach twisted, partly in anger, mostly in hunger. He grabbed his coat, turned off all the lights except the front porch one, locked up, and headed for the pizza shop. It was dark, the streetlights revealing a light snow beginning to fall. The familiar bell jingled at the door. Lights were low, and patrons were talking quietly for the most part. Why hadn't Edwina called?

He found a small corner table and tossed his coat over the second chairback. He did not want to be disturbed. Spencer pulled his cell out and set it on the table, then checked his watch. It was eight o'clock, two a.m. in Scotland. The waitress, someone new, took his order.

Tapping his fingers on the table, he thought about life. Where was he headed? Hadn't he gone after his dreams too? The restaurant. Paying off his school bills. Becoming self-sufficient. Was he any different than Cecelia?

"What have we here? Is that you, Spencer Hallman?" A female voice interrupted his dark thoughts. He looked up.

"Deep in thought, I see." She tossed his coat on another chair and sat down. Uninvited.

"As you see," he grumbled, trying to identify the face.

"Eleanor. Don't tell me you've forgotten me already."

Spencer nearly groaned out loud. His former fiancée's sister. She looked ten years older even though it had only been four years.

"Sorry, it's not a good time right now. Would you mind?" He stood.

"So I'm dismissed?" She remained seated. "Looks like you're not as much fun as you used to be. Of course, you wouldn't be. Sherry said you'd turned sour. Guess she was right."

"Yep, she was right."

"Well then." Eleanor tried to stand, obviously tipsy.

Spencer reached out a hand to steady her. "Looks like you need to go home."

Eleanor stared at him with the eyes of a lonely, lost child. She used to be beautiful. "I'll call a taxi." He reached for his cell.

"I'm not leaving." She tipped her head sideways. "You're no fun. I'll find someone else."

256

Spencer sat down hard and watched her walk away. The devil had come to call. Those days he'd thought were forgotten. One look into a face that had once been beautiful now dredged in makeup and her slurred speech brought back all the ugliness of past days. He couldn't help but wonder where Sherry was and if she'd turned out the same.

The pizza came, and Spencer asked for a box. "I'll take it with me." He dropped a generous bill on the table and walked out into the night. He'd just unlocked his apartment door when his cell rang.

He tossed the pizza box on the island in the kitchen and answered.

"Spencer, it's Edwina. Cecelia just arrived. We've been talking. It's not good, Spencer. She doesn't want me to tell anyone anything. Could you please just pray?"

"Of course, Winnie. Look I don't want you to break your confidences, but you need to let me know she's going to be all right."

"She will. It's just . . . I think I can tell you this. . . . Evan Wyndham is married. He has a wife and two daughters in Italy. He's been married ten years, Spencer."

Spencer slammed his fist on the granite and winced. "I knew something wasn't right about him."

"There's more, but I can't—"

"She's pregnant, isn't she?"

"How did you know?" Edwina was breathless.

"I found pregnancy tests in her trash. She must have found out and took off after him."

"That's exactly what she did. She booked a flight as soon as she knew. She wanted to tell him herself. She—" Edwina stopped, unable to finish. Spencer waited, his mind running wild.

"She surprised him at the address she had. His wife came to the door. It was a pretty bad scene."

Spencer groaned. "What does she plan on doing?"

"Listen, I'm so sorry, but I have to go. She's calling me, Spencer. I'll get back with you."

"Thanks, Winnie." Spencer's mind whirled.

Chapter 66

"Mr. Hallman, call for you," the new girl said quietly the next morning at breakfast.

"What?"

"There's a call for you on the restaurant phone."

"Isn't there anyone else back there who can take the order?" He shot back.

"It's not an order. It's personal."

Spencer walked to the back and snatched up the phone. "Spencer here."

"Alex Dunnegin," came the strong voice.

"Alex. Is everything all right?"

"Me wife is entailed in the business of helping 'er sister. And I am left to be the talebearer it seems."

"Well, it's about time. Women never tell each other's secrets, which is fine and good, except in cases where we guys are left out in the dark."

"Well said," Alex agreed. "But when a lass is in trouble . . . ," he began.

"Tell me all, Alex. I care about Cecelia more than you know."

"That is why I'm charging ahead. Edwina tells me you are aware that Cecelia is pregnant and the man is married."

"Yes, that's about all I know."

"Edwina has told me that Cecelia has made an arrangement to have an abortion. You've got about ten days to make your case, Spencer."

"I'm on my way. If you can sidestep it, Alex, don't mention my coming. I think it's better if I just show up."

"Good. That's what I thought ye would say. Edwina is not feeling well 'erself. She recently miscarried and willna tell her sister, as I well

258

understand. But I will not have me wife traipsing all over London. Not ta mention the fact that we have offered to keep the child if she will deliver it."

Spencer paused. "I'm so sorry about your loss, Alex."

"Aye."

Spencer could hear the sadness in his voice. "You have offered to keep Cecelia's child?"

"Aye. We have and gladly," the Scot informed him.

"And she has declined, of course?"

"She has."

"We'll see about that." Spencer made his own pronouncement more firmly the second time. "We'll see about that!"

"Safe travel, then," Alex said and was gone.

Spencer stood still for a full minute with the phone in his hand. He slowly placed it in the cradle, then whipping off his suit coat and nipping at his tie, called his staff to his office.

Within the hour, he had plane tickets for a direct flight out of Chicago to Edinburgh in the morning. A flight over the weekend was costly, but he didn't care. He had to get to Cecelia.

Alonzo and Rico would have to handle the restaurant in his absence. Spencer asked for a grocery list from the chef and attendants. He ran upstairs to Cecelia's office and grabbed two checks, signed them, and placed them in the vault. Since the beginning he had retained power to sign checks but never had, allowing Cecelia to handle the checkbook.

He ordered extra food and paper supplies to stockpile the pantry and made copies of his suppliers' phone numbers. Back upstairs he figured employee hours and wrote paychecks, then placed them in the vault. Rico would be in charge of knowing the number.

With everything covered, he bid the employees good evening and went to pack. He wouldn't need much and hoped to bring Cecelia home with him. One carry-on was set by the door. He hadn't thought about eating and figured it best to get something quick and turn in. Four o'clock in the morning would come quickly, especially if he didn't sleep well.

Spencer peeled off his clothes and fell into bed, flipped the lamp on to his right, and grabbed his Bible. He needed something to sustain him and push away the dark thoughts that tried to overpower his mind. Sin never left one alone, even after it was over and forgiven. It had ways of reaching into your psyche and reminding you of your failures.

He leaned his head against the soft headboard and closed his eyes. He knew God had forgiven him for his past mistakes. Maybe it was too hard to forgive himself. He opened his eyes, and instantly they fell on these words: *where the Spirit of the Lord is, there is freedom.* He let the words reform his mind and with difficulty shoved out the negative thoughts. Second Corinthians 3:17. He said the words aloud and memorized the passage.

What else was there to do but believe? He chose to let God work it out and closed his eyes again.

The sound of ringing intruded into his dreams. Moaning, he rolled out of bed and remembered his cell was still on the table in the living room. "Yeah," he croaked.

"Your wake-up call, Mr. Hallman."

"Thanks." He'd had enough sense to call the service desk attendant last evening. He snapped the phone closed and made his way into the shower.

He dressed grabbed a cup of hot tea, then stepped out into a windy, overcast winter day. Chicago's streets were jammed with slow-moving cars. "Ah, there will be flight delays."

"Looks like we're in for a big one," the doorman announced and smiled.

"Sure does," Spencer agreed as he waved down a taxi, stepping back from the curb to avoid the splash, then slid into the cold seat. Traffic was moving at a slow crawl as the radio confirmed there were delays at O'Hare.

Spencer paid the driver, thankful to be dropped off at the American Airlines counter. He checked in and heard the announcement — there would be a minimum two-hour delay.

Thankfully, a small shop was open at this hour. He picked up a magazine, a packaged roll and a cup of hot tea. The area was beginning to fill up with passengers who were either too late for their scheduled plane or too early for the next flight. Soon there were few seats left in the waiting areas.

Two hours later he was boarding. Three and a half hours late, but that would mean he would arrive in Scotland the next day by mid-afternoon. He called Alex to tell him of the change in arrival time.

Chapter 67

Edinburgh

The plane landed at 2:15 Scotland time. The sun was shining on the wings as they set down. Spencer had barely slept. The husband and wife sitting next to him had had words the entire time. He wished there had been more seats so that he could have moved

Spencer heard his name as soon as he exited customs. "Alex." He offered his hand.

Alex clapped him on the shoulder. "It seems we have some work to do."

"Sure does," Spencer agreed.

"Looks as though you'd be needin' some sleep first, man."

"As you see." Spencer laughed lightly. "Weather was bad in Chicago."

"That's what I heard. We'll get you some sleep, but there is one wee problem. Edwina, Paige, and I stay at the farm. Cecelia preferred to be alone at the castle, which leaves you two choices. Another room in the castle or the barn at our place."

"I'll take the room on an opposite wing. All I need right now is running water and a bed."

"Then you shall have it. But I warn you . . ."

"I know. She'll have a tizzy fit. But she'll have to get over it. She doesn't happen to be in charge here," Spencer muttered.

"Aye."

Alex clapped him on the back again.

The ride to Dunnegin Castle wasn't long enough for Spencer's eyes tired as they were. "The countryside is beautiful here even in winter."

"Aye. I am a lucky man."

Spencer heard the familiar crunch of the tires in the circular drive at the castle and leaned down to check out the view.

"You are fortunate. Edwina knows you're coming. She called to say she took her sister away so you could claim your space in time for the fray."

"Oh, there will be a fray," Spencer warned.

"Aye. 'Tis expected."

Reardon appeared. Something about him was different, Spencer noted. "He smiles?"

Alex looked up and then caught Spencer's meaning. "A woman."

Spencer's eyes danced as he nodded. "Ah. So that's it. I can only hope for the same."

"Indeed, man." Alex handed him the bag. "I'll wait here for the lasses to return. Then Edwina and I will, as your southern folk say, head for the hills."

"Sounds like a plan."

"We'll eat first." Alex headed for the kitchen. "Bertie is off with her man this afternoon."

"Whoa, so what I heard was right then?"

"If what you heard is that Claude and Bertie are a two-part, you are right. There is to be a wedding soon enough, but of course none of the men aboot the place are to know of it."

Spencer laughed out loud.

"I'm near helpless in the kitchen," Alex admitted, opening the refrigerator.

"Here, let me. I'll get something whipped up. Least I can do."

"Glad to hear it." Alex poured himself a cup of coffee and munched on a leftover scone.

After their late lunch, Alex retired to his office to make calls, and Spencer went to the library to get a book. He would no doubt be spending plenty of time in his room while Miss Cecelia threw her fits.

Soon the sound of female voices drew both men from their safe places. They met in the hall and quickly formed a plan. Not a word would be said. Spencer hiked up the stairs two at a time and saw his bag sitting next to a far door. He dragged it quietly across the threshold and shut himself in. Alex would play dumb; Spencer was to appear when he thought it safe to do so.

Spencer laid himself on the bed, arms behind his head. He heard Alex's booming voice as he hollered good-bye to Cecelia. He knew that was for his benefit. He couldn't help but laugh. The situation was a serious one, but for some reason, he felt no intensity, just peace.

He knew the proximity of his room was at opposite ends of the wing from Cecelia's. But the hall was straight from one end to the other. It was only a matter of time.

The castle was strangely quiet. The dogs had gone back with Alex in the back of the rusty truck. Spencer had heard it backfire once. It nearly threw him into a fit. He just couldn't picture the stately Alex, keeper of the castle, driving that old truck anywhere.

He heard soft footsteps. The front door creaked open and closed again. He went to the window at the end of the hall nearest his room and looked out. There she was, a tiny figure in an oversized parka, hood turned up against the wind, walking away from the castle. He checked his watch, nearly five p.m.

Should he go out and call to her? Or leave her alone? He decided on the latter. Best to give her time. He threw himself on the big four-poster and fell asleep instantly.

Chapter 68

S pencer woke to strange sounds and remembered he was in Scotland. With a quick check of the red numbers on the clock next to the bed, he saw it was after seven p.m. Slowly he came off the bed in his black sweats and stretched, then walked to the window and parted the heavy curtains. Below he could see the dim light of the circular drive. The hills were distant and undetectable through the mists. He shivered.

After a lamp was turned on, he located the switch and turned on the gas fireplace, long ago revamped for present-day guests. Warming his hands, he wondered if life might have been better in earlier ages when men cut their own wood and managed small homes and large families. The friendly skies had interconnected the world until it was mere hours before anyone could be standing on the other side of the earth.

Musing, his stomach rumbled. There was a light tapping at his door. He opened slightly, expecting to see Alex. Maybe the coast was clear.

"Bertie. You're back."

"Tea?" she whispered and slipped through the crack in the door with a small tray.

"It is good to see you, Bertie," he said, noting that she allowed the name Edwina had branded her with.

The woman set her burden on a side table and turned. "Scones and cream until dinner."

"Sounds great." He helped himself.

"Dinner's at half past seven, but I would not appear until after half past eight," if ye ken me meaning." She warned, her dark eyes serious.

"She's about the place then?" Spencer lowered his voice.

"Aye." Bertie was careful not to make noise with the flatware.

"How is she doing?"

"'Tis not for me to say," she stated, then looked around as if there were other people in the room and said in a low voice, "But sir, she walks 'round the brae and then comes to her room. Doesna eat enough to keep a bird alive and the lass speaks not a single word."

Spencer found himself leaning closer. "What should I do, Bertie?"

"Do ye love her, man?" She stared at him eagle-eyed.

Spencer found he couldn't speak. Until this moment he hadn't allowed himself to admit he did love Cecelia.

"If ye cannot answer, lad, ye don't love the lass. And best ye be then to head back to yer home and stay abroad, away from 'er."

Bertie's hands were on her hips. Spencer sensed it was not a good thing. "You're right, Bertie," he admitted, then heard the door close quietly.

Dressing in Jeans and a black sweatshirt, he pulled on tennis shoes and wondered whether he should wait to be called or just get this foolishness over with and make himself known. Cecelia was not the type to toss over one's shoulder and ride away into the sunset. He had to be forthright and wise at the same time. He took hold of the doorknob to do just that and stopped short when he heard footsteps, then a tap at his door. He pulled back his hand like he'd touched fire and stepped back.

"'Tis me."

"Bertie, you scared the life out of me." He said as he opened the door.

"'Tis safe to come down. She has gone with Edwina to the farm for the eve."

Spencer followed Bertie down the stairs while she carried the tray. He offered, but she refused, citing her employment required it of her.

"What are you cooking? It smells delicious in here!"

"Leek and potato soup."

Spencer forced himself to stand aside. The woman knew her kitchen. He respected that.

"Sit lad." She pointed, and he obeyed.

Dishes began appearing at the table. Relaxing, he sat back and enjoyed watching her familiar, quick movements. "What is your favorite meal, Miss Bertie?"

"Call me, Bertie. No Miss needed," she ordered.

Spencer smiled and picked up the spoon. "Will you join me?"

She hustled about, then turned and rather shyly asked, "Would ye mind too much? I've not partaken since breakfast."

Spencer pulled out a chair, gently pushed her into it, and went for her tableware.

"'Tis not suitable, the guest serving the servant." She started to stand.

"Sit, Bertie."

And to Spencer's surprise, she did. But her hands twisted nervously in her lap.

The two ate quietly for a few moments, then Spencer couldn't stand it any longer. "Do you mind talking while we eat?"

Bertie set her spoon down, dabbed at her mouth with the napkin. "Nay, I do not."

"Well then. Tell me about Cecelia."

Bertie pressed her lips together in concentration for a moment and then turned to look him in the eye.

"Lad, the girl is beside herself. That man . . . that man . . . well, suffice it to say, I'd 'ave taken the pitchfork to 'im!"

Trying not to laugh, Spencer agreed with her.

"She's got 'erself a problem that won't go away, no matter what she does. Fact."

"True enough."

Bertie eyed him again trying to determine how much he knew.

"I know, Bertie. A child is on the way."

"'Tis the truth of the matter," she said quietly. "Alex and Edwina have offered to take the babe," she stated, looking over her shoulder.

"Alex told me."

She sensed Spencer was on their side for she said, "Lad, how be it that ye're 'ere?"

It took him a moment to ask himself the question. "I care for her."

"Enough to marry the lass, when she carries another man's babe?"

Spencer twisted in his seat, picked up his glass, and gulped, giving him time. "Bertie, you are bold."

"Well, should we sweep the dust under the carpets?" She gave him the eye.

"You're right. There's no time for that."

"Aye. It's as I see it, lad."

"What you don't understand, Bertie, is that Cecelia has a very large opportunity to do her own television show in America."

Bertie shrugged. "And a wee child is less important?"

"Of course not. But do you see how she sees it?"

"Psssshhhh. A woman doesn't know what she needs while she's . . . she's . . . well . . . in a fine fettle," she puffed out.

"That's true."

"And a child can't be unborn after it is once here." Bertie eyed him. "Fact, lad if ye care a whit aboot the lass, ye'd best be making yer move, else there won't be a babe."

"I know." He shoved his hands in his back pockets.

"Then what's holding ye up?"

"She doesn't care for me, Bertie. She treats me like I'm her brother."

"Ah, lad, then treat 'er like a woman."

"I've tried. She doesn't see it. I can't make her love me, Bertie."

"Now, here." Bertie put down her spoon, pushed her plate back, and set her forearms on the table. "Ye march right on over to wherever she's at, and ye tell her. Don't give 'er time to sass. Just take hold o' her and let 'er know how it's gonna be."

Spencer swallowed hard. If it were that simple, he'd have done it sooner. "Yes, ma'am."

"Now there's a lad." She stood and swarmed away, grabbing dishes as she went. "Dessert is lemon pudding with cream."

"Dessert?"

Bertie brought two large bowls to the table. Spencer smiled. Bertie was simple. He ate until the spoon was scraping the empty bowl. "No need to take the paint off the dish. We have more," she scolded.

"Bring me more then." Spencer laughed.

Bertie headed for the oven. "Now there's a lad who knows what he wants."

Chapter 69

As he was finishing off the second serving of lemon pudding, the front door slammed. Hard.

Bertie and Spencer locked gazes. He felt his muscles tighten.

"Stand straight lad. This is no time to run to the back o' the line."

Spencer stood. Straight.

"Let 'er know ye're here and be done with it."

Spencer looked at the Scottish woman. Her stance, her look gave him courage.

He walked through the swinging door and met up head to head with Cecelia.

"What are you doing here? Does everybody have to be here?" she shouted and pushed past him.

"Whoa, where do you think you're going?" He reached out, snagged her arm and pulled her back.

"To my room. Let go."

Spencer held on.

"You . . . you have no right to be in my business, Spencer. This has nothing to do with you. Can't you just leave me alone?"

"No. I can't." Then, with sudden inspiration, he reached down and picked her up with his arm behind her knees. Then he realized he didn't know what to do with her.

"Are you hungry?" This was one way he could keep her busy.

"I ate a little with Edwina and Alex," she mumbled. "Put me down, Spencer."

"Bertie made some excellent dessert."

"Dessert? What is it?" she asked.

Shocked to the bottoms of his shoes, Spencer announced, "Lemon pudding with cake and cream."

"Sounds good," she answered.

Spencer turned and kicked open the swinging door, carried her in, set her on the chair he had just left, and ordered Bertie to give her dessert.

With that, he exited and took the stairs two at a time. What in the world had gotten into him, he had no clue. It must have been Bertie's look. The ball was in Cecelia's court.

He shut the bedroom door and grabbed his notepad, tossed himself on the bed, back against the headboard, and forced himself to concentrate on a list of things to do once he returned home. Then the thought struck him. What if Cecelia would come home with him and keep the baby? She would have to cancel the show. Nope, she would never do that. What was the recourse then? He could marry her, even though she had no desire to serve God. Could he be faithful enough to draw her?

That would be a big mistake. She would only hate him. So why was he here anyway? He had dashed over the ocean without any answers to the problems that existed. He knocked himself on the temple with the heel of his hand. What had he been thinking?

"Because you love her, you dope." He'd said the words aloud and kicked his shoes off.

For the next few minutes, he let his own words sink in, then heard footsteps on the wood floors. Someone was approaching. He set his glasses on the end of his nose and tried to concentrate on the list he was making.

A slight tap.

"Come in," he barked.

Cecelia stepped into his room about two feet and stopped. "Thanks for coming, Spencer."

Spencer set his glasses to the side and was about to get up when he heard her next words.

"But you can go home. Your people need you at the restaurant. I'll be fine."

He felt the ire rise inside his chest as he stood to face her. "I know where I need to be, Cecelia, and I don't need you to tell me. In case you've forgotten, I know what my duties are. For once in your life, why don't you let someone in? Or are you too afraid? Maybe you can handle all this"—he swept his arm outward—"but I don't know anyone who is so arrogant that they don't need help from someone. You have managed to set yourself up on a pinnacle high enough that many of us could never achieve. Maybe that's your claim to fame. But no one—no one, Cecelia—can do it by themselves, including you. If you are so inclined, go ahead, see if you can handle this alone, but remember one thing. You are not the only one we're talking about here. Yes, I know you're pregnant. I found your pregnancy tests while I was cleaning. And I know that Evan Wyndham is married. So let's just wipe the slate clean right now."

Spencer saw the abject sadness on her face, but he couldn't stop himself. "And furthermore, when you realize you do need someone, they may not be there for you. That's when you'll find out who you really are, Cecelia Grace Giatano. And maybe I don't want to be around when that day comes—when you find yourself alone, filled with regret, and no way can you bring back what you've thrown away. Oh, but you'll have your buildings and perhaps a vacation home on some fantasy island somewhere . . . but by then, who'll care?"

His eyes never left hers. When he ran out of words, he firmly held her gaze. He saw the blank look in her eyes and wondered if she'd heard a thing. She slowly turned and walked out.

Unable to stand still, he put on his shoes, grabbed a parka, stalked down the stairs, and slammed out the door. The evening air was crisp, and it felt good on his burning face. In the throes of emotion, he couldn't even pray.

Chapter 70

The winds blew against him fiercely until he had to lean into them to stand. But it felt good. Good to be released from holding in his emotions. Sometimes, he reasoned, things just had to be put on the table. He was tired of stepping around trying to be perfect. *No one's perfect.* He heard his own voice in the wind. It was time to stop playing games. Thus far it hadn't worked. He'd loved Cecelia from the first time they met, but he wouldn't allow himself to be taken in by her beauty like her other beaus. Which, when he admitted it, weren't that many. Very few times had he seen her go on a date.

It was usually business as usual for her. Part of the reason he was drawn to her. He knew the feeling of loneliness, of stepping out of God's will, and the pain that came from doing that. He had come back to God and now found himself in a quandary. Should he pursue her? Or leave her alone?

The muscles in the backs of his knees were screaming as he walked upward and finally stood looking out over the valley and the castle below. A light snow was beginning to fall. The stream flowed as always, but it was almost impossible to see it. Darkness had come, and he'd barely noticed. There he stood in Scotland at the top of the moors surrounding Alex and Edwina's place, wondering how he'd come to this point.

God, you are there. I know it. I just don't know what to do. Show me.

Spencer prayed the words, looked up at the stars glowing in the black sky, trying to hold himself erect as the wind pounded at him. Swirling, raging winds, just like his thoughts. Suddenly the wind caught his hood, and it flew off, forcing him to turn around to put it on. The wind at his back pushed him down the hill he'd just climbed. It was then a whisper seemed to fly through his mind, soft at first, then more powerful. *Child, don't stand against the wind. Let me do it for you.*

He wondered if he'd heard right, or was it his own scattered thoughts trying to capture him? Just as suddenly as the winds arose, they calmed. He felt the sense of not being alone there in the dark at the top of the hill. His feet slowly began the downward descent, the winds now gently pushing him. Somewhere in that moment he knew what he had to do. Nothing. God would do it. Spencer knew God *had* to do it because he knew what it was to make godless decisions and live with the results. The shame, even though forgiven, remained buried deep in his heart. When he had been lashing out at Cecelia, he had been speaking to himself.

God, forgive me.

Spencer stopped and repeated the words aloud, then slowly made his way back. He had to talk to Cecelia.

Chapter 71

Down below the lights from the castle windows were lit like a beacon in the valley of the dark hills. Beautiful as it was, it contained people. People who had problems. People who needed love. People who strived to fulfill their own dreams when they could have so much more.

Spencer made his way inside and pushed through the swinging door into the kitchen. There sat Bertie and Claude speaking in low voices and sipping steaming cups of tea. Immediately Spencer tried to exit, but he had been seen. "Sorry, I'll come back later."

"Lad, come in. Bertie and I have been idle long enough. Join us."

Any other time, Spencer would have bowed out gracefully, but he needed companionship tonight. "Thanks." He threw his coat on an extra chair and sat down as Bertie popped up.

"I'll get more scones from the oven." She hustled away.

Spencer noted the softness in her eyes.

"Here, lad." She set a fresh plate in front of him and pushed the butter and cream bowls his way.

"Ah, the winds are mighty this eve, are they not?" Claude bounced into the conversation.

"Very mighty," Spencer repeated.

Bertie poured steaming water into his cup. It seemed a godsend.

He wanted to be alone. To think. Instead he put sugar and cream in his tea, via Bertie's style, split a scone and poured cream over it. Then he plopped strawberry jam on top.

The three were quiet for too long, and Spencer looked up. "I'm interrupting, aren't I?"

Both said in their strong Scottish accent, "Nay."

"We were waiting on ye to say yer piece," Bertie said softly. "If ye've a mind to, that is."

Spencer looked down, stirred more sugar into his tea, and put the spoon down.

"I do, but I don't know what to say."

"Edwina has come for Cecelia," Bertie informed him. "Just after . . ."

"You heard then?"

"Truth to tell, lad, I was on my way up the stairs when I heard. And more truth, I didn't leave like I shoulda."

Spencer smiled at her confession.

"It doesn't matter. Truth is truth, right Bertie? And sometimes it doesn't sound too good coming out of our mouths. But we're just human. What can we do?"

"'Tis so," she agreed. "Now Claude here. He can hold onto something for a long time, it not rushing around in his mind like it does mine. I swear and declare, if I don't get it out of me mouth, I'll explode."

Spencer chuckled.

"Like an old tire with a nail in it," Claude said with a wink.

Bertie hit him on the arm.

"Relationships are hard work." The hot cup felt good in Spencer's hands.

"Now, lad, it just takes folks who are willing to give up themselves for the other."

Spencer looked into Bertie's wise brown eyes.

"You're right. But what if they don't want what you offer?"

"You can't make another want you, lad. No one can do that. But one must declare himself. That is the way of it."

Bertie patted his arm, and a look passed between them.

What he wanted was time with Claude alone, man-to-man. Then as if on cue . . .

"Well, I have to be aboot me business. Spent so much time in here with me woman, I'm behind in my duties." He laughed, scooting his chair back.

"Can I come with you?" Spencer jumped up.

"Sure, lad. I could use the help. It's been a few years since I've worked the barns."

Claude winked at Bertie, and her face actually pinked right in front of his eyes.

The two men walked out the back kitchen door, the sound of clinking china in the background. No words passed between them until they reached the barn.

Claude threw off his coat, so Spencer followed his lead. "Gotta put clean hay in the stalls and freshen the food and water tonight," he announced. "Pitchfork's right over there." He pointed, and Spencer laughed out loud. Claude turned.

"Oh, just something Bertie said," he explained. "She's one fine woman."

"That she is," Claude agreed and started his work. Spencer stood for a moment to see how he worked the pitchfork, tossing new hay down over the first stall floor

"First time I've ever worked in a barn," Spencer said. "Feels good."

"That's because I had the stalls cleaned out a'fore ye came." Claude's eyes danced in the lamplight.

Spencer laughed out loud. "Guess that's the truth for just about everything. Someone does the stinky work, and someone else comes along and does the easy stuff."

"Aye." Claude said. A half hour passed while they labored.

"You care about that lass, lad?"

Spencer stopped and noted Claude kept on working so he did, too. "Yes I do."

When they were finished, Claude set his pitchfork up on the nail where it came from and brushed the hay off his arms. "Since ye ain't a Scot, ye may not take kindly to me words. But if ye want that gal, ye'd best step up to it. That's what a Scot would do if he was after 'is woman."

Spencer looked him in the eye. "Thanks, Claude." Claude nodded and with a few words dismissed himself. Spencer heard the man's car pull away.

Chapter 72

Spencer stepped outside and secured the barn door. The winds had died down; he spotted a tiny sliver of moon. Marveling at the beauty of it and seeing the full circle barely identifiable in the blackness, he felt certain things would turn out all right.

What he needed now was a bath. He checked the back kitchen door, hoping Bertie had not locked him out. He shook the hay off his coat and stepped inside, left his shoes at the door.

A low light in the kitchen revealed he was alone. He turned an ear and thought he heard someone about. He walked through the kitchen and slipped up the stairs. It was a shame to have all these empty rooms. Cecelia could turn this place into a veritable B&B in no time.

There was light invading the hallway near his room. "Bertie," he called out.

She appeared, her hand over her heart. "Lad, ye don't sneak up on a Scot."

"Sorry, Bertie."

"'Tis sorry ye *should* be," she spouted, then calmly said, "Bath water is all ready. See that ye leave yer boots at the door." She looked down at his stockinged feet. "Where are yer boots?"

"Left 'em at the door."

"Good lad." She patted his shoulder as she passed. "Good eve to ya."

"Good eve, Bertie." He bowed at the waist and saw her eyes twinkle.

She clicked the door closed, and he headed for the bath. Some soft scent he couldn't identify permeated his senses. What a welcome sight— warm, steamy bathwater. He tossed his clothes into a pile and slipped in slowly, groaning as he settled into the water. Rolling a towel behind his neck, he lay back and couldn't remember feeling so good. His eyes closed of their own will, and he knew why Edwina had come back to Alex Dunnegin.

* * *

For three days Spencer walked the hills alone with God. His thoughts rumbled back and forth from guilt to rage to humble realization he was just a human being. Had his motives been true? Or had he acted out of his own guilt? Would God bless a union such as theirs? Whose job was it to save the baby and Cecelia from what he thought would be her undoing? Was it his? Or was he just trying to make up for his failure to save his own child?

By the third day he knew the answer.

Cecelia had stayed hidden at the farm which she hated, because she did not want to see him. Thoughts fought for preeminence in his mind. Reality struggled with faith in knowing God would work it out. *You don't need me to fix this, Lord. I'll do whatever you want.*

Spencer pulled in a deep breath. He'd finally let go. Now he must find Cecelia.

Chapter 73

Spencer drove the rental car into the circle. Claude had driven him into town.

He heard voices as he opened the front door to the castle. Who would be about on this cold, blustery day? He'd heard locals discussing the fact that there had been little snow last year. And that they were in for a furious winter. Spencer knew it was time to leave, but he felt inclined to visit his Aunt Phoebe in Edinburgh first. Then he would talk to Cecelia.

Alex appeared in the foyer, Paige after him, and then Edwina. Spencer expected Cecelia to be next. "Aye, we have been wondering aboot ya. Snow is going to fly on these hills, so ye'd best prepare." He slapped Spencer on the shoulder. "I see ye've a rental out front."

Spencer was about to acknowledge Alex's comment when Paige ran and jumped into his arms. He'd barely had time to catch her. "Now what will you do, lass, with snow covering the ground?" he teased.

"We're going to sled," she announced and hugged him.

Spencer held her close and then put her down when she squirmed to be set free. The gal didn't stay in one spot a second longer than necessary. Tears popped into his eyes. Edwina saw and moseyed up and patted his shoulder.

Alex was directing his daughter to get her boots and coat and they would go out to the barn and retrieve the sled. The door slammed hard, Paige choosing to take the longest walk around the front of the castle to the barn rather than the short distance through the back. Alex chose the short distance. Spencer smiled and sloughed off his coat.

"You've been out walking."

Spencer gazed at Edwina. "Yep. Thinking."

"Would you like some tea to warm up?"

"Sounds good."

Edwina brought cups to the table. "Spencer, I know you're struggling. Can I help?"

"I wish you could, Edwina. But it's out of my hands. All I can do is declare my feelings; she has to make up her own mind."

"It's hard, isn't it?" she mumbled. "To know what to do, I mean."

Spencer pulled in a deep breath. "I'm going to visit my aunt in Edinburgh, have a talk with Cecelia, and head home."

"I see." Edwina bit her bottom lip.

"Try not to worry, Winnie. I know it'll work out. I've spent the last couple of days praying and walking these hills."

His smile, sad but strong, encouraged Edwina's heart. "I won't. I've learned worry doesn't help at all except make you crazy with it. I spent so much of my life worrying about things that didn't really matter and clueless to things that did."

"You've changed."

"Yes, I have." She paused, then said, "Spencer, if you have something on your mind, you can trust me."

Her sincere eyes and quiet voice nearly caused him to dump all his past failures on the table right there and then. The only thing that held him back was the fact that she had enough to deal with at the moment. He would not be responsible for placing more stress on her.

"Alex said you two would take the baby if she would carry it?"

"Yes, it was Alex's idea," she whispered, her eyes shining with tears.

Suddenly Spencer found himself standing. "Listen, I need to see my aunt. I think I'll drive up there this evening."

"Of course." Edwina knew that look of pain. She'd only recently experienced it herself. "Would you like me to call ahead and tell her you're on the way?" She stepped to a drawer and snagged a piece of scrap paper.

Spencer repeated the number. "Thanks for understanding," he said, pulling on his coat.

"You're welcome," she whispered, but Spencer was already passing through the swinging door.

Chapter 74

Edwina was still standing in the kitchen praying for Spencer when she heard the front door open.

"Did you forget something, Spencer?" She hurried out.

"It's me," Cecelia announced. "Where's he going?" she asked. "Spencer was pulling out onto the main road as Mr. Gillespie was pulling in. He didn't even notice us."

"He's got a lot on his mind, Cece," Edwina stated quietly.

"What in the world has he got to worry about? It's me who's in trouble, not him."

Edwina was slightly disappointed in her sister's words. "It's so cold. Want to sit by the fire in the library with a cup of tea?"

"That does sound wonderful, Ed, but nothing to eat. I couldn't swallow a thing."

"Okay. Snap on the fireplace switch, and I'll be there in a minute."

Cecelia did her sister's bidding and chose the large fabric-covered chair, avoiding the cold leather sofas. She pulled the knitted afghan from the back and covered up, her knees pulled up tight. She thought about Spencer's apartment, the afghan, the leather sofa where she'd slept one night, not having a clue why she had hurled.

He had been so kind. She wondered why she couldn't let Spencer get close. He was a gentleman. A family man. Spencer's kiss had been so tender the day of Edwina's wedding, but it confused her. Why couldn't she let her guard down with him?

What does it matter anyway? she scolded herself. She was a modern woman with modern ways, and her dreams were about to come true. After she got rid of this problem, she would be back to herself. No more morning sickness and everybody staring at her like she had some sort of unnamed communicable disease.

Her mother had two abortions—at least that's all she knew about. Cecelia wondered why she had not aborted her. She shrugged. That's just the way life was.

"Careful, it's really hot, Cece." Edwina handed her sister the saucer.

"Thanks."

Edwina tipped her teacup to her lips after settling in the chair opposite her sister. They both stared at the fire for long minutes.

"So, you're going with me right?" Cecelia asked. "To the clinic."

Edwina hesitated, setting her cup into the saucer and hearing it clatter slightly. Why was she so nervous? "I won't be going, Cece."

"Why ever not?"

Cecelia was staring at her. "This one time *I* need *you*, you can't come?"

"I can't this time. Alex won't allow me," she said softly.

"Since when?" Cecelia shot back. "I need someone to drive me there and back. You know I can't drive afterward."

"I didn't know, Cece."

"Oh, what? Since you've never had an abortion, you're Miss goody two-shoes now? I thought you believers cared about people. That you weren't supposed to judge."

"We do. I do care about you Cece…you know that. Edwina pulled in a shaky breath. "It's just that . . . well, I have an issue of my own."

Cecelia tossed off the afghan and stood. "What? You can't be associated with me if I have this done?"

"Sit down, Cecelia," Edwina stated firmly.

Cecelia did.

"Alex will not allow me to go because I miscarried last week." Edwina hated the tears that sprang to her eyes.

Cecelia stared at her as though she was daft.

"Miscarried?" she repeated.

Edwina nodded. "I didn't want to tell you."

Cecelia didn't know what to say, so she just stared at her sister.

Edwina pressed her fingers to her mouth and let Cecelia process the information her own way.

"Why didn't you tell me sooner?"

"Would it have mattered?"

"Of course." Cecelia pulled the afghan around her shoulders, stood, and walked to the window.

Two long minutes passed.

"I'm sorry, Ed."

The quiet was interrupted with a loud bang and the familiar sound of Paige's boots clip-clopping across the floor. She and Alex were inside. A few minutes later Alex stuck his head in the door, saw the situation, winked at Edwina, and shut the door behind him.

"Why didn't he just come in?" Cecelia grumbled. "Everybody acts like I'm some kind of odd bird. I made a mistake, a huge one, and I'm going to take care of it. Is that so bad?"

"Cece, you haven't said a word about your hurt. You loved Evan Wyndham, didn't you?"

Her sister turned from the window. "What makes you carry on so, Ed? Of course I did. I haven't given myself to every man I meet you know. I'm sure all of Chicago thinks I do. But if you want to know the truth, he's the first man I've been with."

Edwina was surprised. She never judged her sister, but she'd wrongly assumed there had been other men.

"I trusted him. He offered me the world, and . . . I believed him."

Edwina heard her sister's voice lose control and went to her. "I know you did. I know you did." She gently encased Cecelia in her arms.

Cecelia stood firm for a few moments then with slow movements laid her head on Edwina's shoulder and began to cry softly. "I wanted him to be what I needed."

Edwina held her close, and her tears fell onto Cecelia's shoulder. "Every woman needs that and believes that," she whispered.

"Well, it worked for you. But it sure didn't work for me."

Cecelia's words hit her hard. She couldn't think what to say in response. Everyone made choices, and Cecelia's had come back to hurt her. What could she possibly say that could comfort her sister? *Lord, help me know what to do.*

No words came to her lips, so she held her. Each of them with different dreams.

Chapter 75

Cecelia stayed in her room at the castle since Spencer had gone to his aunt's. She was glad for the reprieve. The date for her appointment was getting closer, and she felt certain this was the path she should take.

By the third day Bertie's constant presence irritated her. But then, everything did these days. The fact that Edwina had kept her miscarriage a secret hurt. The fact that morning sickness ate up her desire to walk on the hills or even enjoy food. The fact that Spencer was so distant. But he had tried to talk to her, and when she thought about it, she knew she had been hard as the stone walls that dotted Scotland's countryside.

It was all she knew. To block out anything that hurt too much. And when she had given herself to someone she thought loved her, the world had taught her a familiar evil. Rejection. At the root of her core. She gave love, and it bit her back. Maybe that's why her mother had chosen the same path Cecelia was about to choose. And she had promised herself she would never do what her mother had done.

Wandering about the place, she climbed the third-floor stairs into the sewing room. Bits of fabric still lay over chairs. A tiny ballerina outfit lay on the table for Paige. Dancing classes were starting in a few weeks. She had heard Paige's declaration half a dozen times. Spencer had listened each time like it was brand new information. Cecelia's heart pinched. She wished he'd come back. She needed someone to talk to.

Evening was settling in again. She heard a muffled noise and went to the window. Spencer.

Her heart flip-flopped as she watched him get out of the car and stand looking out at the view. Big flakes of snow danced by the window, and soon Spencer, who hadn't moved, was covered in white. She waited.

He seemed stuck to the spot, his hands shoved deep in his pockets, shoulders hunched against the wind.

Defenses began to rise in her mind. He would come in sputtering about her condition and guilt-tripping her, no doubt. Something she did not need right now. Back and forth her thoughts fought as if she and Spencer had drawn swords and were fighting to the death.

Something drew her away from the window. It was the sound below. While she was musing, Spencer had come in. Slowly she descended the stairs from the third floor and walked to her room and shut the door. With a long look in the mirror, she saw herself for the first time. Her hair was falling out of the ponytail, no makeup. She was sick to her stomach and tired. Tired of everything.

What did Spencer see in her anyway?

She heard his steps as he came up, and the door click shut to his room. More than anything she wanted to see him, but her stubbornness held sway.

While she was thinking, she heard his door again and his footsteps as he descended the stairs. What if he was leaving? She panicked and ran after him.

He looked over his shoulder when he saw movement.

"Are you leaving?" she cried out.

"No. Are you?" He smiled gently.

Cecelia stepped back. Something was different about him. He was calm and self-assured.

"Hungry?"

"Can't eat a thing," she murmured, struggling with her thoughts, hands fluttering aimlessly.

"Me either. My aunt may be elderly, but the woman can cook. She tricked me into coming to see her, you know."

"Really?" Cecelia felt her heart calm. "How did she do that?"

"Well, when Symond called her and told her I was here in Scotland, she said she was ill and that I should get over there right away."

Cecelia felt a smile creep to her lips.

"She was fit as a fiddle."

"So you stayed three days to make sure?" Cecelia was in now.

"Oh yes, she had 'several occurrences,' you know. Tipsy, forgetful, unable to walk."

"Ah."

"But she could whack me with that cane of hers and not miss a beat."

284

"She whacked you?" Cecelia's hand was over her mouth.

"Couple of times. All in fun, but I noticed when she used her cane to tap each shoulder to declare me an English gentleman, she didn't even waver on those *weak* legs."

Cecelia laughed, noting Spencer's merry blue eyes.

"So what's been going on here?"

"Not much. I've been here by myself since you've been gone."

"Peace and quiet then?"

"Too much." She knew her voice wavered.

"Listen, Cece. I've been wanting to talk with you for a long time." He put his hands up in defense. "Not to change your mind. I have some confessing to do of my own, if you'd be willing to listen."

Cecelia felt her ire rise, then fall. She wasn't about to be guilt-tripped again. "All right."

Spencer heard the hesitation in her voice.

"Let me get rid of my stuff here. She sent me home with things to give to my sisters. I'll meet you in the library."

"I'll start the fire," she said and hurried off, glad to have company.

Within ten minutes, they were sitting by the fire in the same two chairs she and Edwina had occupied.

Several minutes passed as they stared into the flames. They were dancing off the walls creating a strange atmosphere, yet warm and inviting.

Cecelia spoke softly. "Edwina miscarried last week."

"I know." He said quietly, his eyes never leaving the fire.

"You knew?"

She looked hurt and so vulnerable. He hesitated. Should he speak the way he intended?

"You know Evan is married?" she whispered, staring into the fire.

"Yes," he admitted. "Alex told me."

She nodded.

"Cece, I came here to tell you about my past."

"Why would you need to do that?" She gazed at him then back at the fire.

"I want you to know the real me."

"Okay." She shrugged. "The floor is yours." At least he wasn't going to lecture her.

Spencer leaned forward and put his elbows on his knees, then gave her a look. She gave him her attention.

"Remember when I told you there were two years in my past that I was not proud of?"

"Mm-hm."

"The pictures you saw in my room when I was a Cubs player—it started then. I had been raised in church my entire life. I dated a girl in college whose father saw promise in me. He was connected enough to get me on the team. Bottom of the list, but I was on the team. I thought my dream had come true. I could hardly wait to get the chance to show them what I could do. And I did pretty well. Thing is . . . I got involved with this girl. Left all my sense behind and got myself and her in trouble."

Cecelia's eyes grew large, and she had to force herself to act normal.

"This is not easy to admit, but I was drinking heavily, into the girls, and pretty much went along with whatever the guys were doing, leaving my conscience behind. This went on for two years. Then I found out. . . ."

Cecelia watched him struggle. He looked up once, she knew, to gauge her response.

"The girl I was dating at the time got pregnant..." Pause. "But she never told me. A few months later one of her girlfriends was drunk and told me what a jerk I was. I didn't even know what she was talking about. Sherry was afraid to tell me. I *was* a jerk back then. She got an abortion."

He stopped and hung his head. Cecelia's heart beat furiously. She wanted to comfort him, but couldn't move.

"I think this is why I've been so hard on you." He looked up and locked eyes.

Cecelia couldn't speak.

"It was a girl. She would be about Paige's age now." He gaze dropped.

"I'm sorry, Spencer." Cecelia heard herself say.

He nodded but didn't look at her now, just kept staring at the floor. Then she saw tears plop down onto his hands.

Instantly she was out of her seat, kneeling in front of him. "I'm so, so sorry." She lowered her head onto his hands and could feel his tears fall into her hair.

Spencer's hand moved to cover her head.

"I . . . I lost something I can never get back, Cecelia. I just didn't want you to suffer the same thing. What I know now is that you have to make your own decisions. I won't stand in your way. God won't either. He'll let you do whatever you need to do. But I want to tell you this—"

He stopped, and Cecelia looked up. She felt both his hands on her cheeks and saw the tears in his eyes as he said, "Whatever you choose to do will affect the rest of your life. It won't go away like a bad dream. It will keep haunting you until the day you die."

His gaze kept her eyes locked onto his, then spoke again.

"I saw Sherry's sister a few weeks ago, and she said Sherry had been married a couple of times and was on the outs again. I could have given her a life, if I would have known. That's why I was so hard on you. I resented you because you have a choice. I guess maybe I thought I could walk in and save you from your hurt, but that would be helping me instead of you."

Cecelia's heart dropped into the pit of her queasy stomach. She sensed he was backing away from her. Just when she was walking toward him.

He dropped his hands and stood. "I'm sorry for judging you. I had no right."

Chapter 76

Cecelia, still in shock, heard the door click behind her. What he had just shared could not possibly be absorbed in her mind. Spencer? A father? No wonder he held Paige so close. Every time he picked her up, he remembered his own daughter.

She buried her face in her hands and wept for Spencer's loss. For her loss. *Why is the world so full of evil? Why do we have to pay for every little thing we've done wrong? Why did God, if there was one, have to be so . . . so . . . hard?*

Everything was such a mess. The one solid stone she could stand on was her business sense. *That* she owned. *That* was safe. Swiping her fingers across her eyes, she stood. Life was hard. But she was harder. Her mother hadn't suffered from two abortions. She never talked about them. Never even let them break her stride. She was still working as an actress on the stage. That had to count for something.

She would take care of the problem. She wasn't Spencer. She wasn't Edwina. She was Cecelia Grace Giatano, and she knew what she had to do. Even if she had to do it alone.

* * *

Spencer packed his things to keep his mind from working. He had told Cecelia the truth about himself. Finally. And he wouldn't blame her for not looking to him for any kind of understanding. He'd let himself down and her too. He was not God. But one thing was sure. He wasn't going to let her walk into that abortion clinic without knowing the consequences. That was all he could do. And he'd done it.

He caught up the new suitcase he'd bought in Edinburgh after his Aunt Phoebe had given him so many items to haul back home to his mother and sisters. He had laughed, thinking he'd need to put "fragile, handle with care" on it because the woman had warned him within an inch of his life that these crystal vases and ancient dishes had better get to the girls in one piece since they were more than one hundred years old. About as old as he felt right now, He wrapped them in his undershirts for travel safe.

Cecelia must have been shocked because he didn't hear anything except the click of her door down the hall. She had nothing to say to him.

Everything was packed and ready. Spencer made his way down to the kitchen to look for Bertie. She was nowhere to be found. It was the weekend, so perhaps she and Claude had plans. He wished he and Cecelia could have met each other as friends. He was her house cleaner, business partner, and everything but what he wanted to be.

Perhaps things would have turned out differently if he'd acted more like a man. It was clear Cecelia thought him beneath her. Or maybe, like him, she was hiding her heart. Shrugging, he set the teapot on the stove and turned on the gas. The kitchen's low lights felt good. His eyes burned.

He carried the cup to the library and sat in a tall-backed leather chair that gave him a good view of the outside. The footlights came on at night and swathed everything in soft whiteness within a thirty-foot range. He saw movement and leaned forward. Claude and Bertie were coming toward the house. The snow created a mirage, and he smiled as they stopped and shared a quick chaste kiss as though someone might be watching them.

Love was everywhere, but he had been so foolish. He should have been there for Sherry, and he'd failed. Would he fail Cecelia too? Somehow he couldn't think like that and got up, set the cup on a side table, and searched for a book. He would get no sleep tonight.

Besides, he had one more thing to say to Cecelia before he left in the morning.

Two hours passed, and he heard nothing from above. It was late, perhaps too late to talk with her. But he would not leave without doing so. He stood and stretched and walked up the stairs. There was a light under her door, so he knocked gently.

She opened the door, and he saw she was drowsy. Obviously he'd woken her. "Sorry, I just wanted to let you know that I'll be leaving in the morning early. Didn't want you to be surprised."

"You're leaving?" she mumbled. "Tomorrow?"

"Yep. Got to get back. *Winnie's* won't last . . ." He started to laugh, but the laughter died in his throat.

"Oh." She nodded.

Spencer sensed she wanted to say more, but didn't. "Well then . . ." He pushed the door open, and she didn't resist. "A hug before I go?"

Oddly, Cecelia stepped into his embrace, and he held her close. So close he wanted to swoop her up and tell her that he loved her. Suddenly he knew it needed to be said.

"Cecelia, God loves you and . . . I love you. I have for a long time."

He held her in his embrace for a long minute, kissed the top of her head, then stepped back and saw the tears rolling down her cheeks. He couldn't abide them and knew he had to get out of there before he ran ahead and tried to play God again. He'd said the words. It was time to walk away and let her make her choices. "I'll see you when you get back."

With that, he left, his steps heavy as rocks.

Chapter 77

Spencer had been holding her up, but he'd left so abruptly she hadn't had time to steady herself. He'd said he loved her. She had pushed him away so many times and was pregnant by another man. How could he possibly love her? Slowly she pushed the door shut and melted to the floor sobbing. She was alone, truly alone.

* * *

Spencer balked at God all night. "Lord, are you sure you want me to leave? What if she . . ."

The memory of the sound of her door closing told him he'd done all he could.

He'd hardly slept. Shoving a hand through his hair, he rolled out of bed with a groan, and finished his morning routine. Once dressed, there was no reason to wait; he grabbed his two bags just before daylight and crept down the stairs, locked the castle door, and shut it firmly behind him. It was up to God now.

It was too early for his flight, and he had to see Alex and Edwina and explain to them what had transpired. He owed them that much. He pushed the snow off his car and drove to the farm. Spencer banged the knocker on the front door. Lights lit the small farmhouse, so he knew someone was up.

Bertie came to the door. "What in the world are you doing here?" Spencer said before he could think. "I was wondering what happened to you."

"Ya missed yer bath service, did ye?"

"I sure did." He welcomed Bertie's voice into his soul.

Bertie leaned closer and whispered, "Alex thought it would be best to leave the two o'ye alone in the castle. I came for me things last night so I could stay here." She winked.

Bertie had no clue that all of her efforts had been in vain. She'd find out soon enough.

"Alex here?"

"In the study. Edwina's still abed, but the little one is up and hopping around. Sledding season ye know."

Spencer smiled and found Alex's office and knocked.

"Spencer. Up early this day?" Alex greeted him. "Come in man."

"I'm heading back home, but I wanted to stop in and let you know how it went."

"Sit," Alex ordered and pulled up his own chair. "So, did the stubborn lass hear ye out?"

"She did. Only things didn't go like I hoped. She has to make up her own mind, Alex. If I sway her, I'm forcing my judgment on her."

"Did ye tell her ye care for 'er?"

"I did, but this time I waited for her to respond. And she didn't." Spencer looked down at his hands knotted together.

"Edwina and I will pray. Sometimes things don't go the way we want, but the Lord has a way in the end. I was where ye are now, just a short time ago. I almost married the wrong woman. So I won't judge, but I do know one thing. It can look like things are heading for bad when they are heading for good. If ye'll have faith . . ."

"You're right, Alex. That's why I'm leaving. I've said and done all I can. I have shared my past with her, told her I loved her."

"All ye can do." Alex dropped his head.

Spencer stood. "Will you let Edwina know? Give her my best?"

"Aye." Alex stood.

"Then I'm off." Spencer shook Alex's hand, then turned to go.

Suddenly he was hit headlong with a small body. "Spencer, can you go sledding?"

Spencer lifted her up, stared into her brown eyes, and laughed. "Not this time, Paige. Maybe another time. I'm off to the States."

"Again." She pouted and wriggled out of his embrace. "Everybody's always going over." She gave her father a look.

"I will not be leaving, lass," Alex answered her unasked question. "Just Spencer, but Lord willing, 'e will be back." Alex saw the relief in his daughter's eyes.

Spencer cleared off the vehicle's windows. He turned in the circular drive and headed toward the main road.

Negative thoughts invaded his mind. He wanted to be sad, but suddenly realized the folly of being in love. Pure madness. Man was so fallible. The wipers swished back and forth reminding him of the relentless struggle to keep going. He'd done all he could.

Chapter 78

Cecelia walked slowly up the stairs much later that morning. Spencer was gone. Edwina would not be able to accompany her. She was alone.

Her feet took her straight to Spencer's room. The bed linens lay crumpled where he'd slept last night. She knew now Spencer was her friend and that he loved her. Now he was gone. Just like every other man in her life. Why had she chosen a man who used her when Spencer was there all the time? She had thwarted his attempts with her foolish dreams and ideas.

She had no answers, tossed herself across the bed and sobbed. She'd held it in as long as she could manage. She wept for herself, for her loss, for her shame and embarrassment. She had let herself down. And now the bitter results were there for everyone to see. She buried her face deeper into the pillows when the scent of Spencer reached her senses. And she wept more bitterly.

Sharp stinging thoughts raged in her mind. How could she have been so foolish? When had she failed? What started this whole scenario? She shook her head, not knowing the answers. The only thing she knew was that in three days she would be heading to London to take care of the problem she herself had created. She had friends there. Surely someone would take her in for a few days. Sitting up and with a vicious sweep of her hand across her cheeks, she wiped away the tears. It was time to stop crying and get up and do what she knew she had to do. There was no other way. She straightened her clothes and left the room more determined than ever.

She showered, called Edwina, and asked if Reardon might be had for a ride into Edinburgh. "I need a rental car, Ed," she stated flatly.

"Just a moment, Cece, let me check with Alex."

Cecelia tapped her fingernail on the window ledge as she stared out over the snow-covered hills and made her plans. First stop would be to several upscale boutiques in Edinburgh to buy some new clothes to make herself feel better and then arrange for the seven hour drive to London where she would do more shopping, get this thing over with, and head home. Simple.

"Reardon will be there in an hour."

Cecelia heard the reticence in Edwina's voice. "Thank you. I do appreciate it. Once I have my rental, I won't be needing his services again. I've arranged to fly home from London."

"You have? I thought you'd be coming back here so I can take care of you, Cece."

"Don't sound so worried, Ed. From what I've heard from my friends, it's no big deal. I'll stay with one of my friends in London. I just thought it best to let you and Alex get on with your lives. You don't need to worry about me. My appointment is Friday. Weather is supposed to be a little warmer and sunny by then. I'll be fine. Besides I'll be back tonight, I'm just going to Edinburgh for the day."

"Cece, I'm coming over."

"No, you're not, Ed. You're in the middle of your classes with Paige and you need to rest. I can take care of myself."

"I know you can, Cece. You've proven that. It's just that . . ."

"What, Ed? You want me to have the child and give it to you and Alex?"

Edwina paused and prayed for wisdom. It sounded so awful the way she said it. "Would you think about it? Please, Cece?"

Her sister's soft voice nearly crumbled the reserve she had only recently built up. "I have. The answer is no, Ed." she said more harshly than she intended.

Silence.

"Well, say something. You asked. I answered."

"I know. I just wanted to be sure."

"Well, there you have it." Cecelia sent the words flying over the line. "Now could we please move on?"

Edwina said, "As you wish, Cece."

"Exactly. Now I need to get ready.

"I love you, Cece."

"I know, Ed."

Edwina heard the phone click. It was time to pray.

Chapter 79

Cecelia picked up her rental and shopped the afternoon away, then decided she would go back to the castle, pack her things, and spend tomorrow night in Edinburgh. She could drive up to London Thursday and spend the night there. *I can handle my affairs without Alex and Edwina breathing down my back . . . neck . . . whatever.*

With her new purchases packed away, she took one last look around the castle. Suddenly she didn't want to leave. Not even Bertie was around these days. Edwina had informed her that Bertie left an hour ago on holiday to Switzerland.

Cecelia wondered if Bertie and Claude had gone off to be married. She nixed that thought and forced herself to concentrate on the Victorian. She would be right where she wanted to be, if this new design show was a success. It would kick her out into the world for everyone to see. Then, and only then, would she have everything she'd ever wanted.

At least that's what she told herself as she dragged the last suitcase down the stairs. Thankfully, she hadn't had to smell Bertie's cooking coming from the kitchen this morning or she might have hurled. Nerves. That's all it was. Soon it would all go away.

Up the flight of stairs one more time, she stopped at the top to catch her breath. She wasn't used to hauling her own luggage. Or being out of breath.

The door to Spencer's room was open, the light from his window grazed the wood floors turning them a bright orange. She felt drawn and walked slowly, heels clicking and echoing in the quiet castle. Standing in the doorway, she closed her eyes and let the sun warm her face. The bed was still crumpled, and she sat on the edge and smoothed her palm over the sheets. There was a paper on the side table. She hadn't noticed that before. She picked it up and read. It was Aunt Phoebe's address in

Edinburgh. She started to toss the paper in the wastebasket and stopped, stuffed it into her pocket, and lifted her body off the bed. With one last look around to be sure Spencer hadn't forgotten anything, she walked out, went down the stairs, and drove away.

Her good-byes to Edwina had already been said earlier. No need to stop at the farm. It was time to get on with her life. Cecelia pointed the car toward Edinburgh. Knowing she would not be back for some time due to the demanding schedule of the show, she meandered the streets and window-shopped. She found herself standing in front of Larceny. She gazed at the door, desiring to step inside for another look, and decided against it. Her Birkenstocks took her away from the memory.

She stepped into her favorite store, Edinburgh Woolen Mill. There she purchased several Scottish scarves, sweaters, and gloves with tartan designs. As she reached into her pocket for her keys, she found Aunt Phoebe's address in her hand. She started to stuff it back in her pocket, but for some strange reason felt compelled to pay a visit to the elderly lady.

Slowly Cecelia walked back to Princes Street and retrieved her car. She would have to buy another suitcase to haul everything on the plane if she didn't stop shopping. Stuffing the packages into the backseat, she stepped into The Tea Shoppe and asked directions. Several miles out of town, two turns, and a cozy tree-lined street, the woman said.

Twenty minutes later the rental was parked in front of a large brick house in an exclusive part of town. Cecelia could imagine herself buying up houses and turning them into B&B's for tourists. Europeans had enjoyed them for years. Her mind whirled at the thought.

She tapped on the ornate door, noting the elegant *R* on the knocker.

An older woman with a white apron appeared at the door and inquired as to her purpose. "My name is Cecelia Giatano. I am a friend of Spencer Hallman. He is Miss . . ." Cecelia felt her face warm at the realization she didn't even know Aunt Phoebe's last name.

"Please step inside out of the winds." The gentle voice was inviting. "Mrs. Reynard is taking tea."

Cecelia gazed at the pictures in the foyer. Royalty it seemed. Yet the place reeked of antiquated castles and matriarchal sentiments. She leaned closer to the oil painting of a woman, evidently the queen of this castle. Was that Spencer's aunt? Not likely, since the dress was from the early 1700s she mused.

She heard soft footsteps and turned, expecting to see the house-keeper. Instead her eyes fell on a well-dressed woman whose stature signaled an extreme level of class. Cecelia straightened her shoulders and moved forward slowly.

"I'm Cecelia Giatano – a friend of Spencer Hallman."

The elder eyes, blue as the buttons on her mother's favorite dress, gazed into hers with a genuine interest that Cecelia found quite unnerving.

"Forgive me child. I am rude. Please come in."

Cecelia followed the woman, noting her elegance of movement and her tallness. *An actress, no doubt.*

"Please sit here near the fire. I find the days cold. Henrietta, bring fresh tea for Miss Giatano."

The older woman gazed into the fire for a moment. Cecelia sat quietly, her hands in her lap, wondering why in the world she had come. She was impeccably dressed in a navy and white dress, her gray hair pulled back in a chignon.

"Are you quite warm enough, Miss Giatano?"

"Yes. Please forgive me for arriving unannounced, Mrs. Reynard. I'm quite unused to knocking at someone's door without invitation."

The woman waved her comments away. "When you are alone in a house as large as this and there is no one about except you and the house-keeper, you are quite satisfied to have visitors."

Cecelia noted her smile and felt her shoulders relax.

"So, tell me about yourself, young woman."

Cecelia gazed at the fire for a moment. "I am a friend of your nephew, Spencer Hallman. I, well, I just . . ."

"Ah, Spencer. A good man. Not enough Scottish blood in him, however. I cannot get him to stay with me. Whyever not I shall never understand, for I have offered him my house upon my death and he has refused, saying something about a business he, and I believe you, own together?"

"Yes, madam. We do."

"Ah, then you are the young woman he speaks of."

Cecelia had no idea what Spencer could have told the woman.

"I…yes, at least I think so…," she said quietly.

"If you are his business partner then I know a bit more of you than you might think."

Cecelia squirmed in her chair. What in the world could Spencer have told her? Thankfully, she heard steps and teacups softly clinking in saucers.

Once the housekeeper had served them, the woman backed out of the room and pulled the two doors shut.

"Why have you come, Miss Giatano?"

Cecelia felt like she might faint dead away. "I do not know." She heard her own whispered words.

Two, perhaps three minutes passed. The sudden sound of the grandfather clock chiming loudly at the other end of the room, seemed to announce impending doom. Cecelia's stomach teetered on the edge as she considered the old adage, *fight or flight.*

"Perhaps you've come to hear an old woman's story."

Cecelia nodded and invited the woman to call her by her given name. "If you do not mind, Mrs. Reynard."

"We shall be Cecelia and Phoebe then?" she asked with a sparkle in her eye.

"Indeed," Cecelia thankful for the tenderly voiced words, sipped her tea and settled herself in the comfortable chair.

"A beautiful woman is born for adversity," she began. "My father was a doctor, my mother a ballerina. He met her backstage at the suggestion of a friend. My mother was born with exquisite features and exceptional talents . . ." The woman's voice dropped off, then began again. "They married, and my mother bore three daughters. I, the eldest, the next, Mildred, and the third, Catherine. We were raised in this house."

"I was beautiful and talented like my mother. She was unable to continue her career on the stage, and so I became her protégé. My sister Mildred spent her life jealous of my position, and Catherine, born with a defect in one leg, walked with great difficulty. As you can imagine, it was I who was chosen to fulfill my mother's dreams. At first I did not mind so much. Dance came easy to me, and with my mother as teacher, I did quite well on the stage."

Cecelia set her cup down on the glass coffee table. The story was so familiar. Stage. Actors. Talent. Beauty. Mothers.

"When I turned thirty, I was at my peak. My mother had lived her life through me, and I no longer knew who I was. It was then that I met a man. He was new here in Edinburgh, a Scot," she said proudly. "And I fell in love with him immediately. He was in charge of cleaning the theatre. Our stage was never so well-kept . . ." Her voice trailed off. "And he was so handsome, although he did not think so."

Cecelia smiled when the woman stopped in mid-reverie to gaze at her. She saw the look of love in those elderly eyes.

"I was terrified when one night, after so many performances, Dominic caught my eye again, only this time he refused to let go of my hand. He pulled me into a small corridor, and we shared what was my first true kiss."

Cecelia's hand flew to her heart.

"Mind you, I was a woman of thirty . . . an old maid in those days. My mother had held me in her power all those years, and I loved her, but I could see my chance of finding happiness dwindling. Oh, there were men. Plenty of them. I was flaunted before them like a worm on a fish-hook, but none were allowed to fish and *that*," she said firmly, "caused men to hate me."

"Why didn't you go away with Dominic?" Cecelia leaned forward.

"How could I? I had, from the time I was born, been groomed for this life. My mother's life. Then my father died at age forty-seven from a fever he caught trying to save a poor child's life. The only way we could maintain our lifestyle was for me to perform. And my sister Catherine had medical costs. It was up to me. . . ." The older woman's mind was working, remembering.

Cecelia closed her eyes and waited.

"Then," she said dramatically, "Dominic Reynard asked me to marry him. I refused of course, citing my mother's displeasure."

"Did he fight for you?"

"Aye. At first, lass."

Cecelia smiled.

"But who can fight against a strong mother? Or one who knew nothing of herself except the stage and providing funds for her family? A year passed. I went abroad to perform—New York and Boston and Charleston, Chicago, and many other cities. When I came back, he was no longer employed at the theatre. I asked the staff, and no one knew where he had gone."

"How did you find him?"

"Patience, lass. God works in strange ways, and we are not always to know it. Timing is everything."

Cecelia sat back, realizing she'd come close to standing.

"Mildred raised two sons, but was always unhappy. Catherine found true love. I learned of it when I returned home. She was happily married; Raphael adored her. For a year, I watched their love grow. Catherine had two sets of twins, the first girls, the second boys. I, for the first time in my life, was jealous of my little sister. Life had given me beauty and talent, but not love. Life had given her plain looks, a crooked leg, and genuine love. I broke my mother's heart and left the London stage, then went away to Bath. For six months I worked as a governess for Catherine and Raphael's twin girls. She was already expecting the second set of twins. She could not climb the stairs without her husband carrying her. Catherine ran the household on the first level, and I schooled her two little girls above stairs. I was never more happy in me life.

"Then one day a man came calling. The housekeeper came up the stairs during our teaching hour and announced there was a gentleman to see me. Of course, I flew down the stairs hoping to find Dominic. What I found was another suitor. An elderly gentleman, whom I learned later was an agent sent by my mother to woo me into coming back to the stage."

"Oh no." Cecelia let the words slip out.

"My sentiments as well." She paused. "After this my mother and I were never to be close again. . . . As it turned out, I was able to speak sensibly enough to send the gentleman back to my mother in Edinburgh with a message that I would never marry if I could not find Dominic. Another year passed, and the boys were born. I was enmeshed in my sister's home and her lifestyle. She was such a balm to my broken heart that I concluded at the last to become the children's Aunt Phoebe . . . and that would be my life's work.

"One blustery winter day someone came knocking at the door. Raphael happened by and saw the man there. He opened and pulled him into the house just as I was descending the stairs with a child on one hip, the other holding my hand."

Cecelia couldn't breathe.

"It was Dominic. Our eyes met. I saw them change as he began backing out the door. I didn't understand at the moment. He bowed, shook Raphael's hand, and fled from the house before I could speak a word.

"Then I knew what he had seen. He had assumed the children attached to me were my own. That Raphael was my husband. I sent Raphael running for him, which caused quite the scene." The older woman stopped and chuckled, her eyes bright, then resumed.

"I ran upstairs and straightened my hair, for I knew I had changed so much from the woman Dominic had loved—the beautiful dancer on the stage to a mere governess with a plain dress. When I descended the stairs, Dominic was waiting, his hand upon the newel post. I can see him as he was then. . . . With our eyes locked, I came down to the third step and stopped. He lifted his hand, and at his touch I melted into his arms, never to leave them again."

Cecelia waited. Aunt Phoebe lifted her eyes and gazed at her directly.

"I became the happiest woman alive. I bore three children in three years. Two sons and a beloved daughter, all of whom have died before me. Dominic could not bear the loss of the children. Even though each was grown and happy, God did not leave them here for us to grow old with."

Cecelia felt tears falling down her face. "Why? Why would God do that?"

"Child, how would I know? I am not God. I am a child of God. Don't you see, he gave me happy years in spite of my slow start?" She smiled.

"You are not angry then?"

"Angry? No. I am happy to have been loved, to have borne and known my children, sad to see them depart, but I know I will be with them again. Is there any higher happiness?"

Cecelia leaned forward at the question. "How could I possibly know?" She lowered her head, put her hands over her face, and cried. "How could I possibly know?"

"Spencer knows of this happiness." Cecelia heard the woman's soft voice.

"Then why hasn't he shared it with me?"

"He has, child. You haven't been listening."

"When? Where?" She lifted her face, frustration nipping at her thoughts.

"Spencer loves you, child. But you have not noticed. Perhaps it was not the right time."

"What do you mean by that?"

"Do you see where you are sitting?"

Cecelia looked around, then slowly began to realize. "You mean I'm here because of God?"

"Why else would you be here, lass?" The woman's smile cast wisdom into the room.

Cecelia couldn't think of a single thing to say.

"God doesna' make mistakes. People do. And He's there to pick up the pieces."

"Why would He want to do that?"

"Because He cares about people. About you in particular."

"That's why I'm here?"

"Aye. I would say God has offered you a choice. But you must decide whether you will take it or reject it. He will leave that up to you."

"But if he's like a father, like churches say he is, why doesn't he *make* me mind him?"

"Did your father make you mind him?"

Cecelia thought for a moment. "No, he never did. He didn't care about me or my mother."

"Well, you see. There you have it. Fathers who care for their daughters love them and teach them. You are accustomed to a father like your earthly father. God is not like that. You are special to him."

"Is that true?" Cecelia felt like a first-grader talking to her teacher.

"Aye, lass. It is true. You have been left to yourself, with no father to show you the way. Spencer came along, but you weren't ready to see the love God has for you. We cannot live in our sin and be happy. We must turn ourselves over to the Christ of the cross, else we will be lost."

Cecelia had heard of these things but never thought about Christ dying or caring for her in particular, just the world at large. "You mean he did it for me?"

"Aye."

"Can I have a father then? A real father?"

"If you want him, he will come live in you. Now and forever, child."

"What do I have to do?"

"Tell him all about your sins, believe that He died for you, give him your life . . . and get ready for the battle of your life."

"What?" Cecelia felt fear creep into her mind.

"You, child, can belong to God. There will be a spiritual battle, but it cannot be won by the evil one once you belong to Christ. God will provide you with the courage and strength that you will need to carry on. Do you want to belong?"

"Yes, I do. I . . . I can't keep going. I'm so . . .tired."

"Then come to my knee, for I am unable to kneel with you, and we will pray together."

Cecelia felt like she was in some other world. She slipped from her chair, knelt, put her head down on the woman's knee, and felt the touch of a gentle hand upon her head. She prayed the prayer that came from the soft voice above her and felt her body relax.

The hand continued to pat her head. No more words were spoken. She remembered Bertie's ministrations and wanted to weep. No one ever treated her with so much tenderness as Bertie and now Aunt Phoebe had. She didn't rise for long minutes. The fire crackled in the fireplace, the blustery winds whistled through the windows.

Chapter 80

Chicago

Monday morning Spencer was showered, dressed, and ready for work. The flight had gone without a glitch. Glad to be back to business, he walked into the restaurant and gathered the invoices from the box, then headed up to Cecelia's office to write checks. She wouldn't be back for a while. As soon as he walked into her place, he felt his heart squeeze. She would come back a different person.

He forced himself to press down any guilt he had of wishing he would have dragged her back home, willing or not. It irritated him that he could not get the woman off his mind. He'd promised the Lord not to interfere and to wait. Why was it so difficult to keep that promise?

Because everywhere he looked, she was there. In the room, her fragrance drifted off the paper he was writing on. Her favorite pen had been left behind on the desk in her hurry to get to Evan Wyndham and tell him about her pregnancy. And then to find out he had a wife and children. Spencer rebuked himself for having been so hard on her.

One thing was for sure. He was glad he'd been honest with Cecelia.

He set up some of the regular accounts to be automatically deducted each month on the computer and wrote checks for the rest, signed them, and set them aside to mail. A glance at the calendar and he realized her appointment date in London was Friday. Frustrated, he pounded his fist on the desk and rose. Helpless, he went back to work with a vengeance. Tossing off his jacket and tie, he put on an apron and began washing pots and pans.

His employees didn't say a word. When he was finished, he put his jacket and tie back on and went out to greet dinner customers. He spent himself in busyness, and it felt good.

The restaurant ran like a top while he was gone. No major disasters. The next day he was more amiable, and the staff began to tell their stories. New clients. A new dish was created while he was gone, tried and tested the entire week, and successful it seemed. Spencer was proud and told his staff.

"You're back!" Becca's voice, loud and happy, sounded over the heads of his diners. Thankfully there were few of them at the moment.

He laughed as she all but threw herself at him. "How's Cecelia?" she asked, immediately concerned as she took a chair at her favorite table. "When is she coming back? I've got stuff to discuss with her. And they start filming again in six days."

"She's doing well. I don't have a clue when she's coming back," Spencer said and changed the topic. "So, what needs to be done at the Victorian?"

"Not much. It's mostly finished, remember?" She rolled her eyes at him.

"Right." Spencer was disappointed. What he needed right now was a hammer and some nails to pound on.

"But if you're looking for a project, I have one." She hesitated, trying to read Spencer's face.

"What is it?" He jumped on it.

"Well, there's this family who lost their home to a fire while you were gone. One of our clients. We had just sold them a small house, and before they had everything moved in, it burned to the ground."

Spencer sat up straighter. "Where is it? Do they have a place to stay?"

"Not far from here, and yes they do. What they need from us is a complete teardown and rebuild. Interested?"

"Yep."

"Well, I'm going over there tonight. Symond is going to join me. The church is showing up full force. Guess there's going to be a big machine—what do you call those things that tear buildings down?"

Spencer laughed. "A bulldozer."

"Right. Well anyway, we're going to dress warm, see what we can do. It's not going to be exactly like summer out there tonight."

"I'll bring our big coffeemaker and one for hot water so we can make hot chocolate for the workers."

"Great idea. Say, would it be all right with you if we girls used the kitchen about three o'clock to make some cookies to go along with that coffee?"

"Absolutely. I'll see you tonight, then. Meet you down here. What time? I'll follow you over." Spencer went to find the large containers.

"We leave here at six," she called to his back.

Cecelia Grace Giatano, I swear, if you don't open your eyes and see this guy, I'm going to grab him for myself. Becca picked up her ice water and swigged.

Three hours later the cookies were being stirred up in a huge bowl with the mixer. Four large batches at once. About five o'clock, Spencer came down with the containers. "Whoa, you girls have been busy. I've got heavy boxes we can line with foil. Would that work?"

"Great. We were just wondering how we were going to haul them without breaking them into a gazillion pieces." Symond smiled, blowing hair out of her face.

Spencer, glad to be busy, hauled the containers onto the elevator with a wheeled cart and returned. Each person hefted a large box of cookies and followed. The group met up with two cars, Symond riding with her brother, glad for the time alone. Becca and the cookies in the other.

For the next three evenings, Spencer and his group of ladies worked alongside many more who hauled out charred wood, clothes, toys, and appliances. They filled a city-sized dumpster twice.Every night he came home and washed the black ash off his body and fell into bed, then woke up and worked the restaurant. In all of that, he couldn't help but notice today was Friday. He'd tried to forget it by tossing the calendar pages in the trash.

Knee-jerk reactions seemed to be running his life lately. He hadn't been able to bring himself to slow down. Something needed done, he did it. He also knew this could not last forever. He had to come to terms with the fact that he had done his best and the rest was up to God.

Chapter 81

Two days later he had forgotten it was Sunday and slept until past noon, missing church. He'd heard his cell ring twice and couldn't even bring himself to wake long enough to answer.

Finally he knew he had to get up and into the shower. His muscles ached from pounding nails. The men had worked through the nights, thanks to the huge lights provided by local contractors, to finish putting the walls up and installing a roof on the new house. The windows would be installed in a few days. Next were the electrical and plumbing guys.

Tossing off the heavy comforter, he headed in and turned the water to warmer than usual, then just stood there, hands on the walls, and let his body feel the gushing water for a long time. Afterward he dressed in black sweats, and running his fingers through his hair, went for a cup of tea. He never had liked coffee much. Tea somehow reminded him of Bertie and the castle. He sipped and wondered if Bertie and Claude were hitched yet.

Today was going to be a day of rest – as Sundays were created for. He had no gumption past the point of eating and laying on the sofa, maybe picking up a book.

That's how Cecelia found him. She'd tapped at his door several times and could hear music playing inside. Finally, she'd stepped in and found him asleep on the sofa, the afghan thrown over him. A book lay crumpled on the floor. She knelt and pressed her cheek to his, feeling his breath near her ear. Suddenly he jumped awake and knocked her backward onto her rump.

"Cecelia." He groaned and was off the sofa helping her up. "I'm sorry, I didn't—"

"Don't worry, Spencer. I'm fine," she said as he helped her to her feet.

"What're you doing back so soon? You should have stayed with Edwina until you were well enough to travel," he scolded her.

Cecelia watched him shove his hand through his blond hair and smiled. Mr. Blue Eyes was discombobulated.

"Sit down. Do you want some tea?" He knew his voice sounded hoarse. "Water maybe?"

"No," she said and stayed right where she was at.

"What do you want?"

"I want to talk with you. Can you sit down?"

Something was amiss. The woman looked like the cat that swallowed the canary. He eyed her again and reached out to help her sit when she pulled away from him.

So that was it. She had come to tell him to get lost once and for good.

"Can you let me speak just this once without worrying if I'm okay or not?" She tipped her head sideways.

"Right." He sat on the sofa. She didn't sound angry.

She took the chair across from him. Her entwined hands rested in her lap.

Spencer widened his eyes to open them further. He had to read whatever it was the woman was about to say. He concentrated as best he could after being woken out of a really bad dream.

"I went to Edinburgh—"

Spencer dropped his gaze.

"—and visited your Aunt Phoebe."

Spencer's head shot up, and he sought her eyes. "You did? Why?"

Cecelia's gaze softened. Spencer waited for her to go on.

"You're quite like her," she said.

"Am I?" Spencer couldn't stand the suspense.

"We talked for hours."

"Hmm. She's a good woman. What did you talk about?"

"Mostly about life. She told me a lot of things, Spencer. She told me about the three children she lost to illness, how difficult it was to lose them."

He nodded sagely.

"I . . . um . . . I'm still pregnant," she announced.

Spencer thought he hadn't heard her right. "You're still pregnant? Are you sure?"

"Well of course I'm sure." She laughed lightly.

He jumped up and with one step pulled her into his arms.

Cecelia felt his tears falling on her head, just like before. She finally felt safe.

"I knew you couldn't do it. But even if you had . . ." He couldn't finish.

"Spencer, there's more." She felt her voice quiver.

He pulled back and bore his eyes into hers to try to read if it were good or bad news.

"Your Aunt Phoebe told me about Jesus. We prayed together."

Spencer's ears were burning. He thought she said she prayed. "You prayed with Aunt Phoebe?"

"Yes. She told me how Jesus died for me. I couldn't believe he would do it just for me. And I hated you for everything because I wanted what you and Ed had, and I didn't know . . . how to find it."

Spencer pressed his fingers to her lips, then held her at arm's length and gazed into her eyes, looking for truth.

"You've got to be kidding." Spencer's voice raised two levels. "You've got to be kidding!" He pulled her to him and swung her around, knocking the lamp off the side table. "God heard my prayers."

"You prayed for me? Even after everything I've done, everything I said to you, the way I treated you?"

"Of course. When you love someone, you never give up. Never."

Cecelia heard his voice lower as the twirling came to an abrupt stop. "I've loved you since the first day I met you." He stopped talking.

Cecelia felt his warm hands caress her face. And he never took his eyes from hers. Spencer lowered his head and showed her with his kiss just how much he loved her. Words could never convey that kind of love.

He felt her snuggle into his arms, and for once she was not stiff, not aching to run from his embrace. The kiss deepened. He wanted a lifetime of these kisses.

"Will you marry me?" he sputtered when he saw the soft look in her eyes.

"You want to marry me?" She pushed him away, and he felt fear strike.

"Why do you push me away?"

"I can't marry you, Spencer. Maybe some day, but not now. . . . It's not right. . . ."

"Hush up, woman. You either marry me now, or I'll . . . I'll . . ."

"You'll what?" Cecelia waited, hands leveled at her still-slender waist.

"I'll die of heart failure right here . . . right now." He knew that sounded dumb, but it felt true. Very true.

"Well then, we don't want you dying." She pulled back more to make sure she saw in his eyes what she needed to know. She did.

"Spencer, if you'll have me . . . and . . . and . . ."

"I want you, Cecelia. You and the baby. We'll be a family."

"Are you sure?" She couldn't help herself. Nothing like this had ever happened to her. This Jesus that she prayed to must have some real power because everything she'd ever wanted stood right in front of her. And she hadn't even seen it.

"I'm sure enough that I'm betting we're having a girl."

Cecelia couldn't speak. Her legs grew weak, and she thought she might die of humbleness. Spencer must have sensed her problem because the next moment he hauled her up into his arms and just held her without saying a word.

She laid her head on his strong shoulder. Joy was a word Cecelia didn't know the meaning of until Spencer put her down, finally. Her heart beat with the silliness of a fifteen-year-old sharing her first kiss. She waited to see something in his eyes that would break the moment of truth and it would all have been a dream. But all she saw was the look of love in those blue eyes.

She reached up and for the first time ran her fingers through his spiky blond hair.

Chapter 82

Nhews of the engagement spread like wildfire. The wedding would be in Scotland three weeks hence. Not on the hills since they were covered in snow, but in a tiny kirk in a little village with the graveyard stones in the woods next door to remind them of how short life was and how important it was to live now.

Cecelia wanted her pictures to be memories not of her dress or her shoes, but of her happiness. Spencer had already made it clear he didn't give a whit what she wore anyway.

Bertie made Cecelia's dress from the pattern she already had, adding an inch to the midsection. The dress was cream with a pink band around the middle, long sleeves, and a simple veil. The pink was for the girl Spencer knew they would have.

Aunt Phoebe rode with Reardon in the car all the way to the church. She wasn't going to miss that ceremony. Alex, Edwina, and Paige stood alongside her. Spencer's parents, Symond, Becca, and two of his other sisters made it over. The fourth was too far along in her pregnancy to come. But the words were spoken and the promises made before the Lord in the tiny Scottish church with little fanfare from outside, but a great deal from those attending.

An after-wedding dinner at the castle followed where laughter and joy reigned more supreme than fluff and finery. And Bertie did make the best scones around.

Cecelia's mother was too busy to attend, having just started her play in Detroit, and Edwina's father was midterm. But that was okay. There hadn't been time to wait. They all knew that before long there would be another celebration, which would require another trip over. And with the current gas prices, well, you know, it just wouldn't be prudent.

Spencer's smile lit up the entire place anyway. Cecelia had no idea that he'd loved her so much. And he told her in no uncertain terms how he had let God do the work because he couldn't get her to understand how much she meant to him, no matter what he did.

Cecelia smiled with a new understanding that God does work in strange ways.

Epilogue

A little girl was born on a warm May evening in Scotland. A head full of dark hair and dark eyes shaped what was to be the beginning of the Hallman Family. Cecelia labored hard and long for Emily Rose, and Spencer said again and again that she would never have another. But two years later, Stella Rose arrived with blonde hair and blue eyes.

Edwina delivered a son to Alex and a brother to Paige, named Aiden Alexander Dunnegin twelve weeks after her sister delivered Stella. The house was alive with babies. Bertie insisted the two mothers stay at the castle together so she could watch over them during the births and then after with the babies.

Bertie decided she loved Claude enough to stop sneaking around in the pantry to steal kisses, but not until he promised to stay at the castle with her after they were married. She would not leave her young charges. Bertie now gave little lasses and the young lad their baths.

Rebecca Burke became manager of *Cecelia's Place*. She chose a large two bedroom suite on the 10th floor – with a view of Lake Michigan. And decorated it to her heart's content. In a year she would be married. She met her man when they were cleaning up the burned out house. That guy was Brad-Pitt cute and could swing a hammer like nobody's business. She fell instantly in love, and besides all that, the man knew the Lord.

Spencer appointed Rico manager of *Winnie's*. Business was up by another 12 percent.

Mrs. Quentin King paid Cecelia full asking price for the privilege of becoming the new owner of the now famous house on the television pilot *The English Victorian*. Cecelia didn't mind signing the papers one bit.

In Edinburgh, Aunt Phoebe's mansion became *The Rose Victorian* which opened when Emily was three, Stella just one. Spencer cooked and hired help to clean the fourteen suites. Aunt Phoebe moved into the cozy carriage house behind the mansion, and luckily Spencer was able to obtain the house two doors down from the mansion for all his girls. Aunt Phoebe loves her new family.

Cecelia even dresses her girls in pink – something she never thought she'd do.